Ou

By T.S. Lowe

The characters, names, and events as well as all places, incidents, organizations, and dialog in this novel are either the products of the writer's imagination or are used fictitiously.

Published by CompletelyNovel

ISBN: 9781849148139

Visit CompletelyNovel.com, your local bookstore, or
Amazon.com to order additional copies.

Front cover by Ryan Kristen Cox

To contact the author:
https://tayslowe.wordpress.com/
or via email
tayslowe@gmail.com

To my wonderful husband, who never stopped believing in me, even when I was a snotty wreck on the closet floor.

Prologue

Hath could not find her papa. Black legs ran about her in the moonlight and people shouted over one another. Mother tugged on her arm with her mouth in that thin, straight line Hath knew meant she was nervous. Not many things made Mother nervous.

"Get in the house," said Mother, but Hath did not think Mother understood. She may not be worried about Papa, but Hath had seen the flash of the Egyptian soldiers' white kilts in the moonlight. And she knew men kill men, not women and children.

Mother tugged harder. "Hath, listen to me!" Her voice pitched high like a cat's.

"Papa!"

"Papa can't come."

Mother almost had her past the doorway. "He's busy."

Straw from the threshold ran between Hath's toes. It was as cold as the night itself, and nearly as rough.

"We have to find Papa! What's wrong with you?"

"We can't help him!"

The house was too dark. Mother had closed the door. Hath shrieked in frustration and jerked her small sweaty hand from her mother's grasp. Mother's nails caught the edge of her clothes, but she had already escaped out the door and swallowed up into the sea of skin and night.

"Hath!"

Hath called for her papa. She could only see clothes, legs, and moonlight turning the entire world black and white. Over the crowd she could hear her mother calling for her in that unnerving cat-like yowl. Bodies rich with the smell of sweat and urine shoved her this way and that, bruising her shoulders, scraping her hands, and stomping on her fingers. For a brief, horrifying second she thought she would be trampled, but then the crowd pushed her out of its centre beside the Nile. She stumbled into the dark silt next to a dock where a group of Egyptian soldiers had gathered. Their spears and swords had been turned toward a small group of men at the edge of the dock. Through their long cinnamon legs she could see a familiar head of wiry black hair among them.

"Papa!" she cried.

But her father did not look her way. Instead, he held up a worn wooden box Hath remembered seeing in their cellar mere hours ago.

His deep voice pounded out against the chaos of the village behind her. "You and your Pharaoh's wickedness end here! No longer will your cruelty cow our people, but our ancestors who you slew to enslave us shall rise tonight and free their children by the power of sacred death! The will of Apep!"

He pointed to the sky, where what could have been a black mouth in the sky moved to swallow the moon.

Soldiers pressed in, blades forward. Hath yelled a warning, but Papa vanished behind the mass of legs. Just as she scrambled to her feet, she heard a splash and spotted Papa once more, now wading in the Nile with the box held tight in his arms. From her new vantage point she could see the other men left on the dock doing their best to stop the Egyptians from following, but they were painfully outnumbered and their blood spilled all dark and shiny on the docks. She pressed her palms to her ears to block out the sound of their lifeless bodies slipping over the edge into the water.

Egyptians jumped into the Nile. Her father had stopped with his face up to the moon in earnest.

"Papa!"

But the sky never swallowed the moon completely. When a sliver was left, it paused. Then the darkness passed over as though it had changed its mind. Her father gave an animalistic cry of despair. The Egyptians sloshed closer, khopeshes in hand.

The blades went down. Papa dropped.

And the box fell with him, lid lifting just before it sank into the depths of the cold, unforgiving Nile.

"*Papa!*" Her eyes stung terribly. Her chest felt empty and on fire all at once. Papa.

"Stop screaming!" A hand wrapped around her arm. She spun, hands raised to slap, to hit—

To see a young Egyptian boy, about her age, with bright eyes like obsidian. The smile he gave her was a tender thing and she felt the horror inside her fade ever so slightly. He wore a burlap cloak and held it tight about him with gold laced fingers, so she could not see what he wore underneath.

"I don't think you want those guards over there to know he's your dad."

She weakly protested. "I am not ashamed of my papa."

"Yes, but now he's dead."

In the shock of hearing it out loud, she became so angry her tiny body flared with fire. She pulled mightily to escape the grasp of this young boy, hissing and spitting like a wild snake.

"Shh! Just come on," said the boy.

"No!"

"Please?"

He gave her that tender smile again and her anger calmed just enough for her to wonder where he had come from and why he was trying to pull her away. But no, she could not go with him. They must go to the river, help Papa, save him! For he could not die so easily.

But the boy was pulling her along through waves of Egyptian soldiers. She was caught in awe of how easily he made his way through, as though by magic.

"Who are you?"

"Where do you live?" he asked, in the way of an answer.

"I can get there fine myself."

He tugged her hard, forcing her forward. "I'm trying to help you!"

"But you're Egyptian! Egyptians killed Papa!"

He stopped, but did not let her go. For the first time she noticed he was shorter than her, but the obsidian eyes had made her think him much bigger.

"I'm nine years old," he said softly, with emotions soft as cicada wings. "Do you really think I could kill anyone?"

This gave her pause. Of course she had not thought that, but...had she? As Egyptians surrounded them she looked into his face, listening to the terrible screaming of her people, the form of her falling father still replaying against a wall of her mind.

"Who are you?"

He gently squeezed her arm. "You'll know soon enough, but I don't want you to get hurt."

They ran, but not far. They broke out of the soldiers and came to the foot of a giant who sat atop a brilliant white horse and wore more gold than Hath had ever seen in her life. Bright colored soldiers, their eyes lined with kohl, sat atop their own steeds around him, encasing him from the battle that lay just ahead.

She ran into the young boy when he slowed. He did not seem afraid of the Egyptian that towered above them, and even smiled as he tugged her down with him into a bow.

"Father."

With her face inches from the dirt, Hath realized who this giant was.

The Pharaoh.

Part One

Of Hath

When Hath was eight years old, she began her work in the palace as a slave due to the mercy of a young Egyptian prince. At such a tender age, she had a hard time believing that she could be killed simply because her father had run into a river with a box and shouted stuff about how the Egyptians had been mean (which they had). However, she had seen enough blood that night to comprehend just how deeply her and her mother were indebted to the prince for their lives.

She waited for him to come to her, to talk, maybe to invite her to be friends or something. You don't just save someone's life and then forget all about them. But as the days went by without a word or a sighting of the dark-eyed prince, she began to wonder if you could.

During the day, she would dust the braziers and little statues around the palace. Oftentimes she would be recruited to water plants with other slave children. Though the tasks were meant to be appropriate for little hands and bodies, she would come home many nights with aching feet and a grumbling stomach to an even more ragged and tired mother. They would eat supper, kiss each other goodnight, and curl up together on their ragged mat.

Then she would dream of the prince.

They were silly dreams, really. In some they would dance around the fire with their arms to the stars, as she had with her father; loving the air in their lungs and pounding the earth with their naked feet. Often times, she would look over to see her prince wearing the same beautiful colored coat as her father had, and before her eyes the prince would grow up big, into a man, and swing her into the air. In other dreams they would chase each other in fields of soft golden grain and splash in a crystal clear Nile. In all of them he would look at her with his kind, dark eyes and give her that disarming tender thing of a smile she remembered all too well.

And when she woke up she would go back to dusting and watering to the deep hum of the empty ache in her chest.

One night she came home to find her mother crying, but with the hard look that usually meant Hath was in trouble. But she did not scold or yell at her. Rather, she pulled out a sheet of lamb skin from under their mat and sat Hath in front of her.

"It's time I explained why Papa died."

This confused Hath. What more was there to explain? The stupid, mean Egyptians had taken one of their shiny curved swords and stabbed him into the river—what more was there to understand? Just thinking about it made her angry and confused and brought back the achy emptiness that was so large she thought her insides had simply vanished, leaving her raw and sore like a dry nose.

She still felt that if she just gone back to the river, there would be a chance Papa had still been there, waiting for help.

"First, Hath, death is nothing to be afraid of, but rather something sacred and prized."

She went on to tell Hath that most people, including the Egyptians, thought that life and the birth of it was something to be celebrated, while death is something to be mourned. Endings were sad to them, and Hath had only to think of Papa to understand how they felt before shaking it off. No, they were the reason Papa was gone. There was no way they could understand her pain.

"But death should also be celebrated," Mother said, eyes already dry. "The end is just as important. Without the end, there would be no beginnings, and death brings with it the afterlife, which is free of suffering, pain, and loneliness."

Hath did not quite understand, but nodded as though she did. Mother explained that just as babies and life are to be protected and respected, so are the dead and death. No one should end someone else's time or bring their death on faster than what is deemed appropriate by Apep. It is just as horrible to bring a baby unprepared and unloved into the world as it is to kill someone before their time without necessary cause, such as self-protection or in an act of war.

"The Egyptians have not done this," Mother said. "They

have killed many of our people for their own selfish gain and then shortened our lives by abusing us in enslavement. Taking away one's freedom is one of the quickest ways to kill someone. We, therefore, are entitled to the right of death in protecting ourselves."

"What does this have to do with Papa?" asked Hath. She was starting to wish her mother had waited until morning to tell her all this death stuff.

"Because Papa was trying to stop meaningless deaths. Papa was trying to free us by calling on the powers of the sovereign of death himself: Apep."

Hath thought back to that horrible night, despite the hurt, to how her father had screamed up at the moon fading back into existence.

"What good is a god of death?" asked Hath. "Wouldn't they just kill everyone, or, I don't know, a lot of people?"

Her mother smiled an icy, chilling curve of a grin. "Only within reason."

On Hath's tenth birthday, she was bought by a noble by the name of Merkha to be a handmaiden to his daughter, who was only a year older than her. Her name was Kasmut.

Kasmut had a liking for dying her wigs red and was overly fond of spending an hour or more in front of her polished bronze mirror in the evenings. She was strict, even as a young girl, and had an odd fascination with political conspiracy theories, such as 'so and so wants to be pharaoh,' and 'the Hittites will rule us one day because of such and such.' At first, Hath was fascinated to hear what, to her, sounded like prime secrets of the kingdom. It did not take her long to realize it all was nothing but her mistress's love for drama.

And so, for the next seven years, Hath would rise with the sun and leave her and her mother's little hut for the corner of the noble one's bedroom, then return in the evening to her mother, who waited with cups of blood, dried plants, and various sharp knives of obsidian.

She did not much care for her mother's lessons on death and the spells that worked because of its power, nor did she care to serve the noble girl who was vain, proud, and selfish. Her mother was a sharp, solemn teacher with bad-smelling practice spells, and the later was quick to smack her if Hath was not quick enough. Hath also lost the company of her old friends when she changed masters, which made her life miserable and lonely.

Until her lady struck up a friendship with the prince himself.

Where before Hath dragged herself out of bed, now she leaped, spurred on with the hope that today would be the day the prince recognized her as the slave he had saved. He would look over at her, a glint would come to his eye, and he would pull her away to some quiet place where they could talk. Soon they would strike up a friendship in the alcoves of statues and pillars, share each others' secrets, and delight in knowing everything there was to know about the other. No one would know of their close relationship, but that would make it all the more sweet.

Hath could see it clear as day as she happily followed her lady around on her play dates with the prince in his various favorite games. She often tried to peek at his face without the prince noticing. Should she be caught looking directly at the prince without his permission, punishment could be painful, but her lady never caught her, and the one time the prince did she looked away too quickly to see his response.

Every day, as she listened to their small talk, she would think: *surely today he will recognize me!*

Though he did stop once and asked after her mother, if they were doing well (a memory which she held tight to her heart like a warm flame at night), it only served to make her hopes fall all the harder when he made no move afterwards to talk to her. When he never bothered to even look her way, the prick of disappointment was worse than if he had never spoken to her at all. At least he remembered her, if only vaguely, but what could that do? She could not be mad at him for his ignorance, for that was how a prince should be toward one such as her. Yet, why did she have to live as a slave, with whom it would never be acceptable for a prince to be friends with?

Then one day, when she was fourteen, as she waited in the

background while her lady laughed and shared pomegranate seeds with the prince, he leaned forward and pecked a teenager's kiss on that stupid, vain, red-haired girl's cheek. His beautiful dark eyes sparkled like mother's obsidian knives and his cinnamon cheeks flushed with the lightest pink.

An icky, nasty feeling Hath had never felt before flooded her insides like hot blood. She wanted to lash out and at the same time wail until her throat broke. She wanted to run through the palace and knock down every stupid, animal-headed god she saw. She wanted to fling herself into furious dance and pound the ground until her feet bled and that stupid, accursed, evil Egypt that had killed her papa and teased her with such a beautiful boy was far, far, far away.

But she did not. She stood still, watching as though through a sheer curtain while the prince and her lady finished their fun and parted. Her body disconnected from her spirit, moving on its own to obey the vain noble's commands.

So when Hath was asked where she had put Kasmut's prized jasper barrette, she honestly did not know. Her mind had been out on a daytime dream. Or perhaps a nightmare.

Though she had gotten used to the other girl's occasional smacks and short patience, it still surprised her when she pulled out the whip from the housemaster's hands herself before telling her to strip and turn around. She had to demand it twice before Hath did, wondering why a noble would lower herself to discipline a slave. She even dared to hope that Kasmut's thin, soft arms would hurt less, but was soon poorly disappointed. If anything, the lashes stung more than the housemaster's.

The stripes of fire across her back brought her spirit back to her with a snap. As she heard the crack of the whip, felt her knees lock to withstand the blows, she recognized the anger in her mistress's work. This was not just discipline. This was personal.

When Kasmut finally allowed her to turn, her vision popped with dark spots and the tip of her neck to the heel of her foot felt as though it had all been melded into one plate of pain. Any kindness in her heart for her mistress died then, and she averted her gaze so as to hide the hatred burning in her gut.

And then she saw it. Dark, handsome eyes vanishing from the crack in the door behind Kasmut. Even as Kasmut breathed her vile curses, she could hear his footsteps tapping away down the corridor.

Afterwards, Kasmut would never understand why the prince avoided her. But for Hath, who gladly kept her mouth shut, it started something within her. The yearning for him twisted until it burned like the sun, both powerful and painful.

He had not agreed with her whipping. In an indirect way, the prince was standing up for her, and somehow it hurt to have a verification of his noble kindness; stinging her in a place no whip could possibly reach.

The Egyptian prince was just too wonderful.

Mother's mouth had taken on that thin-lipped quality when Hath walked in for lessons with her dress whole, but stained with blood from lashings that usually never broke the skin. She quietly ordered Hath on the floor so she could clean and bandage her daughter's wounds. She did not ask what Hath had done. Hath suspected she did not care, though the elder woman wrung the wet rag as though twisting off a rabbit's head.

Though the oil had burned low and they did not have much money for more, her mother sat her down on the floor with the bowls of fish blood and whispered to her spells of dark magic and truths of the end. She also took the rags stained with Hath's blood, sacred and powerful, if used in the right way.

"Listen, Hath," she had whispered. "Just listen. This will help."

Because death always made the pain go away.

When Hath was fifteen, her mother brought home the corpse of a girl not much older than Hath. After Mother had Hath dig up a corner of the house, she procured from the dirt there a familiar, worn wooden box, dark stains dribbling down its sides and a peculiar twisted frame that Hath never noticed before, as though the wood had been forced into a box shape reluctantly. Her mother meticulously picked the old, dried blood within the scratched-out characters on its surface with her fingernails as Hath pressed her thumb down on the flapping skin on the girl's neck to keep the wound open till no more blood leaked out. The bowl she had used to catch the blood had filled to the brim.

Blood. So dark and shiny. The docks that night had been so dark and shiny.

"You need a noble virgin for the best results," said her mother, with the air of reciting a recipe. "But a maid of any station will do."

"Won't someone notice?"

"Those superstitious Egyptians will probably just blame the wrath of some god."

"Doesn't she have a family that will care?"

"Why are you so worried? It's just death."

Hath examined the jewels on the girl's wrist and worried anyway. It had nothing to do with the fact that the girl was dead. Her mother had made her accustomed to corpses long ago. But the idea of facing the wrath of the Egyptians one more time frightened her, no matter how comfortable she was with the thought of her end. Death was welcome. Living a life alone, without her mother or the sight of the kind prince, was not.

Her mother poured the bowl of blood into the blood-stained innards of the box and closed it. She then placed the box in the traditional circle of hair and human bones and put a long black finger to her lips. Hath obediently remained silent and closed her eyes as her mother sang unearthly words in that throaty, thrumming way of hers. It calmed Hath, and she took her first deep breath of the day. All her aches and pains vanished, including the constant throb of her sore heart. Only at times like these, when her mother sang her spells, could Hath think about the prince without buckling agony, and she allowed her mind to drift. Mother sang. Mother was here. Mother was not going anywhere, and everything would be all right, even if the prince never loved her.

Mother's hand wrapped about hers.

"Listen," she sang. "Listen."

The room grew cool, like a breath of winter.

Hath had yet to ask what her mother wanted from Apep this time. Before this, it had been for the god to withhold his hand from crops and turn it to pests, curses of sickness on those with cruel hearts, a heightened sense of His will, manipulation of the body, and the reanimation of animal corpses, among others. But what phenomenal miracle could the blood of a virgin do?

But when her Mother's song had ended and Hath was allowed to wander to bed, nothing had changed. The candles burned the same and the house's walls still had bits of straw sticking out from their mud bricks. Her mother kissed her forehead, then slung the body of the dead girl over her strong back and vanished into the night.

The next night, Mother brought home another body, as well as two men Hath had often seen working in the fields alongside her mother. Hath once more drained the corpse of its blood through the neck and closed her eyes as her mother began the spell, this time assisted by the other two men.

"Friends of your father's," she said once they left, taking the body, this time of an older woman, with them. "Cowards looking for redemption."

"Redemption?"

"Your father is dead and they are not."

But Hath now had concerns she deemed more pressing than revenge, for the prince who had saved her, the prince who had grown up so beautifully, had still not spoken a word to her since he recognized her. He probably did not even remember that she still existed. But every day she worked in the palace, she was reminded that he did. A part of her had supposed he would grow up to be just as greedy and barbaric as the rest of his people, but her experiences in his shadow told her otherwise. The years only made him more kind, and although he struggled with his passions and often made rash decisions, she found that to be his honesty and earnestness showing through.

And it made her love him all the more.

But he would never know. He could never know. She was but a slave, and he the future king of Egypt.

Mother did not bring home another body until the next year. This time Hath had to drain the blood of three girls, all of which were slightly younger than she was. One looked as though she had just made it past the start of puberty. Hath put aside their bowls of blood with cold meticulousness. Death was not a pity. It was a blessing. These girls would never suffer again, but be taken down by the arms of the underworld river, the river of Duat, to a rest prepared by Apep. There they would be greeted by all their loved ones who had died righteously, with their eyes open and their hearts clean of fear.

This time her mother had Hath bring the bowls outside, where a group of ten men stood in a circle, bones dangling from their clothes and sharp obsidian knives in their hands.

"Listen," she instructed her daughter before she began to sing. The men swayed to the music and Hath took the bowls into the center of the circle. She still did not know what her mother was aiming for, nor did she know why the men had returned. But when her mother told her to fill the symbol carved into the ground with the blood, it slowly started to make sense to her. Her belly felt numb and hot at the same time. She could not tell if she was excited or terrified.

A resurrection. But of what kind?

"We will finish what your father began," her mother had whispered to her, as though the blood itself might hear her and warn its still-living kin.

Another year passed without incident. Her mother covered the bloody mark in the yard with a fire pit and took to cooking outside. Death was nearing, and many souls would be set free, she told Hath often, both Egyptian and Kushite. The Egyptians would die, and she and Hath would no longer be slaves. They could live wherever they liked, grow as much food as they wanted and never give it away, and Hath could get married to a wonderful man. She could make her mother grandbabies with skin like rye and hands that could take down the toughest of soldiers with their softness.

Yes. It did sound wonderful. But standing at the end of one of those vast palace halls as her prince walked past the other end with his nose in a scroll, the same hot, numb feeling punched her in the gut. The Egyptians would die and she would be free. The prince's soul would be free from his life—and gone from hers.

And she did not want to have babies with anyone else.

Another year passed, and on the same day under the same moonless sky, her mother and the ten men met together once more. Some carried the bodies of virgins; others carried bottles of sticky, old blood. Bones rattled on their clothes and glowed in the darkness along with the whites of their eyes. The symbol from the year before was repeated all around the fire with more bones, more clumps of long hair, and even patches of what looked like light leather, but which Hath understood to be human skin. Obsidian glinted all around the circle. Her mother sang. Hath once more poured blood late into the night, dreading the morning when she would have to rub her hands raw with lye to get the stains out.

Then the men brought in a live one.

She was beautiful to Hath, with the cream brown skin of the Egyptians and wide, dark eyes framed with eyelashes like a camel's. She had no hair, which told Hath she had been dragged out of bed, having been unable to put on one of those wigs Egyptians loved so much. What startled Hath the most, however, was not that she was alive, but that she was obviously and unmistakably pregnant.

For the first time in her life, Hath wondered if her mother had the necessary cause to kill as she had taught Hath to remember. Death was sacred because life was sacred, and here was life that had yet to be born.

The men easily forced her to the ground and bent her over the last symbol: a simple deep hole in the ground flanked with bones. Hath watched her mother kneel at the girl's side with a sharp, obsidian, needle-like blade in her hand. She stroked the woman's head, which bounced up and down with the force of her panting. With each quiet terrified squeak the woman made, she reminded Hath of a rabbit she had killed that morning for dinner.

"Shh," said her mother. "Shh, only peace is coming."

"Why have you done this?"

Her mother smiled kindly, but to Hath it was but the same chilly smirk. "You'll know. Can I have your name? It's only polite to let Apep know who is coming."

For a moment, the young mother looked as though she was buying into the priestess's gentle tone, and she struggled to breathe easier. "T-Tawaret. Tawaret. What's your—"

The obsidian blade cut the poor woman off. Hath watched numbly as the woman sank lower and lower to the ground, the whites of her eyes widening just like the rabbit's, as her life's blood drained from her neck into the waiting bowl Hath held.

She was glad that it was her mother who squeezed out the last drop of dark, shiny red this time. Hath could not find her limbs anymore. The uncomfortable, tingling numbness had spread to her fingers and toes. She had never seen her mother kill a person before. She had always only seen the results when her mother dragged the body home, and then the look of stillness on their many faces which told Hath they were at peace. The burden of life had been lifted from their shoulders. But the baby—the baby had not even had a chance to learn what it was leaving. Wasn't death so lovely because life came first? This woman was a person. Her baby was a person too. Not a rabbit for dinner.

But her mother had to have a cause. An important one. One that was worth these two lives. Didn't she?

Her mother met her eyes. "Listen," she sang. "Listen."

But for the first time, mortal fear caught up to Hath, and after pouring the drained blood into Apep's box and into the fire, she turned. She ran. Her world blurred in a swirl of night and she could hear the terrible warnings of Egyptians. She could remember the way death screamed the night her father died. The stars were so beautiful. The city was so quiet.

And then she found her feet on the palace steps, gasping for breath and loving the burning sensation of her *living* muscles, her pounding, living heart. Her throat felt like she had drunk sand, and she savored it.

The prince. She needed the prince.

Like magic, he was suddenly there, guided by guards holding torches. Behind her, the sound of a horse racing off into the night made her jump. The sudden movement jarred her into reality.

"Set!" cried the prince—and then he finally noticed her.

She wavered, feeling naked under the starlight. He was looking at her.

"Do you need help?" His eyes were on her—only her!

She gave a choking sob and stepped toward him, reaching for him.

"Prince," she croaked.

"What is it?" he asked, even as he stepped past her with his guards. "I'm in a hurry. Have you seen a woman with child?"

Her burning muscles chilled. Her mouth went drier than any summer day.

That woman...

"Your majesty, look!"

Hath turned around to see a tall pillar of smoke, lit yellow by fire, from where she knew her mother's house was.

She couldn't move.

The prince moved around her. His wonderful smell of the desert after rain whooshed past her, and her knees buckled beneath her. She watched him go and knew it was too late. Her mother only needed one more sacrifice to complete the spell—one more sacrifice done beneath the red moon which had failed to appear for her father.

But even as she watched, the fire died and she knew her mother was too clever to be caught. By the time the Egyptians found the beautiful young mother's body, along with the other girls, with the smell of their drained, burnt blood in the air, the priestess and the men would be gone, for sure.

So instead of rushing to her Mother's aid, Hath slumped against the wall and tried to remember the prince's smell. Just one more day and he would be killed with the rest of the Egyptians. Just one more day. One more sacrifice.

It wasn't till morning, wandering aimlessly about the neighborhood, that she finally returned home. Blood stained the courtyard more than usual and Egyptian soldiers pulled her neighbors from their homes, demanding with knives to their throats. Amidst them, with her limbs askew, was the body of her mother. She knew it was her because just a foot away was her mother's head, her black curly hair swathing it like a pillow. The bodies of the men that had helped her lay about her mother's body in a heap, necks nothing but bloody stumps, with a dot of white where their spine poke through.

She ducked away, horror scrabbling at her throat. Something incredibly deep took up the space where her mother had somehow been within her. From that deepness came a coolness that rushed through her limbs and numbed her fingers.

She was the last, now. The last of Apep. The last of her family's line.

But she didn't have time to dwell on that. They would know she lived here. Master Merkha had made sure of it when he bought her to serve his daughter, in case she ever planned to run. He had allowed her to live with her mother with the thought it would make her a better handmaiden, since her mother had already been one for most of her life.

Death wasn't something to be feared, yes, but in that moment of panic, Hath forgot to remember that..

Your skin, your blood...

The voice reached through her mind like cold water being poured on the back of her scalp. She hunched over with a cry, forearms thrown over her shoulders, then clapped her hands over her mouth. The soldiers! They'd hear her!

Father and Mother killed, haven't you learned nothing? You still have power, you still have blood.

The liquid chill of whatever spoke trickled down her neck to her right arm, which grabbed onto her left without her command and sunk her nails into her wrist. As she pulled it back in horror, faint trails of blood were left behind and words floated up from her memory: the manipulation of blood, and therefore, of the heart, where all memory and thought resided.

Instead of burning the blood of others, the voice whispered, *do the proper rites and pour your blood into the drinks of your masters.*

Heart in her throat like a thrumming, living stone, and her stomach clenching so hard it might rupture, Hath turned on her heel and sprinted to her master's manor, her nails scrabbling at the scratch on her wrist.

Two years passed in a numb haze for Hath. She had squeezed her own enchanted blood into Merkha's drink and all she could think of that knew her secret. Due to this, her heritage was never brought up. For all they knew, Hath had always been an orphan. Where she lived had been forgotten, and she was moved into a chamber reserved for the other slaves and lower servants of Merkha's household.

And yet, a sense of the surreal overcame her, for the voice she had thought had been a figment of her memory never left. It whispered to her, predicting the deaths of the sick she barely knew, and some she didn't know at all. It hummed to her of a place beyond the stilling of a beating heart. It told her she was his, Apep's, the last of his priestesses in Egypt. The black arms that scrubbed the floors and the scrawny legs that followed after her mistress were no longer just her own.

But her loving, wonderful prince was not the same to Hath. Her mother was dead, and he had let her die. He had let her head be sliced off her body and thrown into the streets. Not only that, but when they had met on the porch of his palace, not a flicker of recognition had crossed his face.

Her heart cried out that he hadn't been acting out of malice. His friend's pregnant wife had been mercilessly murdered in his eyes, and he had simply allowed his friend to avenge her. No, not the prince, the prince's father. The Pharaoh had allowed him.

It helped remind her of this whenever she would catch glimpses of the prince's widower cousin, who had been husband to Tawaret. The pain on his face almost convinced her that her prince had been right in killing her mother in causing it. Seti, or Set as her prince called him, was growing thin, his eyes hollow, and his cheekbones sharper. Even to her it was a pity to see such a tall, fine specimen of a human being waste away before her eyes.

And yet, she could not ask her heart to be moved. Seti had killed Mother, the only family she had had left. He had killed her, and every single Kushite he thought affiliated with her. Only by the power of Apep had he never found Hath, his wife's killer's only child, and none of her people would help an Egyptian by betraying their own, whether they knew her or not.

Yet, even then she wondered if her mother really had been

justified. It wasn't as though that young mother had enslaved their people herself, right?

But Hath quickly shot down those thoughts. She couldn't doubt Mother now. She couldn't doubt the god who would free them. Hath didn't have anything else.

Seasons passed, cold, wet, dry, hot, and the sun ever burnt the land with its heavy gaze. Days moved past her like river water. The moon twirled through its phases across the sky till the stars blurred against her eyes. In the darkest of nights, when the moon vanished, she thought she could hear the whispering of her god from the waves of the Nile rather than within her.

Hath, he whispered. *Priestess.*

But she had no reason to respond. Her only reason for existing for Apep had died with her mother, and her reason for living still remained in the prince. Until the day she could not have him, she had to live, but since her mother had left her alone, she had to die. So Hath found something in-between.

One night, a year later, a tall man whose shoulders spoke of years in the Pharaoh's fields came to her door. At first she was frightened, because she was alone in the house with only a small obsidian dagger for her defense. She went to close the door on him quickly, but he stopped her with a large hand.

"I knew your father."

Hath sneered. "Seems my father knew a lot of people. Are you yet one more coward who left him to the river?"

The man bowed his head. "Worse. I ignored your mother as well when she came calling. I was foolish. Afraid of death."

"What do you want?" Now that she knew the man probably wasn't going to break in and rape her, she wanted to get to bed. She had had a long day.

"To serve, to repent. I don't want to live this way anymore, in the dirt, the animal of some other man."

"Then why do you fear death? Because you believe Apep will have no mercy for you? Well, I guess that's what happens when you leave fathers to die alone."

"I didn't think he'd be alone. The resurrection spell was supposed to work. If the moon hadn't..." he paused. "Can I come in? It's not safe to talk of this out here."

"Then go home," she said, and tried to close the door again. He stopped her once more with his hand.

"Please, I beg of you, let me serve you, let me serve Apep."

"Who do you think I am, some sort of priestess?"

"That is what your mother taught you to be, isn't it?"

She hesitated. She had never said so, but it was implied. He took her hesitation for a good answer and handed her something through the door: a small, old box, riddled with carvings. It was the same one her father had dropped into the river, the same one her mother had lost while being murdered by the Egyptian soldiers. Hath reached out a finger in disbelief to touch its rough surface.

"Where did you get this?"

"My brother. He works as a guard in the palace. He was able to smuggle it out of the Pharaoh's treasury, I'm not sure how."

Hath took the box with trembling fingers. Something within her stirred and for the first time the sky held still and she became aware of the breath in her chest. She was alive. Her parents were dead, but she was still alive, and so was the prince. She could still be with him. She could start a new family with him, the prince—and then she wouldn't have to live alone.

The night suddenly appeared more beautiful than ever.

The man bowed again. "I won't bother you any longer, but if you ever need me, Hath, my name is Jee. I live on the north side of town in the west wing of nobleman Merkha. We haven't met yet because I just moved here with my brother from the delta. During the day you can find me in his fields or tending to his animals."

When Hath looked up from the precious box, he was gone. But her heart was pounding in excitement. When she smiled she could feel the strain from the unfamiliar expression on her cheeks. Within her Apep whispered of death, of freedom, both in mortality and immortality.

The rest of the next day she worked tirelessly for her mistress, mind racing with spells. While her mistress visited with her friends, she ran to the throne room. Only servants were inside, cleaning the floor and refilling the braziers with oil. Making sure to look confident in her purpose so no one would question why she was there, she walked up to the throne. Sure enough, the cushion the Pharaoh sat upon had thin, grey hairs. They were small, and almost indecipherable, but they were there. The aging man was notorious for fiddling with his goatee while thinking, and he had probably twisted it around his finger all the same when he allowed her mother to be killed.

With the care of a mother to a babe, she picked up each hair and wrapped them into a ragged handkerchief and tucked it away into her belt.

That night, she opened the lid of the box. Inside were layers upon layers of dried blood, staining the wood a deep magenta. It made her heart leap. What a prize! What a gift! Now with this box, she could do all her mother taught her. The sacrifices were still in force! Tears leaked out onto her cheeks and she wiped at them haphazardly. The dark presence of Apep hissed alongside her happiness.

Once her vengeance was complete, once the killer of her family lay dead, she could cast the spell that would bring about a world with her prince.

With that happy thought, she dropped in the gray hairs of the Pharaoh and carefully closed the box.

Softly, she sung her mother's song. The notes tasted bitter on her mouth, but fell sweet on her ears. It was as though her mother were here with her, coaxing her to listen. Even then, listening to the comfort of her mother's old song, Hath knew she had a reason to kill the young, pregnant mother and those other girls. Apep had instructed her, just as Apep instructed Hath now.

Yes, kill him, whispered Apep. *Hath, kill him who trifled with my servants' deaths.*

She kissed the box, hid it beneath her mattress, and curled up under her meager blankets.

When she would hear from her mistress the next day that the Pharaoh had collapsed with fever, she'd leave her tasks early to make her trek to the farmlands of the house of Merkha, where Jee waited.

The old Pharaoh, the man who had killed her father and then her mother, died.

***

As she wandered after her selfish mistress, she no longer had to avert her eyes out of pain from the beautiful form of her prince. So many methods to choose from! So many ways to have her prince! But first she had to come to terms with the fact that there was no chance her prince, soon to be pharaoh, would fall in love with a slave and make her his queen and royal wife, especially a slave he did not remember. His father being dead did nothing to change that.

So she'd start from there.

Jee took her instructions without complaint when she told him to kill a young Arabian colt. He followed with the loyal duty of any fine acolyte, though she refused to be impressed with the man who had abandoned her father to his death.

She couldn't obtain all her sacrifices at the same time. It would raise suspicion, and she wasn't about to make the same mistakes as her parents. With the blood, she would begin a six month spell, using her own virgin life to seal it. This would allow her to take the body of any Egyptian noblewoman she chose. It had to be one she could be without raising suspicion, but then, what Egyptian would ever guess that their friend or sister or whoever had died and a Kushite had taken her body? The idea was laughable. Still, unpleasant rumors would make it more difficult to win the favor of her love.

She kept particular awareness of the noblewomen she knew over the next few days, but it became all than more apparent that her mistress could be the only choice. There was no other woman she knew better than her, no one more worthy to lose her body. Hath still wore the scars of her lashings across her back as well as the hatred she had felt then.

The colt's blood dried and clotted in the box amidst its perfumes of lemon and spice while the prince started his reign as pharaoh.

Then, eight months later, Jee brought to her whispered news from his brother, the guard, that made her laugh out loud for joy. The priests were looking to present a queen to the Pharaoh. She leaped about her little shack as Jee watched on in confusion. It was so simple! So easy! Apep had laid out the path of truest happiness before her after years of his abandonment, but oh had the wait been worth it! Now not only did she have a chance to be queen, but she could be his wife! Her wonderful, beautiful, kind prince's wife! All she had to do was take Kasmut's place and have herself chosen by the priests to be queen.

But here Hath froze. Her mistress was a spoiled, evil-spirited girl, and those who knew her would never nominate her as anybody's leader, let alone all of Egypt. She had watched herself as her prince's initial infatuation with Kasmut five years ago had vanished and he had grown to avoid her.

Jee became concerned when he came in to find her huddled onto her bed in the corner and refused to respond to his entreaties. He made dinner for her, but she didn't eat; her mind was too busy, desperately thinking of a way to persuade so many minds. Even if she did take the body of someone more likely to be chosen, she wouldn't know their personality, family, and friends as well as Kasmut.

Then, as Jee snored at the foot of her bed and Khonsu hung high above the city, an idea finally occurred to her. She took the box from under her mattress and stroked it. The blood sacrifices her mother offered were still in here, and though depleted, amongst these was the blood of the young mother who had said her name was Tawaret, and the wife of her prince's cousin, Seti.

And lucky for her, Seti, with his sad, stupid face, best friends with the Pharaoh, had recently become royal vizier. There was no one more capable of swaying the court's mind than him.

It was easier to find him alone than she thought. He had been sitting outside in a courtyard, a roll of papyrus open in his hands, yet he was looking out at the water rather than reading. She watched him for what had to have been an hour, just staring, eyes lost. She couldn't help wondering what in the world he was doing. Didn't royal viziers have jobs?

Then, eyes to the autumn sky, a thought occurred to her: The day before her mother's death had looked much as this one. Could it be this was the anniversary of the vizier's wife as well?

Finally, when the last nobleman leaked away from the hall

edging the courtyard, she cautiously approached. Fear pounded in her heart, and yet she felt reckless. He didn't even notice her until she spoke.

"I can bring her back."

He blinked, but didn't move. Hath licked her lips.

"Your wife. She had a birthmark on her upper arm that looked like a bird."

He turned so fast the papyrus crinkled. The way his gray eyes landed on her made her feel like she had attracted the gaze of a cheetah rather than a man.

"My wife is dead," he said, and he didn't have to say the next, obvious sentence that hung between them. By offering to bring back his wife, he knew she revealed her origins. She knew she revealed the shadow of Apep about her, and this man had made it his business to kill every soul like hers.

Why had Apep suggested this man to her?

"I saw her body," his voice cracked. "You were foolish to approach me, Kushite. This will be the last day you see."

As he rose, terrifying and tall, cheetah eyes narrowed, Hath quickly brought out the box, hands shaking. His eyes narrowed on it.

"She's here," she said breathlessly. "I know you have the magic to see truth, so see it and know also that I am the only one left who can bring her back. It wasn't right, what happened to her. I mean you no harm."

Seti snorted, and suddenly there was a knife in his hand. Hath nearly lost her composure. Since when did a royal vizier have a knife? Was he going to kill her himself? Had he really gone that far? The cheetah eyes said yes.

Hath, whispered Apep.

Words came to her mind, and she let them spill from her lips as Seti approached, his hackles raised. She opened the box. At the same time she felt a rush of warmth slide out of her arms, leaving them cold as the winter Nile.

From within the box a mist-like figure rose. It dropped to the stones before Hath and straightened. The autumn light from the courtyard faded where it reached the figure, leaving the hall dark as though a cloud had passed over the sun.

Her mother's last sacrifice was exactly as she remembered her: dark eyed, long hair, and pregnant. The bird-shaped birthmark could just be seen through the sheer fabric of her shawl. Seti stumbled back with a loud, rasping gasp.

"Tawaret."

The mist-like figure opened her mouth in a mournful, silent cry and reached for him, grey, smoky arms outstretched. The knife in Seti's hand clattered to the ground and he reached for her as well, but before his fingers touched hers, she faded away into the air. Sunlight flooded in where her figure had stood.

Hath closed the box with a clack of worn wood. Her arms shook and her fingertips felt numb against the bumpy engravings. He stared at her, face pale.

"I can bring her back," said Hath, "but I need your help to do so. I mean you no harm."

"Do you know who I am?" said Seti, his voice shaking. "Of course you do, which is why I can't believe you of all people could mean me no harm."

"But you don't know who I am," said Hath. "And though I mean you no harm, along with your help I do ask for a price. It is a small one," she said quickly when she saw him bare his teeth. "More than reasonable. I am open to you; use your abilities to see the truth in me."

She watched him hesitate. He dropped the papyrus roll, where it spread out down the steps and into the grass of the courtyard. She held her breath, though the expression on his face told her he had been infected by seeing Tawaret's image, and he wouldn't be forgetting it anytime soon.

Seti looked around, but the hall was still empty. The nobles were at the high nobleman Merkha's harvest feast, and the only reason Seti hadn't gone with them was to keep his pharaoh company during this sacred time of year. He had come out here to idle the time away while Xius did his morning prayers. Hath knew this through Jee's brother.

Seti took a step toward her, and she forced herself not to move.

"What is this price?"

Hath swallowed a smile.

"You must convince the priests and high nobles to offer Kasmut as the Pharaoh's queen."

Seti's eyebrows flew up in surprise. "That's all? What has she to do with you?"

Hath allowed a bit of her smile to show. "I told you it was a small price, and it isn't her I'm asking this for. It's for one of her servants. It involves some long love story with a man who lives here, nothing important to you, but you must let me do what I need to bring back your wife and not allow anyone to know about me. I can't do anything for you if I'm dead."

Seti frowned. "What will you be doing?"

"I'm afraid to say Apep requires the sacrifice of virgin blood for most of his gifts." When Seti flinched, Hath added, "But I will do everything I can to choose maidens of little consequence and to be as discreet as possible."

"How can any god do anything good through something so obviously evil?"

"Is it obvious?" Hath met his eyes, hard. "Is death so evil amongst your people? Death is nothing to be feared, Seti. It is as important and glorious as birth, just misunderstood. What I am to ask of Apep is simply to allow you and your wife to live and die together."

"What about the baby?" he asked.

Hath hadn't anticipated this. She mentally berated herself for not doing so; it was bound to come up. The woman had been pregnant, after all, and that was why her mother had picked her out for the final sacrifice—not for her blood alone, but for the mingled noble blood of her infant. Hath scrambled for anything, but decided to stick with honesty.

"I can't promise the child," she said hesitantly. "The baby has a separate spirit of its own, but its body wouldn't be able to support itself, not to mention being never born the babe would have moved on to rebirth by now. If you allow me to do this, you must also be okay with the chance of only getting Tawaret."

She watched his eyes linger on the box in her hands. Then he looked back out over the courtyard. Apprehension clawed at her throat, though she couldn't see how he could say no.

Finally, he turned back to her, lips pale. “Do what you must.”

“You will allow me to?” she said. “You won't inform the Pharaoh of me? Even after you have your wife?”

Seti hesitated. The pause held an eternity in it.

“I swear it.”

***

Just a month later, on the night of her dear prince's birthday celebrations, Hath's hands shook as she arranged the piles of ash within the box. Jee sat beside her, stony faced and quiet. *Which is appropriate for today*, she thought, as it was to be the day of Hath's death. Funny, that as she prepared her death, she hid in a beer cellar, reciting sacred rites among rats and in the light of burning camel fat.

She stumbled over the chant several times, but managed to pick up the syllables before they completely fell. She tried not to think, but all the while memories of her father kept cropping up in her mind. He wouldn't approve. This was a wasteful spell and it served Apep little, he would say, and mother would agree. But her heart was racing.

Soft now, whispered Apep. *Gently. Soft...*

Somewhere in the distance the music from her prince's—now pharaoh's—birthday party reached her. It sounded almost like a muffled waterfall of voices, edged by the chimes of bells and trill of flutes. Jee left her at one point to stand guard outside as she finished her spell. This was her last chance. She hadn't been wise to procrastinate this spell till a few days before Kasmut's presentation to the Pharaoh, but she had decided with herself to enjoy her own body for as long as possible before she must lose it. Deep down, however, she knew the real reason for putting off her spell: she had been afraid of dying, and was ashamed of it. But, even now, the question she avoided most floated to her mind: would it hurt?

Her tongue cramped again, and she had to breathe her way around a word.

Soft...

She finished the song and closed the lid, careful to not unsettle any of the ash in its delicate patterns upon the bloodstained wood. Jee came in at her knock and looked at the box in her lap. His dark eyes reminded her of the prince's for a moment, but no, the prince's eyes were almond shaped, bright, and kind, not dark holes set into a heavy face.

Thinking of Xiusthamus brought the feeling back to her hands in a rush of warmth.

"Is she out yet?" Hath asked.

"Not yet. But I've counted four goblets so far."

Hath felt a twinge of amusement amongst her unease. Of course Kasmut of all women would know how to hold her drink. Her mistress was immature, unaware, and gluttonous on her nobility to her last day.

Jee left once more to keep watch. On the other side of the cellar doors was a deep staircase that opened up to the corridor that surrounded the Great Hall of the Pharaohs, where most palace celebrations were held. As she sat in the semi-darkness, holding to the box as though it held her resolve, she thought how fitting it was that Egyptians kept their beer close by, being the drunken, greedy lot they were.

Her heart pounded in the quiet. Would it feel like suffocation when her heart stopped? Sweat dripped from the skin behind her knees, squished between her calves and thighs, but she didn't shift to help it, afraid to unsettle the ash in her box. Besides, any discomfort to her body now wouldn't matter soon.

When the door creaked open to announce Jee's arrival, her teeth clenched and her veins filled with a fiery, animalistic instinct to run. She heard Kasmut's muffled screams and nearly screamed herself. But then she thought of the prince—no, pharaoh, with his tender smiles and the kindness and thought of being his wife. The panic calmed to a cool peace.

Jee closed the door behind him, easily keeping the woman contained with his large, earth-worn hands.

Her mistress focused her eyes on Hath and the little camel fat candle. She tried to say something through the cloth around her mouth. Hath braced the box between two sacks of barley and Jee lowered Kasmut to the ground, the latter of which seemed to calm somewhat when she saw her slave. The two Kushites met each others' eyes and Jee undid the cloth around Kasmut's mouth.

"Hath? So this is where you've been, you bitch," Kasmut scowled, though her eyes drooped a bit. "Get this man off of me. I have to pee."

The knife, whispered Apep.

It glinted amber in the candlelight. Kasmut seemed to barely notice it as she was lolled her head about to look at the place, gaze unfocused.

"Hurry up, they're bringing in some somersault people, whatever they're called, but Anui said they could tie themselves up like flax. If I miss that because of you—"

Her sentence was choked off as Jee forced her head down, but kept her face toward Hath by her hair. She let out a gurgled grunt of surprise.

Hath hurried to angle her own neck over the box as she opened the lid and readied her knife on her own throat. The face of her pharaoh burned in her thoughts as she watched her mistress's eyes widen. She didn't hear her drunken curses as Jee brought her nose to nose with Hath.

This was her last chance to back out. After this her body, the one Xius had saved so many years ago, would be dead.

But he didn't remember her, so what did it matter? Life without him wasn't worth avoiding the gift of death.

Say it, hissed Apep.

"Come to my vessel," breathed Hath. She could taste the rotten sweet smell of beer on Kasmut's breath. "Let me into yours. Welcome your final release, and I will take up the burden of beginning. From one who has yet to dabble in making life, I offer my blood, to satisfy your soul for life."

Hath didn't even give herself a breath to think, but crashed her open mouth onto Kasmut's, which had already been dangling open in confusion, and ran the knife hard across her own Kush throat.

It hurt. Her eyes burned with tears and a strangled cry, muffled by Kasmut's mouth, rang in her ears. Kasmut had frozen beneath her lips, and through Hath's open eyes she could see the faint line of the Egyptian's irises contracting till only mud brown was left. But then she felt her lungs seize up. Her vision tunneled, and she found she couldn't swallow anymore. Her body wouldn't respond.

As the darkness closed in, she experienced at thrill of utter terror as her world flip flopped, her limbs disappeared, her senses vanished, and her mind drew blank.

My wishes will be granted.

Hath opened her eyes with a start, gasping furiously for air. Jee hung over her, face as stony as ever. Behind him she could see the flickering of the candlelight and smell the rusty tang of blood and the stench of urine. She felt dizzy, and oddly lighthearted, as though she had just jumped off a cliff and met with no harm whatsoever. She could taste the alcohol on her tongue and feel its familiar buzz in her blood.

"Jee?" she breathed.

He closed his eyes and bowed his head. "Thank Apep."

Slowly, with a hand to her whoozy, light-as-air head, she sat up and let her eyes fall on the dark-limbed, bloody girl across the blood splattered box. The eyes of the body were wide and black in death. Her eyes.

"I kept you upright till the blood flow slowed," said Jee. "I will escort you to her—your chambers to change before I deal with the body. I'm afraid you're in no state to return to any party."

Hath looked down at Kasmut's cinnamon body wearing a urine drenched party dress. The ground beneath her teetered. A sensation of vertigo made her stomach turn.

"Priestess?"

Before she could tell him to back off so she could vomit in peace, she passed out.

***

The words Jee was saying didn't register in her head at first. She could only comprehend the candlelight, flickering against the walls of Kasmut's chamber. The image of her own dead body, which she had seen just moments ago, played against her eyes, and all she could think was how strange it was to see her back for the first time. Was her body still there? Slumped across the stone with her butt in the air?

Her mouth tasted of bile.

"He knows it was us. He knew the moment your body was found that we had something to do with it and is demanding to know when he can expect what you agreed on. He was persistent enough to find me out; I think it might be tricky to hide from that man." She heard a strange ringing as Jee paused. "I don't like his eyes."

"Cheetah eyes," she said faintly.

"And he's demanding to know if we are behind the appearance of some white foreigner who crashed the Pharaoh's party after we left. There are whispers of magic, he says, and he looked quite irritated, mistress. If I don't give him an answer soon—"

"I'll give him an answer." She found herself on her feet without remembering when she had stood. "The box."

"Here, priestess."

"Don't call me that."

She took the box from him and curled up in a dark corner with it. The fire flickered across the blood-lacquered wood, and she ran her fingers along the engravings. No, Kasmut's fingers.

Tawaret. Her mother's victim's round, cinnamon color figure floated to her mind. What would she need to do such an extreme spell? She had heard whispers from Apep of resurrecting the dead, yes, but it had only been mentioned once by her mother, and just in passing, for to resurrect without express permission from Apep was to abuse his power and call upon his wrath. Nevertheless, she reached out to the cool presence that had taken up a corner of her mind whispering spells and prophecy to her. It was time to begin the ritual and fulfill her promise to the impatient Seti.

No, she heard. *No.*

Her numbness was shattered momentarily by a brief, icy spike of fear. Her fingers fell still on the box, their tips upon two markers that looked strangely mouth-shaped.

No? But she couldn't understand. Why show Seti his wife if Hath was never meant to resurrect her? Confusion plagued her mind like fog and she bent over the box with a muffled squeak. Why had she just killed herself and taken another's body? Why had she even tried if Tawaret had been a mistake?

The stranger...

"Hath?"

"Shush!"

She strained her mind, urging quiet every vile impulse within her to reject Kasmut's flesh. The coolness laid a hand upon her thoughts, bringing to mind the image of an ugly, alien, pale-haired woman with blue eyes like the demons her father would tell ghost stories about, late at night around the fire.

Use the stranger.

"Did you say some weird foreigner wrecked the prince's party?"

Jee didn't mention her slip on calling the Pharaoh "prince." "Yes, a white one, and he wants to know where she came from."

She took a deep, nauseating breath. "I have the message for you, Jee. I don't think I can tell you more than once, so listen well and bring over a pot, will you? I'm feeling sick again. That white foreigner is his wife."

Jee frowned. "I thought his wife was Egyptian."

"She is. Tell him her soul had already been reborn and so we had to bring her from the future."

The look on the other Kushite's face would have made her laugh if she hadn't just had her soul uprooted and thrown into an alcohol sick body.

"Um, priestess, did Apep really—"

"Of course not, he's a god of death, not a god of a nonexistent future, but that is what he's telling me to say. "

Jee hesitated, then bowed. "Very well. I'll go convey the message."

But Hath didn't hear him. The sound of her own vomiting echoed back at her from within the basin.

When the sun dawned on her first day as Kasmut, Hath couldn't stop looking at her hands: the way the cuticles met the nail, how they narrowed to a tapered end, and the way the wrinkles made by her new knuckles reminded her of the lines her mother use to draw in the dirt of their backyard.

When she wasn't staring at her hands, Hath was avoiding mirrors, afraid to see the face of Kasmut staring back at her—Kasmut, who was now dead in Hath's body.

Merkha was, of course, concerned about the new anti-social turn in his daughter, but he attributed it to the murder of her favorite Kushite handmaiden—Hath—the night before and told the Pharaoh's vizier to give her time before presenting her to the council. Hath heard all this through low whispers from Jee, who had somehow managed to return and get reassigned from Merkha's fields to guard duty to Kasmut, in case the murderer decided to return.

The first day didn't go on forever, but blended into a second day, then a third and fourth until Hath lost count. Her legs—no, Kasmut's legs—were too long. She moved gracefully in them, but for hours she stared down at her mistress's feet taking her back and forth across the Arabian rug her father had given to her as a birthday gift.

"Priestess," he whispered one afternoon as she sat staring at her hands again in Kasmut's bedroom, "you must come to yourself. You are to meet with the Pharaoh soon, and your father is worried. He is wondering if you would like to pick out a new handmaiden."

"Kasmut's father."

"Now your father."

"Whoever, just tell him no to the handmaiden, and that I'd like to take care of myself for a time. Give him whatever reason you can think of to make that sound believable. Where's the box?"

"Hidden. I am fulfilling its lust for blood until you call for it."

Hath would have cared to know what blood he put into the

box, had she been in her right mind. But instead the only thing she could think through the buzz of her own muddled thoughts was how like dung Kasmut's arms were. The bright, diuretic dung of a sick cow. They should've been dark as the silt of the Nile.

When she finally lifted her eyes from her new body, she didn't know how much time had passed since Jee had whispered to her, but the sun poured in like gold and she reached out to touch it. She had never felt such a warm winter light. It reminded her of the warmth of her prince's gaze, and she dared to smile. Her body might be different, but her heart was the same, and now because of this sacrifice she made, she and the kind prince could be together.

She rose, bathed, and sat in front of the mirror to behold the faint black stubble upon Kasmut's scalp. She kept her eyes on the image in the mirror as she went through the steps of preparing her mistress for the day, except now watching her mistress do it for herself. She lined her eyes with kohl, dabbed her lips with red stain, painted her eyelids blue.

Then she smiled, and for the first time she could see herself in the face in the mirror.

No, this wasn't her mistress anymore. There was but her heart and her love for the prince.

Part Two

Of Annette

Ten years after the death of Hath's father, the new pharaoh and his vizier lounged about a game table. They fingered carved pawns while outside fronds of various trees and papyrus sent shadows spiking across the floor. Bare-breasted maids with thick wigs and kohl-lined eyes held out bowls of fruits and breads. Seti, or Set, royal vizier, deliberately dropped a dog-shaped piece on the Pharaoh's hand to get his attention as he reached for a honeyed roll. The Pharaoh raised an eyebrow. The vizier mimicked him.

"I don't think what you did was right, your majesty."

The Pharaoh put the small ivory dog back onto the Aseb game board. "What, with my last move in the game?"

"With that pale woman. She could have been telling the truth."

"I know you're not as stupid as you're suggesting," said the Pharaoh, hoping Set got the clue and just stopped there.

"But throw her in with the slaves, your highness? As far as I'm aware of, she can't speak a word of our language. She'll be," he shifted to move a clump of his robes from beneath him, "in an unsavory position."

The young pharaoh lowered his chin and shook his head, as though to shake off a fly. Set frowned and took a bite from his roll before saying, "I just don't know. You are impulsive, but never have I seen you act so harshly." Then he swallowed, leaned forward, and asked quietly, "Are you sure you weren't able to decipher which language she was speaking, Xius? I know you've made great progress in just being able to make out what she was saying, but you're still new to…"

To distract himself from the uncomfortable squirm in his gut at what Set was suggesting, he reached up to one of the serving bowls, brought down a perfectly ripe fig, and ate it in one bite.

"I'm just concerned she may be someone of importance to

a country Egypt would rather not be on bad terms with, given her paleness and strange clothing—"

"She was telling us she was from the *future*, Set," Xius said as he chewed. "She could have lied about anything else—she could have even told us she was this, this," he waved a hand, as though to grab the right word from the air, "nameless courtesan from another country of yours. But I will not be treated like a fool. Slavery is being kind. At least she can work her way out, and in the palace, nonetheless. Anywhere else she would've been killed. When she's redeemed herself, I'll set her free. Then we can see about her origins."

Set sighed. "As you wish, your majesty. But don't tell me you're not at least a little uncomfortable."

"Why by Seshat would I be uncomfortable?"

"Because what if she *is* telling the truth? She passed every trial I could think of."

"Then she manipulated you. Now forget about it or I'll find someone else for a vizier, and then what would you do? Loiter around with those stupid peacocks who call themselves noble and sip beer?"

"Well, I'm not unskilled with a bow and arrow. Father was always about strong in body, strong in mind. I could be an archer for Denan."

The Pharaoh only had to imagine his lanky friend on the field next to the burly soldiers to burst out laughing. Set tried to look offended, but his lips curved ever so slightly.

"Come now, I'm not that bad of a shot."

"It's nothing like that, you just look more like a giraffe than a warrior."

"If your highness insists—"

"Oh, enough with that," Xius broke in. "Stop being a woman. I insulted you, pharaoh or not!"

"Very well." Set gathered himself upright and sent him a look of mock seriousness. "Say your last prayer to Thoth, Xiusthamus, for I will have you pay for that mar on my manhood."

Xius grinned. "How so?"

"By beating your sorry pride so badly in Aseb you'll cry,

oh great one," said a tall man from the doorway.

They both raised an arm in greeting as the man they had been waiting for walked through the door. Bald, broad shouldered, and with skin toasted the color of cooked rye by the sun, Denan, royal chief general, towered over Xius. Though Set was the same height as the general, he might as well have been shorter for the lack of muscle he had in comparison. Though a good five years older than Set and Xius, who were both twenty, the age difference never seemed that apparent, even now, with three daughters and a wife at home.

The warrior plopped himself down on the other side of the table, upsetting several game pieces.

"Watch yourself!" cried Xius as he caught a rolling cat and Set jerked to stop a handful of warriors from falling over the table edge.

Denan bowed his head and grabbed a roll from a rather unsettled servant girl, whose eyes kept shifting toward him underneath her lowered lashes.

"Excuse me, your majesty. I can only control so much of this," he gestured to his bare chest and took a bite from the leavened bread. "No one makes them like Wenamon." A look of wry playfulness crossed his lips. "Don't tell my wife I said that, your majesty. She would have my hide."

"Why are you telling me? Set is the one more likely to tell."

Set rolled his eyes. "Now that you are here, can we begin?"

"Course!" Denan said through a mouthful of bread. "I'll play loser—and knowing how this usually goes, that will be Xius." he bowed his head towards Xius. "Forgive me, your majesty."

Xius didn't bother defending himself. Against Set's cool cleverness and Denan's strategic genius, the young Pharaoh knew he was less than a challenge. Though he had wondered why he even bothered to play against them, he simply could not keep himself away from a good game or two. Besides, Denan's antics offset by Set's determination to be stoic were quite entertaining. And after the ruined party of the night before, he could use entertainment; anything to get the foreign girl off of his mind.

Set and Xius carefully reset their warrior pieces across the board's eight and five square rows as Denan chewed. A hawk piece picked out for his pawn, Xius leaned back.

"So, old man, how did that foreigner get in last night?"

Denan lowered his roll, wrinkles spreading up his bald scalp with his frown. "Ah, her."

"Yes."

"I hate to say this, but I'm not certain, your majesty." He gave his roll a hard look, as though it had the answers for him. "Drilled all my men and none of them saw a thing. Nothing came in or out of that hall, and she wasn't part of the Syrian magicians' act."

"Sure she wasn't," grumbled Xius.

Denan gave a short grunt and scowled, the lines carving a formidable mask on his face. "This is wrong. No one should be able to get past my guards, absolutely no one, especially not some flimsy, skinny foreigner. Didn't you question her yourself, Set? What did she say?"

Set selected a cobra pawn for himself, placed it on the board, and wrapped his hands across his forearms. Rather than answering his question, Set gave a quick jerk of a nod and said, "Can you be certain no one came in or out? The whole night?"

Denan leaned towards Set, voice falling into a growl. "My men are plenty alert, or are you doubting my abilities to train my soldiers?"

"Of course not."

"Then what did she tell you?"

Set looked hesitant. He exchanged a look with Xius, who nodded, before answering. "She says she's from the future."

Denan flinched back into his seat, slack with surprise.

"And I could sense no lies in her, nor could the high priestess Isis," added Set.

The huge general now goggled at them both. "*No.*"

"Yes!" Xius said with a burst of indignation. "Said it straight to my face."

"Have the gods bemused her mind?"

"Not as far as I can tell, though if she is being honest, that's the only real answer I can think of," said Set. "Please move your piece, Xius, we don't have all day."

The Pharaoh placed his bird forward two squares and removed one of his warrior pawns to move the extra space. "They might as well have."

Denan tapped what was left of his roll on his chin. "You don't think it has to do with that murdered Kushite slave at Merkha's, do you?"

Set's hand knocked over one of his pieces and Xius started.

"And I am hearing about this just *now?*"

"Well, Merkha informed me because he was alarmed that there was a dead body connected to his family, slave or not. He was concerned for his daughter, who was the one who found the body, but...I don't know. The daughter told me the killer fled before she could get a good look at him."

"Sounds to be merely a spontaneous tragedy," said Set. "Your move, your majesty."

Xius moved his hawk diagonally this time. "He has a point. I don't see what Merkha has to do with this. If you're going to connect him to the incident, you might as well connect all the other nobles who were there last night. There's just nothing to suggest it. Was it perhaps a family member who committed the murder? A dispute?"

"Well, your majesty, that's the thing." Denan frowned at Set's next move, where he sacrificed two warriors to move closer to Xius. "She has no family, and there were no witnesses besides Merkha's daughter, Kasmut, and the slave was known to be a loner. She didn't have any friends, and I'm surprised Kasmut took it so well, though she did look awfully pale. There's just nothing I can come up with as to why someone would murder a slave in front of her mistress like that. And it just seemed like a coincidence that the foreigner should appear on the same night."

The Pharaoh's fingers hesitated on the bird pawn for a minute, counting the spaces between himself and the cobra. Set's eyes searched Xiusthiamus's as they both often did when they tried to decipher what the other was thinking, and for the first time Xius noticed faint shadows beneath his friend's eyes, as though he hadn't been sleeping well, which wasn't uncommon. Glancing back at Denan, and then back down at his pawn, he moved it forward.

"No, I do not think we should be too quick to make connections. The foreigner is just a foolish woman, and a slave now at that. Perhaps the murderer was against Kasmut, not the slave."

Set sacrificed another chunk of his warrior pawns to place his cobra side by side with the hawk.

***

Xius stepped out onto the training grounds to blue skies, beige earth, and the Nile glistening in the distance within a bed of green. A good day to make the annual royal inspection of the troops, which had lined up in the training grounds by company. They stood like stalks of grain, proud, and bare-chested, with their chins up high and their hands motionless at their sides. Despite the cool day, servants followed the general and pharaoh with a canopy edged with tinkling bronze. Denan watched him none-too-conspicuously as they walked amongst the ranks.

"They've done well this last quarter, your majesty," he said, the pride evident in his voice. "The new recruits we gathered from Memphis have had a good number of boys with the sturdiest legs I've ever seen, though that's to be expected from dock workers."

"Good," said Xius, unable to think of anything better to say. He eyed a particularly grizzled soldier who could have been no older than himself but appeared older due to the various broad, patchy scars across his face and body. "What happened to him?"

The soldier in question tensed.

"Bad accident with a skittish bull and plow, your majesty. His right eye is a bit off, but he is far from the least of his regiment when it comes to strength."

The soldier held so still he could have forgotten to breathe, to Xius's chagrin, and he moved on to allow the man some space.

Denan pointed out each squadron and updated him on their training. Several times he had to repress a yawn, wondering why he couldn't just let Denan lead his army as God on Earth for him. His father had only had that skirmish with the Kushite uprising ten years previous, and Set had taken care of the remains of that deranged cult not too long ago. Other than that, his people had known peace and the surrounding countries saw themselves as just short of allies to Egypt. Besides all that, Xius's lack of any strategic prowess should be enough proof that Denan should lead the army instead. Not to mention he could think of better things he could be doing: organizing the mid-summer Sekmet celebration (six months away, but by far his favorite), watching the new dancers, checking on the progress of the new Temple of Horus, etc.

He had just suppressed another yawn when a commotion broke out behind a platoon to the back. Denan stopped mid-sentence to peer around the front line of soldiers.

"What in the name of—"

Shouts rang through the air and soldiers stepped into neighboring rows as a pale figure leapt through. She ran with the spirit of prey, long legs flashing and hair a banner of white behind her.

"Catch her!"

Several soldiers lunged for her only to miss when she dodged their grips. At the last moment before she broke the ranks of the men altogether, a line of five surrounded her. She cried out as a man finally caught her by the hair.

A man with jowls gone purple in fury and a whip in his hand appeared behind the men who had their hands on the escaped slave.

"Bitch, wench, stupid child of—"

He took notice of the Pharaoh and general and froze. His eyes appeared to pop.

Xius raised an eyebrow and the man fell to his face on the ground.

"The slave just slipped away during discipline, your majesty, please, pay her no mind."

"Quiet." Denan scowled as several other taskmasters of various sizes, all with whips, came up from behind and went down as well.

"I can't see how a slave could have caused this much trouble and gotten so far," Denan growled. "Bring her here, men."

The soldiers backed off and allowed the two with a tight hold on her hair and arms to drag the kicking, bucking slave forward, forcing her gaze toward the blue sky and the brilliant face of Ra. They threw her before the shade of the canopy, where she missed catching herself.

“This face looks familiar,” said Denan, giving Xius a wry grimace. The grimace turned to a wince as the general took a closer look at the fallen girl. “Not doing too well.”

Denan had been kind in saying so. Deep, red gashes ran along her arms and back. The servants dress had been yanked down to hang around her hips , where the pale, second-hand linen had been stained with splatters of scarlet. Bruises spread along her skin like dark purple and blue cheetah spots. As she lifted herself on shaking arms, she wearily spat out blood from a split lip and looked up to their legs.

Xius felt his stomach give an awful twist, and he turned on the taskmasters.

“Why is she like this?”

The purple-jowl man glanced at each of his fellows in turn before daring to look up to the Pharaoh’s chest.

“Me, your majesty?"

“Any of you.”

The taskmasters exchanged panicked looks, each trying to avoid being the first one to speak. Finally, the younger of the three spoke up.

“She is disobedient and slow, your majesty. She doesn’t respond to commands given to her, even in Achaean, as you ordered. Today she, well, she kicked Jhara in, ah, an unseemly manner and fled before we could properly punish her.”

Denan laughed.

“So you thought whipping her senseless would fix the problem?” Xius didn't bother to hide his annoyance. “Have you tried Arabic? Hebrew? Syrian? Carpathian? Do you even have a clue if she understood your commands or not?”

The men said nothing. The soldiers around them shifted from foot to foot awkwardly, unsure of where to stand while the taskmasters took up the Pharaoh’s attention and the space.

Denan leaned towards Xius’s ear as covertly as possible and whispered into his ear, “These men are not linguists, Xius, otherwise they wouldn’t be over slaves in the first place.”

Xius gave an exasperated puff of air and all the men about him shifted like grass brushed by a breeze. Then he looked back down at the bleeding slave at his feet. Her platinum blond hair was clotted with dirt, the ends stiff with blood. Her skin had turned pink from the sun, rather than brown, and had begun to peel like a babe's. She was the farthest thing from Egyptian he had ever met—an invader in the purest sense. Coming uninvited to his private court had been enough for a death sentence, but he had never sentenced anyone to death in his year as Pharaoh, especially no woman who had looked as lost and confused as she had. She had had such wide, frightened blue eyes.

"What am I to do with you?" he said, not bothering to tap into his magics. He could see her shoulders trembling as she eased her scraped and dirty knees beneath her. He could feel his friend's eyes on him along with the furtive side glances of rows of soldiers and the taskmasters.

Then, in that brief space of time where only the distant desert winds made noise, the white girl lifted her eyes up his torso to meet his. A foolish act—disrespectful in the extreme—but there were those tearful eyes the color of the lightest desert sky. Her bloody lips quivered, and dark streaks framed her face where tears had turned the dust to mud.

"Please," she said, "Please."

It was strange knowing he was the only one who understood that single word amongst the hundreds who watched on. The power shook him, and he found himself turning to his older friend beseechingly. The general only gave him a weak smile.

"Did any of you attempt to show your commands?" Denan asked. "Hand gestures, expressions."

"Forgive me, your grace," said the young taskmaster again, "but we have other slaves to tend to and we can't afford the time to play charades, let alone with a slave as flighty as she."

Xius bit his lip and glanced back down. The woman was still looking at him, still trembling on her lashed arms, and still weeping quietly. He couldn't just leave her like this. He hated to admit it, but Set had been right. She would die within the week at this rate. He could always assign a personal task master to her, but then he might as well annul her slavery. Slaves lived to be in debt to others and to pay off that debt. They ceased to be so when put above another, and he still felt the need to be repaid for the humiliation she had sought to set on him by telling him such lies.

Besides, he couldn't gain a reputation of taking in foreign spies that had the audacity to wander wherever they damn pleased in his palace. Even Set had agreed to that when they had been debating on what to do with her.

He felt Denan's large hand on his arm. The expression on his friend's face said he had guessed as much as to what was going through Xius's mind.

"There is another option." At this, Denan stepped closer and lowered his voice once more so only he could hear. "That is, unless you are ready to kill her, and banishing her would be as good as death. I know your heart, Xius. I can see it on your face."

"What is it?"

"Take her under your wing as your personal slave. You could use one. And at least until she can learn the language and tell you what you want to know."

"She insulted me, Denan. I can't just let that pass."

"But what does it matter?" Denan thumped a heavy hand on his shoulder. "You are Pharaoh. She can't take a single inch off of your stature or divinity."

He met her eyes one last time before making his decision and focusing his mind on the rough gold medallion hidden beneath the wide, beaded necklace upon his chest. While Set had been mentored in the basic magic of finding the truth, at least to weaker minds, Xius had been taught by his father, who had simply told him, over and over, to focus his attention on the medallion with the person whose language was to be translated before him. He had been going to teach him more—like how to tell which language he was speaking or how to access a written language—but he had died too suddenly. And since the workings of the medallion was something of a royal secret that not even Set knew entirely about.

Well, at least Xius had this.

"What is your name?" he asked.

"Annette," she said.

He snapped his fingers towards the taskmasters.

"I want her cleaned up, purified, and sent to my quarters."

The taskmasters exchanged looks of surprise. Denan thumped Xius's shoulder once more and turned back to his army.

"Men! What is this? Get your asses back into formation!"

As the soldiers scrambled back into their lines, Annette was hauled off by the taskmasters. Having not understood a word of what was going on, she initially appeared to be overcome with terror and Xius found himself almost feeling sorry for her. He shook himself. Having pity on a foreign invader, now a slave at that? What would his father have said? But then her lips curled back, her eyes narrowed, and she leaped so quickly from the slave master's hands he nearly lost his grip on her. Xius's pity vanished as she then proceeded to gnash her teeth at them. Her *teeth.*

Oh my.

***

Set said nothing as he sat next to Xius that night in the empty kitchens, the lines around his mouth tight. Xius chose to ignore him and rather watched in silence as Wenamon, a older man almost as large as Denan, and the head cook, carefully gutted fish and set them sizzling atop the dome roof of the oven. Set tried to get comfortable on the hard wooden bench as his fingernails outlined the grain of the table.

Xius sighed. "What have I done this time, oh chief of my advisers? Are you here to scold me about going beneath my nobility and lounging in the kitchen again?"

"Xius, I'm not in the mood for your attitude."

"Oh, just because we're down here you think you can talk to me however you like?"

"I already talk to you however I like, whenever I like. You gave me permission when you made me your vizier."

"Like you ever needed my permission."

Wenamon gave a cross between a wary and an affectionate glance at the two friends. Knowing it was better to keep quiet, he simply took out a fish for Set and got to work on it.

Set ignored Xius's last comment. "Is it true you have that white foreigner up in your room right now?"

"Yeah. So?"

"How did you go from one bad idea to the next? Don't you know the implications this could cause? Not unless you plan on telling the priest's she's your long awaited bearer of the children of Horus."

Xius's face burned hot and Wenamon turned his back to the two with a amused smile he didn't quite hide quick enough.

"She is nothing near—of course I would never do that!"

"I know that, numskull, but it doesn't matter what I think. The implication remains the same."

"But she would've died if I hadn't done something!"

"As I told you would happen, but dare you listen to me for once."

"I hate it when you act like you know better. Can't you just trust my judgment for once? I'm not stupid. Besides, Denan was the one who suggested it."

"Did he suggest hiding her away in your room?" When Xius flushed, Set pushed on. "You could have handed her over to me or even Wenamon. It wouldn't have looked nearly as bad."

"Because I'm the only one who can understand her, you twit, or have you forgotten?" Xius moved to yank out his medallion from his shirt, but stopped himself in time to notice the two servant girls who had appeared at the steps and did their best to slide in unseen. He moved his hand to his hair to hide his action and pressed on. "She can't do anything useful unless she speaks the language."

Set leaned in to him, that annoying, self-knowing smirk on his face. "I could teach her—and without your 'gift.'"

Xius sneered. "But of course, you know everything."

"Will you two stop acting children and just eat your food," said Wenamon as he clacked their plates, with spiced barley on the side, down in front of them. Xius went to pick up his fish and glared at Set, who was purposefully acting cool to prove he was stronger than Xius's rage. The hot fish burned Xius and he dropped it with a hiss.

Wenamon rolled his eyes. "Patience is crucial for a pharaoh, your majesty."

Xius scowled and leaned his chin on his hand, now glaring at the offending fish. Set blew on his before tearing off a bit with a fin and popping it into his mouth. He delicately slipped the bones from his mouth and dropped them back onto the plate.

"Fine, keep her as your personal slave. You know I'm right, though," said Set. "You can't keep her in there."

Despite the fact that Xius hated it, Set was usually right, though he rarely admitted it. Not like he had to. Set had known him long enough to know how to read his grumpy silences.

At least Set had the decency not to mention that if Xius had just executed her from the start he wouldn't be having this problem. On the other hand, Denan and the priests said Xius's mercy was an act of a sophisticated mind and a cultured character, but Xius knew it for what it really was.

He still remembered the way his gut had squirmed up like

that when he was staring down at her in the great hall, surrounded by expectant nobles and party decorations. She had seemed so small then, and oddly naked in her strange, finely woven clothes. Her eyes had been wide with confusion and so bright, light blue. The onlookers had been waiting for him to declare her death for invading like that, uninvited by him, clearly from a strange land, and staring up right into his eyes without a single thought to propriety.

He was a god, after all.

“Well, let me know if you need me to take the girl. I'm turning in for the night in hopes that when I wake up you won't be a whoring monarch.”

Xius turned to give a retort, but Set was already at the stairs, the tail of his blue robes slipping up after him step by step. The two servant girls had long ago cleaned up and left to their own chambers for the night. Xius knew he should have been to bed himself hours ago.

He finished his meal without meeting Wenamon's eye. Wenamon didn't demand Xius's attention, but rather went back to cooking, giving the Pharaoh time to himself. That alone cooled Xius’s temper and he sighed.

“I know what you're thinking,” Xius said. “Do you want a turn suggesting where I put that girl? Or would you rather I had killed her too?”

“My pharaoh, may I be open with you?”

“Didn't I just say you could?”

Wenamon smiled, though his dark eyes were serious. “It doesn't matter what I think.”

Xius frowned. “Is that your openness?”

“Yes. You worry too much what other people think.”

“According to Set, I don't worry enough.”

“Set only wants to help you. He is your royal vizier.”

Xius leaned his elbows onto the table and scraped his fingers through his hair. “I hate this. If being pharaoh is executing people, praying till your knees get sore, and constantly getting nagged about what I should be doing, I don't want to be it anymore.”

“And building temples,” the cook said wryly, as though

there was something funny about temples.

"I'm not building temples, men with actual lives are."

"'Actual lives' as in what, your majesty?"

"Don't get all philosophical on me, you know what I meant."

The cook washed his hands in a bucket of water, then brought over a plate of his famous honeyed rolls and sat across from the Pharaoh. He appeared older than usual in the weak firelight, and Xius started to wonder where all the years had gone. What had happened to make someone so timeless, age?

"Xiusthamus, you are a good man and have a noble heart. As pharaoh you have no room to doubt yourself, so you should not be afraid of your own decisions. Trust yourself."

"I don't mean to sound rude, but when were you ever pharaoh?"

"Granted," said Wenamon, and he took one of his rolls to eat. Xius ate one as well, feeling jittery.

"I shouldn't have saved her," he said when the fire had burned down to embers.

"Mercy is never a mistake."

"But Set's right, she might ruin me before I've even started." Xius groaned and dropped his forehead to the table. "It's this whole queen issue. The priests have called a meeting with me tomorrow on it, did you know? Something about not upholding ma'at or making babies fast enough, cause that's the other thing pharaohs are good for: breeding god's bodies."

"You dishonor the way of the gods, your majesty. Be careful."

"I'm not meaning to—gah—look, I know my duty well enough, I just haven't found anyone yet and their impatience isn't helping. If this woman is going to affect almost every choice in my life and beyond, I'd at least like to find someone I like."

"What, are you looking for some chosen romance to sweep you off your feet? You can have love without all the bangles, you know." Wenamon looked to be on the edge of laughter, but kept it back with the force of his tight, grizzled jaw.

Xius scowled. "I'm not a child, Wenamon, I don't need

romance. I only meant an appropriate mate. A friend. Someone who can rule this country with me. I don't want to end up married to a queen who makes me feel like I'm alone. Like things are now."

"What are you talking about? You have Set, Denan, me—"

"But only I am Pharaoh." Xius shook his head. "I should be trying to figure out where to put that foreigner."

"Give her to me," said Wenamon. "I will watch over her and keep her out of the mind of the court and Set can come down and teach her. That is, if she has any free time once I start her working for her keep."

"She's soft. She burns in the sun and has blisters everywhere, not to mention she's going to be covered in bandages for a few days from those whips. I'm not sure how good of a worker she'll make you."

"Let me decide that, your majesty. Set and I can probably find out where her people are as well. A cook is a tad less intimidating than God Pharaoh."

This made the corner of Xius's mouth twitch. Him? Intimidating? He hoped. "When shall I send her down?"

"Tonight would be best, so as to avoid awkward questions, your majesty."

Xius agreed, thanked Wenamon for the meal (and apologizing for Set, who had not, the ingrate), and headed back up the stairs to where his guards waited to escort him to his chambers.

***

The door to his room opened silently on well-oiled hinges. The palace had long fallen asleep, and outside, crickets played. The large brazier in the center of his room had been left burning to warm and light his way. He found Annette curled up beside it on a cushion, orange light glinting off her smooth, brushed hair. Her eyes were closed in sleep and she clicked lightly as she breathed in. Bandages laced her arms and covered what portion of her back was shown by the simple, but clean, dress. Bronze chains glinted from her ankles. Her hands had tucked themselves around the cushion, as though afraid it would slip away.

He yawned, crouched down, and nudged her. "Annette."

She didn't respond, tucking her face deeper. He finally rolled his eyes and shoved her over. He was pharaoh, not some slave master. She made a distressed squeak and blinked blearily up at him. Then she registered who she was looking at and her eyes widened. She pulled the plain slave's dress above her breasts in an odd display of fashion and scrambled up, expression stony.

"What do you need, pharaoh?"

"Go down the kitchens. Wenamon, the cook, will take care of you from now on."

She blinked. Then her eyebrows furrowed and her lips tightened.

"Why?"

"You are not meant to ask why, you are simply to go. That is your place."

"A place you gave me, Pharaoh. Where I come from I'm not some slave."

"And wherever you come from must not exist, for there's no such thing as," such a distasteful lie, "South Daka."

"South Dakota."

He thought he had made it apparent that no one believed her, but he didn't want to bother trying to straighten her out. He had already done more than enough. "It doesn't matter, just go before I send you back to the slave masters."

"Why did you send me to them in the first place?" she

asked, expression earnest. "All I did was tell you the truth! Honestly, I don't even look dangerous."

"Which is why I didn't execute you on the spot."

She stared at him. Something broke in her gaze and her face blotched pink with anger.

"You really mean that…"

"You are a foreigner and you just wandered into my private celebration without invitation and then had the gall to mock me by telling me something as farfetched as you being from the future. I will not be disrespected so, but I understand you are just an ignorant, uncivilized foreigner—"

"Uncivilized!"

"—so I expect Wenamon to teach you how to act."

She just stared at him, pink as early pomegranate seeds, then jumped to her feet with a tinkle of chains.

"Where's the kitchens, oh Pharaoh?"

He didn't appreciate the sarcastic tone, but stood and gestured to the doors. "One of my personal guards will lead you there."

"I feel so honored."

"And you are to do everything Wenamon asks of you." He narrowed his eyes. "If you don't I may change my mind."

She said nothing, not even a thank you or goodbye, but went to the door, fists clenched at her sides and chains clinking as they restrained her steps.

"And Annette,"

She glanced over her shoulder, eyes bright and hot.

"Turn from me again without being excused and you will regret it."

"May I be excused then?"

"You may."

And she left, hands shaking as she opened and closed the door. He sighed and went to pull off his bracelets and simple crown. Yawning, he dressed for sleep and headed in for the night. As pharaoh he was expected to rise to greet the sun as it started its journey across the sky with incense and prayers of welcome.

With one last look outside, he drifted off into the downy

plush of his mattress.

***

Set walked beside Xius on their way to the council meeting, stiff and proper as usual while Xius rubbed his eyes blearily.

"I heard Isis caught you asleep in your prayers again," Set said.

"Late night granting your whims," said Xius. "And you try not falling asleep with that incessant humming and incense on half a night's sleep."

Set smiled at this, as though he understood. "I'm sorry about my impatience with you last night. I wasn't a, well, a considerate adviser."

"Play a game of Bullstones with me and we'll call it even."

Set frowned. "Why Bullstones?"

"Because it's the only one I seem to be good at."

"Ah, so that's what you've been practicing in the courtyard. Aren't we a bit too old for these games?"

"Don't let Denan hear you say that. He's older than both of us, and he loves Bullfrog."

Set and Xius fell silent as they came to the doors of the meeting house. They could hear the murmurs of the council members and priests on the other side of the door.

"No matter what it is," said Xius, exchanging a look with Set, "you'll be on my side?"

"Of course," Set smirked. "You may be idiotic at times, but not nearly as much as them."

"Now, that just isn't fair. There's some rather clever old men in there."

"You're welcome for the compliment anyway, your majesty."

Xius and Set entered, heads high. As one, all the counselors and priests bowed to the polished floor while Xius took his place at the throne and Set took his place at his side, head dropped low so it did not rise above his—a feat considering how much taller Set was to his short pharaoh. The throne beside Xius, meant for his queen, was left empty.

"Arise and present your matter," said Xius.

They arose, careful to put their left feet first. The priests' shiny, egg-like heads gleamed in the reflected sunlight from off the smooth floor, and each of the counselors wore a certain elaborate turquoise and bronze necklace around their necks.

The nobleman named Merkha and the high priest, Pawah, came forward. This must be serious, thought Xius, if they were approaching him by two and not just on their lonesome. Having both the High Priest and Head of the Court held authority almost equal to the Pharaoh's. They inclined their heads to Xius once more before looking at somewhere beneath his knees.

"Our pharaoh, morning and evening star to our land," said Merkha, "the priests and we have come to the point where we feel it is our duty to, not only express our deepest concerns, but also to provide a solution, if it pleases Pharaoh."

"Speak on," said Xius. He had a faint sense of trepidation at what he was about to hear.

"As we have spoken to you before, it has been a year so far and yet the Pharaoh has not found himself an appropriate queen to uphold ma'at. We understand that your case is unique given you are the only one of the previous pharaoh's children to survive and also you have not many female cousins your age." While Xius could have concubines older or younger than he, his queen, or head wife, was to be his equal in every way, even age, within reason. "But it has been a year now and we are concerned at the close of this harvest and fear the gods will not take our future prayers and ceremonies seriously if we keep pushing back the fulfilling of their laws.

"Thus, we have taken it upon ourselves to present you with a candidate."

"Candidate?" said Xius. "Since when has my marriage been up for a vote? Or discussion? I will marry whomever I please."

Pawah and Merkha bobbed their heads like chickens. "Of course, my pharaoh. But we understand your concern is the same as ours. She is but a consideration for your highness, and we have invited her here today for your eyes."

Pawah waved behind him and the guards at the end of the hall opened the wide double doors.

Accompanied by a pair of maidens with thick wigs like

helmets, a woman walked in, her hair long and red and a gossamer, transparent robe outlining her fine, pleated dress. Kasmut, daughter of Merkha. Xius felt his stomach drop. He remembered this girl. She had been charming, yes, and friendly, and he recalled when he had been taken in by her. She wasn't bad looking, and never had been.

But then he remembered the unnecessary stone that she had tied on to the end of her whip and lashed across the unknowing slave's back. It still unnerved him. Even if, by some chance, the young Kushite girl had deserved it, Wenamon had always told him that how a woman treats those less than her is a good indication of what kind of mother she would be.

Did these men who presented her to him know that? Would they even care? And that had been so long ago, had she changed?

"At least she's a woman of fashion," whispered Set, mostly to himself.

Xius allowed the corner of his mouth to twitch.

Merkha and Pawah urged her before them till she reached the foot of Xius's throne and crouched to the ground in a huddled bow. Her maidens took their places behind the rest of the counselors and priests.

Xius only had to glance down at Kasmut's dyed red hair to feel an instant twinge of annoyance. Did they not trust him to uphold ma'at on his own to the point they felt the need to play matchmaker for him like parents to a daughter? Even his father with his...peculiar ways had been able to find a wife on his own; why did they feel the need to start with him?

He noticed the counselors and priests tense and did his best to calm himself. His temper was legendary, and he was hoping to make it not so anymore. No temper ever earned loyalty and trust. Even as pharaoh, and even despite Set's opinion of them, he did need their support and advice to run a country. If his father had taught him anything, it was that pride could kill him. Just because mutiny and usurpation was immoral and unlawful and hadn't happened in Egypt for many years didn't mean it couldn't.

Xius leaned over to Set to say only loud enough for him to

hear: "You already know what I'm thinking."

Set glanced up at him. "I wouldn't discount their concern, and I nominated her myself."

Xius flinched. "What?"

"I agree, you aren't some sire to be mated, but they were insistent, and I thought you liked her."

"I use to like her, that was five years ago, you were there!"

"Well, it's better than a complete stranger. Besides," Set examined the woman before them warily, "it wouldn't be too bad of an idea to at least consider her, maybe court her a bit. If you take their candidate as queen it could earn their support and make them feel more comfortable giving you suggestions in the future, as well as speaking well of you to the people. If you don't they may think you do not take ma'at or your position seriously, and therefore they'd be more quickly to murmur or discount your decisions."

"Or it could make them feel like they have a hand over me."

"Xius," said Set sharply, "stop your suspicion right there. You know I won't ever lead you to that."

Xius met his eyes, saw the hard, solid certainty in them, and straightened to face the rest of the room.

"I will consider your generous offer," he said. Instantly a collective breath was released by the counselors and priests. "Give me some time to get to know her, though."

"But, my pharaoh, you've known Kasmut and her family since you were a child and time is growing short—"

Xius ignored them. "Kasmut, stand up. Let me see your face." It had, after all, been quite some time.

She stood gracefully, the barest trace of a smile curving her dyed lips. Blue outlined her eyes and gold and lapis lazuli gleamed around her neck. She was fairly pretty, just as he remembered her. He considered her, leaning his head forward, resting on his knuckles, and tried to see if her face reflected any softness that she had lacked those years ago.

"Do you still care for boats, Kasmut?"

"I think they're lovely, your majesty."

"Then I will send for you tomorrow evening for a cruise

down the Nile. The weather is quite cool this time of year. I think you will enjoy it."

"I have no doubt that I will, my pharaoh."

***

The night couldn't have come sooner for Xius. Wanting to get to bed as soon as possible, he called for dinner in his room rather than stay up to visit Wenamon after hours. It wasn't like there was much to talk about: fell asleep before Ra (might get cursed for that), ate a particularly good slice of beef—and he was taking a woman with red hair out to the river to see if he cared to marry her on punishment of unbalancing ma'at.

He sat on his balcony with his back against the wall as he sipped his stew. The city and palace twinkled with torch and candlelight. Yeah. Nothing much to talk about.

No sooner had he finished then movement caught his eye. He squinted over the balcony and caught a flash of white vanishing behind a wall. As he watched, the whiteness burst into the central courtyard beneath his balcony.

The slave girl. She was running, pale, naked legs stretched out long in the moonlight like an antelope's. Her hair blew behind her and around the shoulders covered in bandages.

He stared, gut clenching. It wasn't until she took a flying leap over a bush and into the underbrush that he reacted, dropping his bowl and running to the door where his guards waited outside.

"Wenamon," he said. "Tell him I saw his slave. She's escaped."

One broke away and sprinted down the hall. Xius closed the door back and stood there, feeling slightly stunned for some reason he couldn't place. The image of the white girl leaping with those long legs stuck in his mind. It was unnatural. What was she running from?

A few minutes later, the guard returned, face wet and panting.

"Wenamon already knows," he said. "He said he let her go on the promise that she would return."

"What?"

The guard bowed. "Pardon me, my pharaoh. Shall we stop her?"

Xius hesitated. What was Wenamon up to? Did he actually believe that liar would hold to her promise? "Yes...and take her back to Wenamon. Report back to me afterward, both of you."

They both bowed and left. He sighed and closed the door, one hand running through his hair. So much for a quiet evening.

"Stupid woman," he muttered.

But he didn't have the heart to call Wenamon foolish for his misplaced trust.

The guards returned, he had already reached the edge of sleep. They lowered their heads to the ground, backs glistening with sweat.

"We couldn't catch her, oh Pharaoh, before she returned to the kitchens of her own accord."

"What do you mean you couldn't catch her?" He wondered if she had noticed the guards and thought differently of escape.

"She was too fast, your majesty," said the other. "Even when we were able to intercept her, we couldn't catch up."

Xius rubbed his gritty eyes.

"This is idiotic, how could a woman outrun you? And a foreigner at that?"

The guards said nothing. This irritated him.

"At least she's returned to the kitchens," he grumbled. "You may leave."

They left him to curl back under his blankets. Right before the dark blanket of sleep covered him completely, a thought occurred to him: Why hadn't he just let her run away? It would have been one less headache for him. She shouldn't have even come there in the first place. And it wasn't like Wenamon would not have deserved it for putting such trust in someone who couldn't even speak Egyptian.

But the only answer that came to mind was how she had look running through the leaves with the slave's gown hitched up to her hips, long legs free, and her hair thrown back.

***

Several of the nobility sat around the table wearing the finest wigs, eyes lined with shades of black, both men and women, mouths open in laughter. Xius smiled, but he wasn't entirely sure what they found so amusing. The chicken before him was fine, though he hadn't noticed the taste yet. His mind was elsewhere, out in the corridor of the kitchens where he had glimpsed the strange-colored slave scrubbing the floor on her hands and knees, long legs once more covered.

"Pharaoh?"

A middle-aged man with a row of ivory around his neck was looking at him. He shook himself.

"What was that, Mephtet?"

"What are your plans with Kasmut? Though it is none of our business."

"Just as I said, a ride down the river. Maybe some snacks and some blankets, should it get cold."

"That includes entertainment as well, I presume."

Xius gave him a peculiar look. "No. Just as I said. The only ones who will be onboard are Kasmut and I, my personal guard, and the boats man."

The nobles all gave him peculiar looks. A few just stopped themselves from whispering to each other.

"But, your majesty," said Mephtet's wife, "Whatever will you do? Just sit there?"

"We'll talk," he said. "Get reacquainted." And hopefully find out if she had changed at all.

"Is that necessary? You grew up together, did you not, my Pharaoh?"

"Yes, but we haven't been in contact for some years, so she could have changed." Hadn't that been apparent? He fingered a drumstick, eyeing them all, more especially Mephtet and his wife, with lowered eyebrows. He wanted to say more, including what he really thought of the priests who set him up with this girl, as well as what he thought of the nobles, but he said nothing.

"What if she gets bored?" asked a rather simple woman near the end of the table.

Xius said nothing. He was done pretending to be interested in this discussion.

A knock came at the door and Set entered left foot forward and head bowed. He lingered in the doorway, hand set flat against his right shoulder to show that he didn't want to speak to the Pharaoh unless he was alone.

The Pharaoh could have danced. He dabbed at his mouth. "Excuse me, but I must attend to other matters."

With that he got up and left with Set. They went into Xius's study, a quiet, small room off the side of the palace filled with scrolls, maps, and various measuring instruments, including an abacus of precious metals and stones. A year ago it had belonged to his father. Even now it still had the lingering scent of him. Rather than upsetting Xius, though, it comforted him as a reminder that his father had only gone to where Xius would in turn be someday as well, with his mother, and all the siblings who had died in infancy.

Set closed the door carefully, then sat himself in the corner on a couch, slinging his long legs over the lion head armrests.

"I hope your day has been more exciting than mine," Xius said as he stretched upon his own silk pillows scattered before a large, open balcony.

"Anything is more exciting than dealings with the bureaucracy," Set said.

"You could have said no when I offered the position to you."

"And say no to the Pharaoh?"

"You find the oddest times to adhere to propriety. If you're going to bring up that unspoken rule, then you might as well get your face to the floor."

"I'm quite comfortable where I am, thank you, your majesty. But I've actually come with the report on the scrying you've asked for."

"And?"

Set's eyebrows scrunched together. "Well, your majesty…I can't say I have much to tell. The aura we managed to glean off her items gave us little to work with. Mostly confusing flashes of…we don't entirely know. Strange rectangular buildings and even stranger metal contraptions. Other than that, Isis and I found the items more curious than useful, especially the peculiar contraption made of the strangest light metal or wood. It was the only thing to have given us any results, your majesty. It was filled with a roll of brown glass that held different shades if you put them up to the light of Ra."

"Do you know what it does?"

"Not a clue. You will have to ask the slave—Annette?—about that. If you'd like, I can question her for you."

"That won't be necessary," Xius waved it aside. "Tell me more."

"There isn't much more, your majesty. Each image was so blurry Isis and I couldn't be entirely sure of what we were looking at." Set opened his palms to Xius, as though beseeching his understanding. "I could be wrong in calling them buildings at all. For all I know, they were weapons or strange animals; the images were borderline incoherent. The gods are determined to be vague in response to our questions. But I left the items with Isis according to her request. She thinks perhaps entreating the patron of the high moon, Khonsu, god of visions, will bring forth more fruitful results."

Xius nodded, then smirked as a thought occurred to him. "Isn't Khonsu the god of fertility and of, ahem, night activities as well?"

Set laid his head on his hand, fingering a potted plant's leaves that hung near the couch. "I suppose so."

"Uh huh," Xius could feel his smirk growing. "And are you joining Isis for this new round of scrying?"

The vizier blinked at the leaf, then scowled heavily at Xius. "She's five years older than me, you twit."

"I don't see why that should mean anything. She's quite pretty, especially the eyes, with a smile I'm rather fond of myself."

"If you can ignore the fact she's hairless like all the other priests and priestesses." Set's expression darkened. "Now I'd appreciate it if you stopped this subject here and now...*your majesty.*"

"But how come? You get along well enough, don't you?"

"Please."

"And it's been two years now since Tawaret—"

"*Xius.*"

Pharaoh or not, Xius closed his jaw with an audible snap. He could feel the forbidden ground he had just stepped on still stinging between them even as Set sat up on the couch and pushed on, desperate to change the subject.

"Didn't you take a liking to Kasmut a few years back? You were what, sixteen?"

"Yeah, before I saw her whip a Kushite slave down because she had lost a barrette."

Set gave him a look that Xius couldn't read and only said, "Ah."

Xius fingered a scroll he had been reading, trying to shake off the embarrassment of not thinking before he talked. It was a story about an ancestor of his who had tamed a wild leopard for a pet to prove his love for a Hittite princess. He wanted to get back to it, but he knew after the lunch with Mephtet and his friends he was supposed to go review last minute touch ups to the temple of Horus with the architects. He sighed.

"I'm sorry."

Set didn't need to ask what for. "Already forgiven, Xius."

"And I don't want to go to the temple."

This made his friend frown. "Why not? It is your temple, in a roundabout way."

"Because I feel more like swimming right now."

"But it's almost winter!"

"Exactly, so no one would be there. I could have some peace and not be harked on to talk and make up opinions where there isn't any." Xius rubbed his forehead, putting the scroll aside. "Talk talk talk talk, is that all I'm good for?"

"It never ceases to amaze me the esteem issues you have as God Pharaoh."

Xius rolled his eyes and shrugged. "I guess we should go."

"Xius..."

"What? Oh, I mean, we shall go."

Set chuckled softly and they left together, the story tucked safely under Xius's arm for later reading.

***

After he finished his morning worship at the temple of Ra, Xius returned to his chambers to find a bandaged form curled up on a pillow from his couch fast asleep, his lunch waiting for him on the table. Wenamon must have sent her up to deliver his food, though why she had fallen asleep on the cushion, he didn't know. Hadn't she been provided a bed down in the kitchen?

Irritated, but curious, he touched some of her peculiar hair and was surprised at the softness, despite the snarls and tangles in it.

When her pale lashes began to flicker he snatched his hand back. Blue eyes, bleary with sleep, looked up at him. The image of her kneeling before him, pleading, with muddy tears on her cheeks, went through his mind.

"Pharaoh?" she mumbled groggily. He wanted to demand why she had thought it was okay to fall asleep in his room, but something stopped him. Hadn't he been planning on talking to her about her belongings anyways? He might as well make use of this opportunity.

"Tell me what the black contraption in your belongings is for."

For a minute she blinked at him in utter confusion before scowling and quickly sitting up.

"You mean my camera?"

"Camera?" What a peculiar word. Though the medallion allowed him to understand her language, this word only brought the image of what he had just asked about, meaning it did nothing for him.

"I can't think of what else you could be thinking of. My camera made pictures of things. When you've taken as many pictures as you can, you take it too a, well, special shop I guess you could say, and they take the pictures from the camera and put them on paper for you to see. Though, that'd be papyrus for you guys, wouldn't it?—your majesty, I mean."

She had lost him.

"Just tell me if this camera can be used to do harm."

"Uh, no?"

"Great, now get out of my room."

But she didn't stand. "What are you doing with my stuff, anyway? And why the disposable camera out of everything?"

"Did I give any indication that it was your right to ask? No."

Her face fell blank and she finally put her eyes to the floor. Though she gave the image of meekness, he could see her fingers clenched till her knuckles showed white. He thought of Set's scrying and the strange, tall buildings he had seen. Granted, it was ridiculous to give any credit to her lie about coming from the future, but she did come from somewhere remarkable to have such strange possessions, clothing, and that soft white hair. And why had she run last night just to return to Wenamon? Had she seen his guards?

"You tried to run away last night," he said. "Why?"

"I wasn't trying to run away, and even if I was, where would I go?"

"Why were you running, then?"

"Because I felt like it, Pharaoh." Her head jerked a bit as though she thought of looking at him, but she wisely kept her face down.

"With all those injuries?"

"My legs are fine, thanks."

"You're not telling me something."

"Why are you asking me these questions if you don't believe anything I say? Are you just waiting for me to confess I'm some alien from Rome or something?"

He frowned. "Rome?"

For a moment, she too seemed lost. Then she put a palm to her forehead.

"Crap, is Rome before Greece or the other way around? Why did I have to sleep through that class?"

He caught on to her words. "You have been educated, then?"

"Of course I was educated, *Pharaoh*. Just because I can't read or write Egyptian doesn't mean I'm illiterate in my own language, your oh noble majesty. "

"Why do you have this abhorring attitude toward me? I've never met such—such rude ingratitude! What have I done to you other than save you from death and give you a place to stay in my palace? I've even given you the opportunity to earn repentance, and yet you feel like you are entitled to have it without questions. Were you a queen in your country?"

"What?"

"You must be to have such snobbery."

"Wha—no!"

"A princess, then?"

"Where I come from there are no royals, your highness."

That took him a moment to comprehend. "Wait, so you're of a tribe then?"

"Do tribes run by democracy?"

"What?"

"Oh, never mind. Sure. I'm from a tribe, your most highness."

It now made sense: why she felt no respect of him as God Pharaoh, why she held such reproach for him, and why she understood no common fear for his power and authority. He had heard tales of barbaric, pale-skinned tribes to the far north who lived in family-like clans with only chieftains to give them a sense of law in its weakest form.

Not for the first time, he asked, "But how did you get here?"

And also not for the first time, she said, with returning impatience, "I don't know."

"Do you have any dealings with the gods? What gods do your people serve?"

She gave him an odd look. "Your highness, I don't know if any god brought me here, let alone the god I know."

"Were you taken here by others? Kidnapped?"

"Ugh!" She finally looked up at him, small nose scrunched up and scowling. "For the last time, I don't know! One minute I was walking around some ancient rock building or other, because my class was being a complete bore and some kid was being an ass, and the next thing I know I'm walking around in your palace. Asking me again won't change my answer."

He ignored her frustration. He had at least one theory verified, and that was more than before. "Did it snow in this, uh, South Daka?" he asked, sitting down at the end of his bed and crossing his legs.

"You mean South Dakota, your majesty?"

"What an odd name."

"It's rocky, somewhat empty, and has a crazy amount of snow in the winter."

He had never in his life seen snow, but he heard it was in the north—frozen water from the sky. "So you *are* from the north."

"I guess you could say that?"

"I knew it!" He couldn't wait to hang this over Set's head. Not only was she no noble, but she was a barbarian. He could justify himself for the bandages on her back and the uncomfortable guilt could leave him alone.

"You're so intuitive, Mr. Pharaoh."

"Are you mocking me again?"

"Your highness, relax. No one wants to talk to someone who's going to get offended every other sentence."

"I am Pharaoh—"

"And I am Annette." She raised a blonde eyebrow. "It doesn't change it. Whether you're walking across a forest filled with mines or a desert filled with mines, you still don't want to walk where there are mines—your majesty," she tagged on quickly. At least he now knew she didn't have a death wish. He had been wondering before.

"This is not about whether you feel comfortable or not talking to me. This is about you learning your place. I am doing you a service. If society didn't have its levels there would be no order, no ma'at, and no one would know who they are to be, and it doesn't matter if you're from lands too barbaric to understand that."

Her eyes flashed hard and hot. "Then why are you still talking to me?"

All his thoughts stuttered to a halt. He didn't know how to answer it. If he wanted something from her, he should have commanded it and then be done, not discuss it. Wasn't he tired of people questioning his judgments? Hadn't Set advised him over and over again to be confident, to not discuss, but to order?

To listen, but not try to persuade? Again, he had fallen out of how a pharaoh was supposed to act.

Scrambling for an answer, he said, “I may talk to whom I wish, and I wanted to assure my vizier that you weren't of noble blood.”

“Well, I’m not. I hope that puts your vizier's conscience to rest, your highness.”

***

The sound of the river as it lapped against the sides of the boat soothed Xius. He had hoped Kasmut would think so as well. Though he remembered the whipping, he also knew it had been years since then, and she had grown. People could change.

A dozen men rowed before him, expressions serene and the barest gleam of sweat across their shoulders.

Kasmut picked up a fan and waved it lazily, the gold bracelets on her wrists jingling.

"It's awfully warm for this time of year," she said, her fan lifting a few strands of red hair. "Don't you think, my pharaoh?"

"I think it is just right."

"Then it is."

They fell into an awkward silence again. Xius was beginning to regret insisting on having no entertainment and plenty of talking time. Maybe Mephtet and his wife had a point.

He looked around for an idea of what to say. He thought of the young slave girl she had whipped so many years ago and dropped the thought as though it had burned him. He was supposed to be forgetting about that. Besides, Kasmut had most likely forgotten about her.

"Pharaoh? May I ask a question?"

Yes, please, he thought. "Of course."

"What do you think of me?"

His insides squirmed. "Why do you ask?"

"That is why you brought me out here—to figure out what you think of me." She turned her black eyes to him, unsmiling. "Is it not, my pharaoh?"

"Well, more or less, but I was hoping we could talk first."

"About what, your majesty?"

"Anything, really."

She blinked, then smiled in a taut way that looked unnatural against her cheeks. "You make me nervous, oh Pharaoh."

"Forgive me, I did not mean to."

She leaned back. "Don't worry. I remember you well enough. Though I would like to refresh your memory on who I am."

***

He got back to shore jittery and uncomfortable. He kept trying to shake off the memory of how close she had gotten; sitting with a leg draped over his lap, lips brushing against his cheeks, or even a hand on his. He had probably humiliated himself and her with scrambling out of the way each time. She had left looking slightly hurt.

Not that he didn't deserve it for refusing to set up entertainment as the nobles had suggested. Why couldn't he do anything right?

He wandered toward the kitchen, hungry, annoyed, and hoping to discuss the whole marriage thing all over again with the nobles and priests. He turned a corner and nearly pivoted on the spot to retreat at the sight of Set leaning against the wall at the entrance to the kitchen stairs. He loved the man, but after his day, he wasn't in the mood to be corrected.

Set met his eyes before he could duck out of sight.

"How was it, your majesty?"

"Awkward," he said, hoping Set would leave it at that.

"Naturally."

"What are you doing here?"

"Meeting with your slave, of course."

Xius blinked in confusion, then caught himself. "Oh, yes, the language lessons."

"Unless...that's what you were about to do?"

In all honesty, Xius had completely forgotten about the slave and his intentions to teach her, but he wasn't about to tell Set that.

"I never told you to teach her," he said, trying his best to sound casual. He heard footsteps coming up the stairs behind them.

"I did offer, your majesty. Would you like me to leave?"

The pale girl in question stepped up from the staircase, straight back, gaze unabashed as usual as she met Xius's eye. He sighed. He'd have to take care of that, maybe clarify with Set that he was also going to have to teach the girl manners.

Set turned. "Oh, Annette."

Her attention flashed to him, then wilted. "Oh. You."

“A bit strange you should call her by name already,” Xius said.

“Her name is the only common language between us right now,” said Set. “In teaching one who you can't communicate to, their name is the first bridge to understanding.”

“Was that directed at me?” Annette met Xius’s eye again. He found her ignorant disrespect both uncomfortable and annoying. “Could you translate for me, Pharaoh? Or should I grovel first?”

“It wasn't for you,” he told her, with the medallion’s magic tingling in his mind and the shape of the strange words on his tongue. “This is Set, you’ve met him before. He has given you the honor of volunteering to teach you of our language.”

“Why couldn't you just teach me?” She shot a glance at Set that looked far from comfortable. “I just had to go through two days of charades, I don’t see how trying to learn from him is going to be any different.”

“Fascinating.” Set nodded.

“Oh, stop trying to be smart, you don't understand a word we're saying,” said Xius, before switching over to Annette's language. “You should have learned by now you cannot make demands of the Pharaoh, foreigner as you are.”

Her eyebrows lowered in a hardened expression and she looked down at the floor without a word.

“What were you talking about?” asked Set. “What did she say?”

“I was telling her you were going to be her teacher,” Xius gestured to her, “so teach.”

“Could you help me for the first few lessons? Just so I have a bank of words to work with?”

Now here was a nice change: being asked for help by Set, though Xius would have to wait to tease him.

“Of course. Now move, I'm hungry.”

“I think you're weird for preferring to eat your dinners down there. You make the servants nervous.”

Xius didn't say anything, but slipped past Annette. Beneath the smell of ash and bread, he thought he caught a faint scent of something flowery and musky sweet coming from her. He almost paused to try and identify it, but continued on, annoyed that he could ever get close to being interested in how a slave smelled.

A large hulking form sat at the table below. Denan turned and grinned broadly at them with goat cheese flecking the edge of his mouth.

"Ah! I thought I'd find you down here."

Seeing Denan was borderline awkward. His huge form made the kitchens seem crowded. A few scullery maids cleaning up for the night lingered around the edges of the room, focused on not looking up and accidentally meeting the Pharaoh's eye. Wenamon worked at the last lit stove.

"What are you doing down here?" asked Set.

"Eating. Also, your majesty, I heard you went on an outing with your future queen today." His eyebrows went high with excitement. "Aphery's been waiting for me to come home with updates on how it went, though she's not the only one. Come, come, delight me with your attempts at romance."

Denan was the only one married out of the three of them. Since marriage was a touchy subject with Set, he had spent the last few years pecking on Xius to get married. Xius had never felt bothered by it, because Denan was a good five years older than him, but now...

"He said it was awkward," Set said.

"Oh, well, that goes away once you're married. Kind of hard to be awkward after you have—"

"We're not getting married," said Xius.

Denan frowned and Wenamon smiled beneath his beard. The foreign slave girl followed Set and leaned against the wall, eyes to the floor. Xius caught a few wary glances from the maids towards her from their folded up bows in the corners.

"Huh," Denan blinked. "Well, um..."

"If this is about the slave she whipped, you're being ridiculous, your majesty. It was just a slave, and Kushite at that."

"No, this has nothing to do with that. She just came on a bit too...strong."

Denan chuckled and wiped at his mouth, collecting goat

cheese on his arm hair. “Of course she's going to come on strong, your majesty, you gave her invitation to! You, her, all alone on the Nile and waving queenship in front of her like a yam in front of a donkey.”

Xius forced himself not to fidget and sat down at the table, where Wenamon handed him a plate. Set sat across from him after gesturing Annette to sit on the floor, which she did with much hesitation, probably unsure if that was what she was being asked to do. She looked up at the bench where the rest of them were sitting.

“Do I have to sit down here?”

“Yes,” said Xius in her tongue before saying, “There was just no connection between us. I can't see myself having to work beside this woman for the rest of my life, let alone having children with her.”

“You can't say that after only one boat ride,” said Set. “And you can always get another wife if she doesn't satisfy you; but honestly, Xius, ma'at is at stake here.”

“He knows that,” said Denan, waving a fish tail at Set. “The man can think, you don't have to do it for him.”

Set sighed and refused the food Wenamon offered him, explaining that he had already eaten. Xius could feel his concern humming in the air as he ate. Denan and Xius chewed in silence while Set rubbed his fingers along the bridge of his nose.

“When you're done eating,” he said quietly, “we can get to the foreigner.”

Xius nodded and glanced at the girl. She had her head down again, but her forehead was crinkled as though she were scowling fire into the stone floor. Wenamon muttered something to her at one point, but she didn't seem to hear. She probably didn't understand.

Denan wiped at his mouth with his arm once more when he was finished and thanked Wenamon for the meal. As he walked out, he shook Xius's shoulder with a warm squeeze.

“It's all right if you don't want to marry her, your majesty. I know you don't need me to tell you that, but sometimes I think you need reminding.”

Set furrowed his eyebrows as he looked at Denan, but Xius smiled, grasped Denan's forearm, and nodded.

"Better get back. I promised the girls a story before bedtime."

"Tell them hello from me."

"Of course, your majesty."

Set shook his head as he watched the general leave.

"He's a bad influence on you. First the slave, now all this marriage fantasy—"

"You wanted to do something with the slave?" Xius was in no mood for Set's 'advice' tonight.

Set pushed aside his plate and turned to the girl.

"Annette, stand up."

She looked up at him, confused until Xius repeated the command to her in her own tongue. They proceeded to teach her, with Xius following Set's lead and translating words for her and teaching her simple commands about the kitchen.

From the shadow of the stove, Wenamon watched as he rubbed ash and dry lye off his thick-fingered hands, a softness to his gaze.

***

Xius looked out at the stars as the brazier crackled behind them. They sipped fine imported wine in nothing more than their underwear, enjoying the quiet and watching from Xius's balcony as the occasional guard walked his round on the other side of the courtyard below. A warm, musky-scented breeze blew in from off the desert sands.

"Why do the gods care about us?" Set asked.

Xius swallowed his wine and answered, "Because we are their creations, children in a way, and therefore their joy."

"Is that all the gods do, then? Do their godly duty over their mortal children?"

"Why are you suddenly wondering this, anyway?"

Set shrugged and swirled his wine. "Everyone wonders it at one time."

"Usually not out loud to a god in person."

Set snorted. "You're still a man, Xius, even if only partially."

"I don't need you to remind me."

"But what's the point? Tending cosmos, punishing stupid children, *having* stupid children. Is this really all so that, in the end, people can be born just to die forever?"

"What's wrong with that? It is the nature of life."

"But why is life even there?"

Xius couldn't hold it in anymore and burst out laughing. Set glared at him but remained slouched against the wall, long legs poking his feet out between the wooden rails of the balcony.

"Very well, I'll play philosopher," said Xius. "Life is there because Ra got bored."

"So, we are the result of boredom..."

"Fine, the purpose of life is happiness. Happiness is when we feel the fulfillment of our purpose."

"And I presume you're going to then tell me that suffering is to teach us how to feel happiness."

Xius raised his goblet to the stars. "Opposites in all things, Set. The law of existence."

His vizier rolled his eyes and took a deep swig of his drink.

After a few minutes, Xius set down his empty goblet and adjusted his body so his feet were also poking out over the edge. “You'll see her again.”

Set said nothing. Then his mouth tightened and his eyes closed.

“It doesn't make any sense. Why must I wait here while she's there? This mortal realm is pointless.”

“Because you like me.”

“Don't joke with me, Xius. I'm not in the mood.”

“You don't like me?”

Xius winced as Set's wooden goblet bounced off his breastbone and over the side of the balcony. He watched it fall, twisting end over end, until the balcony's edge blocked his view.

Xius rubbed his sore breastbone. “Can't say I didn't deserve that.”

“You're an asshole.”

“And you dare slander your pharaoh?”

“I'm drunk.”

“Must be.”

“The slave is getting better at speaking.”

“Good. Now we can forget about her.”

“Not quite.”

Xius lifted his head and propped himself up with his elbows. “What, still think she's a royal? I already told you, she isn't.”

“But she has the character of one. One true to their blood, that is.”

“Come on, you can't be that drunk.”

“Perhaps I am. Though...”

“Though what?”

“The other day, as I taught her, I could feel her mind and see the truth in her eyes. She’s honest to a fault, just like Tawaret. I think she *is* from the future.”

Xius rolled his eyes. “Go to bed, cousin.”

“And the way she holds her head high, even while the servants glared at her—so like her too.”

“I said go to bed. It's a good thing you chucked your cup

because you've had enough—and no, I'm not ordering you another one."

Set glared. "I'm not a glutton, your majesty."

"Go to bed anyway, it's late."

On his way out, Set once more donned his blue coat of office and reminded Xius of the meeting on bread and bear shares for workers in the morning. After he left, Xius wandered in from the night and closed the curtains over his balcony. Despite his humor, Set's words troubled him. Even when drunk, Set often was right. But anything being from the future made no sense. The future was yet to be made. How could someone from a place that had yet to exist be here?

Also, it was more than apparent that two years wasn't enough for Set to forget Tawaret. What if he never moved on?

Too sober and fidgety for sleep, he threw on a tunic and some shoes and headed out for a walk. His personal guard lingered at his chambers at his signal, though they looked hesitant. He wanted to be alone. Besides, he had guards all around the palace. He'd be fine.

The palace echoed with the melody of crickets. Most of the braziers had been put out, but the clear starlight and silvery moon lit his way well enough. He liked the palace better like this. In the empty darkness, there were no judging eyes or expectations for him to be anything other than Xius. Not a god or a pharaoh. Just a man, as Set had said.

Not to mention there was something seductive about the smell of the night. Perhaps it was the perfume of Nut. He felt sorry for Geb, never able to embrace his wife of the sky for danger of smothering life, yet still able to smell her fragrance.

A white figure broke into his line of view. For a minute he thought he had just seen a burst of moonlight through the granite pillars.

"Annette?"

She stumbled to a halt, nearly falling over. With a huff she threw back her thick white hair and looked back to see who had called her name, pale face flushed. Xius immediately flushed at what she had done to the slave's gown she had been given. Besides her usual strange way of wearing it well above her breasts, she had sliced it up the sides to reveal her long slender legs and shapely thighs.

He turned his head away. “What have you done with your dress?”

“You people wear tubes, Pharaoh. I couldn't run at all with it riding up to my waist.”

“What you find in sprinting around like a child, I don't know, but you shouldn't. People are going to think you are a harlot.”

“Oh please, there's no one around. Besides, I tie the tear close when I go back. Now is there anything else or can I go, oh great Pharaoh?”

He looked back at her in amazement. The hard way she looked at him would have suggested she hated him, and the way she held herself, unbending, spoke that she held no respect and no fear of his position whatsoever, as usual. She had been so meek since they had begun her lessons, he had thought she had learned.

“Why are you so angry with me?” he asked. “What have I ever done to you? And what happened to that fear you showed when you begged me for help?”

She flicked her head back and scowled. “Anyone would be afraid after being whipped within an inch of their lives.”

“I thought you spoke Carpathian—”

“I don't even know what Carpathian is!”

“Well, how was I to know that? I don't even know what language you’re speaking!”

“English! I told you the first time!”

Xius bristled and he could feel his hackles rising, as though he had turned into some kind of wild dog. Just because no one was around, she thought she could treat him whatever way she wanted? Or was it because this was one of the few times she saw him without all his finery?

And then suddenly, he decided he didn't care. Moments before, he was happy to wander as neither a god nor pharaoh. He didn’t want to worry about what this slave thought of him too.

“You're not there anymore, I've tended to your wounds—”

"Your servants did, Pharaoh—"

"—I feed you, I clothe you, I provide protection, and yet you've turned on my like some dung sodden bitch against her owner—why? What possible reason do you have to hate me with such—with such passion when you know nothing about me!"

"Why do I need to know you? I don't even care! You throw me in as a slave and every freaking day you treat me as an uninvited invader who snuck in when I wasn't wanted and who should have been killed, and then you call me a liar when all I've EVER done is told you the truth! Well, news flash, your majesty, I don't even want to be in your stupid country!"

He swelled and the blood pounded in his ears. She, slander Egypt, the choice land of the gods? "You foolish—"

But she wasn't finished. "And then you, by some sick twist of fate, are the only person who can understand a word that I'm saying, but you abandon me with a bunch of people who can't and expect me to be useful? Don't you have any idea how *lonely* that is?" Her voice cracked and her eyes gleamed with a threat of tears. The rage had melted from her ever so slightly and for a moment, he caught a reminder of the fragile girl who had pled at his feet. He felt himself waver on the edge of either striking her or pitying her, but before he could decide what to say or do next, she bolted.

"Wait!" he cried.

And before he could think better of it, he ran after her. They raced across the polished floor of the palace porches and against the starry gown of Nut, but for Xius it was like chasing a gazelle.

"Stop!" he panted. Just as she vanished behind a corner and he finally accepted there wasn't even a dream of ever catching up, he yelled. "Please!"

He stumbled, fell to his hands, and gasped for breath. Stone eyes of gods watched from their decorative pedestals. They almost seemed to ask with him: What are you doing? Why is a pharaoh doing such a thing as running, let alone after a slave? Even pleading with her?

He didn't know how long he knelt there, eyes to the floor,

drinking in the air, before pale feet stepped into his view. He quickly got up, ashamed to find himself on the floor by an inferior, and an ungrateful one at that. But he couldn't find the words to scold her when she met his eye once more, so honest and unashamed. He suddenly couldn't find disrespect in them anymore.

"You said please," she said.

"I won't say it again."

But, for the first time, her gaze softened. She folded her arms and leaned on her hip. A leg peeked out from the slit. "What do you want?"

"To understand."

"Sounds almost deep, like a song." Then she smiled at him, a tiny thing, really, but a smile nonetheless. "You must be pretty desperate to say please to a slave, you racist."

He grimaced. "Don't get cocky, or you *will* regret it."

"Or what? You'll kill me? Beat me? But you won't." She leaned forward, almost teasingly. "Because then you would have said 'please' for no reason."

"Why do you resent Egypt?" he asked, too tired to try and defend himself anymore. "You must want something I've failed to give, what is it? What do you want so badly that makes you hate me? Hate us?"

She blinked at him and seemed to withdraw into herself. In an instant she returned to the fragile, begging girl, and he couldn't help but be confused at how quickly she could switch between savage and flower.

"Simple, Pharaoh. I only want a friend."

The stunned silence between them only lasted for a moment.

"Xius!"

Annette ran for it before Xius could stop her. He turned around, ready to shout Set down for his annoying timing, but the urgency on his face stopped him, even as Set reached him at a run, lamp in his upraised hand.

"Just my luck you decide to go on a midnight walk," Set said as he caught his breath. "Denan's gone, your majesty."

"What do you mean 'gone'? Have you checked the unused

barracks? He sometimes likes to go there to think."

"That's not what I mean," Set wiped his brow. "Neither Aphery nor his soldiers can find him. He's been missing all day. We think he's been captured or taken hostage."

Xius felt his stomach jump. "By whom?"

"I don't know."

Part Three

Of These

A week before Denan the General had vanished, Hath sat on Kasmut's bed with her elbows clenched between her knees and a mass of soft blankets clutched to her chest. Jee stood to the side of her chambers, gaze switching from the hallway to the balcony and to the side of the room.

"No one is going to attack me," she muttered.

"I'm doing my job."

"Have you made it? According to all my instructions?"

Jee's thick nose wrinkled. He didn't approve of her idea at all. "Yes."

"Okay, you know what to do with it."

"This is foolish of you. You haven't given the Pharaoh time and this potion is a waste of resources."

"He thinks I'm boring, Jee, *boring*. Ugly is one thing, but there's no way a woman can recover in a man's eyes from being boring, of all things. Wretched, childish creatures."

His eyes narrowed and switched to the balcony. "You are playing with the royal general. You may be hidden, but he is powerful."

"We're not going to kill him," she said, almost scathingly. "I'm going to save him and my prince will finally really see—and we need the blood of a noble anyway if we're ever going to finish my father's spell."

"There is such a thing as trying too hard. There are others of noble blood, after all."

"Just do it."

"I must wait for night."

"Oo, yes, the cover of darkness, how professional of you." She stuffed her face into the blankets, her guts a twist of anxiety. What if she *was* trying too hard? But all she had for an answer to that was her fear and the memory of her spindly dead limbs. She couldn't handle it anymore. She needed her prince. She needed to feel his warm arms and taste of his kindness. The skin she wore wouldn't feel right until then, and she had gotten desperate. What if he never decided? Even though she felt transparent whenever he looked at her.

"Your friends are coming to visit," said Jee faintly, his focus on a point somewhere below Kasmut's balcony.

"Kasmut's friends."

"Your friends, so you should probably stop speaking Kush."

Kasmut scowled. Bit by bit, she felt her identity being sucked up in Kasmut's. The woman was dead! Why did she still feel like her slave? She heard her voice every time she spoke, saw her every time she looked in the mirror, and only Jee mentioned her true name from time to time. She even dreamed of her, standing before her with the whip in her hand, face full of fury. Always with the whip, and this time Hath punishment would be far beyond that of losing a jasper hair-piece.

At least the nightmares made it hard for Hath to feel sympathy for taking her mistresses place in life. Death was a gift. Kasmut would only find peace, and she had lived life long enough to know what Hath had rescued her from, surely. Perhaps death wasn't so sweet as Kasmut had never really suffered in her life, and therefore wouldn't understand the priceless value of the peace Hath had given her.

As Kasmut's friends came by to coax her out, insisting she tell them about her relationship with the handsome pharaoh, she forced on a smile, swallowed her black, Kushite heart, and responded in a perfect imitation of Kasmut.

***

It had been three days since the general's disappearance. Aphery was in a panic over her missing husband, and Denan's daughters wandered the halls of the palace with plaintive faces. One daughter, the youngest at age 5, had even approached Xius to ask if he had seen her papa. Before he could answer her sisters dragged her away.

Also, Annette had not spoken a word to him since that night and Xius hadn't brought it up, at a loss for what to say to her.

Needless to say, he was more than distracted.

And then Set came through the door of the throne room with a look Xius knew all too well. His nerves rankled at Set's forced calm. The scribes and noblemen, who were discussing the annual receding of the Nile, cowered at his feet, hyper-aware of the Pharaoh's bad mood.

"What?" Xius asked him, none too kindly. He got his reward at the subtle, reproachful flitter across Set's features.

"If your majesty is too busy—"

"Just tell me."

Set glanced about the room with a frown. "Sire, are you sure, in front of…?"

Xius only had to glare at the small crowd gathered below him before they scattered. Set folded his hands behind his back.

"Do you remember the murder of Merkha's slave Denan mentioned the night Annette came, your majesty?"

"What about them?"

"Well, your majesty," Set gnawed on the corner of his lip.

"What?"

"Three more maidens were found this morning appearing to have been killed the same way as that slave." Xius fell off the fist he had been leaning his cheek against. "All within marrying age, all with the same sliced throat and drained of their blood."

"Where were these girls found?" He could feel his stomach growing cold.

"Near the homesteads next to the palace, your majesty. Another very worrisome sign. I cannot say that Denan doesn't have anything to do with this. His disappearance is highly unusual, especially given that he has yet to explain how Annette managed to get past his guard. And he didn't find who was guilty of the slave's death."

Xius prickled. "Are you daring to say you think Denan is behind these?"

"Of course not, your majesty. But...you have to admit it is strange."

"How do you know Denan wasn't taken by this killer?"

"So far, only young virgin women have been killed." Set gave Xius one of his narrow-eyed gazes. "I may be mistaken in this, but the general never struck me as the most feminine virgin, especially considering he has three children and a wife."

"That's not what I mean," said Xius, flushing beneath his simple, royal headdress, "What if he got in their way or became a threat?"

"We don't even know who 'they' are or whether the girls were murdered in the first place—"

"Oh Ra, Set, don't tell me you're implying they just dropped dead out of an illness that happened to slit their throats."

Set gave an exasperated sigh, which did nothing to stop Xius from clenching his fists.

"Your majesty," he said while rubbing a forefinger and thumb along his eyebrows, "I only meant that it would be unwise to jump to conclusions. Of course I'm not stupid enough to think their deaths were in any way natural, and you know that. But it could have been suicide, and Kasmut was unable to see the killer. All she could attest to was finding the body—she had even fainted on finding her handmaid dead, poor girl." Set paused, eyes to Xius's white knuckles. "Will you calm down? This is stressful enough for me."

"Stressful for you? How do you think it is for me? I have to keep reassuring Aphery and the girls of things I don't even know when there's a possibility that there are some kind of crazy cultists out there—"

Set stiffened abruptly. "Cultists? I never said anything about cultists."

There came a tangible twinge to the air. Xius was close to

Set's taboo subject. Horrifically close.

"What else could it be?" he said, trying to sound calm. "What is the likelihood that all these girls slashed themselves? And in the same way Tawaret was killed?"

"I took care of all those cultists. There's no way the killers of Tawaret would be doing this under my very nose, right next to the palace. It could just be a man whose mind is bemused by the gods or who has some sick sense of humor. Honestly, that the girls were killed out of some…religious fervor seems rather rash."

Set's expression had turned dangerously cool, and the skin about his eyes paled. For a moment, Xius feared his friend would once more crumple in on himself and grow dead to the world as he had two years ago after the Kushite purge.

As soon as his taunt mood came, however, it left.

"I suppose you have a valid point," he said softly. "But still, we must not be too quick to jump to conclusions. We would have to seek out the religious texts of the banished ones to verify that these are indeed the same cuts; but either way, I made sure all of those bloodthirsty Kushite savages were executed. Unless they somehow converted others while my back was turned—also unlikely."

"By Ra, you're not perfect, Set!"

Set wrinkled his nose and the muscles around his jaw tensed. Xius heard a soft scrunch of material as Set clenched his hands into his robes "I am quite aware of this, and I'd appreciate it if you stopped yelling at me. We have no evidence of anything like this yet besides the cuts, and we have to focus on finding Denan first."

Outside, in the aging light of day, a holy ibis stalked its way through the gardens on long, black legs.

Xius took a deep breath, unclenched his hands, and slipped the crown off his head to run a hand through his hair.

"Set, what if Denan…what if he's—"

"There's no warrior in the land that could best him, not even if he was asleep."

The ibis arched its head back with a tiny snack in its beak and swallowed it in one gulp. It then went back to furrowing through the dewy grass.

Set ran a thumb along the inside lining of his blue robe. “Your majesty, should the general be found to have left for the eternal Nile, I must advise you to keep your head. You are Pharaoh and have no time to give in to your passions just because you are on friendly terms with him.”

“On friendly terms?” he said quietly. “Is that really what you think he amounts to?”

“By the gods—*of course I care!* But this isn’t just about us. This is about the whole country. We are only here to serve the people, and if they see you, their Pharaoh, their God Protector on earth, start wailing and tearing at his hair after all these deaths, no matter how they happened, how do you think they will react?”

Xius faltered and his anger died. Set was right. Set was *always* right.

“Besides,” Set continued, “there’s no need to get dramatic, your majesty; we don’t know what happened yet. For all we know, he’s simply tied up somewhere and giving his kidnappers hell and will be back tomorrow morning.” Set shifted onto one foot and uncurled his arms to his sides. “But aside from cultists, have you asked the slave about the black box yet?”

“Uh, yes.”

“Well?”

Xius could feel the heat creeping up his neck. “Well, I didn’t really understand. She said the stone was some sort of…cam-ah, or cam-rah, which ‘takes pictures.’ Then she went babbling on about hieroglyphics and some shop that makes special papyrus.”

“But it's harmless?”

“Yes.”

Set grunted and ran a hand through his hair. “Useless. Either way, it’s more important to find where Denan has gone and if it has to do with these deaths.”

“Agreed. We can worry about where she comes from later. What of her other items?”

“Just some food and very fine papyrus and writing sticks. We also found a few rocks that look like they might have a bit of quartz in them."

"There we have it, then. Unless she planned on killing someone with pretty rocks, she might as well just be any other slave."

***

Xius did not return to his bedroom until the torches and braziers were lit about the palace and the city sitting at the foot of his grand estate glowed with lamplight. After his meeting with Set, he had gone to the newly built temple of Horus, where he had prayed until his knees felt tender from the hard stone. Now and then priests had ambled by, holding their hairless heads high. Their songs still hummed in his ear, and his nose still burned with incense.

As he entered, intending to shed his jewelry and crown before meeting Set for dinner in the kitchens, he was surprised to find Annette curled up on a cushion next to the open balcony, face up to the night sky. Fine linen curtains flickered toward her in the breeze.

"Why did my guards let you in here?"

She turned and bowed herself into a ball on the floor before him.

"Set sent me. He gave me this weird piece of cloth and your guards took it. I think he's wondering where you are. He was asking me all sorts of weird questions. What's 'Denan'?"

"It's not what, it's who. He's my chief general."

"Oh. So...he's missing?"

Xius grunted in response. He stripped off his pleated temple robes as he made his way to the center of the room by the lit brazier. He collapsed onto the ring of cushions, taking off his bracelets, armband, and heavy, thick-beaded necklace till all he wore was his simple linen kilt and the medallion that allowed his speech with her. He kept it on at all times and had long ago gotten used to sleeping with it, as his father had instructed him to as a way to come more in tune with its magic.

"Your stars are beautiful, Pharaoh. I didn't know there were so many in the sky."

He let his jewelry drop onto the floor. It would be picked up later. "Our stars?"

She blinked and turned to glance back at him across the fire. He wondered at the peculiar intensity her ice blue eyes seemed to always have. There was something unnatural about having one's pupil standing out so. It gave her eyes an almost naked quality.

"Excuse me, your highness."

And she turned back to the stars. He once more found himself growing agitated. He couldn't tell if she was being polite or sarcastic. Besides that, it had become more than apparent that he could not get both of the things he felt he needed from her: the respect he deserved and openness with him. He was even more annoyed at how comfortable she made herself in his royal chambers without even asking for permission. But, she would speak to no pharaoh.

With an inward sigh, he decided.

"What do you mean 'so many'? Have you never seen the sky at night?"

"Yeah, it's just where I come from it's hard to see the stars. Most of the time, you hardly see them at all."

"Why is that?"

"Light pollution. You know when you sit by a fire and the stars don't show as well against the light? Same concept—your highness."

"Are your cities really filled with fire?"

The corner of her mouth twitched. "You could say that, your highness. That is how I had to describe it to your vizier."

"That must be a lot of maintenance."

"I guess you could say that too, your highness."

A brief silence fell and he took his time pulling on his sandals. The kitchen floors weren't the cleanest of places.

"Come on. Back to the kitchens. You've done what you were sent for."

She did as told and followed him. At one point she asked if it was weird for a royal pharaoh to be somewhere like the kitchens and he, wanting her to continue being comfortable enough to keep talking, told her yes, but that he didn't care. Besides, he went down to visit his father's old friend, Wenamon, who had been a sort of uncle to him growing up.

Down below, Set sat at the table with a writing stick and an unfurled roll of papyrus. She sat next to Set and sighed when Xius gave her a pointed glare to move her to the floor.

"That's a bit unnecessary," said Set as Annette slid down to the ground.

Xius ignored him. “Why did you send her up for me?”

“Because I wanted you to translate a few words for us before I give her the lesson for tonight.”

Xius stiffened, “I thought we agreed that Denan came first?”

“Before finding out where she came from, yes, but I still have time before bed to teach her a bit. Besides, I find it relaxing.”

“This isn’t a time for relaxation, Denan—”

“There’s only so much I can do. Denan’s first captain has already sent out the search party for tonight, and you did give me the duty to teach her as well. Do you expect me to go out into the streets in the dead of night and search as well?”

Forcing out a breath, Xius dropped down onto the bench opposite of Set and leaned his forehead on his palm.

“Fine. What words do you need?”

“There’s no need for the attitude. Denan will be found, I swear it.”

“Just tell me the words already.”

Set gave him a list of them that he had heard in English, which Xius then would give the equal word in Egyptian for, which Set would then write down on the papyrus. The sound of her own language at first caught Annette by surprise, but when she realized what was happening she went back to the propping her cheek up with her hand and staring at the fire still lit in the last oven.

As Set finished scratching down Xius’s last answer, Xius met Annette’s unaware gaze. The light of the fire turned her hair orange.

“Where’s Wenamon?” he asked.

“He turned in for the night,” said Set. “Was feeling a bit off, apparently.”

“As well as the other servants?”

Set stopped to look up curiously. “Why so interested in servant schedules?”

“Because Annette’s just sitting there. I figured she’d have work to do or something.”

“She’d finished up before I came.”

“How do you know that?”

Set blinked at him as though the answer was obvious. “She told me.” And then he went back to the papyrus, probably to reread what he had written.

This got Xius thinking though. He couldn’t quite remember ever seeing Set so relaxed with a slave before.

“Set, in teaching her—how is that relaxing?”

Set paused again, but didn’t look up. “I’m not sure.”

After a few moments, though, in which Xius fell into thought, Set made corrections, and Annette sat ignoring them, Set said: “She truly does remind me of Tawaret.”

Xius remembered their conversation of the other night and took another look at Annette’s obvious foreign features. Tawaret had been tall, taller than Xius, and painted with the traditional brown Egyptian hues, while Annette was just as tall as him and alien. He couldn’t see any resemblance whatsoever.

Seeing the look on his face, Set hesitated. “Remember when she caught me drunk in the stables with Denan?”

Xius burst with laughter, startling Annette, who didn’t seem to be able to follow their conversation.

“Don’t get me started,” chortled Xius, “I just managed to forget.”

And he had had to forget, for every time he remembered his cool, collected friend naked and dancing about with the huge bear of a man before the horses, it’d be a while before he could shake off the mirth.

The corner of Set’s mouth twitched. “But remember that look she gave me?”

“Look? Ra, Set, she barely gave you a glance before leaving you to it and sending over every woman she could find. Served you right for getting so plastered.” He managed to smother down his chuckles to ask what this had to do with Annette.

“Well,” Set looked down at the girl, who on meeting his eye frowned in confusion. He gave her a soft smile. “She had that same look at me earlier. The same as Tawaret. I think I actually got afraid.”

Recognizing the warmth in Set's gaze, Xius sobered. "Set…"

His friend looked back at him, expression blank and warmth forgotten. For a minute Xius thought he had been mistaken.

"Yes?"

His stomach gave an uncomfortable twist. Xius rubbed his eyes hard. It was too late for this. He should just be happy that Set had been able to talk about Tawaret without changing the subject or breaking down. Even though Xius hadn't known her as Set had, he missed her as well. She had only ever been kind and warm to him.

"Nothing. I'm going to bed."

Set nodded. "Sorry for keeping you up."

Xius made his way to the staircase. Annette straightened.

"Good night, Pharaoh."

He glanced back at her and felt the uncomfortable twisting again. He couldn't see Tawaret at all in her disrespectful gaze.

But he nodded to her nonetheless and went up the stairs.

***

"Pharaoh!"

Xius stopped with armfuls of scrolls, somewhat alarmed, as Kasmut strode over to him with a bright smile.

"Would you like some help with those?"

"I can manage quite well, thank you."

"May I ask what they are, your majesty?"

"Poetry."

She blinked. "Poetry?"

"Yes. I had some emissaries send me poetry from the areas they were in, translated into Egyptian." He readjusted his load and tried to his best to look polite. "How can I help you today, Kasmut?"

"Well, I just thought," she tucked her hands in front of her and looked up at him from beneath her lashes, "that since you wanted to know more about me, we could do something together. Something fun."

"What did you have in mind?"

"Nothing much. Just a dinner in my quarters with some entertainment, unless...would you be so kind as to share your poetry with me?"

The answer was no. He rather enjoyed indulging in this particular interest by himself ever since Set and Denan had laughed till they cried when he recited a poem to them without knowing what it meant. Being younger and more naïve than them, he hadn't realized the topic of the poem at the time.

But he couldn't tell Kasmut that. If she was to be his royal head wife, he'd just have to find out if she'd laugh at him too.

"I, um," No, stop, he was Pharaoh. "Of course. One or two would be fine. But I can't spend too much time with you, today is Sobek's Rinsing and I have to be at the Nile in an hour or so."

"What are you doing after?"

"Leading a search party."

"The General's still missing, then? I'm so sorry, I hope he's okay."

She followed him to a small courtyard that branched off the guest quarter's reserved for high priority guests. His sweaty hands unrolled the first poem and he sat down next to an ancient olive tree.

"Love, I do not know you," he started. "Though the salt brine and whales sing, I cannot see you on the rocks. Dusty winds will always blow away."

When it became apparent to her that was the end, she made a face. "That's...what is that?"

"Hittite. Though I've never bothered to ask a Hittite about what it was about. Didn't think it was important."

"Uh huh. All right. Can I hear another?"

"Um," he rolled to the next section of the papyrus. "Here's one, Carpathian: Hark, red suns only mean heaviness, dark skies twilight, and I care not for your bed, nor for your roof of brambles, nests to swallows, dusk to dawn. A rocky path invites me with spilled wine, a belly empty, an eye full. The sea crosses my brow. "

A sparrow landed on an olive branch above him and twittered a song. Voices echoed down the hall against the patter of sandals.

"What does it mean?" she asked.

He shrugged. "I don't know." He didn't much like this. His mind wandered to ideas of how to get away.

"Why do you enjoy reading it if you don't understand it? And why do you even care for such lowly poetry? I'm still surprised the Hittites even write poetry, they seem too violent."

"Didn't you hear it?"

"Hear what, your majesty?"

"The sound. The way the words worked after each other, like a song, even in Egyptian."

She tapped her nails together and rolled her shoulder back into her scarlet hair. "A song, huh? Is it easier to hear in their native tongue? I'm sorry, am I stupid for not hearing?"

He rolled up the scroll. "No. I was just wondering. I need to go now, Kasmut. Dinner tonight?"

"Oh, yes," she smiled. "I'll send a servant for you."

He nodded to show he heard and left. After dropping off the poetry in his study, he continued on to the front of the palace, where Set waited for him.

The sun blazed down. Set stood with a hand cupped above his eyes. Two guards knelt on the ground with their horses beside them.

"Your majesty," Set bowed."We must show Sobek we are making the effort. I'm afraid the litter is out of the question."

"I've done this before, Set. I can ride a horse. I prefer it, even."

Set gave him a blank look."Then you would have remembered those were my lines for the ceremony. Just get on the horse, your majesty, we are going to be late."

Down in the bulrushes, the sun turned the Nile into a giant, shifting mirror of light and he had to squint to make out the forms of the ceremonial procession. His guard rode close, with Set alongside him.

"The men will be waiting for you afterward. I still don't agree that this is the appropriate time for a search."

Xius replied with a noncommittal grunt, shielding his eyes. At least they were on the east side of the Nile, facing away from the late morning sun.

His dark steed gave a snort and shook its head of the morning gnats. A tall statue with a crocodile head stood upon a tiered pedestal just out of the reach of the river. Once they made it into its shadows Xius dismounted, followed by his guard and Set. Several people ambled up and down the steps to the temple just behind the statue, including Isis, followed by several of her priestesses. Incense wafted about them, swirling to the throb of their chants. Being a priestess, all her hair, including her eyebrows, was gone, leaving her scalp smooth and her dark eyes somewhat too large for her face. Yet, despite her hairlessness, she was beautiful with her high-cheeked noble face, thick purple lips, and brown-cream skin. Ever since Xius was a child he had thought so.

"Isis."

Those too-big dark eyes found him and she bowed. "Ah, Son of the Gods. And Seti," she smiled at Set.

"Haven't heard that name in a while," said Set. Then he cleared his throat, straightened, and put his hands before him as though holding up a box. "I can witness that the Pharaoh made the effort required to come here."

"And I receive it." She gestured the other priests forward. "Take your places."

As the priests scrambled about them, Xius bent in to Isis with a, hopefully, hidden smile. "You know, it was more the horse's efforts."

"Hush, have you no reverence? You, out of all people, should be in earnest for the gods' assistance."

He was properly cowed and bowed his head. He allowed the priests to approach him and peel off his garments till all he wore was a linen kilt. The last to come off was his crown, replaced with an eye of ash upon his forehead. Incense filled his nose when they swept the burning sticks before his chest, where his heart, the seat of his soul and thoughts, resided.

Isis lifted her voice in prayer, and Set stepped up to Xius's side, also in his kilt, with the ceremonial Feather of Truth strapped to his forehead. He crouched till his knees were just above the ground, chin to his collar bone. During this ceremony, Set was to take the place of ma'at, the order of all things, and would guide Xius to the proper respect to present before any god. Thus, Xius followed into the squat.

He tried to keep his mind focused as Set whispered the prayer to Sobek to him and he echoed him for the river to hear, knees still just above the mud. But by the time Set had finished telling him the prayer and he could stand, Xius's thoughts were to the last time he witnessed this annual ceremony to beseech the favor of the river god for a plentiful flood. His father had been in his place, graying but strong.

And now, with not a sibling to pass the crown on to, nor a wife to produce children, Xius had already lost his general and friend and allowed a killer near the palace.

The cold water of the Nile lapped up his shins. Silt squashed up between his toes and sucked in his heels. Set walked beside him.

"Do you have an offering?" Set asked.

Xius blanched. "I was supposed to bring an offering?"

He didn't have to see it to know Set was looking to the sky in exasperation, as though Nut herself could fix Xius's forgetfulness. “Something you promise to do in return for Sobek's blessing. Something that would please him.”

What did you give a river? Xius scrambled for something, all the while feeling goose bumps erupt over his skin from the chilly water. He could feel his feet sinking deeper.

He looked down into the depths of the Nile, where the water turned murky from the dirt he had unsettled. A slender movement of green caught his eye as a fish darted downriver.

His father would have thought of something grand. He would have known the river as he should have, like a brother.

Xius knelt into the river, and Set flinched.

“Xius—” but he stopped when he heard Xius whisper.

“Sobek, I know so little about you and your ways, so forgive my meager offering to do the best I can do, as a pharaoh, as a friend, as a man, and...” Xius hesitated. “And to do even more, if needs be, just, please...” Xius closed his eyes tightly and felt the cold water brushing past his skin. He could no longer feel his toes. “Please help me find him.”

He didn't know if Set heard all that, but he hoped not and stood, the linen of his kilt clinging to his thighs. A breeze blew over him and his teeth started to chatter. He clenched his jaw to stop them. Set's hand on his shoulder felt marvelously warm.

“Now seal the promise with the sign,” said Set, and Xius held his hand to his right shoulder, keeping his fingers straight. “Good, now we can leave the water.”

Complete silence reigned over them as Xius and Set sloshed out of the river, shivering and legs wet with silt. Isis smiled at both of them and wrapped a thick wool blanket around Xius.

“It is well.”

No sooner had she said this than murmurs broke over the priests. They looked up, following the collective gaze upriver to where a woman made her way to them, her brilliant red hair standing out against the green bulrushes and blue sky.

“Help!” she cried, “There's a man back here in the mud; he's injured! I think the crocodiles got to him!”

Could it be?

“Kasmut?” Xius held onto his blanket and made his way to

her through the priests. “Who did you see?”

“I'm not sure, but I think,” her lip trembled and her eyes were wide, “I think it's him.”

He didn't have to ask more, but hit the banks running.

“Lead the way!”

Kasmut nodded and pivoted on the spot to run alongside him. Upon his other side came Set, easily keeping up with him on his long legs.

“What are the chances?” said Set.

“As good as anything else.”

The bulrushes swallowed them, their sword-like fronds stinging as they slipped across his skin. He kept his eyes on her bright red hair as she pushed aside the fronds.

They came to a narrow clearing on the banks.

“Here,” she said.

He scanned the area. Still, he saw nothing. Set stepped out in front as Xius's guard came out from the bulrushes behind them. Something wasn’t right about the mud, right at the edge of the river. He trudged across the sludge to it. Yes, yes it was a man, nearly covered in mud. Set and he dropped to the man's side, throwing decorum aside, to wipe enough mud off of his face to make certain. Xius's breath caught in his throat.

Denan. He’d know that broad, bald head anywhere.

Heart in his throat, he met Set's eyes. Kasmut hovered a few feet away, hands balled up against her breast. Meanwhile, his guard filed out behind him. As Set pressed his fingers to Denan's throat, fear clenched Xius so hard he thought he wouldn't be able to breathe.

But then Set looked up and gave the barest of smiles. Xius put his wrist to his general's open mouth and felt the faintest of breezes.

“Help me!” He lifted up one side of Denan and Set the other. His guards nearly tumbled over each other to reach their commander.

“Your majesty, we can take him—”

“No! I will see to it personally that he gets to the palace. Help me get him onto my horse!”

“But sire, any of our horses will do.”

"Just move! Quickly!"

They rushed to obey, each putting their hands beneath a leg and Denan's back to lift him up between them while Xius and Set each took a shoulder. Through the fronds once more they went in an awkward, sideways, running gait.

"Don't you die," Xius heard Set grunt. "Don't you dare die, Denan."

The priests watched, the spot of sunlight on their heads gleaming like a third eye. They muttered in surprise as the guards and Set heaved the limp body across the shoulders of Xius's large black stallion. Xius, having always been the smallest of Set, Denan, and himself, was barely able to slip behind him comfortably and still reach the reigns. Kasmut watched with the priests, her hands now clenching her skirt. With one arm gripping Denan so he did not fall, he kicked his horse slipping and popping out of the mire of the Nile silt and back into the city.

Covered in black mud, half naked, and carrying a man twice their size, Set, Xius, and their guard attracted more than enough stares upon entering the palace. At the Pharaoh's bark, though, all hit the floor running to comply. Before he knew it, not just one physician, but seven came running as though chased by Ammit herself, eater of unworthy hearts. Each was followed by a stretcher.

"Only the gods can save you if this man doesn't live," he growled as he loaded Denan into one of the stretchers with the help of his guard. The healers paled at the sight of the general. Men picked him up (quickly turning red in the face from his weight) and trundled off. Xius moved to go after them. He had only gone a few steps when a muddy hand caught his equally muddy forearm.

"They'll do everything they can, your majesty. You will only get in the way," said Set.

"But he's dying!"

"That may or may not be. I could hardly see anything amidst all that mud, I might've been mistaken."

"Let me go."

Set's expression softened. "Xius, you have done all you

can."

Scowling, Xius wrenched his arm from his grasp like an angry adolescent. Though he refused to look at his chief advisor, he didn't attempt to follow after the physicians again. Set was right. Set was always right. But he hated it. He hated how helpless he felt. What was the point of being god on Earth if you couldn't do anything!

And then he noticed the whispers. Courtiers and palace servants had tried to place themselves inconspicuously beside pillars or behind corners. Merkha was amongst them, whispering something to his brother, who gave him a look as though he couldn't believe what he had just heard. Were they here to behold Xius's helplessness? Mock him in his royal robes, caked in mud? Or to fascinate themselves with the tragedy of his fallen general?

Set reached out to him once more.

"Let's get washed, your majesty."

This time, he didn't fight Set's touch.

***

Set left him at his quarters and returned, still muddy himself, with Annette at his side carrying a basket of soaps and towels. He left once more with a quick bow, explaining that it was inappropriate to appear so ungodly filthy before the Pharaoh and promising to bring back food. Xius was touched that Set went through the trouble of tending to the Pharaoh himself, but then again, it just showed his apprehension. He became a workaholic of sorts whenever troubled.

Annette bowed before cocking her head to the side, eyebrows furrowed and lips tight with a held-back smile.

"Whoa, what happened to you, Pharaoh?"

"Did I ask for an interrogation? No."

He had thrown himself onto his couch, not caring about the still-damp mud smearing all over the white fabric. She made her way over to him.

"You look…" but she snapped her mouth shut. Cautiously, as though trying to not bother a drowsy lion, she sat herself at his side. "Um, Set said he wanted me to help you wash up."

He said nothing. When she continued to look at him, waiting, his ire rose up again.

"Don't look at me with those ugly eyes!" he snapped. Of course it was a pathetic lie. Before he could feel guilty, however, she turned around, set the basket at her side, and didn't move.

After a few minutes he began to feel his frustration subside. Without giving it much thought he reached out a hand and touched her strange, white hair. So soft. Unable to help himself, he moved to stroke it, running his fingers through it as though it were a pelt from a prized cheetah. To his mild surprise she didn't pull away or glare at him for the intrusion of her space. He found the texture relieving. He just had to listen to Set. He had done all he could. Yet Denan's breath had been so faint.

He was acting like a child—no, an infant. It was disgraceful. He pulled his hand away from her hair.

"Pharaoh?" she turned her face partway, but kept her eyes to the floor.

"What do you want?"

"Would you like me to get you a cloth and a bowl of water, then? I mean, you look like you don't want to move."

This startled him out of his self-loathing. Had she really just offered to—of her own free will? Then, it occurred to him what she must be doing and any good feeling fled.

"I don't need your pity, *slave.*"

"I don't pity you," she snapped, and it was almost a relief to hear her old resentment. "I just wanted to help you feel better."

"Just be quiet."

She turned her head away again. This time, when he had calmed down enough to seek the comfort of her soft hair once more, she pulled away from his reach. When he finally stood to go to his bath, which lay down a staircase behind a tall statue of Bastet in his room, she handed him the basket and gave him such a sharp glare that he didn't bother expecting her to help him. He was too tired to fight her stubbornness, so he went and bathed himself.

When he returned, Set was just walking in, a tray of Wenamon's delicious honeyed rolls in his hands. Annette still sat sullenly next to Xius's mud-stained couch. He looked from Xius to Annette, mouth quirked and eyebrows raised.

"Did you bathe yourself?"

"My arms work quite fine, thank you," said Xius as he flung his wet towel over his banister.

Set sighed, shrugged, and put the tray down on the small table next to the couch before sitting down on a chair. He attempted a small smile.

"Well, I guess we won't have to go out and search today after all."

"How is he?"

Set's smile melted away. Xius's heart sank.

"I'm afraid, your majesty, that they have uncovered many injuries beneath the mud, with quite a few showing signs of infection. He has lost a lot of blood."

A cool breeze blew in, making Xius shiver. He shut the blinds over the balcony and picked up a honey roll, although he didn't feel like eating.

"He...he will be fine, though. Denan is the strongest man I know," said Set.

Xius didn't care. Helplessness overwhelmed him. Behind him, Annette murmured a name. To his surprise, Set instantly gave her his attention.

"What was that you said?" Even more, his tone was warm. Kind.

"Denan hurt?" she asked in awkward Egyptian. Her accent, however, made the word so exotic that for a moment Xius was taken from his anger to listen in fascination.

"Yes," said Set. "Very much so."

"Found Denan?"

"Yes."

"'Infection' means?"

Set opened his mouth, then stopped, at a loss for words. He looked at Xius to explain, though the Pharaoh didn't see why he had to. He should have been on his way out to check on Denan, not here trying to eat sweets. Annoyed with himself, he dropped the roll back onto the plate. Nevertheless, he translated the word into her language. Her eyes widened.

"Have you summoned his family yet?" he asked Set.

"I did the moment we arrived, your majesty. Are you feeling well? You have been fasting all day; you should eat." Set lifted the plate.

Xius waved it away in aggravation. "I'll be fine, I need to see him."

"Salt water!"

Set once again glanced at Annette.

"What was that?"

"I know how kill infection," she grimaced to find the right words. "Hot salt water, honey…plant."

"Your people know medicine?"

She did not look amused by Xius's question. She spoke back in her own tongue: "Of course they do. Far better than your people, I should say." Her expression softened. "But I think I can help him."

She did not know what she asked. To put Denan's life in

her hands would carry a weight Xius knew, in her position, would be fatal for her if she failed. Xius and Set weren't the only ones who cared for Denan, and no Egyptian would take well to a foreigner attempting the medicine of barbarians on an already dying man.

Set, however, took it in stride.

"Very well. I'll get some salt."

"Watch yourself. I give the orders around here. Why are you listening to this slave girl?"

"If she really is from the future, your majesty, there's a good chance she knows things we don't. I know Denan's family won't want her about, but it's important she be there to explain to you what she means."

Xius couldn't believe his ears. How could Set be so calm and sure about this? He hadn't even flinched when he had said the word "future." However, no matter his inhibitions, if her strange medicine could possibly save Denan…

"She's an absolute idiot when it comes to proprietary, you know that. The situation's going to be already tense, you know how Aphery is."

"She can't be worse than you."

Xius took the last remark in stride, impatient to get going. She hesitated when the lanky vizier gestured to her and headed to the door. They headed out down the hall, Annette properly keeping her head below Xius's shoulder. The guards next to his doors bowed as they left.

"Now, remember what we've taught you. Don't meet anyone's eye, do not speak unless spoken to—"

"Be a good little slave, yeah yeah, I'm not an idiot, and yes, I understood you."

"Then you should know the gravity of this situation."

"Somebody's dying, I sort of figured it wouldn't be a party."

"But should you fail...I don't know if we can protect you. His life will be on your hands."

She snapped to a stop. Set looked back when he noticed they weren't following. He didn't bother to ask for an interpretation of their discourse, but watched silently as Annette stood frozen at Xius's side, eyes still to the floor.

"Pharaoh, I'm not a doctor, I can't guarantee anything."

"Then why did you say you could help?"

"Because I think I can, and...I want to try. He's your friend, isn't he? You've been all depressed and stressed ever since he went missing."

A tingle of shock ran through him. Why should she care if he was upset?

With a new uncalled for surge of giddiness, he nudged her forward. "Come on. I'll say that I ordered you to. I'll take the blame."

"But—"

"Come on. Salt, right? And honey?"

"That medallion of yours is remarkable," said Set.

Xius fingered it against his chest. "My mother told me it was made by the god Thoth for Osiris, the first Pharaoh, so that he could make better peace with his neighbors. My father, however, thought it was for domination; that we may better rule over subjects who speak a different language, so they could keep no secrets."

"What do you think?"

"Does it matter? I can use it however I wish."

"Well spoken, your majesty."

When they finally entered the room where Denan was being kept, the physicians bustled about him, cleaning what was left of the blood on his chest and painting symbolic salves across his wounds in prayers to Imhotep. They bowed to the side like grain before the wind as Xius stepped forward.

"Denan?" He took in his friend's new clean state. Blood leaked through bandages about his chest, arms, and legs. Set came to his side, and the white slave fell on her knees beside Denan. Her light blue eyes appraised the large man, and she bit her lip.

"Well?" Xius asked.

"Do you know what aloe is, Pharaoh?"

His mind magics sent him an image of a plant with thick, waxy leaves, but he was no herbalist. For all he knew, the plant didn't even exist in Egypt. Thusly, he shook his head. She sighed.

"Well, I was never entirely sure about that one, anyways." She turned to Set and, in Egyptian, said. "I need hot water, salt, honey."

"How much?" he asked clearly and slowly for her. She wrapped her arms in a large circle to vaguely indicate how much water she wanted, then made a small oval with her hands that looked to be about a pound for salt and a pound of honey. Xius scowled.

"Do you know what you are asking?"

She blinked at him.

"No…?"

"Salt is expensive! How is it going to help Denan besides preserve his body like a mummy?"

Set simply nodded and summoned a man to his side to fetch the objects.

"It's an antiseptic," she said.

"Anti-what?"

It didn't take long, and once the items were before her, all watched in interest as she poured the salt into the water and mixed it. She frowned as she lifted her hand out of the large bowl of water.

She pointed to the water and said something, but her pronunciation was so horrible not even Xius could understand it.

The servants exchanged confused glances. Set gave Xius a raised eyebrow.

"What did she say?"

"I'm not a translator, you're the one who said you could teach foreigners."

"I can, but that doesn't mean instantly."

"Pharaoh, this water needs to be hotter." Annette had given up trying to get the others to understand and had turned to him. Set waited on him, which made Xius growl. Denan was dying and suddenly his life depended upon everyone understanding a slave's sloppy Egyptian.

"She said it isn't hot enough."

For the next hour Xius had to clench his teeth in the corner and do his best not to start tearing at his hair. Annette peeled away all the bandages and draped rags of hot, boiling water and salt over the man's wounds. Halfway through he thought he heard Denan groan, but the man was unconscious as ever. The physicians wandered in and out with more hot water and salt, watching with fascination at the white girl's work. By the time the mattress beneath Denan had been soaked with salt water, his wife and three daughters had arrived.

At first they seemed more alarmed at seeing their God Pharaoh with a glare ready to kill than finding their father on his death bed. The tiny four year-old ran to her father's side first. Her loud cry of "Poppy!" startled Annette and she dropped a rag back into the bowl, hands noticeably bright red from the steaming water. He felt his chest tighten. Annette stared at the little black-haired girl as she reached out to tug on her father's fingers.

The other two girls followed, one seven and the other nine. Their mother, Aphery, stood in the doorway with her hand to her mouth. Xius could see the tips of her black wig shaking.

"What happened to him?"

"We don't know yet," said Set. "We found him at the riverside this morning."

It was difficult to meet her eyes. Denan had been under *his* protection. He didn't want to see her accusation gazing out at him.

Aphery at last took notice of the white-haired girl draping rags over her husband and pulling others off for re-warming. Her younger daughters had already surrounded her and were sticking their fingers into her strange, pale mane. The oldest only had eyes for her father.

"Mama, is he dying?" The sound of those words stabbed at his heart. But before he could figure out what he could do, Annette opened her red hands to the girl and shook her head.

"No. He well. See?" She gestured to Denan's face, which had filled with color since she had begun. Xius thought he could make out twitches in his expression. The nine-year-old obviously could. She called to her father as Annette moved to her side and pushed one of the rags into her hands. The girl stared at her as the white slave gave a gentle smile.

"You can help." Her Egyptian was broken, but precise this time, and relief spread over the nine-year-old's face.

"What do I do?"

Annette pointed to her eyes as a mime for "watch," then showed how the girl should keep the rags steeped in the hot, salty water and drape them over her father's wounds. When the girl lifted the first rag from off her father's chest, she flinched horribly at the sight beneath. For a moment, Xius thought she would faint. Their mother ushered the other two away to spare them the sight.

"Nephy, get back here. You should not see your father in such a state."

"But I want to help!"

Xius could see her hands pinking from the heat of the water.

He couldn't understand. How had Annette known that the best way to comfort the girl was something so out of propriety for a girl of noble blood? Sweat beaded on her pale brow from the hot water. Strands of her white-blonde hair stuck to her cheeks and neck as she carefully, almost lovingly, led Denan's oldest daughter by the wrist to show her how to drape the cloth across her father's wounds.

Lip quivering, Aphery also asked for a rag, leaving the younger two on a couch next to the door. Now three women picked rags out of hot salt water and spread them across Denan's various cuts, both deep and shallow.

"Sire, shall I find a distraction for the little ones?" Set asked.

"Yeah." Then he turned to the flabbergasted physicians. "Where is the honey the slave requested?"

Set ushered the two small girls out of the room. A gangly old man scrambled about for a pot, which he then scurried to display to him. Xius gestured to Annette.

"Follow her instructions. If you don't understand, I'll translate."

He ended up having to translate the entire time anyway, for Annette gave up on trying to explain in Egyptian. The other two physicians hovered uncertainly about them as the two women, one physician, and the small girl smeared honey over his gaping wounds and bandaged them up tightly. Then the three physicians moved Denan to a new mattress and tucked blankets around him.

Something strange was going on within the young pharaoh. It was too hot for comfort, and he had the overwhelming urge to reach out and touch Annette again, against his wishes, but he remained. He ended up ordering in two more beds for Aphery and Nephy. Most of the healers scuttled out the door and as soon as they found themselves with nothing to do; all too glad to escape the oppressive tension of the room.

Outside, the sky was brushed with the rusted colors of sunset. Deep reds hinted at an oncoming storm. He couldn't help but think that Annette looked like a protective goddess standing over the others, but quickly shook that stupid thought from his head.

"Come, Annette."

"But—"

"Is there anything more you can do?"

"No, but," she looked back. The compassion he saw there seemed to dwarf whatever he had managed to feel and increased the strange urge to touch her. He nearly reached out then and there to bury himself within her soft, white mane.

With gritted teeth, he held his arms to his muddy sides.

"You have worked hard. It is time to rest those hands." They were still too pink for his liking. "Aphery can watch over him."

"Is that her name then? Aphery. How pretty."

With that, the three of them left to give the family some time alone and Xius and Set dismissed Annette to go back to the kitchens. Xius gave one last look at her red hands swinging at her sides as she walked away before remembering that he had a dinner date with Kasmut that night.

***

It was getting harder for Hath to remember her name. Playing the part of Kasmut came so easy to her, unless she was with the Pharaoh. But she wanted him to see her for who she was, not as Kasmut, maybe even have the chance to teach him the breathing, fire-like dance her father had taught her.

So when he took Denan from her hands without a second glance toward her, she wondered if she should have been more like Kasmut in seeking attention. Each night she closed her eyes to his face in her mind, each morning she woke up with the hope of talking to him again, and every minute she longed and planned how to spend more time with him. But still, his mind was always somewhere else when she spoke to him in the halls, always worrying about someone else, his eyes always straying to somewhere other than her.

Even if he married her, would he always be looking elsewhere? Pharaohs can, after all, have any woman they wanted.

But no, she would be Royal Wife, she would make sure of it. Even if he found others, as long as she was first in his life, she would be content.

She hadn't realized how obvious she had become in her intentions until Jee whispered to her one night at dinner with Merkha's second and third wives, who barely gave her a glance.

“You might scare him away at this point," he said.

“You're not exactly in the right position to be giving me relationship advice," she said. “When have you ever been married?”

Jee's expression hardened. “I never had the means to care for a wife. It has nothing to do with my courting abilities.”

“Sure.”

They were interrupted by Merkha's second wife, who demanded to know what Kasmut could be whispering to a slave that couldn't be heard by all of them. The third wife said a snide remark about not being entirely sure of Jee being a eunuch or not and he and Hath had to stop their conversation. While Hath finished her dinner in silence, she listened, half-interested, to the wives talk of the deaths of virgins and whispers of the return of what they called "the slave cult." Hath only felt a jerk of nervousness in her gut, but knew Set would keep his word, and she shrugged it off when one of the women stated that the number of the deaths was unknown, but could be nearing any number. In her mind, Hath remembered like a cloud dream that there had been only two dead girls before her blood sodden box.

They picked up later when Hath took an evening walk in the courtyard.

“I am only doing my best to help you," Jee said softly, even though no one was in sight. “Apep must have an important plan in place for when you become queen.”

“What couldn't I do for Apep if I was queen? By the gods, Jee.” Then she reconsidered her words. “Thank you for your efforts, though. To be frank, I was thinking the same thing.”

It wouldn't do good to make an enemy of her only ally, and a questionable one at that. He had abandoned her parents, after all.

“You've already saved his friend, what more—”

“And he's barely bothered to thank me!” hissed Hath. “No, you know who he really thanks? That ugly albino foreigner. Apparently she salted him like a piece of venison and now everything is golden, and though I'm sure she was stuffed away into the kitchen, I know he goes down there occasionally.”

“He's been going down to the kitchens since before she came—”

“I know that.”

“Then why are you so concerned?”

“Because *I* was the one who made the effort to save him, and she's taking all the credit! I risked our safety with this whole plan for what?”

Jee made gentle shushing sounds and glanced around them. “Priestess, please, it's only been a few weeks and there's got to be a lot on the Pharaoh's mind.”

“I can't think of what,” she said.

“And besides, the foreign girl has already been forsworn to the vizier. You don't have to worry about someone so ugly stealing away the Pharaoh. And she's a slave.”

“The Pharaoh made her that, though" said Hath, and,

getting too upset to deal with him anymore, she stalked ahead, leaving Jee to trail after her.

That night, though, as Jee went to bed and guards took up their post at Kasmut's door, Hath tossed and turned, occasionally losing her thoughts in the soft glow of the coals in the brazier. Anxiety gnawed at her, and yearning twisted up in her gut. The ache for her prince made tears bud at the corner of her eyes. She had already done so much, already so perfectly close, so why must she wait longer?

But on the edge of her mind was a faint fear of what might happen if Xiusthamus really did fall for someone else. What if he found someone else to be his first true love, his Royal Wife, his queen? Even deeper down, so deep she didn't even dare to acknowledge it, she wondered what would happen if he ever found out what she had done to get his attention. Would he be flattered?

No. She knew him too well.

***

Hath woke up when Jee nudged her with a tied roll of papyrus in his hands. If there was anything Hath valued most out of the small luxuries she now got as Kasmut, it was her sleep, and she had been certain Jee had known of this.

"What?" she said, none-too-kindly.

"This was waiting at the statue of Seshat by the banks."

She frowned. It had been the appointed place they had given to Seti in the case he felt the need to contact them concerning his wife. She had hoped to never get another message from him after the arrival of that ugly white girl, and what Jee was doing way down there in the first place, she didn't care to know. Probably peeing into the river late at night. She wondered if she should feel bad that she didn't worry about whether he'd get eaten by a hippo or something.

"Give it here." Too bad the loaf couldn't read, her eyes didn't want to work right. In the moonlight from her window, she rubbed the last of the fuzz from her eyes and read the neat handwriting.

"I think it odd that the mistress of your friend just so happened to find the General."

She frowned. What an odd thing to write. So what?

"There's more," said Jee, mouth in his deep, solemn frown. "The man was waiting for me by the statue. He knows we've been killing for more than the spell for his wife. He told me to tell you to stop, or that he'd have us executed, agreement or not. It's only due to his gratitude for having his wife that he has allowed us to live this long."

Hath yawned. It was too late for this. Couldn't the stupid vizier have waited until morning?

Jee looked displeased by Hath's lack of reaction.

"That man is dangerous." he said. "I'm starting to think getting involved with him was a mistake."

"No it wasn't," said Hath, annoyed. "There's a reason Apep told us to tell him we brought back his wife. I'm surprised that sappy-face Seti, with all his brains, hasn't worked it out yet."

When Jee just frowned, Hath sighed. "Okay, give him this

message, I don't care how you do it: if he dares to threaten us, stop us, or stick his nose where it doesn't belong, we can easily recant the spell that holds his beloved Tawaret to this plane."

Jee scowled. "That won't stop him for long, priestess. That man will find us eventually."

"Yes, and by then, we will have killed him first. Now get going. I'm tired."

But even after Jee had closed the door, a bit of unease knocked around behind Hath's relaxed demeanor. This had been the plan originally, and yes, it would hold Set for a time. But by then, Apep would have had a curse in place for the man with the cheetah eyes. Hath couldn't go astray with a god directing her.

And with that comforting thought, she managed to fall back asleep.

***

"Your majesty, ten more maidens have been killed, five of whom were just found this morning outside their individual homes. Each died of the same wound as the three maidens found in the east homesteads of the palace. None of my men can report of seeing anything, and we have yet to find witnesses. According to our reports, the girls just vanished. No one can say where they went, only that they were found dead within a few hours of going missing."

Xius groaned and ran his hands through his hair beneath his crown.

Denan's second in command, a young captain by the name of Ptahmese, the nobleman Merkha, and the high priest Pawah waited, kneeling upon the ground with their gaze set respectfully at his feet. Xius readjusted his simple white linen headdress. If only Denan were capable of giving him advice now.

"Great pharaoh," said Pawah, "these deaths have reached the people of Waset. I fear that if we do not confront them before the rumors get to them, they may find diverse paths and leave the gods who have graced them so."

"Prepare the people for my presence tomorrow, then. I will be speaking to them."

As Pawah quickly scribbled down his words, the captain bowed in compliance.

"Yes, your majesty."

Xius excused them, but Merkha lingered. Leaning back into his throne, Xius eyed the nobleman bowed to the ground. The fatigue wore down on the young pharaoh like scarab beetles scrambling over his eyes and weighing down his skin. He looked outside, trying to demand the tension gone from his shoulders. Between the pillars, the sky was blue and the sun hovered off the edge of noon with a hint of clouds on the horizon. If only it were night. Then he could sleep this away.

But that was the problem. He couldn't sleep. Not with Denan possibly dying a few walls away.

With a sigh, he turned his attention back to the crouched nobleman.

"What do you want, Merkha? Certainly it must be something of importance for you to have lingered after I excused you."

"Your majesty," he said, voice muffled by the floor, "it concerns my daughter, Kasmut, who we have offered as your future queen."

"Yes?"

"She's...she's changed, your majesty. I don't know what has happened, but I was hoping, since she is so eager to please, if you could inquire as to what's on her mind."

Xius raised an eyebrow. "Changed? How so?"

"Well, she, well, nothing has changed much in her actions. She still dresses the same, talks to me the same way, enjoys the same things—it's not as though she is acting withdrawn or anything. I suppose it's just something in her manner toward me, and the way she talks to me. I'm her father, I've known her all my life, it's just...I'm not quite sure what to think."

"So you're saying she's grown distant?"

"I suppose so, your majesty."

Xius sighed again and dug the balls of his hands into his eyes. Noblemen. Always thinking their little troubles were his business to solve. When he had dined with Kasmut a few nights ago, she had been every whit kind, happy, and presentable. He could barely see anything of the cocky, spoiled child he remembered. Maybe that was what Merkha referred to, but he couldn't very well tell one of the high nobles, his own uncle even, that his daughter had just decided to act her age.

"Merkha," he said as patiently as he could, "Kasmut is a woman now, and one facing marriage, even. She is going to be distant; she's not a child anymore who answers the every beck and call of her father."

Merkha said nothing, as was right.

"Now, let that put your mind at ease. It's the only answer I'm going to give."

"Yes, oh Pharaoh."

Merkha was excused and Xius was left to slump in his throne and stare at the ceiling in. He let his mind drift about like dragonflies on the riverside.

He woke up with jerk. At first, he muddled in a state of confusion as to where he was, how he had fallen asleep, and what had woken him. Set's hand was on his shoulder. Dark circles had come under his eyes as well.

"You'll break your neck sleeping like that," he said.

"Set," Xius groaned and rubbed at his face. "How long have I been here?"

"How should I know? I wouldn't say too long, though. It's only about lunch. Your lady has been nagging me as to where you are."

"Who?"

"Kasmut, Xius, wake up."

"Oh. What does she want?"

"Who knows, maybe she just wants to be with her possible future husband. But she said something about Denan and was wondering how you were feeling."

"I haven't said anything to that, and you know it." He picked the sand out from his eyes and blinked hard. "Ra, I'm exhausted."

"Let's get some food, then. I'll finish things up with the temple of Horus and you can get some sleep. I'll wake you up for your prayers in the evening."

"You're a god."

"I'm glad you've finally recognized that."

Xius chuckled and pushed himself to his feet. "Humble, are we?"

"Just following your majesty's example."

"What about all those self-doubts of mine you're complaining of? Have you decided it's all just false modesty then?"

"Oh, yes, your majesty."

"How's Denan?"

"Still asleep, but his fever has broken. The physicians are hopeful." Set paused. "Perhaps the foreigner's medicine really did work."

"You're the one who had the faith in her to begin with. Are you saying you were just pretending?"

"I was hoping. Is that so wrong?"

“If it is, we both were wrong.”

They dropped by the kitchens to grab a light lunch (Annette was "out for a break" as Wenamon said) and ate it in the eastern courtyard. Set told him what he knew—which wasn't much more than Xius—as well as his theories. But they didn’t mentioned Denan anymore.

As to the killer, though, Set could no longer ignore the possibility of the Kushite cult Xius had referred to.

“I was able to scavenge out some of their old writings,” said Set, “which is something, considering it's an oral tradition. But the cut is the same, and all of the girls were unwed and young. Whoever is doing these killings is collecting their blood into the 'Bowl of Apep', which is supposed to be this strange wooden box. Most of what I got was off captain reports from your father's reign, so as for what they are planning to do with this blood...”

The skin beneath Set’s eyes had paled to a caramel and his gray eyes quivered from one spot of the garden to another. Unnerved, Xius put a hand to his shoulder.

“Set...”

“Yes, your majesty?”

“What are you thinking?”

Set turned his face away. “You don't want to know. But there is something I have discovered that you do need to know: the Bowl of Apep that I acquired two years ago...it's missing.”

When they separated, Set to the temple meetings and Xius to his bedroom, Xius's mind was abuzz with memories, both of two years ago when Tawaret was murdered and of long ago when his father had taken him along to behold the ugliness of those who worshiped gods of death. A cold chill settled upon him, unrelated to the winter season. There had been so much blood. And the girl, the girl he had begged his father to save, had that been a mistake? Had it been a mistake to hide who her father was?

Again, he wondered: Was it his choice back then—to save a slave—that caused Tawaret's death? Was that woman who had led the cult that killed her the same slave girl he had had compassion on?

His thoughts weighed so heavy on him that when he heard music he was confused as to what the noise was. It sounded so contrary to himself at the moment. He followed it, not entirely sure why, just drawn by the fact it sounded so happy and he himself was so sullen. He passed a few halls till he turned around a corner to a bright and sunny scene, overcast by wide, green leaves in the servant's courtyard.

A set of musicians sat on the grass with lyre, drums, and flute playing loud and lithely. Their eyes shone with joy as a familiar white woman danced before them, her long antelope legs peeking out from her dress. The ties she had used to lace close the slit of her dress had been left to curl at her feet, and her long white hair spun out about her like a veil.

But the sound of her laughter sounded strangest of all, and as she turned he saw the wide smile that composed it.

Had he ever seen her actually happy?

The moment he recognized what he saw he ducked away, his whole body hot. Wenamon had said she was on a break, but...well, what did he expect? Nothing, really. He had never wondered what she did in her spare time. Ra, he had never even thought about what she did in her usual time. What did she do? Clean. Cook, naturally. Though did it really matter?

He turned to go back to his rooms, more flustered than he had a right to be.

Behind him he heard the lyre player call for a halt in the music. He had plucked one string a bit too hard and needed to replace it. He paused at the sound of Annette's heavy Egyptian, thanking them and giving clumsy praises. They laughed and corrected her grammar, while another asked about what kind of dance she had done for them.

***

That night, after his nap and dinner, Set and Xius once more lounged on his balcony drinking wine and admiring the night. The brazier crackled with fire behind them, radiating warmth onto their backs.

"How do you know?" said Xius, dipping his fingers lazily into his wine and watching the red liquid drip off.

"The way she is, the way she talks," Set shook his head. "She isn't mad, Xius."

"Hmm." The image of her laughing face as she danced flashed across his mind, and he took another swallow of wine to push it away. Even now, the memory threatened to heat up his skin.

After a moment filled with the strums of crickets, Xius asked, "What now, then? Theoretically, if she is telling the truth."

"I don't know. But first we should probably leave her where she is. Wenamon's fond of the girl, and he's taking good care of her. It's helping her to adjust."

"But why? Why would she be here? Nevermind how."

Set's fingers tightened on his goblet. He took a quick sip and didn't answer. The stars were bright and spread out like a rainbow of jewels. Annette had said she couldn't see the stars in her time and had been so fascinated by them. He tried to remember what her face had looked like then, full of awe.

"Have you decided on Kasmut yet?"

Xius sighed. "How am I supposed to decide my eternal companion in a few weeks? Although," he brought his cup to his lips, "she found Denan. She saved him."

"Nice of her and all, though what by Ra was she doing down there in the first place? Last I knew of her she was a delicate woman who squirmed at the thought of mud."

"She's changed a lot," said Xius.

"You would know," said Set half-seriously.

"I wonder what brought it about."

"Growing up?"

"No. That couldn't do this much change. It's like she's a different person entirely. I don't even recognize her anymore."

Xius took a drink, then squinted at the sky as though Nut held the answer. "Don't you remember what she was like at the coronation feast?"

"I fear, your majesty, that I am not as hyper-aware of pretty women as you are."

Xius kicked Set in the leg, which only made him laugh, so Xius punched him for sure measure.

"The balance of the universe lies within the status of my bachelorhood," he said, scowling as Set rubbed his arm and rocked back and forth with a smirk. "Become a single pharaoh and then tell me you're not paranoid of women."

"Paranoid? Is that the word?"

"Oh, be quiet."

Set looked at him from the side, his long dark fingers rolling his empty goblet across the stonework of the balcony. A beetle crawled up the banister by his shoulder and Xius casually flicked it into the grass below.

"On the topic of women," he said, "I may have one in my own sight."

This hit Xius like a bull and he made a show of falling onto his back.

"Don't lie!" he cried.

"I wouldn't do such a thing to the Pharaoh," Set said, his cheek twitching. "I am still a man, you know, it's not the end of the world if I like a girl."

"Of course, but..." Xius thought better of it. If Set was willing to forget about Tawaret, then Xius would too. "Gods above, who is she? Tell me now."

Set laughed, and the sound was so carefree and happy it was disturbing. Perhaps Xius had gotten so used to his friend's depression he had forgotten he could laugh like this.

"I'll tell you if she agrees."

"Agrees to what?"

"What do you think, you twit? Besides, if I tell you and she ends up hating me you'll never let me live it down."

"I'm not that merciless."

"But you're that vengeful. That, or you'll try to force her to marry me."

Xius couldn't help but smile. "I can't say I wouldn't do that. Very well, don't tell me. But I will have to shun you until you do."

"Agreed, then. I will now consider myself your worst enemy."

They chuckled and chatted till Xius could feel himself nodding off, and even Set leaned his head against the wall with half-lidded eyes. They bid each other goodnight and Set left Xius on the balcony with only the stars to distract him from his thoughts. Even exhausted and feeling a bit too much good-will from the wine, it didn't stop *her* from finally creeping back into his mind, white hair about her like an aura and face alight with laughter like a cloud lit by the sun.

And then, as though summoned by his thoughts, a flash of white from below caught his eye. Across the courtyard, through the alabaster pillars, Annette appeared, sprinting down the hall.

Without thinking, he stood up, threw on his tunic and sandals, checked to make sure his medallion was on, and walked out of his room. He made his way down the polished, granite halls and found himself near a barely-lit edge of the palace that held a view over the glittering city Waset, in an area with the fewest guards.

Sure enough, as he walked around a corner and into the gaze of sitting, animal-headed gods, Annette appeared at the other end of the porch. She jerked to a stop, covered breasts heaving, face flushed, and pale hair sticking to her face.

He didn't move. It was almost as though he were afraid to startle a wild animal.

When she started to make her way toward him, eyes bright with starlight and expression peeved, he realized what he was doing and forced himself to exhale. He was being an idiot. A complete idiot.

"Annette," he said.

"Do pharaohs often go for midnight strolls?" she asked haughtily. "Got to worship some star god or something? That is what pharaohs do, right?"

"When will you let go of this contempt?"

"I'm just annoyed that my nice Zen alone time has been

interrupted, doesn't matter who. Don't take it personally."

"Zen?"

"You know, peaceful place? Good mood?"

"What are you doing up this late? Don't you have work in the morning?"

"I'm running."

"I can see that, though I still think you're strange for doing so for no reason."

"I have plenty of reason," she scowled. "You try getting sucked back in time and becoming a slave in a desert." But before he could think of how he was supposed to respond to that, she said, "It was nice seeing you, good night, ta-ta."

Then with a scowl and a sloppy bow, she ran past him.

"Wait!"

"Now what?" she cried.

"I...I want to run with you." Where had that come from?

She seemed to be thinking the same thing. "Why?"

He could feel his neck burning and glowered at her. "Can't I have a reason for running as well?"

She snorted. "I don't know, is something chasing you?"

"Oh, yes, Ammit with a craving for my heart."

He succeeded. The corner of her mouth twitched. "What the hell is Ammit?"

"Let me run with you and I'll tell you."

"I could just ask Set, you know."

"But he can't speak your language."

She bounced her head. "Touché." Then, with a hesitant smile, she turned back, gestured to him over her shoulder, and started out at a slow jog.

The first few minutes of following her in the semi-darkness beneath Nut's veil he spent demanding of himself why he had the urge to run, of all things, and with the woman who bothered him so much. But then once his lungs began to burn and the night air became the finest cool water against his skin, he thought maybe he could understand her attraction to running so late. Occasionally she would glance over her shoulder to see if he was still following and give him the barest glimpse of a smirk, as though laughing at him. Instead of irking him as it should, he found himself embarrassed and just a little bit hyper-aware of how stupid he must look straining himself like this.

Then she took a flying leap off of the palace porch and her bare feet landed on the packed dirt of the road. He froze on the edge.

"Stop!"

She did, fists hanging at her sides.

"What?"

"It's dangerous to walk at night barefoot. There are scorpions and serpents! You won't see them till you've stepped on them."

"Huh," she said, then turned back toward the road, where the city of Waset glittered with the barest trace of candlelight. Beyond that was the Nile, a rippling reflection of the night sky on earth. The longer she stood there thinking about Ra knew what, the more agitated Xius got.

"Come back," he said.

She looked back at him, a peculiar expression on her face.

"Let's go swimming," she said.

"Are you mad? Don't you know what's in the river?"

"Parasites, germs, mud."

"Crocodiles! Hippos!"

She gave an exasperated sigh. "Isn't there anything fun to do at night that doesn't involve dying? Besides," she stole a glance of the sparkling view, "I can't tell you how many times I've looked at that river, wanting to touch it. I wonder why I haven't by now."

Looking at her outlined by starlight, hair aglow with silver and long legs framed by her cut dress, he remembered her words the last time they had met out on her run. He hesitated. He thought of Set, he thought of Denan, then he thought of Kasmut.

And then he decided he didn't care. In the dark, at this almost magical time, he would forget for a while that he was pharaoh. Just for tonight. Just for this moment.

"You want to swim?"

"Didn't I just say I did?"

"I have an idea."

She followed him to his chambers without once questioning him or acting suspicious. Her trust both annoyed and enthralled him. She either didn't know what could happen to someone like her or didn't care. When they passed by his guards, he didn't worry about them telling the court about his sweaty, breathless appearance or the fact that the strange slave followed him. They obtained this position by proving the tightness of their lips.

"What does your room have to do with swimming?" she asked.

"Just come on, you'll see."

He lifted the tapestry behind the statue of Bastet for her. Down the dark stairs they went, and at one point he thought he heard her trip and catch herself against the cool stone walls.

Then when his private pool came into view, she took a loud intake of breath. He let her take it in, pleased his privilege had finally gotten through to her in at least one way. The stairway had curved down to a man-made, granite-lined pool filled in by a carved trench of the Nile. Tightly woven pillars and trees made an impenetrable wall all the way around the pool, allowing only a low hole cut near the bottom. A wooden screen allowed water in and kept crocodiles out.

The next minute, she cried out, "Marco polo, you're it!"

He started. "What?"

"Just get in!"

Her exuberant expression, so like the one that had been following his thoughts around all day, overwhelmed him, and before he knew it Annette had pushed him waist high into the freezing water.

"What by Ra are you doing!?"

"We're playing a game," she said breathlessly, cheeks pink with excitement. "You're it, so you close your eyes and try to find me. You say Marco and I'll say Polo."

"Marco Po—what?"

"Just do it! I bet you can't catch me."

Then he realized her hands were on his arms. They were pale and fine-fingered.

"Close your eyes!"

He did so, confused and just a little bit curious.

Then she forced him to spin.

"What are—"

"Eyes closed, Pharaoh!"

He squeezed them shut. Cold water splashed up his chest. He couldn't feel his toes anymore.

Then her hands vanished. He stood there feeling rather stupid in the cold water, listening to the crickets and the faintest rustle of papyrus. Now what? He self-consciously stuck his hands out in front of him.

Tentatively, feeling stupider by the second, he said, "Marco?"

"Polo!"

He jumped when her voice sounded just behind him and he whirled around, bare feet feeling their way along the stone-paved bottom. He waved his hands wildly, but only got a quiet giggle for his efforts.

"Marco."

"Polo!"

To the left—he strode forward—nothing.

"What is the point of this?" he asked.

"You've got to catch me!"

"Why?"

"Because I don't think you can."

He lunged and her hair slid past the tips of his fingers. The shocked giggle from her sent a tingle of warmth into his stomach. He found himself smiling too.

"This water is freezing," he said.

"Oh no you don't! You can only say Marco."

"Then you should only say Polo."

"Polo."

This time his fingers brushed her arm, which hadn't been in the water long enough to lose its warmth.

"I should have something for demeaning myself to your Marco Polo-ness."

"Polo."

"At least it's better than running. What is a Marco Polo anyway?"

"Polo—o."

He jumped and she leaped out of his way with a rush of water.

"Marco Marco, first you run by yourself like some soldier in angst and now you play children's games. Just how old are you?"

"Polo, Pharaoh, can't you follow the rules?"

"I said Marco."

"Ugh, Polo."

"Marco."

"Po—" she shrieked as he lunged for her and his hands found her arm. Just as he did, though, his feet slipped on the slimy bottom and he went down head first. Freezing cold went up his nose, into his ears—

He came up, gagging, to the sound of her laughter. He wiped the water from his eyes. Her eyes were squinted closed by her round cheeks, and her hand was to her forehead.

"Oh, man," she said, then laughed some more before saying, "Okay, whew, my turn."

"Why are we doing this?"

"You ask too many questions. Now come on, spin me." She closed her eyes tight, still smiling. He rolled his eyes, wondering how she could stand this icy cold water, but not showing himself as weaker by getting out. He took her by her shoulders and spun her. He tried once to tip her over into the water so she'd be as pathetic looking as he was, but she just laughed and righted herself.

Then, once he stopped, he tried to sneak away as quietly as possible, lowering his nose to the top of the water. She kept her hands to herself.

"Marco," she said, all too seriously.

"Polo."

They played like that until Annette finally confessed that her feet had gone numb, having only been able to catch him twice, though even those faint touches made his skin prickle. Xius found he couldn't stop grinning, and when Annette climbed up the steps beside him, he shoved her back into the water and jumped out of her reach. She tried to glare at him, but it was ruined by her twitching mouth.

"What kind of man are you! Pushing a girl!"

"You pushed me plenty of times."

"You're such a jerk, and if I wasn't freezing I'd tell you to face me like a man!"

He turned, arms around himself, freezing, breeding goose bumps by the thousand, to show her mock confusion. "Do you mean—"

"Oh, stop thinking so hard, you'll hurt yourself," she said, stepping up next to him and throwing her long, wet hair over her shoulder. She was shivering hard, her lips pale. "I'm sorry for getting you wet, Pharaoh."

He laughed, then stopped, suddenly realizing what he was doing, what he had been doing. Then he heard her teeth chattering.

"Come on, let's warm up by the fire," he said.

Up by the brazier, they sat themselves down. For once, Xius didn't feel the oddness of sitting at equal levels with her. It was almost as though he were alone with Set, not Annette the slave. Yet an uncomfortable pressure lingered in his mind, constantly demanding an explanation for his actions. He shook it off, too afraid to face it.

Annette got as close to the fire as humanly possible without burning herself. Xius glanced up to make sure the balcony was closed off from the night sky and drew close as well. When the silence pressed on between them, the pressure in Xius's mind increased.

"I think Set likes me."

Xius looked up sharply. "Likes you?"

"Yeah. Like, really like." Her pale lashes were spread across her cheeks. "I don't know much of anything about how you Egyptians do things, but...I don't know."

A strange sensation, colder than the water but just as wet, slid down his chest. He searched for what to say.

"Why are you telling me this?"

"I...well, I haven't told anyone."

"So you're telling me?"

"Well, yeah, I mean," she hesitated. "Never mind, forget I

said anything."

"It's bothering you," he said, both curious as to why and surprised. "Is it?"

She tucked her hands between her thighs and put her forehead to her knees. "Yeah."

"Why?"

"Just forget, it, I shouldn't even be talking to you like this, huh? I'm just a slave after all."

The pressure broke through. His insides felt hot and cold at the same time. Hot with guilt for how he was betraying ma'at, the order of things, and cold with the thought of Set in love with Annette.

"Why are you worried about Set? Any attention from him, if you're right, should be an honor."

"Forget it," she said, and time Xius heard a hint of the girl who had pled with him all those weeks ago in the dirt. She stood up and moved to leave, once proud shoulders and defiant demeanor wilted. He stood up as well, intending to stop her, and yet he couldn't move.

He shouldn't be doing this.

"Annette,"

She opened the door.

"Annette, don't ignore the Pharaoh."

She flinched. His guilt grew all the more painful when she turned and lowered herself to the floor in a bow. He couldn't stand it, he couldn't.

"Just go," he said. "Thank you for..."

But she was already gone.

***

When the Pharaoh found his chief general awake and exchanging smiles with his wife on a sunny morning, he rushed to his friend, beaming.

"Ah, your majesty." The general inclined his head the best he could. "Sorry to have caused you so much concern."

"You're going to need more than an apology!" He patted the head of one of Denan's daughters who stopped by him to bow. "How do you feel?"

"Like my rights of death were only half finished. I hear you have a miracle worker on your hands."

Xius's stomach dropped. He had hoped to forget about Annette for the time being.

"I guess you could call her that."

"My wife has been going on none stop about her. You'll be doing me a favor by taking my place for a bit."

Aphery bowed her head. "It is only natural, your majesty. She did save my husband."

"She's nice!" chirped the nine-year-old, who earned a harsh hush from her mother. She smiled sheepishly at the Pharaoh as her younger sisters giggled at her.

Xius smiled at the children. "I wouldn't say it was entirely her. It could have been luck, I mean, she didn't do anything special, from what I could see, besides salt and honey."

"There's more to medicine than just mixing together this and that, Xius, honestly," said Denan, as though amused at the idea. "Do you know if she was a physician among her people?"

"I doubt it. I think she's from one of those tribes to the north, and that should explain enough to you about their medicine."

"Do they even have salt up there?"

"I don't know," said Xius doggedly. "But what happened to you? I doubt you just floated down the river for however god-forsaken time you were gone."

Denan grimaced, but inclined his head once more.

"Ah. Figured you'd come for that. Aphery, please take the children outside."

His wife didn't question, but herded the little girls outside the door. Xius settled into a wicker chair beside Denan's bed as the great man coughed and cringed. He cursed quietly.

"For future reference, salt treatment isn't the most painless."

As the general collected himself and his thoughts, he looked over the balconies of his own room, which were boarded up for the storm. Xius could hear the sound of wind rolling about.

Denan let out a slow hiss.

"To be honest, I am not quite sure what happened."

Xius waited impatiently. He looked over Denan's bandages once more and tried to decipher how deep the circles under his eyes had become.

Denan rubbed a thumb across the stubble on his jaw line. "I was just walking back from the evening drills when I heard this scream, a woman. Naturally I went to figure out what was causing all the commotion, but when I came around the corner, someone knocked me out." Denan scowled. "I'd like to know how they accomplished that—before I throw their corpses to the crocodiles, mind you. As to why they would have wanted to do that to me," he shrugged. "I think I was just in the wrong place at the wrong time. Next time I woke up it was in the river with Sobek's monsters looking at me like the plumpest bull they'd ever seen."

"Any guess as to who it was?"

"If I had one, do you think you'd be asking this? Even half dead I could have dispatched a soldier to you to tell you." His face fell hard. "Forgive me, your majesty. I'm afraid I don't have anything of use to tell you."

The General looked as though he felt those words more than Xius ever could. If Xius had been in a better mood, he would have taken to comforting his large friend, as nothing bothered Denan more than feeling he hadn't been useful, but his temper had flared, and therefore taken up the greater part of his focus.

"They'll never come near you again," he growled. "Whoever they are. If they ever show their ugly muzzles, I'll..." Xius trailed off, unable to think of anything awful enough. All the stress that he had barely kept tethered the weeks before seemed to be pouring out all at once. The armrests of the wicker chair crunched as his hands clenched about them.

"I can take care of myself."

"But, I am Pharaoh—"

"Yes, your majesty." Denan smiled kindly at him, disarming Xius of his sudden intention to dispatch half the army to comb the city. "Therefore your safety is much more important than revenge on my behalf. Besides, if you take away the joy of doing that myself, what will I do with myself? I'll be fit to cry, and no one wants to see a grown man of my physic bawl like a baby."

Of course he would say something like that. This was Denan he was talking to, the other half of Set. While Set had always been his voice of logic, Denan had been the calming force in his life. As a child, Xius had, much to his mother's exasperation, been known as the most temperamental child in the whole palace. It wasn't until his father had wisely set him and a cousin, Set, up on a play date and had a captain's son—who so happened to be the much older Denan—be their guardian that Xius became tolerably obedient and somewhat amiable. Having Denan missing the past week or so had been misery, not just on Xius's part, but on everyone else's as his frustrations reached their maximum. Set could only bear the weight so far.

Yet it ashamed Xius how dependent he was on his friends. Certainly, now that he was an adult he could handle himself. But he, even as pharaoh and after all they had done for him, couldn't find a time when he had been any real use to them. Why he was such a temperamental child and sometimes an even more temperamental adult, he didn't know. No one did. His mother believed it was because he felt everything on a much deeper level than the average person, whether it be happiness, sadness, hate, love, or anger. But for some reason, the anger was noticed far more often than any of the others.

He dropped his head into his hands.

"I'm...so useless."

"No need to fold over yourself like that. If anyone is

useless it's me. Trained all my life to defend myself against any man, and I got downed before I could even blink. That's pathetic."

Xius only shook his head. He didn't want to hear this.

Denan waited, but Xius kept his face in his hands.

"Your majesty…" Denan hesitated. "Xius, do you know why I allowed myself to become your friend?"

"Because my father told your father to tell you to be nice?" he said dully.

"Like I would have listened to my old man, but no. I've never told you this, but I hated you at first. Spoiled little brat who threw fits at a moment's notice, always following his own idea of 'right' no matter what anyone said." To Xius's chagrin, Denan made a disgusted noise.

"Then why did you stay?"

"Because you were as angry as me—well, as much as a seven year old can be. Instead of trying to comfort me, you were angry with me. And that by itself made me respect that bratty, little kid. You were sad with me, you were happy with me, you ranted with me—-you never tried to tell me my feelings were bad or how to behave. I had parents for that. You were my first comrade. And I also know now more than ever that if you had a chance you would kill the men who did this to me and my family with your bare hands, pharaoh or not, because you are personal like that, where everyone else holds such things at arm's length." He stopped, frowning. "Not saying you should do that. Please don't. At least, not without me. Ammit herself couldn't stop me from missing out on so much fun."

The young pharaoh looked up to meet the tired warrior's face. He could feel his throat tightening.

"That was unnaturally—what's the word, womanish of you?"

Denan laughed, but stopped quickly with a cringe at his wounds. "Hardly. If anyone's womanly it's you."

"Oh, so one minute you give me a speech about how wonderful I am just to insult me the next. Well said."

"It is my duty to make sure you are properly humble

before the gods. Our salvation depends on it."

"Don't remind me! If anyone's salvation depends on me, oh Ra, I don't want to think about it."

The large man tried to restrain his chuckles in his throat this time.

"So, that white girl, she *is* the same woman you enslaved for wandering into your court, right?"

Just the beginning of that sentence threatened any good feelings he had.

"Yes, but I've already told you all I know."

He could feel the other man examining his face and shifted uncomfortably, and he just looked at him, face blank. After only a second the general gained a familiar glint in his eye, the same as when he was onto Set's strategy in a challenging game.

"Did something happen between you two, your majesty?"

"Nothing at all."

But Denan's eyebrows were knitting, sending wrinkles over his bald forehead. The corner of his mouth twitched upward.

"I haven't seen that look on your face since Kasmut—"

"I better let your wife back in," Xius said quickly. "You are married to her, after all, not me, and I bet her worry puts mine to shame."

Before the general could find another chance to question him, Xius fled. Aphery wasn't far down the hall, talking to some noble women with their own children as she waited. They bowed as he approached.

"We're finished, Aphery, if you want to go back."

The woman gave him a grateful, happy smile with her respectful bow. The children didn't need a second invitation and came scurrying down the hall to the door. Only the tiny four-year-old remembered to bow to him with her mother before dashing inside the room after her sisters. This made him chuckle, and he thought to himself that if he never had children, he would be more than happy to offer his household to Denan's. But thinking this sobered him and, not knowing what else to do, he wandered off.

Eventually he came to the wide, empty west porches of the

palace, watching the rain dye the world dark and drip off the roof. He sat cross legged on the floor and leaned against one of the towering pillars. His mind worked through the mire that was his thoughts: Denan's kidnapping and near assassination and the dead women—how did they connect? He almost didn't want to know.

And then there was Annette, laughing in the water and shouting "Polo" while her skin shone with starlight.

The earth gave off a musky aroma as though Geb was doing his best to seduce Nut into sinking down from her arch into his arms, despite the jealous will of her father. From where Xius sat he could see children from the village dancing with mud splashing up their sides on the edge where the palace grounds began and the village ended. He was hit with a crazy urge to join them. Their dance somehow seemed more religious than any ritual Isis could perform. Their innocent happiness rising to the gods could only be the sweetest incense, and gratitude tasted sweeter to the gods than any sacrifice a priest could give. Perhaps he had not been grateful enough, or simply he had not married when he should have, and these murders were his punishment.

He shook his head. He was doing it again.

Lightning flashed with a great boom of thunder, making the children shriek and run for cover. Xius closed his eyes and leaned his head back against the pillar.

I only ask to be a true pharaoh. To have the power to do as the Pharaoh must do. That's all I ask.

And yet, it wasn't. He really must be ungrateful.

***

Cinnamon faces turned up at him atop his royal litter. Somehow, along the way, he must have inhaled a mouthful of sand, and he swallowed in an attempt to wet his mouth. The parents of the dead girls had to be somewhere in this crowd. What were they thinking as they looked up at him, short, plain, and dressed in royal robes? Did he look like an imposter?

"I've come to tell you," he said, but drew a blank. The speech he had prepared for himself vanished. "I've come to tell you..."

He gulped again. On the other side of Set stood Kasmut, her eyes respectfully averted to the ground, red hair like fire in the sunlight. She had come to support him, and he could see her cheeks pulled back in a reassuring smile through her red wig.

He thought of the families in mourning for their lost daughters and tried to imagine what he would tell Denan if one of his daughters were the ones with a slice at their throat and all their blood drained.

But that was the thing. There was nothing he could say. It would be too horrible. But he had to say something to them. As Pharaoh, God on Earth, he was supposed to protect them.

He closed his eyes, dug deep, and imagined Denan bright in his mind before he opened his eyes.

"After examining the cuts on the bodies and the status of the women who died, we have come to the conclusion that one more of the Kushite cult of Apep remains, somehow, and is loose. I do not know why this sickness of the Kushite's still plagues us. We have done all in our righteous anger and power to cleanse us of the lot of them." In his mind, his father's voice echoed that he should never tell the people he didn't know something, but rather find out before they ask. He felt his throat clamming up again, so he pushed the memory aside. "Be on your guard. Do not let your children out of your sight, especially your unwed daughters, for they are especially at risk. Our soldiers will be patrolling the city at all times for suspicious activity. We—I will be investigating these deaths, and I swear by the holy light of Ra, I will find these cultists who have dared to escape death. The gods will not let these wretches escape again."

That was it. He couldn't think of anything more to say.

Somehow sensing this, Set's gentle touch sat him back down in his litter.

"That was good, your majesty. It was short enough to be remembered and long enough to make an impact. Is there anything else you wish to do?"

Xius moved to ask if it really had been enough when he noticed Set's face. It was the most unusual color, and his expression was abnormally flat—not that Set was one for many expressions, but the stoniness almost was an expression unto itself. He looked ill.

"By Ra, Set, are you well?"

"Quite well, your majesty."

Even his voice sounded stiff. But before he could ask more the litter carriers lifted him off the ground and away. Set stepped into a small, horse-drawn chariot to ride behind him with Kasmut at his side. She had turned her face to him and her reassuring smile from before the speech was still in place. Scribes on horseback set out in all directions, having copied down Xius's speech as he spoke it.

On the slow way back to the palace, Xius tried to smother the feeling of wanting to hide himself in his room and never come out again. That was a pathetic speech. What had happened to the one he had prepared?

Back at the palace, Kasmut approached him with confidence.

"You were marvelous, my pharaoh."

Xius said nothing. She took a step closer.

"Don't be embarrassed."

"I would never imply such," said Xius coolly. "I am Pharaoh."

"Excuse me. May we walk?" she gestured before her. The procession that had followed Xius, including the litter carriers, guard, priests, and upper noblemen, flowed past them like river water. Merkha inclined his head to him with a smile toward his daughter before heading off on his way. Set had vanished to who knew where.

They walked down the halls, greeting the nobles they passed and making small talk. At one point they found themselves quite alone.

"Really, my pharaoh, you did quite well."

"As you and everyone else will say."

"No." She turned soft eyes to him. "It expressed all that needed to be said about yourself and your heart. All your kindness, all your earnestness."

Xius flushed at this, and just a tiny bit pleased, but shook it off. "I ignored all the rules my father told me about speaking to the people."

"You aren't your father."

"You're right, I'm not." Then, in a brief moment of weakness, probably brought on by her compliment to him, he said, "He was strong, confident, and in control. I can't even control my temper."

Her hand touched his arm and he involuntarily flinched at the touch. Her hands were cold, almost clammy.

She withdrew quickly. "Forgive me."

They paused by the central courtyard to observe it silently. A few servants walked by behind them while trying to hush their giggles and failing miserably. The urge to hide himself away somewhere increased.

"I saw you the other night, Pharaoh." She bowed her head to allow a curtain of her red wig to slide in front of her face. "You're quite elegant when you run."

A sharp jab went up his spine and he stiffened, but while he was still scrambling for what to say, she spoke again, softly, and in a tone he couldn't make out.

"What do you think of that foreigner, may I ask? I do not mean to offend, it's just...if I am to be your wife, I want to know where we stand."

"I—" of course she'd want to know that, and all of his indecision suddenly gave way and he knew he couldn't risk her refusal of him. "I think nothing of her. She is but a slave."

"Then why do such an unseemly thing with her so late at night? And with her running around half naked."

"In her culture that wasn't the case; she does not know any

better. I was trying to learn of her country from her."

"Ah, I see. Does this have anything to do with your strange fascination with foreign poetry?"

That was just as good as any excuse, he figured. "Yes."

"Could you share her poetry with me some time?"

"Of course." He'd have to remember to ask Annette for some poetry. He didn't much care for lying.

"And, also..." she hesitated, and in that brief moment she was nothing like the Kasmut he remembered, all the way down to the very feel of the air around her and the sound of her breath. It struck him that he was looking at a different person, someone with a different name, a different life, but he paid it no heed. What a strange thing to feel.

"Yes?" he asked, trying to sound kind.

"Is there anything I can do to please you?"

When had she become so blunt? He always remembered one of the things about her that frustrated him most was how she never seemed to say what she meant and only what she knew he wanted to hear. Rather than relieve him, it unnerved him, but he tried not to show it. Kasmut was looking at him in earnest now, honesty in every line of her face.

"Why do you feel you must please me?"

"Because," her eyes flickered to the side then to somewhere on his chest, "I would like to be with you, my Pharaoh. I want to learn more of what it is you need."

All sorts of uncomfortable heat ran down his neck.

Trying to think of something to tell her, anything, he found himself blurting out, "Play a game of Aseb with me?" No sooner was it out of his mouth than he wanted to hit himself. He sounded like a child.

She looked surprised as well, but smiled happily. "Of course! Do you like Aseb?"

"I like any game, really," he said. "Even though, I have to admit, I'm not very good at them." The urge to hit himself grew. Now he sounded positively meek. A pharaoh was not meek.

But Kasmut looked even more pleased now, and the warmth radiating off her face couldn't be faked. In that moment it hit Xius with the force of a bull that Kasmut loved him. Truly loved him, and he couldn't even remember the last time they had spent any time together before the priests had offered her to him as a candidate for marriage.

"Meet me here after dinner. I'll have a game set up in the courtyard."

***

"He was lying."

Jee frowned over the soup he was stirring over the fire back in her old hut. Most days Hath lived where Jee use to be, in the household of Merkha, but for the first time she and Jee had returned to her childhood home back within the slave district of Waset, as Hath had been annoyed with the gossip and snide remarks of Merkha's wives. They thought she had gone shopping, and she had a small package of hair pieces beside her on her old bed for evidence.

So far, she and Jee hadn't spoken, and these were the first words of the night.

"Who lied?"

"My prince. He lied to me about that ugly white foreigner." She hugged her knees to her chest and her stolen dark eyes narrowed. "I heard their stupid little game in the water. Markha Po po, or something like that. He told me he had been asking her about poetry. I couldn't understand what they were saying, but it did not sound like poetry. It sounded like flirting." Her voice became muffled as she buried her face in her knees. "If I had known he had a taste for foreign slaves, I would have stayed as Hath. Curse it all, curse it to the shit pile."

"Why not just kill her?" asked Jee. "Her blood might make a good spell."

"It's not that simple anymore. I'm Kasmut now, I can't just walk into the kitchens without notice, and that damn Set has his eye on her. He'd notice too soon if I were to take her somewhere."

"Then what about me?"

"He knows you, Jee, he'd rat us out in a second. Damn it all, she was supposed to only attract the bastard vizier."

"Some things can't be helped."

"Be quiet, I don't need your comments."

Jee fell silent. Hath kept her face buried in her knees, caramel forehead furrowed, until Jee handed her a bowl of soup and went to scoop himself some. She stared into the broth and the floating bits of vegetables and meat. The humble meal enticed her more than the luxurious foods of Merkha's mansion any day. A thin smile made its way onto her face.

"Mother used to make me the most disgusting soup when I was sick. Either she was sneaking me some potion without telling me or she was a horrible cook when it came to that particular recipe." Then her smile dropped and her eyes went wide. "That's it."

"What?"

"I'll just use the same spell I used on that old demon of a pharaoh. She'll get sick and just die, poof! Getting a piece of her hair should be easy; she has an ungodly amount of it."

"By then, wouldn't Set have a reason to reveal us? I mean, having his wife die a second time—"

She sighed. "Gods, how do you live being so simple, Jee? There's no way he can blame us if she just gets sick, and now that Kasmut is already in the priests' favor, I'll just kill him if he causes any trouble. It will be marvelous!"

Jee frowned. "I see complications in this, mistress."

"Nonsense, it's perfect. My prince will be left to me once more." She smiled and hugged herself.

"But don't we need him to finish your father's spell?" Jee's frown deepened till his face was parted in two. "The blood of the general proved to not be of noble enough bloodline. It was smart of you to test it before killing him, but it was wasted effort from the beginning."

"How was I supposed to know? And as you said, we can always find some other noble, maybe even Seti-sap-face himself."

He sighed and blew on a spoonful of soup. "I fear your arrogance in all this, mistress. You're powerful, yes, but Apep is the one who is behind it all, and the god of death bows to no one, especially not someone alive. Somehow, I can't see him being too preoccupied with the revenge of a petty crush."

There was a crash as Hath threw her soup bowl at the burly Kushite, splattering him up to his chin in broth and vegetables. He blinked, spoon still held halfway to his mouth. Hath bared her teeth at him.

"Don't act like you know the will of Apep more than me," she hissed. "It is *I* who hears his voice, *me* who works his spells. That is why you came here, isn't it?"

"Forgive me." He put his spoon back in his bowl.

"I need you to drain another girl of her blood tonight. All of it, just in case Seti proves to be a liability."

"Mistress, all this to kill a slave? Couldn't you just use poison?"

Hath glared. "And risk being caught? Or even worse, poisoning my poor prince? She works in the kitchen, Jee. Gods, just do as I say. I'll worry about getting some of her hair."

Jee didn't look like he believed in her, but under the fire of her glare he bowed his head, finished his soup, and headed out to begin his task without another word.

***

Down in the kitchen, Xius hung his head in his hands as Wenamon put a plate of fried bird meat in front of him. When the Pharaoh had entered, all the servants except for Annette had scattered, all too aware of their unworthiness to be in his presence. Annette, however, barely noticed him. She shoveled ash from one of the ovens with a glazed expression, as though her mind was deeply involved in something other than her task.

"Kasmut really loves me, Wenamon," said Xius quietly.

"And that's a problem?"

Xius said nothing. To his surprise, Wenamon chuckled, and Xius's head snapped up in anger.

"This is not a laughing matter!"

"Forgive me, your majesty, but let's just say you're not the only young person here with romantic issues that logically shouldn't be issues in the first place." Wenamon's eyes went behind him to where Annette shoveled the last bit of ash into a bucket, seemingly unaware that her dress was now a sooty, splotchy mess. Her once white hair was now gray and tied into a knot on her head.

For a moment he watched her, then averted his eyes to his meal and forced a bit of meat into his mouth.

"You're not going to ask who?"

"I'm hoping it's not who I think it is," said Xius calmly. He felt oddly numb.

"Why is that, your majesty."

Xius shrugged and shoveled more food into his mouth. He had thought he wanted to be here with Wenamon, away from the other nobles and priests, who would undoubtedly be wondering about his marriage to Kasmut. Wenamon sighed.

"Well, I advise if you still are going to meet up with Kasmut, you should get a bath. I can smell you."

"I don't smell," said Xius.

"Of course not. Why not take Annette to help you? She is, after all, your personal slave."

"I can bathe myself, and even if I felt like it, I have servants for that."

"Ah, yes, but she's convenient. You don't have to make an

effort to summon anyone, your majesty."

Xius thought he could hear another meaning beneath this, as though Wenamon was almost asking him to take Annette with him. Another glance at the girl showed her kneeling in front of the oven, face blank and having yet to realize that a full bucket of ash was still shedding ash in her lap.

"She's filthy," Xius said.

In response to this, Wenamon just nodded, still smiling. "That can happen when you find yourself on the end of unrequited love, I dare say."

Xius snorted. "She should be flattered."

"As should you, your majesty."

Despite his annoyance with Wenamon's vague reasoning, Xius did feel the crispy dry layer of sweat on himself. Who knew speeches could do that. He finished his meal, stood up, and focused his thoughts on the medallion hidden beneath his clothes.

"Annette, come."

She looked at him blankly. "What do you need?"

"A bath."

The patches of her face not covered by soot turned red. Despite his distractions, he smothered down a laugh. What had she to be so embarrassed about? Did she think he asked her to fondle him or something? Dance naked? But once she had put her bucket aside, she got up to follow him back into his chambers. She fidgeted while waiting for him to peel the rest of his jewelry off until all he wore was his kilt and the eye of Horus pendant about his neck. Fetching a fresh kilt from a basket beside his bed, he ushered her on.

"Come on. You know where it is."

She jumped nervously into action, going toward the statue of Bastet. Behind the catlike goddess hung a thick, woven tapestry of various dyed wools. Once a side of the tapestry was lifted she disappeared behind it with him following. In a little carved shelf in the stairway, she took out fine wool cloth and sweet smelling soaps.

Down at the pool, this time in broad daylight, he couldn't help but remember the starlit game of Marco Polo. Yes, this was her job as his personal slave, might as well put her to work. But this had been the first time they had been alone after that night, and he still wasn't sure what she thought of him and why he had lost himself so.

He stepped into the water, watching the light fraction and flicker upon its surface. How did taking a bath become so confusing? When he had walked waist deep into the water and she didn't follow, he turned around. Annette stood in a patch of sunlight with towels and lye for him clutched to her chest. Even through the fine layer of soot, her hair burned white gold and brilliant, her face pink like a pond lily in her shyness.

A sensation as though his ka was escaping came over him. This couldn't be a girl. This couldn't even be a woman. Even as she tried to hide her face behind the bundle of towels, bright blue eyes peeking out over the linen, he couldn't reclaim his runaway ka.

He beckoned her down.

She tensed, but placed the towels down at the side of the pool and took up the scented fine soaps and washcloth. Instead of undressing to the necessaries, however, she plunged in fully dressed with legs pinched in as far as they could go while still allowing movement. First, he stared. Then, as she gave him the full brunt of her embarrassed, reproachful face, he threw his head back and hooted with laughter. All his humiliation from the day, all his confusion and stress, melted away. Once more the magical feeling of the night came over him, and he felt himself relax.

"Isis, Annette, what was all that?"

"What?"

"You look, good gods, like you tried dying your face with pomegranate juice while trying not to pee yourself. And you didn't have to keep your dress on."

She hid her face. Her voice, however, held a biting tone. "For your information, *Pharaoh*, I may be a slave, but where I come from no one dresses like those slave dancer *whores* of yours in public, or for any king, for that matter."

"Though you were once poor, you certainly don't have the manner of one. Only nobility have such modesty. But I guess it would be so with your people if it's as cold as I think it is. Is there snow there?"

"Only in the winter."

"Nonetheless, if it's cold enough for ice to fall from the sky, it's god awfully cold. Thus, more clothing."

She lifted up the soap and cloth gingerly, as though trying to keep water from getting on her still dry and sooty top. "Do you want me to do my duty or what, your majesty?"

He smiled wryly at her, stepped down to the floor of the pool, and turned his hands outward to her in invitation. She grimaced when water reached even higher on her as she stepped toward him and rubbed soap all over the rag. The touch of her fingers as she placed her rag on his body sent an unbidden shiver of goose bumps across his skin. The end of her white hair floated across the surface as she moved about him, ash running off in a trail behind it and catching momentary flickers of sunlight through the canopy. He watched in fascination.

By the time she came back around to his front, her blush had faded. Pale lashes fanned across her dirty cheeks, and her lips had parted as she worked. An image of her laughing and dancing on antelope-like legs came to his mind.

Her lashes lifted and he was caught in the blue. Such peculiar eyes, so unlike the dark ones common to people of the desert. Air became sticky in his lungs.

"Care to lift up your arms?"

He did so and she proceeded to scrub along his sides and the undersides of his arms. Soap residue lined her arms like creamy sleeves. The strange warmth from the day she had healed Denan burned his chest. Before he knew what he was doing, it spoke for him, needing to do something, anything.

"What do you want?"

She paused and looked at him uncertainly. "What was that?" Diamonds of light played over her face, reflected from the water.

"What do you want? Nobility? Jewels? A white Arabian steed?"

She gawked at him and lowered her hand from his raised arm uncertainly. After a few brief seconds in which he traced the lines of her mouth and her platinum locks with his eyes, she frowned.

"Are you okay, Pharaoh? Did something happen? I've heard from Set that there's some crazy person killing people—did you see something? Did someone really important die?"

"No. No, I just want to know. What do you want? I..." Feeling the heat rise up his neck and his throat constricting, he lowered his arm to rinse it off. He should have said nothing. Why did he always have to act so idiotically? It was unseemly of a pharaoh. But before he could recant his words, she spoke.

"Well, I'd really like my shoes back."

His heart leapt. Was that all?

"Those strange things?"

"Hey, Egyptian shoes suck and make my feet smell. They're also hard to run in." She turned to fetch a bottle of fragrant oils and soap still on the steps for his hair. He caught a brief glimpse of the transparent, wet portion of her dress sticking to the curves of her waist before she came back and did his best to not draw her attention to the effect it had on him.

"Hard to run in? How is that important?"

"I like running, I thought you'd figured that out by now," she said, the bottle in her hands. "It's something I used to do when I was back home."

"Were you a messenger?" Out of curiosity, he glanced down at her body. Instead of seeing the lean machine of a runner, however, he made out supple softness and curves down to her ankles, which sent the hair on his arms prickling. Lucky for him, she was preoccupied with untying the stopper on the bottle.

"No, not like that. My parents moved too much for me to do anything long term. I just, well, whenever I got frustrated or upset I liked to run, and sometimes if the track team was out practicing I'd go race them. I'm a sprinter, you see."

Forcing himself to look away from her rippling figure beneath the water, he furrowed his eyebrows at her. "I don't understand."

"A track team was, um, crap. I guess those type of sports are for the Greeks, um...they were a group of people who like to race for sport. You know, like competitively. They practice and train to get themselves as fast as possible."

"That sounds like children and soldiers' play."

"Whatever. The point is, they were a bunch of people who liked to run and it's sort of a big deal where I'm from. There's two different types of running: long distance running, which depends mainly on endurance, and sprinting, which focuses on speed. I don't have the endurance to be a long distance runner, not to mention I'm lazy, so I'm more of a sprinter."

Xius scratched his neck. "So strange. Having running as a…wait, did you do this for your living?"

"A hobby. Crazies are those who do it for a living. And there really isn't any way to make a living off of it, I would think, your highness."

"So very, very strange…and moving? From place to place? Was your family nomadic?"

"Nah. My stepfather just had a job that jumped all over the place, so we had to move from town to town where his work went."

"Sounds difficult."

"It was." She paused as the stopper finally gave way with a pop. Water licked at the bottom curve of her breasts as she stared into the bottle's depths. "It is."

He lowered his head to allow her to rub the contents through his hair into a wispy lather. He had had others wash his hair before, but what he did not expect were her nails, which weren't rubbed away like most working servants' or slaves'. Surprise overtook him as they pleasantly scratched his head. He wanted to melt to the bottom of the pool.

"Uh, Pharaoh, you're going to drown yourself if you keep dropping like that."

He didn't care. Drowning didn't sound so bad. Why hadn't any of the servants had long nails?

Once she had finished scrubbing, he leaned back and allowed himself to float peaceably across the pool, watching the great palm leaves shift in an almost non-existent breeze. Annette, however, quickly got out while he wasn't looking, and when he had the chance to turn back to her she had a long towel tucked tightly about her. Her face was pink again, though clean of soot. He chuckled. He had half expected her to start another game before getting out.

"What are you so nervous about? You didn't act like this the last time we were here."

She glared. "It was dark then, and I'm just not comfortable with all my assets showing through a wet, white dress, okay?"

He shrugged, though secretly disappointed. Her determination to hide herself just made him want to see all the more.

She paced along the edges of the pool as she waited for him. He sighed at her poor etiquette before finding his feet on the bottom of the pool to make his way toward her. Her hair was at last clean and out from its bun and gleamed once more in the scattered sunshine. As he stepped into the towel she held out for him, he reached out a hand to touch it. Silk ran against his fingertips. She appeared to ignore his touch as she tied the towel about him and it encouraged him to step closer and greedily reach his hands through. Before he knew what he was doing he had his face in that mass of beautiful, gleaming silk, breathing in her scent. It was sweet, like the aroma of an exotic flower he had yet to place.

"Um, Pharaoh?"

He flinched back.

He cursed and brushed past her to the steps. On reaching his room, he moved to the golden chest in the corner where he had stashed the camera. By the time Annette came up wrapped tight in a towel, he had turned around, pale shoes held out to her as though in offering, feeling stupid and flustered.

"Here," he mumbled.

At first she just stared at them in disbelief. She reached out to touch them. Before he could think of more to say, she pulled back her hand, her expression suspicious.

"What do you want from me, Pharaoh?"

"Nothing. You just said you wanted…besides, they are just taking up room and are of no use to me."

Still, she kept her hands pressed to her chest, fingers curling around the edge of her towel. She even took a step back as though to flee. Throwing proprietary to the wind he placed the strange shoes on the floor before her.

"You may take them or not, they'll stay here until you decide."

And with that, he left to change into the dry kilt. She purposefully kept her eyes to the floor as he peeled off the wet kilt behind the pseudo-screen next to the chest. When he came back out she was crouched on the floor, poking them.

"If you're wondering if I hid scorpions in them I can assure you I did not. If I had wanted to kill you, you would know."

Oddly enough, this gave her the courage to pick up the shoes and pull out the strange, woven sacks within them. She beamed.

"You kept the socks too?"

"Is that what those are?"

Satisfied, she took the shoes with her to the couch, now white and unstained once more, and proceeded to slip them on. She tapped her feet together quietly as he dried his hair.

"Pharaoh," she hesitated and pulled her hair behind her ear. "Can...can I say no if someone wants me to marry them? I mean, being a slave and all. No matter who they are?"

Pulling a blanket off the end of his bed and wrapping it around himself, he sat down and crossed his legs. The liquid cold feeling was back to sliding down his chest. "Why would you want to say no to Set's proposal?"

She flinched horribly and gave him a wide-eyed look. "I didn't say anything about Set, and I was just saying figuratively."

"Then, figuratively, why would you want to say no? I can think of no greater honor, and you'd no longer be a slave. You'd be a fine lady, which is also why it's unheard of."

She looked away. "I just don't want to be made to, that's all. And no, he hasn't proposed to me."

"But you think he might?"

She stared at his doors as though seeing something in their carved wood. Then, softly, she said, "I'm not a slave. You have no right to make me one, and no one has the right to make me do anything."

He felt the challenge in her voice, heard the threat upon ma'at, the defiance against his authority. But…it slid over him.

Instead, he wondered at her in utter amazement.

"Annette..." he said softly, for there was pain somewhere in there as well. "I don't think you understand."

"Oh?" She turned back, eyes alight with fire, though she spoke with equal softness. "And you do?"

"Whatever country you come from, you're not there anymore. You're in Egypt, outnumbered a million to one. You're a foreigner here, and a stranger at that. What I did for you really was kindness. It's not just my arrogance or taste."

She opened her mouth wide to retort, to yell, but then she stopped. She wilted and the fire died. To him, the way she slumped in her seat was sad.

"You didn't answer my question," she said.

"Since you have no father or guardian to protect your hand for you, yes, you would most likely have to marry him, if only out of extreme obligation. You would never get such a miraculous chance again."

"You people are so old world."

"That's how it is."

And Xius found he didn't much like it either, but why, he couldn't place. There was no way he, Pharaoh and God on Earth, could have her. An ignorant savage, a foreigner, and now a slave at that, could never be respected as queen.

He didn't bother to excuse her and left her there on the couch. She knew enough about decorum by now to know she couldn't leave until he said she could, but she didn't complain. At one point he asked for her help in getting ready for his game with Kasmut, but otherwise he left her to her own devices. A few minutes before the sun shone just right on the measurements for wintertime on his wall, she spoke.

"Pharaoh, can we be friends? I know there's a whole bunch of bad juju and no no rules about it, and I'm not even supposed to be talking to you, let alone be alive in your opinion, but—"

"Yes," he said.

"Yes? That's it? That easy?"

He smiled at her. “I'm Pharaoh. I can do as I please.”

“Such as hang out in the kitchens rather than eat with the rest of the nobles?”

“High nobles, to be exact, and that's only when I don’t feel up to giving them the honor of my presence.”

“You sound like an arrogant jackass, you know that?”

“Set tells me I have self-esteem issues.”

“Huh.”

“And Annette?”

“Yeah?”

“That's not my opinion, that you should be dead. I like—I'm glad—I'm happy that you are alive.”

“Why? So you can feel up my hair? What was that for, anyway? It's probably because you've never seen such freaktastically light hair before, have you? Come on, admit you think I'm a freak.”

Despite her teasing smile and lightened demeanor, it just made him want to bang his head against the wall until his forehead bled rather than answer her.

Part Four

Of What Will Be

The courtyard had too much green for Hath. She turned in a circle, feeling the crisp winter air and remembering a less green, much poorer place. Winters had always been a time for dancing amongst her people. Dancing, and gratitude for the harvest. Before that night when the Egyptians ran loose, Papa had pulled her into a drum circle of friends and family. They were singing, and mother's voice had been the most beautiful of all. She didn't sing for death then. She sang for peace.

Papa had spread out his long black arms. Bright-colored cloth had dangled off his shoulder, and Hath had thought him a most beautiful bird.

"Lift up your arms, small one, lift them up and hug the sky," he had said, and she had done so, laughing. They spun in circles around each other and tapped the earth with their feet.

"Feel the dirt," he told her. "Feel the air, can you reach the sky yet? You're already touching it."

She could barely hear him above the drums the others played and her own heartbeat. Round them, a few others completed the circle around the fire, beating the ground with their feet and hugging the sky as Hath and her Papa did. When she started flapping like a bird for a lack of any other dance moves, her father had flung his wiry head back and laughed, and she remembered how his white teeth stood out against his skin. At last, when her legs burned and she could barely breathe, the drums finished in a boom and everyone sang with joy. Papa had scooped her up—she had been so little!—and thrown her above him. In that moment, she felt as though she really had wings and it wasn't just some six-year-old's experimental dancing.

"Life is marvelous, isn't it, my girl?" he had said. "Be grateful for every bit of it. For all that dirt and air and sky."

"But it's hot," she coughed. "And I'm all sandy and sweaty."

"That you are. But think of how much hotter you'd be if you weren't sweaty, eh?"

"Papa, you say silly things."

"Do I? Why do we dance, Hath?"

"Because it's fun?"

"Because it's gratitude in action." He poked her in the chest, white teeth still gleaming. She had thought him so beautiful then, his sweat making his skin look like polished obsidian and his colorful robe like rainbows.

But that was a long time ago. Papa was dead. Hath looked around the green courtyard and wondered what her father would think if he saw her now, standing in a stolen Egyptian noble's body. He would have probably asked her when was the last time she had remembered to be grateful for all that she had, including her healthy strong body, and danced, and she wouldn't have said anything. Nothing at all. Because the last time she had danced was the winter before he had died.

She leaned back and felt the sun on her face, trying to pretend it was her own skin she was feeling it in. *Mother,* she prayed, *if death is so wonderful, why does it make me feel so sad?*

But she already knew what her mother would say to that: it was only sad because Hath was still alive and still wanted to be.

"Kasmut? What are you doing out here?"

Hath sighed heavily. She may not have a father anymore, but Kasmut did.

"Enjoying the sun, Father," she said, being careful to pick up the clean accent of the Egyptians. "Have you need of me?"

"Get back inside, quickly."

"Why? What's wrong?"

"One of our slaves has gotten the sickness. We're leaving."

This startled her. She hadn't planned for anything like this. "What?"

"Haven't you heard, you silly girl? There's a plague about, and I don't plan on sticking around once it hits. Who knows how many have gotten it throughout the country."

She put a hand to her mouth. A plague? "Um, what is it?"

Fat Merkha made an angry grunt and reached out to grab

her wrist. "Just come already."

"Of course, I just want to know what it is. Fascination with the abomination, Father." She gave him a friendly smile, though her insides felt like shattered bits of wood. But why should she be worried? Nothing like that could've happened; the white slave girl was just taking her time dying.

"It's sounding like ameese."

The wood-like feeling prickled up her back to the point of pain. She yanked her hand from Merkha's, and he swiveled around with his bushy eyebrows lowered like storm clouds over his eyes.

"What is the meaning of this?" Once he saw Hath's face, however, his expression softened. "Now now, Kassy, there's no need to be worried. I'll keep you safe, and its mostly amongst slaves anyhow."

"Is it really ameese? Do you know the symptoms?"

"I said it sounds like it. I'm no physician, love, now come on. I've already had your things packed."

"B-but where are we going?"

"Where else? We're going to the west home."

Hath frowned. "West? But only the dead—"

"We'll be dead if we don't go, and it's only temporary. Surely the gods won't curse us for living near resting grounds. As long as we don't disturb any tombs, we should be fine."

"But just how far away from Waset is that?"

Merkha looked at her in concern. "We were there just last spring. Don't you remember?"

Hath mentally smacked herself. How had she forgotten that? Kasmut had taken her with her, Hath being her personal maid and all. She smiled stiffly. "Of course, Father, forgive me. I'm just a bit shaken up by this...whole sickness...thing."

"Well, try to hold off on your nerves until we're on our way. Come, now." Merkha took her hand again and pulled her toward the house, and she grudgingly allowed it, though the moment the sun slipped away from her skin she missed it. This stone mansion felt too cold, too unnatural. It should have smaller rooms, a thatch roof, and a warm, well-used hearth nearby, no matter the time of year.

"What about the pr—pharaoh?"
"He'll be fine."
"How can you be sure?"
"By Ra, have you no faith in the gods, Kassy? He's the only one of his line, you'd think the gods would care just a little about their advocate."
But this only made Hath's alarm grow. Why were others getting sick with the symptoms she had only cursed Annette with? And why hadn't she heard of the white girl's death yet if others were already dying?
She had to find Jee.

***

"Workers on the delta have reportedly fallen very ill, your majesty," Set said during his morning report to Xius. The Pharaoh himself sat in his throne room, trying to shake himself awake from the lull of his morning prayers to Ra in the newly completed temple of Horus. "It has taken a few days for the news to travel upriver to Waset, but by now all of them and their families have fallen ill. They were the first, but this morning some merchants who have traveled up the river from Memphis were found ill with apparently the same illness. We're not yet sure if they will recover."

Xius rubbed his eyes. "Do you have a report of how many have gotten sick?"

"Not yet, but it's apparent that it has become an epidemic."

"Do you have an idea as to what kind of sickness it is?"

"So far it is sounding like ameese."

Xius wasn't sure he heard right. "That can't be it."

"I'm afraid so, your majesty. Isis and Pawah have already sent priests to the shrines of Sekhmet to begin their prayers."

He had heard of whole Libyan tribes in the outlands dying off because of that, but it had always been far back in history, not anywhere close to the safe walls of Waset. "Do we have any idea where it came from? A wayward magician's curse? Bad food?"

Set's mouth made a grim, thin line. "The priests will have a theory for you you're not going to like, your majesty."

"What? That the gods are angry with us for allowing the savage Kushite cultists to have their way this long?"

Set said nothing, just gave Xius a particular look. The Pharaoh read his friend's eyes, interpreted the thin mouth, and dropped his head into his hands with a moan.

"No."

"You have dawdled too long, Xius."

"But it's just one man's marriage!"

"And you are the living reincarnation of Horus, guardian of Egypt and son of Ra. If you fail to have children, the holy bloodline of the gods will be lost and there will be no connection left between the gods and us mortals."

“At least breathe when you lecture me.” Xius leaned back, resisting the urge to grumble like a child. “But why does that mean Sekhmet has been set loose to right it? Yes it is ma'at, but if it's not being upheld, I should be the one that's punished. Not my people.”

“You are but a vessel, your majesty, an advocate for the people. Your faults are theirs as well.”

“I know that, it's just—it doesn't make sense, justice-wise.”

“That's what it is, Xius,” said Set with a growl. “So stop whining like that and sit up straight. The priests will be coming any moment now.”

Xius prickled. “Why do you have to demean me? I'm the one who's pharaoh, not you.”

“Because I'm your friend, and I know you don't want to look like a weak fool.”

Xius scowled and hung his hands off his knees. “Well you don't have to be an ass about it.”

Xius figured Set would feel unappreciated or annoyed with him as he usually did, but Xius, also as usual, didn't care. He was caught between appreciating Set's frankness with him and hating it, which, he suddenly realized, was exactly the way it was with Annette as well.

There was a knock at the great double doors to the throne room and Pawah entered, leading the procession of hairless priests behind him. They approached with the overwhelming scent of incense, and once they reached an appropriate distance they curled themselves up on the floor in bows. Set stepped aside and took his place by the throne.

“We have come before you in place of the gods we serve, great Pharaoh, and pray we will do their intentions righteous justice.”

“Go on,” said Xius.

Pawah stood, bald head gleaming in the morning sunlight from the porch on one side of the throne room. The other priests were still little hills behind him.

“I'm sure you have heard from your royal vizier about the sickness that has taken lives along the river to the north. We ourselves have heard of this from our priests down in Memphis who have fallen ill to the same sickness and passed away." When Xius nodded to confirm Pawah's assumptions, the head priest hesitated. "Priestess Isis prays to Sekhmet, ferocious giver and protector of plagues, but I and the others fear she comes on account of your unfulfilled duty to ma'at. It is not right that you should have ever been allowed to rule alone—not that we are implying it is within our right to say what you can or cannot do."

Why do people tend to say that before they do exactly that? Xius thought scathingly.

"So, on behalf the of the gods," said Pawah, "we must insist the high Pharaoh marry within the week, as soon as possible, for the sake of his people and this plague. We beg of you. No god can rule without their other half; it is against ma'at."

Xius exchanged glances with Set, but the only thing Set's look said was, "I told you so." He hated that look.

Hot, writhing guilt rose up from his gut and Xius clenched his hands together on his lap to hide how they had begun to tremble. "Are you implying that this plague is my fault because I've waited this long to find a queen?"

The priests fidgeted, including Pawah, who said, bluntly, "Yes."

"And you say the gods told you so?"

"Mainly Hathor and Best, but that's as far as we can glean."

Xius caught the tiniest shiver of uncertainty coming from one of the younger priests just to the left of Pawah. It turned the heat of guilt to rage, and he saw Set shift out of the corner of his eye.

"Your majesty, calm yourself."

"They have no proof," he said, a bit too loudly. The priests flinched.

"You know as well as I do that it is foolish to tempt the gods for proof when they have given you their word," said Set.

"They have given me *their* word, not the gods'."

"And are you any more qualified to hear their words than they? People are dying, Xius, get a hold of yourself."

But Xius had had enough. With a snap of "He would see to it," which he didn't much feel like saying, he stood without excusing them and strode out of the throne room, with Set behind him.

"Your majesty, you can't just leave them like that."

"I can do whatever I please, Set. I'm tired of you and all the rest of them telling me what I can and cannot do."

"Where are you going?"

"Wherever I want."

"Xius—"

"Be quiet!"

"Will you calm down and listen to me?"

"Can't you just leave me alone? My marriage is supposed to be the most intimate thing I'll ever do and they're diving right into it as though it were a public bath—gah! I'm done with them! Especially when they have the audacity to blame something like that on me without any proof! I will care for my country in my own way."

Set seemed almost panicked, but he never panicked, so even as he yanked his friend to a halt, his expression was cool and serious. "You're not thinking reasonably right now. Stop acting like a child and calm down. Look, you use to like Kasmut, and you said yourself she's changed for the better. There's no reason to be so resistant! And she isn't the end all, you can have more choices in the future."

Xius yanked his arm from Set's grip and stomped away. Thankfully, or wisely, Set didn't follow, and the young pharaoh didn't much care where he went. Nobles who passed him pressed up against the walls, murmuring to each other and watching in amazement. It just made him angrier.

And then suddenly, the halls became empty, and as they did he started to hear a sound: a flute, piping high and sweet. He followed it, too morose to go through the effort of turning around and figuring where else to go where he could be alone. Then he recognized the servant's courtyard ahead of him, the same one where he had found Annette dancing with the musicians. Anger momentarily forgotten, he eased his way around the corner with anticipation.

Sure enough, there she was, sitting amongst the musicians, slave's gown once more stained with soot as she listened to the flute player with the others, eyes closed. He watched until the musician finished his song and the others began their critiques before he stepped out without thinking.

All eyes fell on him. He didn't know how he had thought it could be otherwise. The next thing he knew, the musicians had dropped to the ground, bringing Annette down with them.

"Uh," He mentally smacked himself and straightened. "I wish to speak with Annette. The rest of you are excused."

The musicians glanced at Annette in amazement as they filed out past Xius, bent in half, with their instruments clutched to their chests. Once they were alone, Annette stood up, brushed off her skirt (which only served to dirty her hands), and looked him in the face.

"Hey," she blinked. "You seem off. What's wrong?"

"Nothing," said Xius automatically. "Set is just being irritating." Among other things.

"For someone you hang out with all the time, you two seem to get on each other's nerves an awful lot."

"We grew up together, so I guess we just know each other too well."

"Well, what did you want to talk about?"

"Not much, I just..."

Annette waited, but Xius couldn't find anything to say. The anger still simmered somewhere at the bottom of his lungs, but it was cool enough now for him to realize he had acted like a complete idiot and that Set was right. But what else was new? Xius would perpetually play the fool and Set would always be the one trying to save him from it.

But he also realized that, either way, he'd have to agree to it. The priests carried out the will of the gods, and to defy them would be asking to dangerously unbalance ma'at to the extent of stopping the sun from ever rising in the sky.

He had to come to terms with the fact that, by the end of the week, Kasmut would be his wife. He hadn't the time to look into other options anymore.

A small, dirty hand touched his arm. He felt a jump inside

of him, like a cricket in his gut, at the kind way she looked at him.

"You just ended up here, didn't you?"

He had to resist the bad habit of looking down at his feet. No leader, even in front of friends, should appear doing such. "Yeah."

"How's Denan? Maybe you can go visit him, talk to him about it, because I'm not even going to pretend I understand the intricacies of the relationship between you and Set."

"It's not just Set," he said cautiously.

"How does being pharaoh work, anyway?" They sat down beneath a gnarled olive tree, one of the few in the servants' courtyard. He looked around to make sure they weren't being watched, then rested his arms on his knees.

"You're going to have to be more specific than that," he said.

"Okay, do you get to do whatever you want? Is anything you say how it goes?"

Her question rankled so much with what had just happened that he glared at the sandstone paving beneath his feet. "No."

"I take it that's one of the things bothering you."

"The priests," he said in a low voice. "They think a disease in lower Egypt is there because I unbalanced ma'at by not getting married when I was crowned pharaoh."

There was an awkward pause. Her foot traced circles in the light sand layer on the ground.

"Huh, that's—What's ma'at?"

"It's the way things are, the way they must be, in order to keep balance in the universe. It is justice, the laws of nature, and the laws that govern the inner nature of man."

"Deep. So...you're not married?"

He gave her an odd look. "I said that, didn't I?"

"Like you don't have some concubine or harem stashed away?"

"No."

She closed her eyes and nodded as though contemplating some deep philosophy. "Yeaaah, you're weird."

This irked him. "What?"

"Aren't all kings around here supposed to have loads of wives and a whole room of women just for their pleasure?"

He flushed. When she slowly raised a suggestive eyebrow, he stood up.

"Look, if that's what you think of me—"

"I don't know what I think of you. You're the first pharaoh I've ever met."

"Well we don't stash women away to take advantage of, at least the righteous rulers don't. I can't say all of my predecessors have been good."

"But all of you Egyptians are pligs, aren't you? One of the nobles I had to deliver lunch to had three wives—three!"

"Pligs?"

"Having multiple wives."

"Only if a man sees fit for another wife and if his first wife allows it. Most, however, are satisfied with one."

"Weird."

"How do your people do it, then? Never marry at all?"

"We only have one wife, ever," she said. "Having multiple wives is more of an anomaly in my country, and most look at it as just plain wrong, or a way for a man to marry younger and younger wives to please his pervy lordy self."

"Is that how you think of us, then?"

"Well, it's one of the biggest reasons why I don't want to marry any of you. Though, granted, there are lots in my time who have multiple sex partners without marrying any of them—though I'm not one of them."

He shook his head and put a hand against the olive tree. "You're such a fool," he sighed. "Look, Annette, Wenamon won't be able to take care of you forever. Do you want to work in the kitchen for the rest of your life?"

"I don't want to plan any life here! I want to go back home."

"What do you hate so much about this place? I still can't understand."

"Probably because you've never seen where I used to live." Her eyes were so focused and strange in their brightest blue, that he almost missed what she said next. "Where I lived the homes were always cool when we wanted them to be, or always warm. We had instant hot water, instant cold, and diseases that would kill people here were just a nuisance there. I miss my bed, I miss my clothes," she gestured down at her sooty, mangled dress. "I miss people who speak my own language, I miss my friends, I miss my *family*. Would you want to stay in a strange place forever? Away from absolutely everything you've ever known?"

"Of course not," said Xius quickly, growing uncomfortable with her intensity. "But you need to prepare for the chance that you might never go back home."

"But what if I do? What if I have a chance? I doubt there's a nice little magic road to come back here, so why get married? And heaven forbid if I had kids!"

"Then you make this your new home. It's what every woman does when she gets married—she leaves her parents and makes a new home somewhere else."

"But I don't want that somewhere else to be here!"

His head was starting to hurt and he rubbed his temples in an attempt to alleviate some of the discomfort. He thought he could understand, but it eluded him, and as far as he was concerned she was acting like a child. "We don't always get what we want."

She leaned on her hand, expression weary. "I know. I'm sorry for frustrating you, Pharaoh. You're already being so nice as to keep talking to me...thank you."

He stared. It was the first time she had ever thanked him, and the pleasure it gave him was borderline overwhelming. Every trace of his previous annoyance vanished.

"You're welcome."

She stood up beside him. "Is there anything I can do for you? Make your day better? I can pull pranks on those priests—though they might have me beheaded for that."

He chuckled and lowered his fingers from his temples. "I'm the only one who can authorize executions."

"Doesn't mean they wouldn't be mad enough to take it into their own hands."

"True, true."

"Besides, I can relate to the whole forced marriage."

Xius hesitated and glanced around him again. It suddenly occurred to him how strange it was that the servants' courtyard, which was heavily frequented, had been empty for so long. The only relief he had was that no one could possibly understand what they were saying. "Has he asked you yet, then? Set?"

"I never said it was Set."

"But it is, isn't it?"

She sighed in exasperation. "Yes."

"Then how can you suppose he's even thinking about it?"

"Well first off, because you supposed it. Secondly," and by now her nose had turned pink, "would it hurt your royal highness to be told your royal vizier is a horrible kisser?"

Uncomfortable tingles ran up his back, making his scalp prickle. He found himself staring at the wall, unable to comprehend his own thoughts. Annette waved her hand in front of his face and he flinched.

"What?"

"You zoned out for a bit. Can you answer me?"

"I'm sorry, what did you ask?"

"Wenamon told me that Egyptian men don't often do such things unless they intend to marry you, or you're a whore—which I'm not—but did I translate what he said right? I felt like he was talking to a two-year-old with how slow he was going."

"Most of the time it is the case," said Xius evasively, and now he was looking over his shoulder in earnest. "Where is everyone?"

"Are you okay?"

"Yes, I—do you love him?"

"Wha—no! I mean, he's all right."

"And he kissed you?"

"Plural."

"More than once! What did you do?"

"Well I didn't *ask* for it. What do you think I did? Walked around with my lips puckered out and fluttering my eyelashes?"

"Ra, why are you telling me all this?"

"Because you *asked*, and frankly, you're the only who can clarify to me how your whole Egypty culture works without speaking Arabic to me, or whatever it is I've been learning." She pouted. "Why are you freaking out? I thought you wanted me to marry him."

"He hasn't proposed to you yet."

Her eyes grew wide. "Is he going to rape me?"

"Good gods and crook of Anubis—where did you get that from?"

"Then why else would he be getting all weird and smoochy?"

"I don't know, can we stop talking about this?"

Holy Ra, he was blushing from his head to his toes, and yet his chest was so full of icy liquid at the thought of Set kissing her that he thought he might drown. He leaned against the wall in an attempt to not give away the sudden turmoil she had inflicted on him. He glanced down the empty hallway around the corner.

"I should be getting back to Set. We had a dispute to figure out between the nobles and this whole plague business."

"I didn't...do anything wrong, did I?"

"Annette, I said I would be your friend, and as long as I don't have anyone breathing down my neck, I don't mind it if you speak your mind."

She cocked her head to the side. Then tipped it to the other side. "That's still so weird to me."

"What?"

"That you actually gave it to me. Everything up to this point has been do or die with you. I still think there's something else in that furry head of yours that's involved."

"Perhaps I was just tired of fighting your ignorance."

"Then propriety must not mean that much."

"Think what you will, I need to go. And please, if you're not fond of Set, don't lead him on. I, personally, wouldn't appreciate it, as he is my friend."

Her nose pinked once more, and this time it spread to her forehead and ears faster than he could blink. "I don't lead anyone on, Pharaoh. If there's anything I don't do, it's lie—not in word, action, or deed."

He simply nodded to this, and left without another word.

The halls were still oddly devoid of servants, and when he finally found Set leaning against a statue of his late great-grandfather, he only needed to catch a glance of the look on his face to know something was wrong.

"Set?"

"It's hit Wenamon."

***

For once, Hath was alone. She huddled in a corner of Merkha's courtyard beneath the fronds of a broad-leafed tree and breathed in the cold night. She wore no blanket, and she didn't want to. The feel of her hair prickling on her skin somehow distracted her from the icky displacement she constantly felt by not being in her own body. A small man-made waterfall tinkled somewhere in the gardens. The little tufts of grass beneath her legs pricked them like straw.

But the stars...she had her back up against a stone wall, with her head almost touching her shoulder blades. Still the same: jewels splattered against a swirl of violet and navy. Hath thought that if she ever flew up and touched it, the sky would feel like the fine fur of a cat, and the stars would be cool as polished, untouched gems tended to be.

A bush rustled next to her and Jee appeared, stone faced and huge. Her peace shattered.

"Your father is looking for you," he said, his low voice rumbling through the ground beneath her.

"Kasmut's father."

"Yours."

Hath closed her eyes. "I'm not leaving this place."

"But this plague—"

"Oh, by the gods, Jee, will you focus? We need to find out why the spell reacted this way. It should have only targeted that ugly woman."

"Healthy as a horse," said Jee. "My brother checked in on her. The chief baker, however, has fallen ill and Annette has been taken in by our good friend, the vizier."

Tugging the red wig off and throwing it against the ground, Hath ran her hands over Kasmut's bald scalp, missing her thick, black hair. She dug her nails into the skin and demanded of the strange darkness of Apep within her gut: *Why?*

"Do you have any excuses to give to your father?" said Jee.

"I'm not leaving."

"You're small and thin."

"Any one touches me and I'll kill them."

Jee gave her a deadpan look. Hath ignored him.

"Why did the spell react this way?" she muttered, picking a zit she found on her head. "It's not like I could've confused her hair for anyone else's. I'm sure I didn't make any mistake in the process, it's an extremely simple spell, and if I had done anything wrong it simply shouldn't have worked."

"Maybe this plague is just a fluke," said Jee. "And your father will be here soon."

"Kasmut's, and no, this is my sickness."

She left no room for argument, and Jee didn't try. He just stood there, expressive as a stone. A few of Merkha's servants could be heard pattering about the grounds in search of his daughter.

The darkness within her stirred. But instead of words hissing and twisting into her mind, all she felt was a chilling, deep, indefinable loathing as she brought up the image of the white girl in her mind. There was no answer. The spell had rebounded off of this girl rather than infect her, but what power out there was greater than death?

"Where did she come from?" asked Hath.

"Rumors are she came from the north," said Jee, "but I would hope you have more use of me besides gossip. The lunar eclipse is close, and I've only managed to glean—"

"Eclipse?" Hath dropped her hands, glaring at Jee. "Where have you heard this?"

"Our people have astronomers," he said, a faint sound of anger to his words.

A new thought occurred to Hath. All this time her focus had been entirely on her prince. Yes, she knew Jee had come to her to finish the spell her father and mother had been killed for, hoping to redeem himself by finishing their work, but she had never really *thought* about when that time would be. She knew she needed a lunar eclipse, but since the last one was only two years before, she had assumed the next wouldn't be for many years, if in her lifetime at all.

In fact, she hadn't even bothered to ask. And though Jee was insulted by her question, she really didn't know any astronomers, because the ones she had known died with her mother.

"When?" she asked.

"One month," said Jee, expression cracking into a frown. He never smiled, this man. He was all disapproval, all grim. He didn't have to say anything for Hath to know he was disturbed to find out she hadn't bothered to know when the next eclipse was. He probably had thought her obsessed with her parents' old spell like him. She hadn't bothered to correct him.

"Mistress!"

Hath cringed and Jee stepped out of the way. Three maid servants ran to her, expressions dismayed. They babbled about Merkha's distress, about the plague, about her safety, and gave random assurances that they only thought her noble for wanting to stay by her pharaoh's side.

As Jee said, she was hardly weighty enough to resist physical force, and the next thing she knew she was being plopped back in front of the broad Merkha, who had sweat pouring down his jowls.

"Kassy," he said, looking down at her with dismay, "why are you acting like this? This is unlike you."

Fear tickled at Hath's heart at the thought that this man could see through her, see that the soul of his daughter was gone, but she shook it off and bowed her head to the floor.

"I'm staying here."

"But there's a plague—"

"You're overreacting, Father. It's just a sickness going around that you're afraid of because vomit is involved."

"People have died already, and don't interrupt me."

"Not that many have died yet. I'm sorry, Father, but I ran because I couldn't handle your irrationality."

There was a stunned silence. Merkha's feet shifted in Hath's view, and she wondered how she had never noticed how ugly this man's toenails were. They were well trimmed, but flaky and an unseemly puce yellow.

Had she gone too far? She had heard Kasmut talk to her father like this on occasion, but even when she had just been a slave, she had cringed at the brash disrespect. If she went too far, surely pain would come. Besides, if Merkha happened to force her out, returning to the palace would only seem strange and give her the reputation of being rebellious and contentious. She had enough of a job on her plate catching the prince's attention with that.

"Kassy," he cooed, sounding anxious, "please, try to understand. We'll just be gone until this all blows over. You wouldn't be away from the Pharaoh for long—"

"But the priests have been pressing him to be married within the month, maybe even less than that. If I leave now, he may find someone else to fill the place, out of desperation."

"What? Where have you heard this?"

She thought fast. Surely she couldn't mention her connections to Seti, who had been keeping Jee posted on her progress as queen. Had she spoken too soon?

"Who else?" she said, throwing it to the wind. Before Merkha could make a stab at who she mentioned and end up digging up a lie, she continued, "Please, Father, we'll be okay. You know how I love the Pharaoh, you know what kind of opportunity this is for our family. It's just a little sickness, we don't know how far it will spread. It might just be a seasonal thing."

"But...they say it's..."

"Exactly: 'they say.' I've already told you all this before, and I'd appreciate it if you didn't drag me before you like a child." Hath did Kasmut's trademark sniff with nose in air while hunching the left shoulder. She remembered how she had mocked Kasmut for this quirk of hers, and she never thought her hours of mocking the same move would end up being a service to her. Her gut still squirmed nervously.

Merkha bit his lip and looked back to where one of his wives stood half-hidden in the doorway, as though she were playing pretend spy. Hath barely withheld a snort.

"I'll talk to your step-mother about it," he said. "She is worried about the children, after all."

"Be a man, father, it's you who is afraid of this disease, not them."

"You know no such thing!"

"Yes, I do. Now if that's all, I'd like to go to bed. I'm tired."

"I still can't believe he let you be raised like this," said the woman from the doorway.

Merkha prickled, inflated, but it was a weak attempt at anger. When his eyes fell on Hath, all she could see was sadness. It irked her that a man who had boasted to have such maddening pride in his spoiled brat of a daughter should look down so sadly at Hath now.

His shoulders slumped. "What has happened to you?"

Hath went cold. "Father?"

Merkha just gave her a sad smile, shook his head, and turned. "I'll see about your staying here. Try to get some sleep, love."

Confused, chest prickling with unease, Hath turned around and ambled to the bedroom that was not hers.

***

Nut's nighttime dress glimmered at him through the doorway to his balcony. Firelight flickered orange and purple shadows across the walls. Dinner had just ended, to Xius's relief. He could hardly swallow enough food through his hyper-awareness of how often his vizier would look over to Annette in the far corner of his chambers where she clutched a pitcher of wine. Xius wondered if Set drank too much to give her an excuse to draw near and pour more for him. But he was thinking too much. Far from relaxed, he lounged across the cushions about the brazier and fingered the medallion around his neck.

The thought of ameese crossed his mind and he wished his drink was stronger, perhaps the wine of Sekhmet herself. But no sooner had the thought left than another unpleasant memory took its place.

After explaining to Xius how Wenamon and a few other servants were found sick with symptoms of ameese, he had revealed to Xius his affections for Annette and begged him to allow him to get her away from the kitchens and the ameese that dwelt there. Xius agreed, sick with concern himself for Annette's welfare, but then when Set insisted on taking her to his own chambers, Xius had to use every ounce of his self-control to calmly tell Set that it simply wasn't appropriate, since he had yet to announce their engagement. They had agreed to have a light dinner of dried fish and figs in the Pharaoh's quarters to discuss it, but ended up sitting in silence and drinking morosely. In the end Xius promised Set to send her after him to a chamber prepared for her, without really caring to, and let Set teeter off to bed.

After all this, Annette still sat in her corner in his room. The emotions burning in his chest urged him to go to her or at least show her some attention, but Set's intentions toward her still rankled in his mind. He should have told Set about his familiarity with her. He should have told Set that she didn't want him, feared him, even. Xius himself shouldn't even be near her now, not with the feelings that had been growing over the last month.

He poured himself another cup. To Duat with this.

"Annette?"

He expected her to brazenly meet his eyes as she always did, but she did not.

"Are you going to sit there all night?"

"If that is what your highness wishes."

He prickled. He knew that voice. Osiris damn it, he knew it and hated it.

"What is it?" he grunted.

"What?"

"You're getting depressed again."

"Why does it matter, if I may be so bold to ask?"

"It's annoying."

"Excuse me, your highness."

He growled to himself. Out of all the times to be evasive...

"That was not a request. That was a command."

To his satisfaction, he thought he could hear a bite of irritation when she answered.

"I don't know what's going on here, so, naturally, I'm a bit freaked out. I'm dragged here by soldiers who I think are going to beat me up just to find out Wenamon is sick, though no one will tell me how he is doing or if he'll be okay. Then there's the whole Set thing, ack!" She slapped her hands on top of her head and groaned. "Did he really ask me to come stay with him, or had I heard wrong? Like, in his room stay with him? Damn it, I hate being the idiot. I hate having to second guess if I heard someone right because they speak a damn stupid other language!"

He took a sip of the wine.

"And it just reminds me why I hate…" she stopped with a snap of teeth.

He fingered his cup, feeling a sinking sensation within him. "Let me guess. It's why you hate me?"

"I don't hate you, per se."

"I'm the one who made you into a slave, which you hate, and that's the reason you're so miserable, even if I can't comprehend why. The only slaves I've seen treated as well as you are few and far between and are more pets than slaves."

Her silence was enough answer for him. He considered the rippling surface of the dark wine. The quiet was comfortable, edged with only the gentle noises of leaves and various insects outside. The fire crackled and popped now and then.

A murmur came from her corner, almost too quiet to hear.

"Sometimes I've thought to ask you to just kill me and end it so maybe I can wake up from all this and…and go home…"

His hand clenched about the cup. That was it, then. There could be no question about it.

"Very well. You're no longer a slave."

She lifted her head to gawk at him, blue eyes wide.

"What?"

"You heard me. You're not a slave anymore. I am Pharaoh, what I say is law. I'll have it written in the records tomorrow, then you can go off and do whatever you damn please, even refuse Set, if you want." He took another comforting sip of his drink.

"But…but then what am I?"

"Well, what do you want to be?"

"I-I-I don't understand."

"What is there to not understand?"

"You! I don't understand you!" she tugged at a piece of her hair with both hands. "I mean, for the first few weeks you'd practically scream at me if I acted above my station. Now you're so…so nice and talking to me like a normal person and I don't understand what happened. Did I do something?"

He shrugged, heart in his throat. "I guess you could say that." He waved a hand to the cushions opposite of him. "Care to sit with me?"

Her gaze narrowed. "Depends. What are you drinking? It's not what you've had me pouring."

"Just some wine."

"The kind with alcohol?"

"I presumed so." He sniffed at it. "At least, that's what I hope it is. Ra, what I wouldn't give to be drunk now."

She cocked her head at him, something he was coming to find endearing. "Why's that?"

In answer he groaned and let his head fall back on the backrest of cushions. He heard her bare feet smack against the granite floor, having tucked her precious shoes beneath her cushion, and then slip down on the pillows a bit away from him. She said nothing, but he could feel expectation, however patient, hovering in the air. He slid his hand down his face.

"The sickness I told you about this morning? It's here. And, well, it might just be my fault if we all die now because of it, though I don't even know if it would change anything if I married this second. Strange to be most responsible, and yet the most useless in doing anything about it." He took in a deep breath and lifted his head to take another deep swallow of the wine.

"Set was right, then."

"In what?"

"That you…that you care very deeply, maybe even too much so."

He snorted. "Did you think I was an arrogant bastard? Because you were right, I am."

But she gave a certain smile and his stomach flip-flopped. The warmth he had been trying so hard to ignore that day constricted his chest once more, filling him with the urge to reach for her, touch her in some way. Aggravated with himself, he tipped his head back and finished what was left in the cup.

"What's everyone getting sick with?"

"Most likely ameese."

"What's that? Is it like a cold or a flu?"

He nodded. "More like the common stomach sickness. There's fever, shakings, vomiting, etc. But then it grows more severe when the ill person loses all desire to eat or drink and the fever overwhelms them. They're skin turns grey, cracks, and bleeds. Some say near the end they grow mad. They die within a matter of days. There are some who think it is simply because they drank filthy water, but it comes out of nowhere."

Annette pulled her legs up to her chest. "That sounds…ugh. And you say Wenamon has it?"

"Unfortunately." He moved to pour himself more wine just to find the bottle empty. He grumbled at it.

"So…does that mean Wenamon...he's going to die?"

"Precisely. Isn't there anything stronger than this?" He knocked the bottle off the table. "I can still think."

Her hands clenched one another till he could see the white of her knuckles.

"Isn't there any way to help him?"

"You tell me. You're the one with the advanced medicine." He glared at the fallen bottle.

"I already told you, I'm not a doctor."

"Pity, because as far as anyone I know is concerned, there's no cure."

After a few minutes of quavering silence, filled with his grumblings, the fire, and her quiet breathing, she looked out onto the banister thoughtfully.

"Pharaoh?"

"Hmm?"

"Set said it was the Nile workers and the merchants who got sick first, right? Did the merchants come up here by boat?"

"Yes."

"Then don't you think that it might be the Nile that's making them sick? I mean, maybe there was something in the river, I don't know, something rotten in the water itself that got to the workers and then the merchants."

"If it is, that just makes it worse. So much worse. All our farmlands would be soaked with the sickness when the floods come." Feeling particularly worse now about the whole thing, he reached for the bottle and handed it to her. "Tell those fools out in the hall to refill this. And tell them something stronger this time."

She grimaced. "I'd rather not, your majesty."

"Do you want to be a slave again?"

"No. I just don't feel too safe being stuck in the same room with a drunk."

He considered this and wondered if he cared if he did something stupid with Annette around. He decided all he needed to make his situation worse was to force himself drooling on her just to regret it in the morning, so he flung the bottle back down and sank into his cushions to sulk.

"You'll be staying in a chamber prepared for you by Set. One of my men will escort you."

She flinched. "Now you tell me?"

"I've had a lot on my mind."

She sighed, seeming to forgive him, and tucked her chin between her knees.

"It will be all right."

"How do you know? Why would the gods, who brought this plague upon us, take it away out of the goodness of their hearts? According to the priests, if I don't get married by the end of the week, we're lost. How pathetic and wrong." Then, like the dawning of the sun, an idea shone through his bleary thoughts. He didn't *have* to marry Kasmut, per se. All he had to do was marry, they weren't specific as to who. He felt his heart pick up a notch and he glanced over at Annette in the light of the fire. All he had to do was ask; perhaps she wasn't as adverse to him as she was to Set, and who cared about the court who would bring up her foreign heritage! At least he'd be married, and that's all they really asked.

An upsurge of emotion came from his gut, warming him better than the wine ever could, and bringing with it thoughts and dreams he had not even dared to imagine before: a life with Annette by his side, having children with her, forever learning of each other and the different worlds they have partaken of until it was as though both of them were natives of both lands. She wouldn't laugh at his poetry, he knew for sure, though just how, he didn't know. They could play games in the water as they had that night, run as fast as they could beneath the stars, and dance to the musicians together. He could touch her without apprehension, kiss her—

All thoughts froze there. He remembered her icy blue eyes and had been and her hot intensity beneath the servant courtyard's cypress.

She only wanted to go home, far away from Egypt.

And then there was Set...

He got up and went to the door to order more wine instead.

"You should probably go to Set's chambers now," he said. "Since I was the closest thing to having any claim on you, being your master, he asked me for your hand and I gave it. Though you're not a slave anymore, according to prudence, you two are engaged and it is inappropriate for you to stay here for the night."

She gave a surprised, dismayed cry and he did his best to ignore it as he sent one of his guards off to fetch the wine. This time, he ordered wine of Sekhmet rather than the weaker wine of Baset. After what he was about to do, he'd need it. He could already feel the acid-like pain growing just below his ribs and rising into his chest, because even if it was possible now to keep her, to love her, she hated him and Set was his best friend.

"I won't!" she said. "I'll go back to the kitchens if you send me away!"

"And risk catching ameese?"

"If ameese is as contagious as you claim, none of us are safe from it, including you. Don't you know how diseases work?"

The ache in his chest was making him grumpy. "He won't do anything to you, and even if you aren't a slave, I am still Pharaoh. Do not defy me."

"I'm not Egyptian!"

"*But I am god!*" he shouted, afraid of what he might do if she stayed in his room any longer while the dream of her still sung in his mind. "Go to him *now!*"

Something broke in her expression and instantly he regretted what he had done. Her eyes grew shiny, but not a tear dropped. She stood, stony faced, dress still stained with soot and dirt.

"So much for not being a slave," she mumbled, and padded out of the room.

***

"How is Wenamon?"

Set looked up from the scrolls before him. The shadows beneath his eyes seemed more prominent than ever, and his expression was wan. He sighed, rubbed his temples with his thumbs, and leaned back against the cushions he sat in. Unlike Xius's chambers, Set's were smaller, with bare walls. Potted plants made up most of the decorations, though here and there were statues of Thoth or the continuation of a wall mural of women dancing in a brook. Mostly, however, it was filled with cubbies of Set's personal papyrus rolls. Annette had been placed in a modest, but royal chamber next door, though Xius knew for a fact that she was rarely in there.

"His daughter has been caring for him," Set said. "She just sent word to me this morning that he has fallen into the gray fever. It shouldn't be long now. Three days at most."

"Who else has contracted it?"

"Mostly slaves. Though that's not accounting for the rest of lower Egypt. The delta has been hit the worst, for some reason, but I can't tell why."

"Annette mentioned the river."

Set nodded. "Still, I can't see any reason how the river could be the cause."

"We found Denan in the river. Maybe it has something to do with how he got there."

"Now you're just blabbing whatever comes to your mind."

Xius ran a hand through his hair and wondered if he should cut it. "You never know." He then smiled broadly, though it felt stiff. "When do you plan on marrying her? And why didn't you tell me before?"

"Because I don't broadcast my love life, and I don't plan on moving on with anything until this all settles down."

"What if it doesn't settle down? All the more reason to secure things."

"Xius..."

"What?"

"You've given me your permission, now step out of it."

Xius huffed. "You're always in *my* love life."

"You're not married, and until you do, it's my job. Speaking of which," Set turned his attention to Xius, who stood over him. "Your week is about up and you haven't done anything."

Xius tried his best to look innocent, even though his stomach squirmed painfully. "I haven't had the chance to talk to Kasmut about it."

Set threw up his hands. "Damn it, Xius, you've been avoiding her."

"No I haven't!"

"You're pharaoh, don't play coy with me. The sun might not rise tomorrow if you simply 'haven't had the chance.'"

"I have my reasons."

"Of course you do."

"Why are you in such a bad mood today? You may be my friend, but you shouldn't get too much in the habit of speaking to me like this."

The vizier scowled and turned back to his reports. "I'm not sleeping well."

"Have you talked to the physicians about it?"

"I'm fine, now go find Kasmut. I've already informed the priests of your consent to marry, so she's probably already heard it as well. It's not good to start a marriage with her thinking you don't care."

Xius cringed before leveling an icy glare at Set. His skin tingled with the speed of his rising ire.

"When did I tell you to do such a thing?"

"You already said you would, so I took the liberty—"

"*Took* is the precise word!" His ears pounded as he dug his nails into his palms.

With an uncharacteristic, closed-mouth yell of irritation, Set met his glare with an equally ferocious one. "What are you so angry about? You're acting like a child."

He opened his mouth, but froze. Annette didn't want Egypt. She wanted nothing to do with it, including him, and Set was his best friend. And it would be much easier for a slave to be a viziers wife than a queen.

Before he could say anything he really regretted, Xius

pivoted on the spot and stomped out of Set's chambers. Guards stepped out of his way and straggling priests flattened themselves against the walls. He couldn't talk to Kasmut like this, but even as he thought about it he couldn't shake away his aversion of her. There was nothing wrong with Kasmut, granted, but from what he knew of Annette, the moment he married Kasmut, all chances with the white foreigner would be non-existent. But how could he think like that? There wasn't any chance with her in the first place.

It wasn't until he found himself at the top of the stairs that led to the kitchen that he realized he had gone there without thinking. He stared down the clay and limestone bricks and sighed. Now more than ever, he needed Wenamon's quiet acceptance and his honeyed rolls. He swallowed hard. The old chef didn't have long now, and there had been nothing he could do.

He heard footsteps and froze when a familiar white-haired girl appeared around the curve of the stairs. She was rubbing her eyes, so she didn't realize he was there until she was just a few steps beneath him. Then, on seeing him, she moved to retreat back down the stairs, but seemed to reconsider as she eyed him.

"Pharaoh?" She then sighed and nudged her chin over her shoulder. "Come on. I know what you want."

"What are you doing here?" he asked. "I thought we told you to stay away from the kitchen?"

"Do you want your treat or not?"

"Treat? Do I look like a dog to you?"

She gave a familiar sarcastic, deadpan look. "Yes, I'm stupid enough to treat the ruler of Egypt like a dog. Now come on already. You look like you're about to cry."

He spluttered in protest, embarrassed—of course he wasn't about to cry! But then he caught the edge of her kind smile and the wave of her long ponytail across her curved hips and found himself trailing after her. Down below, the kitchen was unnaturally empty except for two maids who watched over some bread still cooking on the curved walls of the ovens.

"Where is everyone?"

She shrugged. “Beats me.”

Then he caught the cautious way with which the two servants glanced at her before shuffling out of her way, as though afraid to be touched. Annette said nothing as she took a bowl covered with a cloth next to one of the ovens. When the servants noticed Xius, they bowed themselves as low as they could, nearly dipping their black braids into the fires they tended.

He rubbed his arm absentmindedly. “They're not talking to you?”

Annette said nothing. She sat him down in his usual place at the table and took off the cloth.

“How's Wenamon?” She pushed her hands into the waiting brown ball of dough.

“Gray fever is upon him.” His throat tightened again and he swallowed in an attempt to loosen it. He had just noticed purple bruises along Annette's arms, between her elbows and shoulder in ugly blotches, as though something or someone had hit her there.“Why didn't you go back to Set?”

“What does that mean, the gray fever?”

“Answer my question.”

She fell quiet, though her hands didn't stop. His eyes trailed to another bruise, barely visible above the line where she had pulled up her dress to cover her breasts. The servants would have thought her strange modesty arrogant, wouldn’t they? He glanced back at the servant girls by the oven and resisted the urge to interrogate them.

But this wouldn’t have happened if she had just stayed upstairs with Set.

“Annette—”

“I don't want to marry him,” she said harshly. “I don't want to be near his room, I don't want to be near his bed—”

“I told you that you could trust him.”

“I don't want to marry him.”

Xius sighed. “Without Wenamon here to protect you, I can't say what the others will do to you.”

With a loud bang of wood, she slammed the ball of dough back into the bowl, making him jump. The muscles along her jaw tensed and her blue eyes held the ice he had met on those starry nights. Her cheeks had flushed a lily pink.

"I can take care of myself," she hissed. "Now stop pissing me off."

"How am I doing that?"

"By not telling me about Wenamon. You said some people die from this."

"Most people die from ameese," he said. *If not everyone.*

She made a most unfeminine growl. "What's wrong with me being different, anyway? Wenamon didn't have a problem with it."

When Xius didn't say anything to this, she muttered curious profanities, including something about bastard xenophobic Egyptians. They fell into silence, only broken up by her occasional curse as she molded balls out of the dough and slapped them down atop the ceramic oven. She gingerly fingered the bread as it rose, then flipped it with some tongs to cook on the other side.

"There's some lady asking me about you," she said.

"Who?"

"I can't remember all your weird names. Katmaha, Horus, Blah-something-Patah, I don't know."

He ignored her blatant disrespect for the moment. "Kasmut?"

"Sure."

"What's she been asking about?"

"What we talk about, mainly." She peeled off the cooked roll and slapped on another piece of dough. "I can understand Egyptian just fine, but speaking it is a different story. I don't think she likes me much, though."

Instantly, he stiffened. "Is she the one that hurt you?" She gave him an odd look and he scowled. "Those bruises stand out like the sun on your skin."

"What made you jump to that conclusion?"

"She's beaten slaves before."

"I'm not a slave."

"You are as far as she knows."

"But you said I'm not!" She slathered honey on the roll

with such vigor, a few drops sprinkled up her flour-dusted arms.

"Marry Set and you won't be."

"You never said I had to do anything for it, what kind of pharaoh are you?"

"I meant it will be much easier to revoke your status if you just marry him. If I just go and tell the scribes you're not a slave anymore they'll start wondering why you're wandering around the palace eating food you didn't earn, and I'm not sure what to make you that would change the life you have now without causing complications. You technically can't be of any use until you learn our language and way of life."

"Gah! You know what? Whatever, just eat your pastry and finish your moping so I can leave."

She flipped over the dough on the oven before slumping onto the bench across the table from him, fingers buried in her hair and face pressed against the skin where her elbows met. Xius heard hiss-like whispers behind him, but when he looked, the servant women had averted their gaze. He could practically smell their contempt, though, in the way their shoulders hunched over their ears and their hands tremble in their work. They may not be able to understand the language they spoke to each other, but Annette's actions and tone toward him were blasphemy in their eyes. He picked up the roll and nibbled on it. It didn't melt in his mouth as Wenamon's would have, but he found it comforting enough.

"How did you know?" he asked her.

"Hmm?"

"The rolls."

"I'm not blind. It's what he always gives you when you come down in a bad mood. I know they're not as good as his—"

"They're fine."

They fell once more into silence. A few servants trickled back down the stairs, and as he heard their gasps he also caught glimpses of their appalled looks toward Annette. The unease in his stomach twisted into a knot.

"Annette, I insist you return to Set."

"And watch him read when I'm not dodging his attempts to be romantic with me or sitting alone in my room with nothing to do? No thank you."

He slapped his hand to his forehead. "You'd rather be beat on than receive his affections? Just what are you so afraid of?"

She got up to flip the next roll and said nothing. The hiss of whispers was growing louder. She had yet to notice the honey on her arms as she sweetened the next roll. Her expression had softened, but not in a kind way. If anything, it made her look tired, even haggard.

"I'm just trying to figure out what to do." She said softly. "I was leaving right when you came, stop stressing yourself out." She handed him the roll. "But what's going on with you? Getting forced to marry whatsherface?"

"Yeah."

"Is she pretty at least?"

"I don't care." He took up the next roll. "I'm taking this to go. I can't stand these whisperings."

"Care if I come with?"

He smiled at her to show she could, and they headed up the stairs together.

"So, what's the great mighty ruler up to today?"

"Hunting down my wife-to-be."

She barked a short laugh. "She avoiding you?"

He hesitated, then realizing no one could understand what they were saying anyway, he said, "more the other way around—sort of."

"What's wrong with her?" she asked as she walked beside him down the hall. He noticed a few more servants ahead.

"Nothing—and could you walk behind me and keep your head down? You might not care about getting bruised, but I'd rather you not."

"Why can't you just tell them off?" She did as he asked, though.

"Because then the nobility and priests will start asking why, and the less attention you get the better."

"Why?"

"Ra, Annette, can't you just trust me? I don't have the luxury to explain all the intricacies of politics to you."

"Don't you?"

He hesitated once more as he felt the suspicious gaze of the servants behind him. He didn't even know where he was going, all he knew was he wanted to be away from there. He passed his honeyed roll gingerly from one hand to the other and took a bite. There was something he had to do tonight, what was it? But then, glancing back, he was hit by her coy gaze through curtains of white gold—hair the color of electrum, most beautiful metal of the heavens. All thoughts of Kasmut slid from his mind. Set's anger, the priest's expectations, the plague, suddenly it all seemed just a little less important, or at least put off for the time being. Heat ran through his veins and warmed him all the way to his toes.

But he couldn't forget.

"What do you want?" he asked warily. He could feel a reason behind her following him.

She lifted her chin. "I want to see Wenamon."

"No."

"Where is he?"

"Even if I told you, you wouldn't know. You've never stepped foot outside of this palace—unless you just suddenly appearing in my court had a side trip through Waset."

"As far as you're concerned." Her lips pressed into the smallest of mischievous smiles. He wasn't swayed from giving her a harsh, reproving look. She had the audacity to roll her eyes in response. "Oh, don't get started on me, Pharaoh. Just tell me where he is."

"No." He moved to leave.

She ran ahead of him and threw her arms out to stop him. "Xiusthamus, he's *dying.*"

The sound of his name coming from her sent a shock through his system. Usually she just called him Pharaoh, as was right, seeing only those with authority or express permission could refer to him by his given name. If anyone had heard, beatings would be the least of his worries. "Annette—!"

"And he's the only father I'll ever know here!"

This made him pause. He had never thought of how far Wenamon's and Annette's relationship would have gone. He had only suspected Wenamon's guardianship over her had been out of duty and compassion. One look at her told him she felt every word, though, and would not be moved. Her blue eyes, so full of expression, were hot.

"Tell me where he is or I will run out there and find him for myself."

"You know nothing about the people in the city—"

"—and if anyone tries to stop me, I'll just run. No one can catch me."

"Arrogant, are we?"

"No one."

They stared each other down. Lucky for them, the hall was empty, and he was grateful for that. He looked into her eyes and recalled the last time he had gone to Wenamon's home. He knew it was stupid, but she wasn't the only one who had thought about visiting the old chef, despite the plague. Set would have him tied up like a calf and thrown him into a box before he let him and the woman he loved go anywhere near one with the plague.

But he knew Annette enough to know she would be true to her word. Set wouldn't want her running around the city at night, either.

He sighed. "Xius."

Her arms slackened. "Eh?"

"Call me Xius. If we're ignoring the fact that I am god and you are not, then you might as well call me Xius, though bear in mind that you'll be massacred on the spot if anyone hears you shouting my full name like that again. I'll take you to Wenamon, tonight."

She looked flabbergasted. "But you just told me it wasn't a good idea for us to be seen together."

"Yes yes, pharaoh, slave, Set's fiancé, politics, Kasmut—none of it mixes, which is why we'll be going at night."

She frowned. "Won't they be asleep?"

He huffed. "I know you love to forget it, but I'm *Pharaoh,* Annette."

"Uh, so...?"

"So I'll send a message ahead for them to expect us." He turned away from her, unable to look at her surprised mouth in a perfect "o" a moment longer. “Meet me at the front porch of the palace after the second guard.”

“I don't even know what the first or third guard is, dude.”

“By the crook of Anubis, don't call me 'dude,' and *fine,* meet me there when the moon is at its zenith.”

“Sure, fine. Go do your wife hunting now. I got chores to do.”

“No you don't, Wenamon's sick. Set's in the main hall, go to him.”

“What?!”

“Go!”

“All right! All right! Jeeze.”

But he didn't hear her leaving. Curious, he peered over his shoulder. Yes, she was still there.

“Thank you,” she said softly. “I'm sorry for complaining about Set. If it will really help, I'll try to like him. I don't want to cause you any more trouble, really—” she peeked back at him and smiled. “Unless it's really funny, of course.”

With that, they parted ways, and Xius found himself wandering to the eastern courtyard where he knew, somehow, that Kasmut would be waiting for him with a game of Senet on her lap and a nervous grin. He'd sit down, return the nervous grin, and say words he knew were still undecided in his heart.

***

Xius examined himself in the tall, polished bronze mirror. His head was covered by a traditional, plain white headdress and his tunic was of the roughest linen he could find. Denan had lent it to him with disapproval in his eyes, but Xius already had enough practice with ignoring that look in particular and walked out with steady steps. He had washed the traditional kohl from his face and had patted himself lightly with dirt. All his jewelry was gone, except for his medallion, which he swung in his hand indecisively. He had a thick, dark cloak hanging around his shoulders and another folded up underneath one arm. At the last moment before he walked out the door, he tucked the medallion into the twisted cloth belt around his waist. Best not leave that behind, just in case. He didn't trust Annette's speaking skills, despite all the extra hours she had spent learning at Set's feet rather than cleaning stoves.

The thought sent the familiar cool liquid disgust through his chest that gave him the urge to punch something—or more specifically Set.

A lone man from his personal guard trailed after him as he made his way down the hall. He had shed anything that signified him as anything more than just a friend, though the way he carried himself and the sword on his waist would make him hard-pressed to fool anyone.

He saw the gleam of her electrum hair in the half-moon light before he saw the rest of her. She turned on hearing his steps, her blue eyes silver and her arms bare. He tossed her the cloak and tucked a hand into his belt to touch the edges of the rough gold medallion.

"I figured you didn't own one," he said in her language.

"Duh, you took everything I did own." She fingered it. "Wow, you Egyptians wear cloaks?"

"What's that supposed to mean?"

"Nothing. I just always thought medieval knights wore these—and princesses with poufy dresses." She wrapped it around her shoulders with a smile. "Thanks anyway. It is rather cold out here."

He almost didn't hear her gratitude, too caught up trying to understand what she had said. Figuring it a waste of time to ask, he began going down the grand stairs of the palace. He wondered when was the last time he had walked these steps at night and found he couldn't remember.

"So, how far away is he?" she asked.

"Not too far. Wenamon's family have long been servants to the royal family, so their home is quite close to the palace grounds; but besides that, I have a few things to go over with you. First, you are to speak Egyptian to me from now on. No one must know about the medallion."

"Why? Think someone might try to steal it from you?"

"Being able to understand any language is great power for any ruler of men. Also, I'd rather not have the attention."

"Um, okay then. Does that including your guard here? Nice disguise, by the way." The guard in question, unable to understand what she was saying, didn't even realize she was talking to him. She sighed. "You know, the fun insulting-people-without-them-understanding wore off real quick. Okay, Pharaoh. No English."

"And secondly, you are not to refer to me as 'Pharaoh' outside of their home. If someone in the streets should hear it could cause...complications."

"Let me guess—royalty's not supposed to wander around at night?"

"It's a vulnerable position, and—"

"No need to explain, I'm not stupid, you know."

"And last, no talking to anyone. We say hi to Wenamon, you can ask his daughter some questions, whatever you want, but with anyone else, don't even make eye contact. Now, if you're not an idiot, as you say, I don't have to give you any more rules."

"You didn't even have to give me those, really."

"Good. I'm taking my hand off the medallion now, so from here on out you speak my tongue. Is there anything else you'd like to say before then?"

"Um…tally ho?"

She gave him a weak smile. The guard gave no indication that he was annoyed by a foreign conversation going on beside him.

Xius took his hand out of his belt and concentrated on counting streets when they reached the gates leading to the city. Rather than go out the gates, they slipped through the doors the guards used. The guards themselves recognized their king instantly and bowed them out with a quiet salute.

The homes next to the walls were elegant, to be sure, but not the grand estates of the nobles, which often took up whatever untamable hills lay next to the river. Houses grew shorter, their roofs slowly turning from baked cement mud to thatch, and soon Xius found the street he was looking for. It was empty, but clean, and a lone candle lit up a house at the end. Keeping his cloak close around his face, he led his guard and Annette down the narrow road.

Wenamon's daughter opened the door on the first knock. Her face was wan and pale in the dim light, and she looked to be in her mid-thirties. She was bald, having left her wig off for the night, and she wore a light blanket over her slim kilt. She bowed them in, respectfully keeping her left foot forward and her eyes averted. Annette looked as though she wished she could see everything at once, and Xius scolded her with a glare. She turned away sheepishly.

"He's this way," said the daughter in a whisper.

The guard took his post next to the front door and she led them to an adjacent room where the lone candle he had seen from outside burned. Inside lay a bed with Wenamon's mostly covered form in it. As Annette rushed forward and leaned over her friend, Xius took in the room. It smelled faintly of bile beneath the overwhelming scent of hibiscus and peppermint. Several clay pots had been stacked against one wall, and on the other wall was a trunk of sorts, probably filled with personal possessions.

"How is he?" asked Annette in her heavy Egyptian. Her fingers were very lightly touching the old man's brow, which was beaded with sweat. His dark skin had the trademark cracked and grayish hue. Wenamon looked to be asleep, though Xius couldn't hear a single breath from him in the silence.

"Waning," the daughter whispered. She looked lost.

"Earlier this morning he thought I was my mother, but after supper he thought I had turned into a crocodile or at least that's what I could gather." She closed her eyes and put trembling hands to her chest. "When night fell, so did his awareness. At least he sleeps now."

Annette's fingers continued to pitter down Wenamon, lifting and touching like rain drops, checking his fingers, his arms, the skin beneath his eyes.

"He—he needs water," she said.

"He can't keep it down," said the daughter.

"But his skin..." Annette fumbled, unable to use the right words. Her gaze flickered to Xius, but he shook his head. He knew what she was thinking. She bit her lip and drew back to his side, blue eyes shining. Her teeth bit into her lip so hard, Xius feared she'd draw blood.

Feeling disconnected, and almost afraid, he took his turn to approach Wenamon. He didn't touch him. The old man who had laughed at his love life just a few days earlier now looked dried and gray like ash before him.

Everything he had planned on saying, that he had been dying to say, died on his lips.

The candlelight smelled of animal fat. The walls were bland and plain, so unlike his own. A small statue of Bes sat in a small alcove above the head of Wenamon's bed.

But he had to say something. This might be the last he ever saw of Wenamon, but...it wasn't like he could hear him.

A muscle twitched on the old man's face.

"Prince?" Wenamon muttered, not much more than a croak.

Xius smiled. It had been over a year since the Chef had called him that. "Yes, old man?"

"You're an idiot. Your father's going to find out you came here."

The man's throat was so dry Xius could barely understand him. "You sound like...well, shit."

"Brat," he croaked, tilting his head to his side. "Good."

His daughter came up to Xius's side, keeping her head bowed respectfully. "Father, how are you feeling? Would you like some water?"

He muttered something. All Xius could make out was the word "prince," and his throat tightened uncomfortably.

The daughter wavered, uncertain. Xius could almost hear the conflict between being unable to refute the Pharaoh and taking care of her father twisting in her mind. He glanced at her, then back to the old, dry face.

"Don't worry, we're leaving soon. Thank you for troubling with us this late at night."

"Oh, no, it's the greatest honor, your majesty. The highest honor."

Xius nodded, watching Annette out of the corner of his eyes. She was still biting her lip, eyes bright. He wondered why she was trying so hard not to cry.

Carefully, he took up Wenamon's bandaged fingers. The old man rolled his head to face Xius and mumbled something else without opening an eye. The young pharaoh felt the need to say something profound, something to encompass all his gratitude to the old man for putting up with him while he was growing up, but nothing came to mind. Feeling faintly like a fool for coming here at all, he stepped away from the daughter and father.

"Come, Annette," he said.

The guard closed the door behind them. Xius took a deep breath of the cold night air. Annette sniffed. They walked back to the palace without a word and came upon no one. At the porch of the palace Xius excused his guard, who left without another word. Annette's warm hand wrapped itself in his. Glass-like trails of tears ran down her cheeks. The shock of skin against skin contact with the woman he refused to love paralyzed him momentarily.

"Xius," she said. "Xius."

Then, heart aching, trying not to cry himself, he lost his mind completely. He stepped in and kissed her lips, swollen from her gnawing. She tasted of salt, warmth, and savory sweetness and her exotic, flowery musk. Keeping her hand clenched in his, he lined his bare arm against hers, hungry for the feel of more skin, and wrapped his other arm around her waist.

He panicked when she pulled away, not because he was afraid of her rejection, but rather because he was afraid of what waited for him outside the bliss of her touch: Kasmut, ameese, Set, pharaoh, gods, death cultists—He reached for her again, but she pressed her hands against his chest.

She shouted at him in her tongue, but he couldn't understand a word. The medallion was still in his satchel, but the ice of her tone cooled him back to his senses. He recoiled back from her as she continued to babble and he slipped a hand into his belt.

"—would you do something like that? What happened to the whole Set-and-future-queen crap?"

"I..." and there it was. She couldn't have said it better.

He wanted to run. He wanted to turn on his heel and flee like a child.

But she was looking at him, waiting, angry with bewilderment.

"I love you," he cried. "I love you, and I don't know why—"

"Don't know why?" she said, offended. "Great way with words you got there."

"No! I do know why, just—just—"

"Just what? Felt like I needed a bit of kissing to cheer me up? Wanted a bed warmer? Make up your mind already, and hell, stop being such a *jerk!*"

And before he could think of an answer she turned to the side and leapt into an all out sprint. He moved as though to follow her, though he already knew there was no way he could keep up. Calling her name, he tried anyway, at least for a few steps until she vanished from his sight.

***

Hath stood on her toes, just on the edge of falling. She could almost feel the tingling, rising urge to dance. Maybe this time, she thought, just maybe—and with that thought she caught herself from falling forward. She thought she could hear drums on the edge of her memory. The cool winter air leaking in from the blinds over her balcony brushed past her bare arms. *The drums.* She closed her eyes and focused, once more standing on her toes.

For once, she gloried in being in love.

She fell, brushing her feet forward as though to swing them up into the air. They caught her, and she spun, hands to the ceiling, Kasmut's laughter sounding closer to her own every day.

She kept replaying the scene in her head. How Xius had found her in the courtyard, played halfway through a game, then had taken her into the quiet privacy of his throne room, with the doors closed and no one in sight, and asked her to be his queen. He said he had already informed the priests. The priestesses of Hathor would come find her in the morning to begin her purification process. He had looked so self-conscious, so wonderfully and delightfully *boyish* and imperfect that she hadn't been able to restrain herself from finally throwing her arms around his neck. He had felt so warm, so hesitant, and she had never wanted to let go. After dreaming about it for years, watching from a distance, suffering under the knowledge that it could never be, she could finally hold him as tightly and as long as she wanted.

He had let her hold him, and for a minute she thought there to be something more in his hesitance, but she comforted herself with the knowledge that, should there be any doubts, she would be sure to do all she could to wipe them clean from his mind in the upcoming years. Oh! Just thinking of all the time they would have to talk, to play, to dance under the sun and deep into the night in each other's embrace made her want to scream with happiness.

Before she had released him to attend to his other duties, she had kissed him upon his kind, wonderful mouth. She had never kissed anyone before, and she didn't even know how to tell if someone was kissing back, but at the time she couldn't find the mind to care.

And now she turned into another step, feeling out each part of her father's dance, remembering at the speed of molasses, but growing quicker. It was coming back: the sound of drums, the thrumming of her blood. Even if her body wasn't her own, her soul was, and that was enough for Hath, even if the children she would have with her prince shared none of her Kushite heritage. It was the least she owed Kasmut for taking her place and pushing Kasmut on to join her deceased mother in the afterlife. And the children would still look at Hath as mother, and Xiusthamus as their father.

She could almost see them: those soft little hands reaching for the blue sky as she taught them how to dance. She would be able to teach them that much, at least.

She relished how her breath slipped down her throat and filled her chest. She was alive. Blessedly, wonderfully, gloriously alive!

"Priestess,"

Jee stood in the doorway, somehow managing to look far too large to be able to fit through. She stopped once more on her toes.

"I don't understand," he said, and his thick features looked honestly confused. "We are no closer to fulfilling the blood lust of the curse."

"So?" she said. "Jee, can't you smile for once? Your life might get better if you did."

His thick brow lowered and wrinkled over his dark gaze.

Hath barely gave it any notice, and moved into another step. "And I told you, don't call me that."

"I knew it," he said.

Hath paused. She couldn't understand the chill that suddenly came over her. She put both feet on the ground and faced him squarely. "Jee?"

"Apep doesn't care for the Pharaoh," he looked up, "does he?"

"Of course not," she said, uneasily. "Apep wants him just

as dead as the rest." But he didn't care about the time, did he? Whether the Pharaoh died now or in his old age, what did it matter?

"And he will be."

"I don't know what you mean." Something cold came over her, and it wasn't the winter breeze from the balcony. It suddenly hit her just how much bigger Jee was compared to her. Thoughts of his disloyalty to her father prickled in her mind, but she couldn't see how abandonment concerned anything that Jee was saying now. If he abandoned her now it was probably for the best, and it wasn't like anyone would believe the word of a slave when it came to the future queen of Egypt.

"You never meant to complete your parents' work."

"That's not true," she said quickly. "I—"

"But, of course, I've known this for a while. At first I thought you intended to take the blood of the Pharaoh, very clever indeed, or maybe to do even more chaos under your rule, but..." he stepped into the room, which seemed to shrink in his presence. "You don't intend to hurt the Pharaoh, little, gentle Hath."

She prickled with both indignation and fear. "I killed myself," she hissed. "I sliced my own throat for this, and you call me gentle?"

"You poisoned your adversary indirectly," Jee shook his head, "and even then you didn't bother to do it correctly."

"That wasn't me, there's something about that ugly girl." Jee was moving closer to her now. Any happy feeling in her heart vanished as she felt the wooden doors to the balcony pressing against her back.

"No one living can reflect the power of Apep."

"Which is why there's something about her!" Hath clenched her fists and stood as tall as she could. "Why are you acting like this? How dare you question me! I hear the voice of Apep, I—"

And that same voice writhed up from within her, dark, fuming, like an uprising of bile.

Have been corrupted.

The words came to her so sharp, like a sickle to her soul,

that she hissed in pain.

And it kept coming.

Repent, you liar, of the filthy rot in your heart.

"Apep has been merciful," said the great black slave. "He has given you time to remember your purpose. He has given you all the tools necessary, given you lives, still hoping the daughter injured by loneliness would act on her natural instincts to serve his purpose as Egypt's queen."

"Wait, Jee—"

"At least it was clever of you to obtain the last needed sacrifice of noble blood."

She hardly knew what he was saying anymore. "I know! Kasmut's blood—but there should be half of the needed blood in the box from the last ceremony, and I was planning on finding another noble, one that was less conspicuous—"

"I have refilled it."

Hath stopped. "What?"

"At your command," he inclined his head ever so slightly, bright eyes still on her. "I have drained the blood of Egyptian virgins into the box. There is enough."

Her heart stammered in her chest, and her mouth felt dry.

"Jee," she clenched her hands into her stomach. The words of Merkha's wives floated to her mind, of the rumors of multiple murders. "I told you only two. Just how many have you killed?"

For the first time, a smile spread across his face, revealing his white teeth that shone out against his dark purple lips. She had always wondered what it would look like when Jee finally smiled, and now realized she didn't want to know. It was predatory, it was sly, it was bloodthirsty and it was proud of the death it had wreaked.

"Plenty."

***

Set found Xius on his balcony in what the Pharaoh hoped appeared to be a drunken stupor. He had a bottle of wine in his hand and hadn't answered the door when he had knocked. Maybe it would save him from being asked too many questions. Of course Set realized he hadn't drunk a drop, because his lips were dry and his eyes were bright and sober.

But he still flopped his head as though he were drunk when he looked at Set. Depression could do that to a man.

"I didn't say you could come in," he muttered.

"I came to ask if you know where Annette is. It's almost dawn and she's missing from her chambers."

"Maybe she went for an early morning run," said Xius, flopping his head back to the horizon. Set took note of his rough tunic and frowned.

"You're covered in dirt. Where did you go?"

"To see Wenamon."

Set stiffened. "In the middle of the night?"

"Obviously. Couldn't go during the day without a damn entourage, could I?"

Set inflated for an angry scolding, then paused, a hint of horror coming over him. "You took Annette with you, didn't you?"

"She sort of twisted my arm."

"You're Pharaoh!"

"Damn right."

"You took Annette to a diseased house!"

"Yep." So far, he had been successful in blocking out any unpleasant thoughts about his stupidity this evening, but Set's presence aggravated it, coaxing it into a flame of guilt. He had kissed his best friend's fiancé. Damn him, he had confessed his love to her even!

Instead, all he could force himself to say was, "She really doesn't want to marry you."

"I know, stop avoiding the subject."

"What subject?"

"Why by Sekhmet did you take her!?"

"She was going to run out into the city by herself if I

didn't."

"So you decided to escort her instead of telling me?"

"Who are you, her father?"

"*I love her!*"

Xius almost shouted back, "Well so do I!" But, luckily, he made a gagging noise instead, which made Set flinch.

"Are you choking?"

"I'm fine."

"Then it isn't funny. I won't let this by."

"Well what do you want me to do? It's already done."

"Help me find her, please!"

"Can't you order the guard to do that?"

"You were the last one with her, where is she?"

"Ra, I don't know, already! The last I saw of her, she was running off somewhere."

"Where?"

"Away from me." And at that Xius finally unstopped the wine bottle and took a deep swig, closing his eyes to avoid the look he knew Set would be giving him.

A heavy silence fell between them, filled with the sound of Xius chugging the wine. He put the bottle down with a cough, wiping his hand haphazardly across his mouth.

Set took the bottle away from him.

"What did you do?"

Xius turned his face away, hoping the shadow of the early morning and the dying firelight would hide his guilt. When he continued to withhold an answer, Set leaned towards him. He smelled of old parchment and the childhood blankets Xius used to steal from him to build forts in his bedroom. The scent knocked all thought from his mind, along with the breath from his gut.

"I'll have you remember that there is someone out there killing young virgins," he said softly and without accusation. "Please, Xius, I'm worried. Don't make me call the palace guards and include her in the palace gossip any more than she already is."

Xius closed his eyes. If she saw him again, she'd probably just run. But the reminiscent smell of fort blankets melted him.

"All right. What do you want me to do?"

"Have your personal guards look on the north side of the palace. They'll keep quiet about the search. I'll take the south with my own. If they find her, please have them escort her to bed. She's lost enough sleep as it is."

Xius wavered at the warm concern in his friend's voice. "Set..."

Set was already halfway to the door. "Yes, your majesty?"

"I..." He stood up, hoping the height would give him more courage than he had, not that he had much height in the first place. "I did something really stupid that I never planned on doing. I didn't even check to make sure she wanted it."

He never felt less like a royal pharaoh in his life than he did then. Set didn't even look back at him, but Xius saw the muscles tense in his neck.

"Oh," he said, and Xius knew he understood.

"Set, I'm sorry."

"Just help me find her. Please, your majesty."

He emphasized the "your majesty" with such crisp finality it could have been a slap. Then Set was gone, and Xius was left with his head empty and his gut writhing

Rather than send out his guard, Xius picked up his cloak from off the floor, hung his medallion around his neck, and left. It wasn't like he'd be getting any more sleep tonight, and the palace already knew the Pharaoh took nightly walks whenever he pleased.

It didn't take him long. He found her as he walked through the central courtyard to the north side of the palace. She had fallen asleep sprawled across the soft grass beneath a cypress tree. She had wrapped herself up in her cloak like a cocoon, and her hair was tucked under her head like a pillow.

He kept his distance. The torches in the hallways around the courtyard had been blown out, leaving the stars bright above him. He took a breath to wake her up and hesitated. Then, bracing himself, he hissed her name. When she didn't respond, he spoke a little louder and she jerked awake. Her eyes instantly fell on him.

He gave her a weak smile. "Set got me to come help look

for you. He's worried."

She blinked owlishly at him, then dropped her gaze to her hands as she curled herself up into a sitting position. "Oh."

"If you don't want to go back, I won't make you."

A cricket creaked beside him. Somewhere in the distance he heard the slap of sandals as a pair of guards made their rounds.

"No, I'll go back," she said. "You...you were right. I really have been ungrateful. Besides, he's been nothing but kind to me...and I've been a jerk to worry him like this."

Seconds passed, but she made no move to stand up. Xius dug his fingers into the grass and started systematically pulling it up, exactly six strands at a time.

"You don't want to belong here. It's understandable," he said quietly.

"I don't even know why he likes me so much."

"If I answered that question, that would be too flattering."

She snorted. "You're biased."

He counted out six more strands of grass and pulled. They made small snapping noises as they parted from their roots.

"What's the Pharaoh doing sitting on the ground with someone beneath him, anyway?"

"The Pharaoh may do as he wishes."

"Of course." She pulled in her legs and wrapped her arms around them. "You know what I miss most? About my time, that is." It felt odd to him that she was able to say that so easily, and even stranger that he swallowed it with just as much ease. "The music. I'll never hear an electric guitar again or a violin. I won't get to hear symphonies, rock bands, synthesizers, pianos, or gosh, freaking *Queen*! But," the gentle smile she sent his way was plaintive. "I can still hear English. I guess I should count my blessings."

Was that the only thing she valued about him? That he spoke her tongue? The thought made his chest hurt as though he had cracked his breastbone.

"What do you like?"

Her question threw him off guard. "Like?"

"Hobbies and stuff."

Before he thought better of it, he blurted, “Poetry.” At her raised eyebrows, he unfolded his legs to stand, saying, “We should get you back to your chambers.”

“Whoa, wait, why are you acting so embarrassed? I didn't even know Egyptians had poetry.”

This made him stop. Before he knew it he was five steps toward her and rolling in rage.

“Poetry is the blood of civilization! What did you think us, savages?”

“Not at all! Though,” she smirked, “welcome back. Gloomy doesn't suit you at all.”

“We *do* have poetry.”

“Yes yes, like what? Recite some for me.”

“Recite you poetry?”

“Yeah!” she patted the grass in front of her. “Don't tell me you can confess your love to me but are too embarrassed to recite a little poem. It can't be that bad.”

“I'm not embarrassed!”

“You're so-o embarrassed. Come on.”

It rubbed his pride all wrong to do as she said when he felt so offended, but just moments ago he had been certain she would never talk to him again. Smothering his pride and feeding his hope, he dropped onto the ground with a muffled "plumpf" and folded his arms across his chest. She just kept smiling, tucking her cloak around her tighter. He tapped his elbow as he thought.

“Now, I don't know how this will sound in your language. Poetry is not just the meaning of the words, but the sound of them fitting together, like a song.” He hesitated, feeling like a complete goat with its horns sawed off. The last time he had said this it had been to the teenage Set, who laughed him silly. Kasmut hadn't laughed at him—but then again, he was Pharaoh.

“That's fine,” she said. “Just take off the medallion and recite it to me in Egyptian once you're done telling it to me in English.”

Xius rubbed his elbow hard with his middle finger, then relaxed his arms against his gut and closed his eyes. It helped him to remember better.

In the pond nearby, a frog croaked.

"Oh sun, why do you burn me? I only seek the end of days and nights, where I can sleep without the pain of the lotus petals dried in my eyes. My lover doesn't seek me, my friend doesn't keep me, and no family will bear my name long after the wind rubs it away."

There was a splash as the frog jumped in, and another frog replaced it. It croaked as well.

Before she had a chance to comment, he lifted the medallion over his head and recited the poem again, this time with the familiar roll of the syllables and consonants against the roof of his mouth. The music calmed the nervous shivers in his stomach and stilled his hands.

"That's...beautiful. You're right, it does sound just like music," she said once he had slipped his medallion back on.

When he opened his eyes, her smile was gentle. If anyone voiced their thoughts when they shouldn't, it was Annette, so he knew he could trust her to mean what she said. It made his heart flutter a bit.

"Did...did your people have—what kind of poetry did your people have?"

Annette frowned. "Well, all sorts. Though," she put a finger to her lips, "now that I think about it, I guess you could call lyrics modern-day poetry. I couldn't recite any classical poetry to you, besides 'Homework oh homework I hate you, you stink.'" Xius chuckled at this. "But I know my fair share of lyrics."

To the sound of frogs and crickets, Annette recited to him lines of songs about hard times, poor times, losing your love, falling from the sky, and chasing after mirages. Once she would finish one, he'd prompt her for another, and after the first two he kept his medallion off in order to hear the music of the words as they were meant to be heard: in her own tongue. Now and then she'd prompt him in return, and he too would recite poetry. The medallion was left in the grass beside him until the green light threatening dawn shaded pink. Throat raw, yawning, and realizing with a growing dread that he had morning ceremonies to do in a less than a few hours, he noticed Annette had stopped mid-sentence, her eyes closed once more, head against the tree. Wearily, he leaned forward and shook her awake.

"Come on, bed," he said, picking his medallion back up. "I'm surprised Set hasn't found us by now."

"I am sorry," she said in Egyptian so heavy and slurred he barely understood it.

"What for?"

"Saying you were mean."

He smiled. "You mean a jerk?"

She nodded sleepily. "You are not mean. I was."

And with that, they tottered off together into the palace. Once he found Set and handed her off to him to take to her chambers, Xius shuffled his way to his own, trying to ignore how willingly she had allowed Set to take her hand. As he collapsed on the bed, still with his cloak on, dirt-dusted skin, sandals and all, he realized that if the only reason Annette wanted to be around him was because he could speak her language, he would be okay with that.

***

A knock came at the door and Merkha opened it half-way without stepping through, round face wan.

"Kassy?"

Hath did her best to ignore his voice. The fingers of priestesses fluttered about her, weaving rare winter blooms through her hair and cleaning her feet with frankincense. She wore only a light shift, and for a moment she wondered if she should be embarrassed in front of Merkha. Father or not, he was still a man. She had never bothered to ask Kasmut.

Judging by his nervous stance, it could be either.

"You do know no man is allowed in during the bride of the Pharaoh's nuptial preparations," she finally said, hoping she sounded more aloof than she felt. Her happy, giddy joy of before had been tainted by the intimidating presence of Jee nearby and the box full of blood hidden beneath her bed.

"I won't come in," he said quietly, "I...I only wanted to talk to my daughter before..."

He sounded so small. It really was pathetic. Hath's father would have bounded in, hollering like a baboon for happiness that his precious daughter was being so well married.

But would he have? After all, her husband to be was none other than the Pharaoh, the one destined above all to be slain by Apep. Her father might have been standing next to Jee instead, grim, expectant, and holding the box out for the blood of Kasmut that she had stolen.

"What do you want to talk about?"

"Well, you are marrying so well. I just went to Hathor's temple and I swear all I could see was gold and peacocks. No woman will ever have a finer wedding than you, and I know how much you love the Pharaoh, yet, of late, and I only say this because I love you, but..." Merkha hesitated, hand still on the door handle. "What is bothering you, my Kassy?"

What was bothering her? In a flash it all ran through her head and the irony of it made her want to laugh out loud, especially at the thought of telling Kasmut's ruddy fool of a father. But when she looked up to meet the nobleman's eyes, a smile prepped on her lips, the flabby, pathetic man had vanished into the concern and love he showed. It was in the way his eyes softened on the corners, the tilt of his mouth, the cautious way in which he stood by the door.

She wasn't Kasmut. And yet this man loved her. In a way, she really had become Kasmut.

Throat clenching, heart aching, Hath turned away, unable to keep up the smile any longer. She watched the bald head of a priestess bob above her feet as she prayed. Lotus leaves blanketed each one of her toes.

"I don't want to hurt him," she heard her voice saying.

Merkha cocked his head to the side. "The Pharaoh, Kassy?"

But she couldn't continue. She had already said too much.

"Oh, Kassy, why would you ever hurt him? You've risked your life staying behind to love him. You worrying about it just shows how much you care for him."

"But how do you know I'm not lying?" Hath asked, keeping her eyes to the woman washing her feet. "What if I'm...just going to hurt him? What if I'm just using him for my own wants? Just using him to be queen."

"Oh, Kassy,"

The rock in her throat hardened. Those two words had held so much warmth—too much. She could almost hear the old resonance of her own black father in those two little words, and the man hadn't even said her name!

She should feel guilty. She should feel so guilty it made her physically ill. She took this man's daughter away from him—but no, Kasmut wasn't gone. Just waiting for him. It had only been temporary. It had to be.

"You won't hurt him," he said.

The words felt oddly prophetic to her, and she managed a laugh. It was a throaty, broken sound, and she knew it sounded more like sobbing than laughing, but she turned to show him she had no tears on her face.

"Father, you really shouldn't be in here."

He bobbed his head, still with that concerned little smile, told her he loved her, and left.

When had she gotten so weak and sentimental?

***

The night found him once more on a mess of cushions around the fire of the brazier, sipping a golden cup of wine. He was wondering how drunk he could get without actually getting drunk. The note announcing Wenamon's time of death sat near a discarded papyrus roll listing the number of growing cases of ameese. Annette watched him from the corner while she fingered through a pile of his scrolls. She had said she couldn't sleep and had dropped by for a distraction. Seeing as Xius understood himself to be her only friend, he allowed her in, thinking she would need him if she wanted to talk about Wenamon. At the same time, he couldn't help but be worried of what Set would think if he found her in here at who knows what hour it was. However, he knew he wouldn't, because once Set fell asleep, he was down until Ra made it through his battles once more to bring light to the world.

He sighed to himself. He really shouldn't continue this habit of staying up so late. He glanced over to the girl, who was supposed to be choosing a story for him to read to her, to find her glaring at him in displeasure.

"You're at it again," she said.

He didn't have to ask. "Yep." He took another swallow.

"What are you, some kind of alcoholic?"

"Have you ever seen me drunk? How long have you been here now, two months?"

"About. Maybe more. I don't know your measurement of months."

"Well, what are your months?"

"Between thirty and thirty-one days?"

"Sounds similar enough." He sipped his drink. It was pleasantly warm from the fire. "Besides, this drink is so weak it would take hours for one to fall into a stupor because of it. Why are you so attentive to my drinking, anyway?"

From her shadowy corner she bowed her head, suddenly quite shy.

"Come on, let me into those fair thoughts of yours."

"If you must know," she put down a scroll and smoothed her skirt unnecessarily, "I'd rather not have to push away your royal ass from doing anything particularly stupid with his hands and get killed by an angry Kasmut. You are getting married tomorrow evening, I'll remind you, in case you're too drunk to remember."

"I am perfectly capable of controlling myself, and for the last time I'm not drunk. Why don't you come sit by me? I'll prove it. And it must be cold over there in your little nook."

She hesitated, but got to her feet and came to sit at his side. He noticed she kept a few feet between them. Taking up another cup and the wine bottle, he offered them to her, but she declined. With a shrug, he put down the bottle and cup next to his own and leaned back against the cushions.

"I won't bite you," he said. "You can relax."

Still keeping her eyes on him, she leaned back on the cushions as he did. After a few minutes, her face softened.

"What are you thinking about?" he asked.

"Well, I've never noticed it before, but you have…a rather nice face."

"In 'nice,' I hope you mean attractive or handsome. I would loath to discover men of your time with faces such as mine are considered womanly."

She grinned. "No, it would be considered a nice face in my time too."

"Tell me, just how different is your time from mine, anyway?"

"Oh gosh, very different. For one, we don't need horses anymore. If anyone has horses, they keep them mostly as a hobby, not out of necessity."

"Have you found a better animal?"

"No. We don't even use animals anymore."

Whatever he had been expecting, this wasn't it. He couldn't help but stare.

"Do you plow your fields by hand? How do you get anywhere? Do you walk? Do those shoes of yours give your people extra endurance or strength?"

"We use machines, silly. Come on, you have some of those, don't you? Pulleys? Those weird little pumps you use to irrigate your crops? Ours are just run by these things called engines that are made of all these moving, metal parts that use explosions to get everything moving."

"Explosions?" He thought for a moment, tapping into his pendent to try to understand. The images that flashed through his mind baffled him. "The gods must have muddled the minds of your people."

"Not really, though I guess you'd think that way, especially since we zoom around in cars at 80 miles per hour on a daily basis."

At first, he didn't understand. When he once more tapped into his pendent to translate what was a "miles per hour" and then realized just how fast that was, he choked on the wine he had just been about to swallow.

"W-wait," he wheezed, "are you saying that…" he did a quick calculation in his head. "That these…things of yours could travel from Waset to Memphis in a matter of…of a morning?"

"Oh yeah," she said, nodding, her demeanor completely nonchalant. She stopped nodding for a moment. "Where's Memphis again? I know Waset is Thebes to me, but…"

"It's by the delta."

"Then yeah, I think our plane landed somewhere around there when my classmates and I got here. We had to take a bus ride to reach the temple sites and I think it only took a few hours. It seemed a lot longer with Leah prattling to me about her ex-boyfriend." She rolled her eyes. "I swear that girl knows nothing of the troubles in this world. A nuke could pulverize the town next over and she'd just twist her hair and wonder if it would make her miss her show." Annette blinked, then gave him an apologetic grimace. "You didn't get a thing of that, did you?"

His automatic response was to nod, but he stopped himself mid-drop of his chin and shook his head. He put the cup of wine back down on the table.

"Care to explain? We're not going anywhere anytime soon."

She thought for a moment, then gave him a hesitant smile.

"Well, first off, a plane is one of those metal contraptions that we use to travel, except in them, we fly rather than go along the ground."

"Like birds? People?"

And with that they started a long dialogue deeper into the night with Annette expounding for him the stuff of dreams. Flying men, tools that gave blind and deaf men the ability to see and hear, strange glass and metal machines that made reality and fantasy not so different anymore, and huge portals that allowed you to watch an event happening on the other side of the world. By the time her voice grew hoarse, Xius had never felt less tired in his entire life. His mind whirled with the impossibility of it all and the fight to try to understand how it could be. By Ra, what would the gods give man in the next few thousand years that made these sort of things possible? Or was Annette herself truly crazy, as he had originally thought?

His bottle of wine sat empty next to the fire. He had emptied it as he listened, too enraptured to realize how much he had drunk. While his mind stayed intrigued, he grew increasingly more relaxed. His thoughts became bouncy and unfocused. At one point he almost got distracted by how fast his hand seemed to be able to move before remembering she was talking.

Their conversation turned back to Annette.

"Your mother was unwed?" Xius found himself more surprised than he ought to be. It wasn't unheard of. What was wrong with him? "Did your father die?" That would be horrible.

"No. He divorced her when my sister was only a baby. Since she got married when she was straight out of school—you know, like, really young—it was really hard for her to take care of me and my sister."

"Divorce?"

"You know, when two people don't want to be married anymore so they ditch each other."

"But...didn't your father try to provide for his children even though he no longer found pleasure in his wife? Why were you, as you say, so poor? Did your father not have a prosperous craft?"

"My father was supposed to give child support, but the idiot was too busy spending all his money on his new girlfriends. Please, your majesty, I'd rather not talk about him. He was…weird."

Xius frowned to himself. Certainly, he wasn't unfamiliar with sleaze such as she depicted her father to be. But they were rare, weren't they? And even as he thought on it he felt faint anger. If he should ever find that man, oh, wouldn't he be surprised to feel the Pharaoh's wrath.

"Did your mother remarry?"

"Oh…yeah," her face darkened. "She did."

He didn't like her response. Maybe he should move out of the area of her parentage.

"Um…your sister, is she your only sibling?"

"No, though she is the closest to me. We lived through a lot of crap together. I have two brothers my mom had with my stepdad. They're crazy." She smiled at the memory, and he was glad to see the darkening expression leave her. His oddly slippery attention, though, jumped back to the flying machines.

Somehow, their conversation led to women fighting in warfare, and Xius found himself unable to hold back his disgust. His thoughts wandered back to her family. He suddenly couldn't remember why he wanted to avoid it at all.

"If your people are so advanced," he asked, "why do they do such barbaric things as allow their women into war or leave their women to fend for themselves and their children?"

"I guess it depends on your perspective. To them, allowing women into the army and letting them do everything is advanced and humane—allowing freedom, they say. Equality."

He grimaced, raising an eyebrow and wondering if this was one of her sarcastic jokes. "But that makes no sense. It is not ma'at. All have their role, man and woman. If one were to try to take the role of the other there would be imbalance, one would be overwhelmed as they tried to do everything and the other would be forced out of the picture." He paused. "Is that why your father left you and your mother? Did she begin to crowd him out?"

Annette stopped mid-yawn to shake her head wearily. "He

just didn't like her anymore. It happens a lot, actually. In my country there is no such thing as having multiple wives at the same time like men do here. If any man were to have another woman other than his first wife it is considered adultery of the worst kind and she'd have the right to leave him. Same with a woman if she went with another man. But...I guess it isn't any different where divorce is concerned. A lot of people stop liking the first person they married, so they divorce them—you know, annul their marriage as though it had never happened—and go find someone else."

A new, apprehension pricked his thoughts: Was this how Annette would be in marriage? But then as she bowed forward, curtain of hair slipping off her shoulder to catch the light of the fire, he found he couldn't figure out why he cared. He had never seen hair of electrum before.

"That's..." Maybe she really was a goddess. "That's uncouth. It is the privilege of having a woman that makes a boy into a man. To leave behind that which he swore to care for deprives him of his manhood."

She pulled down a strand of hair to weave between her fingers. "It's okay, it's not all of them. A lot of them stay married to the one for their entire lives. It's just...I don't know what's going on." She kicked her feet onto the marble pedestal holding up the brazier. "What about your family? Do you have any siblings?"

Xius blanched. "Um, uh...yes and no."

She looked at him curiously, and he hated how hyper aware of her gaze he had become. Had her eyes always been this blue? How had he ever been able to move, let alone speak, after seeing such eyes? His foot tapped unnaturally fast, blurring in his vision. How strange. The couch swayed before he realized it was just his eyes swaying back and forth to the shaking of his foot.

"What do you mean 'yes and no'?"

"They all died when they were little more than babes. It's something to be expected of children. Only the strong bear through."

"Not where I come from, your highness. It's rare for kids

to die."

But before he could properly consider what exactly she had said, she was talking again.

"But didn't your dad have lots of wives?"

Xius shifted uncomfortably.

"No, my father only had one wife due to his…eccentricities."

She cocked her head to the side. "Eccentricities?"

"Yes." He hesitated. She would learn of this eventually once she learned the language, if not from Set, then from some other person in the palace. Still, would she think less of him? What did her people think of these kinds of eccentricities? "My father, he had, ah, a preference for the, um…company of men."

He braced himself as his words sunk in.

But she hardly reacted at all.

"Oh, his swing swung the other direction, got it."

"What?"

"He was gay. You know, instead of wanting sex with women like normal guys he went for men?"

He winced. Did she have to be so blunt?

"Weirdness. Didn't think Egypt was into that sort of thing. So, how'd you come to be, then? Can gay guys still have kids?"

"In order to maintain ma'at, my father needed to marry a wife and produce children for the gods, and yet it was difficult for him, naturally. That is when my mother came in. She was quite the woman to sacrifice her needs in order to help my father achieve what needed to be done for the kingdom. She…she was my father's best friend."

She cocked her head again, this time to the other side. She didn't look like she thought less of him. He could feel that strange warmth curling in his chest once more. For how often she found ways to mock him, she was remarkably accepting.

"So, was it ma'at that he have children or ma'at that he should be married to a woman?"

"Both. He was pharaoh. It is important that the Pharaoh have a Noble Wife at their side and children to carry on the life force of Horus. It is part of the important power that allows him to rule."

He poured himself another cup, forgetting his bottle was empty and feeling confused when he rediscovered that it was. "What did your people believe? Obviously not in the order of ma'at."

She rubbed her eyes hard. "Look, that's a really loaded question, and I know you're really curious right now, but would it be alright with you if I went to bed? I can hardly keep my eyes open."

And he could see the truth of that. The night had grown very old and she had sagged ever closer to him. He was tempted to tell her no and keep her talking both for the sake of his curiosity as well as to see if she would slip far enough to fall onto his lap. Her hair could spread out on the cushions, and he could run his fingers along her long swan neck and shoulders. But as her head bobbed, he softened.

"Of course." Then, tipping with good will and filled with the image of her unbelievable skin, like ivory, he gestured to his own bed. "If you like, you may sleep in my bed. I wouldn't tell Set."

She stiffened at this, blinking hard to rid the sleepiness from her eyes. "Xius…" then she reconsidered and eyed him suspiciously. "No, I'll go back to my own room, thanks. You know it wouldn't be right—pfft, why are you even asking? I figured this would be something that is the same in all cultures."

As she moved to get up he caught her arm clumsily. When had he gotten so out of balance?

"It is all right. You are no longer a slave, if station is what you are concerned about. I would be pleased to share anything with you, even if…" he hesitated. Wait…what was he saying? He took quick stock of himself. His mind had grown foggy, slower, and he felt far too good-natured after the death of a close friend. But what was he doing? He was to marry Kasmut tomorrow—Set had mentioned Annette's softening toward marrying him with such hope.

But Xius found he suddenly didn't care about Set or what he thought, nor did he find Kasmut to be all that important. He was Pharaoh, and Annette looked as beautiful as the goddess

Nut herself. A night with her would be exaltation.

His eye trailed down her forbidden curves as she said: "Come on, piece it together, num nuts, stop being so slow. You…you said you liked me, didn't you? Well, what do you get when you have a guy and a woman he's rather fond of in the same bed? I'm not stupid."

"Well then," his smile turned wry, "just marry me instead of Set."

She violently yanked her arm away and took a step back. "Don't joke with me, Pharaoh." For a moment he thought he saw a flash of ice in her eyes. It only emphasized the striking blue against the dark of her pupil.

"I'm not." Yes, he had said it without thinking, but he knew what he wanted. It seemed the natural course of ma'at that if he wanted her, he should marry her. The priests wanted him married tomorrow, yes? They hadn't said anything about who, they had just assumed it would be Kasmut. And so what if she was foreign? So what? If he changed his mind tonight, would there be time for Annette to finish the purification rites before the ceremony? His muddled mind was making it hard for him to remember just how long those rites took.

But her expression had gone cool.

"Even if I did love you, I would never marry a pharaoh."

He winced and released her wrist as though burned. What an odd thing to say. "Do people in the future hate my kind?"

"This has nothing to do with what Americans think of Egypt. Remember back in the courtyard, Xius? I wouldn't be able to handle watching you pick up concubines and other wives." And almost as though to prove her point, she shuddered. "Nor do I want to return home one day to come back pregnant to my parents or leaving behind children. No…I can't marry at all."

"But Annette," he had to stop the desperate sinking sensation that wanted to pull him under before it drowned him. "What if you never return home? You'll be alone for the rest of your life. With me I can give you all that you could ever want! I could give you a family, I will love you—"

"Along with woman A, B, and C—"

"No!" and now he was on his feet and toe to toe with her. "Annette, my father only had one wife. It is the Royal Wife who chooses the other women. I will only be yours for as long as we live, and even beyond that, if you will just take me."

She gapped at him, seeming to falter in her determination. She brought a hand to her mouth, and then looked away.

"You're drunk." She gave him her back and made her way to the door. "I'll pretend this didn't happen."

"I am serious! I'll break my engagement with Kasmut tomorrow if you'll just believe me!" He moved as if to follow her, but tripped on his awkward feet. She caught him, barely, and stumbled back just enough to soften her fall with a soft 'oomph!' against a wall. Whatever he had been intending to say got lost somewhere in his wine laden mind as her scent flooded his senses. Her neck cupped his face as though carved for it, and the parts of her body that his own pressed against lit up with breath-snatching fire.

Yes. Exaltation.

And it slipped from his hands. He could only stare at the floor and wonder where she had gone.

"You don't want me that badly. Just forget about all this. I'm not worth it. I don't belong here, now go to bed and sleep it off. You have a wedding to prepare for tomorrow."

He truly would was as an eccentric like his father.

Somehow, he found his way onto his bed and slipped beneath the blankets. The fire crackled. Had she just left? Yes. There was no other way he could feel so alone. It ached at him and throbbed until he made his mind up to crawl into Set's room without his notice, like they were seven again, and sleep on his sofa.

But before he could follow through with his plan, he was asleep.

***

"You're drunk. I'll pretend this didn't happen." She wouldn't have understood it if the girl hadn't suddenly spoken in Egyptian, if messy, broken Egyptian at that. The Pharaoh, in his drunkenness, had spilled from her language and back into his own some time back, and lucky for Hath, she got to hear all of his confession.

"Annette, I am serious! I'll break my engagement with Kasmut tomorrow if you'll just believe me!"

Hath pressed her head to the door. The royal guards had given their future queen her privacy with the Pharaoh by stationing themselves at either end of the hall. A buzzing ring had filled her ears and her chest. She couldn't feel herself breathing, and she wondered what would happen if she walked in now. Would it stop being real? Or would she just faint?

His hesitancy made sense now.

The slave girl said something else, this time in her own language, and while Hath couldn't understand what she said, she heard enough to know she was right behind the door. Fear pricking her heart, she clutched her chest, as though afraid her heart would crumple beneath the weight of her lungs, and ran down the hall. The royal guard watched her go with slight interest, and maybe concern, but she didn't fear their attention.

How could her prince...how could she...and with a slave, the very thing she used to be before killing her body and stealing Kasmut's. All that sacrifice, all that pain, and her prince fell in love with a slave.

The gossamer thin and soft as silk wedding robes, which she had worn to bed in her excitement, billowed about her, which made it no wonder when she slipped on them. She just caught herself from breaking her face on the granite floor. No one saw. No one was around. And somewhere, above her, a waxing moon shown down. The eclipse would be soon now.

She wanted to bleed. She wanted to hide, crumple into a corner, tear Kasmut's throat out as she had done her own and watch the blood pool about her.

"Priestess? Are you well?"

She flinched and turned her face away from the rumbling

sound of her Kushite tongue, hiding it behind the miles of pleated, sheer fleece.

"Not now, Jee."

"I've just come to check on my priestess."

"Be careful what you say. Some of the nobles understand Kush."

"And even if they did hear, it is already too late."

She hugged her middle. That's right. Soon, they would all die. Soon, all this would end. This pain would only be for a short time.

But that didn't stop it, and she barely swallowed down a moan of agony. Her prince...her prince would never be hers. Even in this short time before the fall of Egypt. There was never even a question whether or not he would be worth it, for now he wasn't.

"Mistress—"

"Go away!" she croaked.

There was a stunned silence. She thought she could hear the man smile, somehow, someway, but when she peered up through the sheer cloth, all she saw was his stony face, blank and dark as ever. He jerked his head in a bow to her, then walked off down the torch lit, granite hallways. The eyes of gods watched him as he went, carved into the limestone and painted with brilliant hues. She remembered a time when she had dusted those same gods, and ducked her head down once more.

What had she done? Her life was gone, her body was gone, and now she had lost her prince as well. Why hadn't she done something more drastic against that ugly, foreign invader? Why had she just waited in confusion when the spell had bounced off her? Why hadn't she sent Jee in with a dagger? To hell with whatever Set did after that, she could've just killed him as well.

But it would've made the prince sad...she would've had to see him weep...

And even now, crunched against the floor, a swath of red hair and wedding clothes, the thought of making the prince sad hurt more than the thought that he loved another.

Part Five

Of What Is

He woke up that morning with the feeling that his organs had forgotten exactly where they should go in his body. With a groan, he reluctantly sat up on the edge of his bed and hung his head in his hands as a dizzy spell hit him.

"What by Ra…" He waited for the dizziness to pass. This was the strangest hangover he had ever had. What happened to the good old-fashioned headache?

At the door he met Set, flocked on each arm by servants ready to bathe him for the evening and help him choose his wedding clothes. His friend flinched as Xius quickly let them in then collapsed onto the closest bit of anything that could serve as a chair.

"Gods, your majesty, you look like a famine."

"It's nothing. Just a bit lightheaded this morning, that's all."

"Maybe you're dehydrated. Try drinking some water."

But by then the room had stabilized enough for him to confidently get to his feet. The strange, misplaced organ sensation, however, remained. Set asked if this was why he hadn't made it to the sun ceremony, and if he should call for the physician. Xius refused him.

"I'm fine. I have things to do this morning, anyway."

After making sure breakfast was served and all the servants had what they needed, Set excused himself, mumbling about something that had to do with flowers and leaving. Xius was glad. He didn't know how much longer he could handle the guilt of his actions from the night before.

He chewed his breakfast in silence as the servants bustled around him in hushed reverence, contemplating the strange, woozy desire to go back to sleep. Though he had hardly eaten anything the day before, the food tasted bland on his tongue. Eventually, he gave up on it and stood, just to be hit with another dizzy spell. Catching himself against the table, he watched as the earth teetered like the deck of a boat. In this state, he couldn't imagine staying on a horse to make it to Ra's Temple. Figuring it was, as Set said, mild dehydration, he decided he would visit Denan first as he waited for it to pass. As before, the world eventually righted. The servants complied and backed off when he told them he wanted to visit his friends before they began the wedding preparations.

The two guards standing at his front door peeled off and followed him closely until they reached his destination, whispering to him that Kasmut had come to visit the night before, but seemed to reconsider before she had even knocked on the door. But Xius felt too muddled to find a response to this before they took up post outside of Denan's door.

He was surprised to find Denan alone, with no chirping daughters or wife about him. Not only that, but Denan was sitting up on his own, staring at a board speckled with tiny figurines and holding sticks in his hand. He looked up as Xius entered.

"Ah! You've come just in time. I have no idea what genius of mine made me think I could play this by myself." As his dark gaze examined Xius more closely, he frowned. "Are you okay, your majesty? You're looking a bit…peaky."

Xius waved him off. "I'm fine, I'm fine. It is only brief spell. I've been overly stressed the past few days. What is it you are playing?"

"Just some Senet, your majesty. Come, pull up a chair."

"You know I'm not much of an opponent. Why don't you just call for Set?"

Denan scowled. "Have you seen him lately? Crook of Anubis, that man should be sleeping! I don't want to encourage his insomnia by inviting him to a game. Besides, you might be lucky, your majesty."

"Do you know how many times you have told me that?"

"Ra, just sit down."

Complying gladly, he reached for a wicker chair by the wall and pulled it to the other side of the board. The chair had become heavier than he remembered. Taking his own handful of polished, ebony sticks, Xius started the game and moved his pieces forward. As he did so he asked questions about the coming marriage ceremony. He also went into depth about his troubled thoughts and feelings on the subject. By the time Xius had come to somewhat of a stopping point, Denan had already defeated him by a bare one square and they were halfway through another game.

"I'll be getting back to duty as soon as Aphery is convinced I'm not going to keel over and die, but until then, is there any news on the cultists, your majesty?"

"No. I told Set to let me know when anything new comes up. He's been seeing over it personally; I'm sure you can understand why." Xius took some time to move another pawn of his and gather courage for the question in his mind. "Aphery was betrothed to someone else before you married her, right?"

Denan nodded and dropped his sticks across the board. As he counted them, he said, "Couldn't resist my charms, I say. The bloke took it hard, but you know what they say: It isn't over till she moves in her favorite chair, so all's fair." He moved a small statue of a cat before looking back up at Xius to find him bent over the board, a hand to his face. "Xius? What is wrong?"

"Just…just bear with me a moment. Just a bit of nausea." He shook his free hand, as though hoping it would somehow convey an easy laugh. "Pre-marriage nerves, and all..." More like dread. If he was lucky, he was sick and he could call it off, even if only for a little bit longer.

"What?" Denan's wide face crumpled in concern. "Perhaps you should head back to bed, there is a sickness going around."

Xius shuddered as he clenched and unclenched his suddenly clammy hands. "Perhaps. But I still need to visit Ra's temple after this. I have to prepare myself for the wedding."

"I doubt Ra would appreciate you getting sick over his feet. As your friend, I suggest you go back to bed. Appoint someone else to go to the temple in your stead, or maybe even move back the wedding date."

Xius was about to argue more when the dizziness came back, aggravating the nausea. He groaned.

"Fine, fine. You win."

Watching Xius struggle to stand, Denan said, "Would you

like my help, your majesty?"

"I appreciate the sentiment, but no. I doubt you're ready to stand yourself."

"If it means assisting my pharaoh, I will stand."

"I'm short enough, there isn't much to move. I just need to wait for the dizziness to pass."

When it did, he stood. "Thank you, Denan, for listening."

"Any time, your majesty. May I ask one last thing?"

"Of course." Now that he was standing and the dizziness had passed, his nausea had abated to bearable levels.

"That white girl, Annette. Doesn't Set have his heart set on marrying her?"

"Yes. What about her?"

Denan appeared to consider his words carefully as he cleaned up the Senet game.

"You love her…don't you?" he said.

Were Xius's feelings that transparent?

"If you must know, yes, but it isn't going anywhere, so do not start on me."

"Does he know?"

Xius hesitated. When was the last time he had seen Set? His mind felt fuzzy. "I think. Please don't tell anyone."

Denan did not frown, but there was no sign of his happy smirk, either. Finally he shrugged his huge shoulders and went back to shuffling all the ebony sticks together.

"If it is my pharaoh's wish, I shall not speak a word on it." Now a faint smile came to his lips. "I wish you luck in your pursuits."

"Why do I get the impression I'm amusing you?"

He left wondering why he felt so ill. The two guards waiting for him instantly appeared at his side. Xius lifted a thumb over his shoulder.

"Watch over my general. I didn't see anyone in there with him."

A guard nodded and walked into the room. The last guard stayed by his side, looking stoically ahead. Xius felt particularly anti-social, but he knew it would be a bad idea to dismiss the last guard, so he continued on through the halls. As another wave of nausea came over him, he went toward the courtyard, head filled with the fresh breeze of palm fronds and fountains.

No sooner was he coming upon the west hall of the courtyard then he heard a commotion of voices up ahead, intermingled with the occasional crack of a whip. Xius frowned. What kind of uncouth master could be disciplining their underlings here? In full view of the nobles? Though tired, his aggravation turned him around the last corner just to leave him frozen in astonishment.

Three young men, servants that did heavy work in the kitchens by the look of their clothes, had gotten their hands onto a familiar fair figure. One held a whip with tiny stones tied to the tails in his hand and was just bringing back his arm for another lash while the other two held onto her. Even from his distance he could see the scarlet lines cutting through her dress and lining her arms.

Despite his fatigue and queasiness, rage stronger than he had never known erupted within him. He strode forward, sheer murder in his heart.

But someone else got there first. Tall and wearing the traditional blue robes of right hand to the Pharaoh, Set stepped in. With a fury to rival the gods', he punched the man with the whip in the face. Then, with teeth bared, he whirled around on the other two and kicked them aside, allowing Annette to crumple free to the floor.

"What by the *name of Ra* do you think you're doing!" seethed Set.

Xius wasn't about to let him have all the fun with these men, but before he could get close enough to make his presence known Annette leapt to her feet and, without even looking at her rescuer, dashed off as fast as her legs would take her. Set called after her, moving as though to give chase, but both he and Xius knew that no one, let alone themselves, would ever be able to catch her. So instead, his tall friend whirled on the men.

"I will have you know," he snarled, "that you have not even the barest inkling of the crime you have done!"

The men squashed themselves against the floor at Set's feet. The exertion of the run had taken its toll on Xius and he could feel all his insides pitching and protesting in their confusion of being arranged wrong.

The world had started to teeter again.

"Set," he gasped, "we have to catch her before she does anything foolish. She's scared, she's hurt—"

"You think I don't know that? Why was she out here in the first place? And without a guard?"

Set's fury stunned and infuriated Xius. Just because he was in love with the girl didn't give the fool the right to lose his cool at his superior. But as the world finally made a complete twist and his stomach lurched, more important things came to his mind and he stumbled to the edge of the courtyard.

His chief adviser turned away from the idiotic soldiers at the sounds of Xius vomiting.

"By the gods, are you all right?"

He wanted to tell the idiot, 'Of course, I periodically vomit in front of the whole world for enjoyment,' but all he managed to do was wipe his mouth with his robe, move onto his knees, and then pass out onto the stone floor of the hall.

***

Throwing up became like breathing. After an eternity of dry heaves mixed with expelling fishlike water, the vomiting finally ended and the fever began to take over. He couldn't eat. He couldn't drink. It was as though his body had forgotten the actions it had known since birth. His skin itched and cracked and the light entering his room frequently changed colors. He soon couldn't tell the difference between sleep filled with feverish dreams and the delirium that was his consciousness. Always the world turned. Demons from Duat came to visit him frequently, whispering of his proximity to them and how he had failed. How he had failed and had been destined to fail, and that he didn't mean a thing. Other times they would be Egyptian faces asking him where the pain was and praying fervently over him. Once he begun to refuse food and water, they stopped offering. The demons sneered and barked his failures.

"Stop it," he'd whimper. "Stop it."

But the demons wouldn't. And soon Ammit herself stood by his bedside, her large crocodile jaws snapping, lion legs scraping along the floor. He knew what she had come for. She had come for his heart, as she did for everyone she approached, but he couldn't remember ever weighing his heart against the Feather of Truth. And where was Osiris? Where was Osiris to welcome him, as pharaoh, with open arms?

"You never were a true pharaoh," hissed Ammit. "Your father's foolishness destroyed ma'at and destroyed you. You are not of Horus. Horus hates you. That is why all hate you."

And he'd moan in pain and itch wherever his weak hands could reach. He rolled onto his side, waking to find that he was not looking at the same side of his bed as he thought. He could make out the familiar form of Set, tall and lanky, weeping with abandon at his side.

"I'm so sorry," Set cried. "I'm so sorry, this is all my fault, I can never be forgiven."

Even with his head pounding and his body hot with pain, Xius reached out for his friend. Why did Set weep so? How could he fix this?

With his arm as heavy as though it were made of gold,

Xius reached to just touch his friend's head, and Set looked up, tears pouring down from his gray eyes.

"I'm so sorry," he whispered.

"For what?" Xius tried to say, but his voice came out in a dry rasp.

"I let them go when they came to me. Those Kushites. I couldn't stand living anymore. I was desperate. Please, understand, I could just eat, I couldn't sleep, I needed her… I needed my Tawaret."

This only confused Xius. What was he talking about? But now Set was sobbing harder.

"They said that her soul had been reborn, because she had unfinished business to do as a mother, and they would bring her back to me. I was so desperate, Xius, so desperate. They said they would help me if I made sure the court and priests nominated Kasmut as queen and allowed them to do the sacrifices necessary to resurrect Tawaret's soul, if I kept quiet. I don't think Kasmut has anything to do with them, though, I think it has to do with a black slave of hers. I don't remember him being around before her previous one was killed, and the girl seems just as confused by his appearance as I am—but besides that, I didn't think they could do this much harm. But then the bodies piled up, Denan went missing, and then you fell sick—I woke up then, I swear, I tried to stop them! I tried to fix my wrong, but then they threatened Annette, and I—I just couldn't. I couldn't. Not her, not after all the sacrifice that had been done to bring her here."

Xius was wavering in and out now. He thought he could see a shadow moving over Set's shoulder. It had wings and darted out the balcony. Outside the sky was dark. Where was Annette? She should be beside him. Sleeping beside him.

Through his feverish mind it somehow clicked.

"Annette," Xius rasped.

Set buried his face into Xius's blankets. "I couldn't let her die, not after all I had done to bring her here. I couldn't lose her again."

"You brought…from the future…?"

"Yes! They were the ones who killed Kasmut's slave in

order to do it, and I almost didn't go through with it, but right as I decided to break the deal she appeared in the hall during that party, all pure and white, like a goddess of clouds, and I just knew…"

Xius blinked away the shadows. This had to be another delusion—another nightmare. Set would never do what he just said he did. It was too unlike Set. Set was cool, logical, intelligent, and reasonable at all times with bursts of occasional, but justifiable, fury. Set always controlled his passions. Set would never behave so irrationally.

"I'm so sorry. Oh gods, Ra, Osiris, I am so sorry. I'm like that evil god Set himself. I was named so appropriately at birth."

Panic fluttered in Xius's chest and he pushed through his weariness to grab onto Set's arm.

"You…" he swallowed hard to wet his broken vocal chords, "you have to stop this plague—-"

"How? It's already reached Waset. Already we are receiving reports of the dead. Egypt is dying and it's all…it's all my fault—"

Xius gripped Set's arm with all the might left within him. He called upon whatever strength the gods could give him to hold on hard and stared harshly into Set's watery, gray eyes.

"Stop this. Don't you dare let Egypt fall. Never. Give all you can, even your very life. If you did start this, you can end it. *End it now.*"

Then his body gave a great shudder and in the blink of an eye his strength was gone and the darkness ensnared him. The great coils of Apep slithered up and pulled him down into the icy waters of the river of death. He could only cry and be smothered as water flowed down his throat and suffocated him.

Now and then he'd catch a flash of white hair and chase it, aching with want for what it could entail. He wanted to live, to hold her sweet flesh and hear her laugh and even the sarcastic remarks that sometimes got on his nerves. He wanted to see her children, wanted to show her the wonders of his own world as she shared hers with him. Most of all, he wanted her to smile as she had that day he had caught her dancing in the servants' courtyard, with her hair bouncing about her like feathery wings. Where was she? Why couldn't he reach her?

And then, opening his eyes, he saw her: a vision of beauty standing beside him, looking down at him. He couldn't quite focus on her face, but he could see the sadness in her eyes. His heart ached. Oh, how he had longed to see her, but not like this. Not sad. Happy. Dancing and laughing on her long, antelope legs.

The vision reached out to touch him and her hands were like ice against his face. He gasped.

Another vision appeared beside hers, and it was tall and dressed in blue robes.

"Help me get him to the pool."

When the tall man just stared at her, she gave an angry puff of air and the cold hands went down to his neck. She pulled something over his head, rocking his world and making him whimper as the movement hurt his head. He itched. His body ached. She handed it over to the other person, who nodded when she spoke and slipped his arms underneath Xius's body. He could feel every particle of his clothing slide against his tender skin and he cried out, begging for relief.

His head pounded rhythmically. Geb must have been laughing, for earthquakes shook his world. Demons screeched and lost dead pawed at his soul, desperate for his saving power. He could hear the river now, hissing as it moved over its stone sides. He could imagine its endless depths, falling into the true abyss of nothing.

Then the arms dropped him in.

Ice cold as he had never known it engulfed him. His strength spent, he struggled anyway and clung to the arms that held him in.

"Don't let me fall," he wheezed. "I beg of you, not there, not there."

"I won't. It's okay, Xius."

A demon guffawed and Xius opened his eyes. The two visions were there again, both Annette and what could only be his friend Set, except he wasn't crying anymore. Had something happened? But as Xius focused on the white face and blue eyes of the woman he loved, he didn't care. This had to be the cold waters of the underworld Nile. Death had claimed him, and the things of Egypt simply did not matter anymore. He couldn't do anything about it. And if Annette was here…hope filled his heart and he reached for her, forcing through the heavy darkness to touch her face. It was real. It was soft. He let out a shuddering breath that felt like fire against his throat.

"Ah, my lily," he breathed.

"You're going to be okay, Xius. Just relax. The cold won't hurt you."

"I know it won't, I have you. Stay with me?"

She seemed to pause, but said, "Yes. I am sorry I didn't come sooner. They wouldn't let me in."

"Curse them." But it was getting harder to speak now. His teeth were chattering, threatening to bite into his tongue. The cold surrounded him, licking at his skin. The rush of the water was getting louder, the cackle of the demons fainter. They were leaving now, put off by the faint glow Annette gave. Then, he really did know. Annette had to be a goddess. No one could be so fair, so beautiful, and be alight with such radiance as she. She must have been a goddess sent down to lead him through the afterlife as all pharaohs are guided.

Shudders racked his body so intensely that his bones creaked with pain.

"When will the pain pass?" he asked.

"It only will if you stay with me."

He felt a weak, reassuring smile on his face crack his lip. "I promise I won't leave you alone."

And he felt her then. He could feel her arms gripping beneath him in the water, holding him up and back from falling into the abyss. He struggled his hands to those soft, warm arms and gave a relieved, quaking sigh. Clinging to them and the warmth they offered, he turned his head and pressed his face into the flesh of her upper arm, praying to smell her flowery smell.

He did. And it nearly made him weep.

"I am so sorry."

It was Set again. Xius frowned but didn't bother to

respond. He was too tired. He was too at peace. If Set were down here too it only meant that he had died as well while saving Egypt. But either way, it didn't matter anymore. They were of the dead. As soon as he could stand they would continue their journey down the river of the dead through the trials to test his power. And at the end of the trials, past the judgment of Osiris and the Feather of Ma'at, lay eternal life in bliss and splendor. There, perhaps, he could see Annette's world. And maybe, in that beautiful heaven, she'd finally marry him. They could be together, forever, and watch their heavenly children grow and begin their own life in mortality.

***

The vizier stood with his shoulders hunched to his ears like a cat ready to pounce. Even in the darkness of the night, his cheetah eyes glittered, deadly and fierce.

Hath did not fear him. Apep filled her to the brim, and blood, dark and shiny like that horrible night, stroked her numb, throbbing broken heart. The only question that went through her mind was why he had insisted to Jee that she be the one to meet him. She had enough on her hands trying to find another sacrifice of noble blood to finish her father's spell, otherwise Jee would be looking to her, or more specifically, to Kasmut's blood.

Her hand checked the hood around her head and the cowl about her face. Even her hand was gloved.

"What have you done?" asked the vizier.

"What do you mean?" she asked.

"Your man lied to me, I know it. You two are part of this."

"And what gave you the idea to question us in the first place?"

"Oh please," sneered the predator before her. "A famine comes a mere month after I let you loose. I know your god has this power, and I know you've been killing those maidens. Your ghastly purpose goes too far!"

Hath sighed. This was dull. "Fine."

The vizier flinched. "What do you mean 'fine'? Don't mock me."

"You're a love-besotted fool who has a sappy face," said Hath breezily, "and you bastards deserve this plague."

And, just as she expected, the coils of the viziers muscles released and he sprang forward, the same blade he had threatened her with the first time appearing in his hand. She didn't even flinch and Jee stepped out to stop the lanky man. His large, earthen hands looked as though they could snap Seti's wrists with ease, and they covered his hands so completely that Seti was forced to drop his knife.

But the cheetah eyes stayed on Hath, burning with deadly intent. She looked back, examining him as though admiring a particularly fine-looking tree. It didn't matter anymore. Nothing mattered. Even if she killed this one for his noble blood and saved her own skin, as they had been planning, what would happen after? What would she do? Would she have to live like this forever?

If she did live...she would have to watch the prince die. The pain reawakened her, and she closed her eyes. She knew what she wanted.

The last thing she wanted before she died…

"If you want to save your stupid country," she said, "you need to reverse the first spell by returning what was given."

Set looked confused for a moment, then his eyes widened with horror. "No."

"Stop being ridiculous, it's either her or the rest of your damn countrymen." Hath swung a hand to the west. "Meet me by the Nile on the date I will message to you and I will reverse the curse. All you have to do is give her up to me."

"No," Set said, now in a venomous growl.

"You'll change your mind once Xiusthamus dies," she said softly. "Which I pray he does not. I hold nothing against the Pharaoh."

"And yet you poison his nation?"

"I'm of Apep," she said, opening her hands to the side in a gesture showing just how helpless she felt. "I am but a tool to his will. Bring her. Her blood will reverse the plague, you have my word."

And with that, she turned, having nothing more to say to the man. Jee put a quick hand to the back of the vizier's head, successfully knocking him out, and slung him over his shoulder.

"I'll put him where he won't be found," said Jee.

"I don't care where you put him."

The broad man gave her a searching look.

"Why not let this plague free?" he asked. "The eclipse is only three days away. Will her blood really end it?"

"More or less. The spell was originally aimed to only kill her. Once it's satisfied, it will stop." Hath muttered. When he continued to watch her, waiting for an explanation, she snapped, "Go away already."

"Shall I prepare for the last day?"

"Sure, just take that idiot away from me before he wakes up."

With his now trademark face-splitting frown, Jee left Hath to find some dark corner to stuff the vizier. She wandered the halls of the palace, empty, sleepy, and quiet. The night sky looked so bright above her, and she breathed it into her belly. *Please, fill me up,* she thought, *I feel so empty...so very empty.*

In pain, desperate and tired, she peeled off the cloak and cowl and threw them into a courtyard she was passing. She needed him. She didn't care if he didn't love her, if he didn't even want her, she needed him. She wanted to see his kind eyes, to hear his voice, to kneel by his side as his queen, which she would have been yesterday if he had not fallen so ill.

The guards looked up when she approached. They didn't ask her any questions. They just stepped aside and let her pass. Trembling with the will to not cry, she slipped through the doors and closed them quietly behind her.

A lone physician sat at his bedside. The luxurious finery that lined every inch of the Pharaoh's chambers was lost on her, as she had eyes only for him.

"My lady," the physician stood and bowed his head low. "The vomiting has passed. I think he is asleep now."

Her prince was sweaty, his complexion gray and his lips trembling. She picked up one of his clammy hands and examined the bloody cracks that had appeared along his fingernails. She kissed it and pressed it to her breast as the pain within her gave an awful twang.

She had caused this. Her jealousy had caused him this pain, and now...now he would die.

"Leave me, please." she told the physician.

"But, Kasmut, he may need—"

"Just for a little bit. I won't be long."

The physician hesitated, then left. The door clicked closed behind him and Hath sighed.

"Oh, my prince," she murmured, kissing his poor, sick hand once more. "Oh, my prince."

There was so much she wanted to tell him and to hear him say. She still wanted to know his dreams, his fears, his wants, his ambitions—all of it. She still knew so very little.

At long last, she let her tears come. They felt hot and tickled her chin and nose as they dripped down and onto his arm.

"My precious prince," she choked out. That's all she could say. There was just too much.

His lips opened in a small gasp. His eyelashes fluttered and her heart stopped, but the next word out of his mouth made her cold.

"Annette."

His dark eyes were on her, but they didn't see her. They were filmed over with fever; he was too sick to see. He tried to open his mouth to speak once more, but only air came. The hand she held began to tremble.

"Please," he said.

Hath took a deep breath. This time, it reached her belly, that cool smell of air from the night outside. She had done this to him. Her.

"Just a minute," she told him softly. "I'll go get her."

"Annette?" he whispered.

She stroked his face, loving the curves, cherishing the feel. "That's right. I'll go get Annette."

It wasn't hard to break from his weak grasp. She left the chambers and turned to a guard.

"Where can I find the fiancé of Set? The white girl." She couldn't quite bring herself to say her name a second time.

The guard gave her directions, and before she knew it, she stood in front of a humble door just next door to Seti's rooms. She knocked. When there was no answer, she lost her tenacious patience and walked in. Inside wasn't anywhere near lavish, but comfortable and refined—the envy of any servant of any rank.

On the plush bed, her figure spread out as though she had just fallen upon it, was Annette, sound asleep.

It was the strangest moment in her life. Her rival, the reason for all her heartache, lay vulnerable and prone before her, but Hath found herself more interested in the fact that this was probably the closest she had ever been to the girl. What was it about this ugly girl that Xius found so appealing? Her pale skin looked a bit tan, like desert sand, almost, and her white hair could've been that of an old man. No one with any sense would keep that ungodly amount of hair in the desert, winter or no. Hath wondered faintly if the girl had lice yet. That much hair just asked for it.

Maneuvering around the bed, she looked closely at her figure. She wasn't scrawny. She held enough fat to portray the curves that marked her as feminine, but that was all. Hath frowned even deeper. Not to mention the strange girl had pulled her dress up to her armpits. Who does that?

The thought that had hit her the moment she entered the room wiggled itself to the forefront of her attention. She could kill her, this girl. She didn't have to wait for Seti to do the job for her (though she had hoped to have one last laugh at his sappy face); she could do it right now. There was even a small knife next to a polished, bronze mirror. It would be so easy to slit her throat while she slept. Hath had slit so many throats in her time that the girl wouldn't feel a thing.

She took a step toward the mirror, reaching out for the blade. Yes, it would be so easy. Then the plague would end and the prince might live, might still marry her. She would save all of Egypt from this plague.

The metal felt cool and smooth against her fingertips. She looked at the mirror, something she generally tried to avoid, and saw the image of Kasmut staring back, eyes swollen from tears, swathed in beautiful layers of sheer coats and pleated skirts.

And it gave her pause. Kasmut's face. Kasmut's body. Where was hers? Jee had said he had taken care of it, but where had he taken her old body?

What would her father say?

Death is holy because life is holy.

The knife clattered back to the tabletop. Her fingers went to her face. What had happened to her? She couldn't do this to the prince. She couldn't cause him that pain. He needed this girl, he had asked for this girl. Besides, Hath had already died.

She slowly turned back to the bed.

"Hey." She reached out, but feared touching her. She was afraid of what she'd do if she did. "Hey, wake up. Can you hear me?”

Annette moaned and threw an arm over her face.

“Hmm?” she paused for a moment, then shot up, eyes wild. “The Pharaoh—is he all right?” Then she noticed who was there and her eyes widened. “Kasmut?”

Hath's stomach clenched. This girl knew her?

“He wants you.” Hath said. “You should go to him.”

Annette didn't move. Her face had, if possible, gone paler.

“Lady Kasmut,” she hesitated, “I...I didn't...”

“I know you didn't.” Hath said quietly. “Otherwise he wouldn't have begged you so desperately.”

Annette looked pained. It was so strange to Hath how someone so alien could express emotions like every other human did. “Lady Kasmut, I just want to go home. I didn't mean—I didn't ask for him to—”

Hath lifted her hand sharply. She didn't want to hear any more. The fact that this ugly girl didn't have to try where Hath had tried so hard almost made her jump toward the knife again. But she thought of the prince, thought of his poor, sickly form, and remembered her place in it all.

“Just go. Your Egyptian is horrible, by the way. I can't believe I can understand you.”

Annette said nothing to this, her hands tucked to her lap and her eyes watching her through her mutant pale eyelashes in apprehension. She stood, careful to avoid touching Kasmut, and made her way to the door. She left without another word, probably not wanting to test her luck with the still legal future queen of Egypt.

And Hath let her, hands fisted at her sides. The moonlight glinted off the knife. It reflected against the bronze mirror.

She couldn't do this anymore.

***

Xius awoke to the rustle of wind through trees. Every part of him hurt as though he had been beaten from head to foot and then scraped along the desert sands behind a horse. Why did his skin feel so raw? Even as he moaned, the sound reverberated through his head with a throb. His tongue had swollen in his mouth.

"Are you awake?"

Somehow, he was able to pry apart his eyelids. Annette, skin paler than usual and her hair a messy fluff on the back of her head, sat at his side. He opened his mouth and breathed to speak, but nothing came. He grunted and put a stiff hand to his face. It was then he noticed why his arm was so difficult to bend: bandages lined the entire appendage. He stared at it, then remembered. Ameese made the skin turn gray and crack. Fearful, he took a glanced at his hand and nearly choked on his inflated tongue: ashen, dry skin that had sucked in around his bones, tendons, and veins.

He suddenly wished he hadn't woken up.

"It's okay," said Annette softly. "I think you have severe dehydration. I know you don't want to, but I'm going to make you drink this. It's the only way you'll survive at this point."

From beside her she picked up a tall cup of water. Xius grimaced at it, feeling the very skin on his face stretch and itch in protest. She looked forward and gestured to someone he couldn't see.

"Come prop him up for me. He's finally awake."

The tall form of Set appeared. He had thrown off his elaborate blue robes and now only stood in the traditional kilt. If Annette looked exhausted, Set looked worse. His eyes were swollen almost shut and his lips were dry and flaking. He reached for his shorter friend carefully and helped prop him up. The entire time Xius tried not to panic at how fragile he had become. He was practically a mummy! Why did he regain consciousness now? Weren't victims of ameese supposed to die in complete madness? And where were the physicians who had attended to him? Had they left him for dead?

He stopped in his thoughts for a moment, trying to

remember his strange dreams. Hadn't he been dead anyway? Surely he had seen and felt the dark depths of the river of death.

Annette sat beside him and put the brim of the cup to his lips.

"We'll take it slow."

He nearly choked on the liquid's warm, bitter flavor and spluttered it out. Enough of it made it down his throat to just wet his vocal chords.

"What by Ra's in that?" he wheezed.

"Just a little bit of salt, some ginger, and some mint."

"What for?"

"Salt will help balance the electrolytes in your system, and the ginger and peppermint will help with any nausea you may get by drinking this, because plain water's kind of rough on the stomach. Now open your mouth, let's try this again."

He was so curious and confused by what she meant by "electrolytes" that despite the horrible taste, he soon had the first few swallows down his throat. The feel of something going down into his stomach was such an odd sensation after who knew how long of nothing that he shuddered. He looked down at his torso. All he could see were bandages and grey patches of skin, but at least he didn't look emaciated. He went to ask them how long it had been, but she stopped him with more of the warm beverage.

"You have to keep drinking this, but only in little sips and very slowly. After you can get a few cups of this down I'll start taking out the salt. Too much salt can just make dehydration worse."

Set watched all this with the muscles of his face tight with anxiety. Xius had just finished the first cup of Annette's brew and was wondering what it could mean when something came to his mind, something he had thought had been a dream…but couldn't be. He felt his sensitive stomach clench. At the look on his face, the white girl pulled back apprehensively.

"Try to relax. It's important you don't throw up again. The ginger and peppermint should help. Relax."

He took a deep breath and tried to do so, but his eyes were on Set. His friend met his gaze unwaveringly, held by a sadness that was as deep as the river of death had been. Xius ran a hand through his hair, crisp with dried sweat, and grimaced.

He tried clearing his throat. "Set, have you told her?"

Set's face darkened and Annette busied herself with a pot of boiling water on the brazier and a pile of herbs and salt on the table. As she bent over her task, something fell from underneath her shirt with the glimmering eye of Horus. Xius stiffened and noticed for the first time the lack of his pendent about his neck and the fact that Annette had spoken perfect Egyptian, though electrolytes were definitely not part of his vocabulary.

"Why is she wearing that?" he demanded of Set in his wisp of a voice.

"She needed help taking care of you," he said quietly. "Your condition was desperate, so rather than bothering with trying to communicate in Egyptian, she took your pendant. She couldn't carry you to the pool by herself. At first she put it on me, but she's been insisting on figuring out how to use it. I think her knowing a good deal of Egyptian already is helping, but still—"

"What pool?"

"Your pool, the one behind Bastet."

"Gods, what did she do?" His throat suddenly stuck again and he coughed to clear it.

"She just held you in the cold water until your fever went down. It was so simple I was surprised. The physicians always thought the heat was Ra's assistance in burning off the evil curse plaguing the body, but that icy water was how she got your fever to break. It's why you're able to speak with us now, though I think it is strange that something so simple, that has been tried before, works in a curse illness such as this. Not to mention how easily she managed to use Thoth's medallion without any training at all. There's something strange about her..."

Xius blinked hard at this, taking a moment to allow the pain of his body to pass. It felt as though Annette's brew just aggravated it. But Set had a point. How had she so easily used the medallion? It had taken years of training for him to get to his level of ability, because the medallion needed a measure of mind magic. Once, Set had been able to use it, but it had been clumsy, although not surprising. He had mastered the mind magic of seeing truth, so using the medallion should be instinctual for him, if nothing else. Was it possible Annette had a gift in the mind magics without having to be taught? And how had she been able to use the water to heal him?

When she came to him with another cup, he held out a hand to her.

"I would like my pendant back."

She only took a moment to hand the cup to Set before pulling it off and handing it to him. Once he tediously slipped it over his head, he turned back to Set. He pressed the ball of his hand into one of his eyes. "You didn't answer my question earlier. Have you told her?"

Set didn't make the mistake of glancing at Annette. His eyes were riveted on the king.

"No," he whispered.

"Nothing at all?"

"No."

Xius's voice was starting to go out again and it pained him to speak, but he pushed on in earnest. "Don't you think she deserves to hear the truth? Of why she was harshly yanked from all she knew to this strange world? Of why even now her life is in—" but his voice broke before he could speak the last word.

Set flinched as though the Pharaoh had struck him a physical blow. Handing the cup back to Annette, Set put his hands to his face.

"Oh, Xiusthamus, you say that now without even knowing the full extent of what kind of danger I have put her in."

A distinct anger rose in Xius, making his body tremble and his teeth clench. Annette grew alarmed.

"What's wrong? Please, relax, your body can't handle stress right now!" Obviously she had not caught on entirely to the Egyptian, now that she no longer held the medallion. Xius had meant it that way. He wanted Set to tell her, to look into her face as he did so.

His dry throat wouldn't allow him to say anything, but he

glared harshly at Set till the man finally looked up and registered the holy wrath aimed at him. He dropped his head back to gaze at the ceiling as though in prayer.

"I drew them out. They're the reason there's this plague, not ma'at—I told them this wasn't part of the deal, but the priestess told me how, probably smirking beneath that stupid cowl of hers the whole time." He took a great breath that made his shoulders spasm and dropped his head back into his hands. "It's her life. Her peon told me the details later, that we'd need to pour her blood into the Nile. All of it. She doesn't belong here—she was what was bought, so she is logically the price their god would demand to take it away. Only then…only then…"

But Set couldn't finish, nor did he need too. Xius now felt sick for entirely different reasons. He wrapped his arms across his midriff, unable to keep his eyes away from Annette, who in turn was looking at Set with a look of concentration on her face.

"Xius…who is the 'she' he is talking about? And I know that word he spoke. It's blood, isn't it? Her blood and the Nile." As though she could already sense herself in the conversation, the cup in her hands began to tremble and brew dripped onto her hands when she handed it to him.

Xius gulped the drink hard past his thick tongue. "It's nothing. I'll…I'll tell you about it later. Now, you wanted me to drink this, right?"

Swallowing her brew became harder than ever. Not only did he have no taste or appetite for it, but now he dreaded not dying. Living would entail he meet this horror. What choice could there be for him, the Pharaoh? Simple. Between Annette and his people, there was no choice—if the heathen Kushites were correct.

But he swallowed it anyway for her. He swallowed it knowing that if he drank this brew and whatever she gave him, she could finally get some sleep and at least a little bit of comfort before…before…

Set had begun to weep again. Annette's lips parted in dismay.

"He's been like this the whole time. I thought he'd be

better when you woke up. Not very manly, is it?" Annette brought the second empty cup back from Xius, biting her lip. She gazed down into it, slumping as she sobered. "Xius, I…I'm not stupid. This has something to do with me, doesn't it? And that man…"

"If you ask me now I will banish you," he said harshly in her language. "Just for once, don't question me."

She clutched the cup to her stomach, eyes quivering on him. For the first time he noticed the new bandages on her arms and peeking out over her shoulders and felt a new twist in his gut. Damn bastards and their natural prejudice. It was almost as though they had known she had always been destined to die. He wanted with all his heart to claim the Kushites as liars and kill them, but it made sense. If Annette was the whole reason this had begun—at the same time, Xius could feel his fury mounting. Was he to be commanded by these black beasts of men? By Kushite slaves, of all things? No. His original plan had been to slaughter the whole lot and pour their blood on the steps of Ra to appease the gods. What had happened to that?

"Set, get a hold of yourself. Did you take this Kushite into custody?"

The gangly man pressed a palm against his temple before looking up. "No, your majesty."

Xius's dry throat couldn't take the explosion that rocketed from his chest. He nearly threw up again he was so angry. Forced to take a quieter tone, he growled, "By Osiris, when did you become so stupid?"

Set bowed his head. "Forgive me, but they would only agree to meet me alone, and the man was twice my size."

"Haven't you thought to get the slave's name? Have the slave masters deal with him?"

"They would have threatened Annette..."

"And they aren't now?"

The vizier said nothing. Xius was too blindingly furious to speak further.

At that moment, however, his body had had enough. A wave of dizziness overtook him, making his vision grow dark for a moment, and he fell back onto his pillows with his head rolling to the side.

When he woke up, Set was gone and a physician now worked together with Annette, who acted wearier than ever. The old man kept shooting distrustful glares at her as she stirred the herbs into the hot water and gave them to Xius. It was only Xius's angry bark that kept the old man from beating her when he saw her looking so frankly into the Pharaoh's face. Because of the shout, his dry throat went out of commission for the next hour. Annette, however, had a face blank as stone, eyes empty and hollow. This frightened him more than if she had asked him the question of whose blood the Nile craved.

He comforted himself with his rage, using it like a balm upon his pain. He would not bow to these slaves' demands. He didn't care how Annette had been brought here. He was pharaoh, and he would slay them all with his own hands. Surely the god of death would also be pleased by their corpses enough to lift the plague. And yet a small voice of doubt whispered in the back of his head. What if the plague didn't go away when all the Kushites were dead? He thought to call Isis, the only diviner he trusted with this horrible secret, but when he summoned her the messenger came back with horrible news.

"She is on her deathbed, your majesty. She, too, has been struck by ameese."

What kind of power did Apep have to strike down the very priestess of Ra, progenitor of gods?

He smothered the thought, drinking another of Annette's now less-salty brews. It had begun to taste of minty ale and he had given orders to the physicians to give the same treatment she had given to whoever else had fallen ill.

Still, he knew it wouldn't be enough.

When he began to eat again the day after, he found he had to command her to eat and drink as well. The night before, she had slept by his side, not caring that he probably smelled of sweat and whatever else. But still she was so deathly quiet. He would speak kindly to her, stroke her face and inquire over and over as to her thoughts. Yet she just looked at him, reflecting tiny images of him and his trepidation on the glassy surface of her eyes.

Set returned on the evening of the second day. His eyes weren't puffy anymore, but his fatigue brought him down to his knees.

"I can't find them, your majesty. Not a trace at all."

Annette floated over to Set to place one of her cool, pale hands on his head. He flinched at the touch, but leaned into it. Xius averted his gaze. Could Annette really be Tawaret's soul reborn? Then again, the Kushites could have summoned any strange girl from the future and claimed she was Set's wife. But that wasn't what made Xius uncomfortable. He couldn't look at his best friend. He couldn't, not while the darkness of Set's actions mucked about his insides. There was a part of his mind concerning Set where he had not yet dared to go. Just recognizing it was there brought him such agony that it took his breath away. No, he couldn't be around him.

"Set, go eat a good meal and get some sleep."

He didn't thank him for his efforts. He didn't give him recognition for his exhaustion; he couldn't, because he knew why he was doing it.

"Yes, your majesty."

Set bowed his face to the floor and left.

Annette stood there and watched him go with an unreadable expression. The palace was unnaturally quiet for that time of day, with so many having fallen sick. He had to decide how to end this, and quickly, or else not only might Isis die, but so many others as well, perhaps even all of Egypt.

Sitting up, he swung his legs off the bed, catching Annette's attention. She cocked her head to the side as he planted his feet on the floor with grim determination. Then, with a deep breath, he pushed himself up.

His legs wobbled horrendously. Right as he began to topple, stomach protesting at his effort, Annette caught him. He leaned against her shoulder.

"Thank you," he smiled, not sure if his face still remembered how. "Would you mind assisting me to the pool? The smell of my sick body will kill me if my weakness doesn't."

She blinked and frowned, but she supported him to the

statue of Bastet. For once, he was glad for his shorter frame, for had he been as tall as his friends he may have squashed the slender woman. On the other side of the heavy tapestry the cool winter air swept upon his overheated skin like a blessing. It felt good. He shivered.

He collected the soap and hair tonic himself, as well as the towels, before they headed down the closed-in stairway to the pool at the bottom. There, the sun shone down gray through clouds blanketing the sky like smoke. He stepped into the water, finally letting go of Annette to hand her his bathing supplies. He bit his tongue at the water's chill, but its buoyancy compensated for his weak limbs. Annette appeared pale and still in the dim light, like a statue.

"Come in, Annette. Wouldn't you like to bathe as well?"

She looked down at where the water lapped at her toes. Hesitantly, she dropped a toe in and shivered.

"Cold," she said, looking back up at him in concern.

"Don't worry about me, the water feels quite fine, and I'm getting stronger every hour. Come in, my lily, and bring the lye and oils with you."

Though the wrinkling of her nose said she would rather not, she slowly stepped deeper into the water. He watched as goose bumps riddled her skin and went to her, arms raised to bring her to him. Again, she showed her fragility when the cold made her wince, but she allowed him to embrace her. Carefully, he took her hair from where it was twisted up upon her shoulder and dipped it into the water. He could feel the knots and snarls and dirt that had accumulated in it from the ashes of the fire. He asked if he could wash her hair and she sat on the steps, dropping her head into his hands to allow her long mane to spread out across the water and over his lap. As he rubbed his fingers and myrrh through her hair, he tried to read her blank expression.

But the silence gave him too much time to think. He didn't want to think. He didn't want to think about what he would have to do as pharaoh—as justice—if they survived this. He also didn't want to think about the lonely years he would have to live afterward. His feverish vision of death seemed welcoming to him now. Ah, how sweet it sounded to slip into death, to float and to dream until the gods picked him up from the waters like a reed.

"Xius…"

Her soft voice startled him from his reverie.

"Yes?"

Her lips quivered as they hovered on the edge of a word.

"You think you need my blood to save Egypt…don't you?"

He could feel whatever color was in his face vanish. He couldn't tell her now. He could never tell her. His heart pumped a slow, painful rhythm in his chest.

"No."

She lifted her eyes to him. "You're lying."

"No. It's not just your blood, it's your life."

He could feel her freeze underneath his fingertips. Trying to control the pressure welling inside of him, threatening to make him burst, he methodically weaved the water through her hair to rinse it of the sweet oils.

"How could my blood possibly stop a plague?"

"I-I do not know. It is what the Kushites claimed. Their logic is since you were what was received in return for the first sacrifices, you being in turn sacrificed would reverse the plague. I didn't ask for details. But I—"

"Wait—they think *they* brought me here? How am I involved in this?"

He closed his eyes.

"Annette, you will not like what you hear."

"Tell me."

He trembled and bowed his forehead to hers. His thick, dark hair poured around her face. He tried to take a breath, but his lungs had tightened.

"Set made a deal with them to bring you here. They claimed you are the soul of his dead wife reborn. In return, he had to allow them to have their way, to allow them to do their rituals for a short time…"

And when this was all over, Xius would have to kill him.

He pulled away. He didn't wait to see if she had caught her head as he dropped it, but swam away to the other side of the pool, half-burying his face within the water. It felt like ice. She slipped down and went sloshing after him.

"I thought you said Set—I thought his wife—"

He didn't hear whatever she said next. He had dunked his head and clenched his eyes shut. Why hadn't he died from the ameese? Pharaoh. What a laughable illusion. He was no pharaoh. He was a slave lower than all the people, for his sole purpose was to be the bloody sword of justice.

He eventually had to come up for a gasp of air, broken by a sob. Annette was there.

"Xius—" she stopped. Her own expression tightened in dismay. Mouth pressed tightly shut, she took his hand and led him back to the edge of the pool against his will with tears mingling with the water on his face. She took up the soap and rag and scrubbed at his skin. It took him a moment to realize that, for once, she was not hiding herself or her wet, transparent dress, and it only bothered him that he had to be depressed in order for it to happen. Once she had washed his hair she brought him out of the water in the same unashamed fashion. He couldn't help but catch a glance of how the cloth stuck to the perfectly formed roundness of her thighs and hips, but he looked away so fast he thought he could hear his neck crack. No. Not now. Not at a time like this.

She dried him off and then assisted him up the stairs. His weakness aggravated him to no end. In the room, she dug out a dry kilt for him and averted her gaze as he clumsily peeled off the wet and slipped on the dry. He could hear her teeth chattering the entire time.

"I'm sorry, I didn't think the cold would affect you this badly."

"Not that it matters much," she said flatly. "I'm going to die soon anyway."

Her words punctured him more than Set's imminent execution. He fell against his bed and buried his face in his arm. He could only fight to breathe now through his stiff lungs. He listened to her shuffle around the room to the fire to dry off with an extra towel.

No. He wouldn't live through this. He refused.

"You won't die."

For a moment he thought Annette hadn't heard. But then a weight fell in beside him on his bed and he could feel her curling up within it for warmth.

"What do you mean?"

"I will not let you die, and if you must for the sake of Egypt, I will follow."

There was a stunned pause before she exclaimed, "That's crazy! You're the Pharaoh, your people need you! And maybe it will work; I don't know any of this magic stuff." Her voice stuttered to a halt. He could almost hear the gaping hole she was feeling in her breast striking fear into her with its breath.

"I will not live without you," he said.

"Stop being so dramatic; you're being stupid."

And that angered him. After all he had done, she still refused to take him seriously? Ignoring his protesting muscles, he flung back his arm from his face. Before she could know what was happening he was on top of her, pressing himself against her soft breasts and stomach and kissing her. She was too stunned to react, let alone fight back, and he relished the feel of her soft lips. He only pulled away long enough to take in the soft, white skin beneath her face before kissing her cheeks and along her neck as well. When his kisses finally made her shudder, she pushed him off, easily overpowering him. She scrambled off the bed and made a beeline for the opposite wall, where she sank wide-eyed. He wiped at his mouth.

"What the freaking hell! What was that for?"

"What do you think, dimwit! For the love of Hathor, why do you insist on defying every word I say?! I know you don't care that I'm pharaoh, but for once in your life give my title a little credit!"

"Oh, are pharaohs extra honest in their love confessions?"

"Gah!" He tore at his hair. "Don't you know what I'm risking in throwing myself before you? You, a foreigner, who come from a people whose love only lasts so long! I offered to make you queen and you spat in my face." He grew quieter. "It's like…it's like I'm worthless to you. It's like my power or what I am, let alone who I am, mean nothing. And I'm tired of it!"

But she was shaking her head. "No! It's not like that at all. It's because of who and what you are that I don't believe it. You're just...just so much more worth it than I am. I mean," she smiled weakly, "how could a great pharaoh like you love an ugly, annoying thing like me? I'm not worthy of being a queen, let alone worthy of you, so earnest and full of feeling."

He listened intently, hungry for her rare, innermost thoughts. It amazed him to hear her call herself ugly. Was she not considered a beauty in her time? For shame! He would loathe seeing what her people called beauty if that were the case. But that thought took a back seat to the guilt creeping up his neck for his behavior. He had probably frightened her away from ever getting close to him again. What little he had glanced of her body had been every bit as beautiful as he had imagined. He sighed and lay back down on his bed.

"Why must you be so silly?" he grumbled.

"What?"

"You're like a child nearing adulthood, with knees wobbling at the idea of your own strength."

"Whatever that means."

Eyes downcast, she drew in her legs to her chest. Xius watched, debating whether he had strength enough to reach her. Already impatient with himself, he stood up anyway, clinging to the frame of his bed for support. He made it and gratefully fell at her side, but she didn't move. He reached out a hand to touch her face, perhaps get her to look at him so he could get a hint of what moved about her mind, but he reconsidered and dropped his head with a weary sigh.

"Why don't you run away?" he asked.

She glanced back at him, then looked back to her knees. "What would be the point of that?"

"It seems like the normal action anyone in this situation would take, especially since you have nothing to lose. We're not your people. Aren't you afraid?"

"I'm terrified."

"Then what keeps you here?"

For a moment he wondered if he would even get an

answer. Then, she spoke.

"Well, it would only get worse if I ran. More people will die, just like Wenamon did, and I don't know what I'd do once I was out there anyway. I might get ameese myself, for all we know. It would be selfish on my part. There is something great and magical that I don't understand that brought me here. Who am I to say what can and cannot stop it? Maybe those cult guys are right and I can make use of myself. Besides, dying can't be too bad. People do it every day."

Xius scowled.

"Annette, what are you really thinking about?"

She hugged her legs tighter to her and bent away from him. He ignored the warnings in his head and put a hand on her shoulder. Rubbing her head on her knees, she spoke in a cool, controlled voice.

"To be honest, Pharaoh, my life back home wasn't all that great either."

Ah.

"How so?" he asked.

She made a noise of frustration. "It just wasn't, okay? I'm not suicidal or anything, if that's what you're thinking."

"What am I to think? As far as I'm concerned, you loathe your life here and were hoping to find your way home. Now I hear you are willing to die without achieving anything whatsoever, including seeing your family again."

"Why do you care? I thought I had to die to save your country anyway." She turned her head away from him, pressing her cheek to her knees. "Just leave me alone."

He was under no obligation to leave her, being pharaoh and all. Thus, he lingered. In her words, he thought he could make out the lines of her heart and the shape it had taken worried him. What had defeated this usually defiant, passionate person? One who had let nothing, including him, take charge of her life before?

"At least tell me..." Tell him what? What could she possibly tell him that could change anything? With a defeated sigh, he leaned back against the stone wall and bowed his head. "Forget I said anything."

Time passed between them in silence. Too weary to stand, he didn't bother to go anywhere, and neither did she. Coals in the brazier crackled and popped. No wind whistled through the trees, and even the air tasted still and stuffy. The clouds persisted and no sunlight came in to break up the gloom. Now and then the thought of Set would pass through his mind and he would leave it to linger and rot without touching it. Eventually his stomach began to protest, and he allowed himself to dimly meditate on what he felt willing to eat. Sometime after it begun to rain lightly. The aroma of earth's oils celebrating at Nut's offer drifted in from outside, easing his soul.

He took a deep, full breath of the smell and savored it.

"My mother…my mother was always running."

He closed his eyes and listened as Annette's voice drifted to him through the sound of rain.

"We've always been moving, even before my mother remarried. She would find a job, work there for a few months, maybe a year at most, then for some reason she'd grow restless and run away by moving. At first she was her usual self: vivacious, loud, sarcastic, inappropriate, always wanting to be in two places at once and filled with so much spirit it's surprising she doesn't launch off and go flying into space." She gave a small chuckle and quieted. "But…with my stepdad…she wore down. He does that, you know—doesn't handle stress well. He's very friendly and fun when life is well, but, due to his shifting job, it doesn't always go well. He starts drinking and then it's like he changes completely. But she's still running from job to job, place to place. Always running."

Xius ran a hand through his hair, a familiar dark feeling constricting his heart. Was this something he really wanted to hear about how her and how her people lived? Was she the exception in her culture or the norm? At least it explained her hyper attention to what drinking habits he had. An image of a street waif came to his mind. Yes, he knew what happened to the children of drunkards or men who were insecure with their ability to provide. Had she truly been one of those? A small, dirty child in the street, getting in trouble, stealing food—then, realizing this was Annette he was talking about, he shook his head. No. It simply wasn't in her personality. Whatever her mother's weariness (and he had seen the wives of such men and knew what Annette referred to), her mother had done a good job in raising this daughter.

"My mom is so depressed at times she can hardly leave her bed, so it's up to me to look out for my brothers and my sister. I wish I could fix everything and I still get angry, so angry, with how things are, and I did everything good kids are supposed to do. I did well in school, I never got into things I shouldn't, I tried to never talk back, but soon it wasn't just talking back I had to worry about. I couldn't talk at all. He's scary, you know. His eyes pop and, well...

"I saved up to go on a school trip to Egypt during one of our good times, I guess. I had to work real hard but I wanted to get away from home. I wanted to go far, far away, just for a little bit."

Pausing for a moment, she glanced back at him. Whatever she saw made her bare her teeth. "Don't you dare pity me! I can survive through anything! And it wasn't *that* bad."

Xius flinched, thrown off by her sudden change in mood and the angry fire in her eyes. It reminded him in a brief flash of an injured animal. He frowned at her, taking the hands back that he had placed around her shoulders.

"Then why aren't you surviving now? Why aren't you daring the very desert itself if you're so indestructible?"

The fire faltered and she retreated. "Because…because I'm tired. And why does it matter? I am not needed. My step-father even told me himself, and he had a point." She grimaced. "Besides, I've always wondered what it was like on the other side of the fence, you know? Death might not be so bad."

"Death is not so bad for those who are ready for it," said Xius.

"And…" she turned around to meet his eyes. "I can't keep running like my mother. I've already seen the results of that. I want to help you. You're all I've got in this world. You need me. So I will give you what you need; I will help you. It's been a while since I've had a friend I could really talk to." She let out a dry, bark of a laugh. "How ironic that it's in ancient Egypt of all places, where no one understands me. But, really, Xius," her eyes grew soft and she gave him a kind, wan smile. "One is only as happy and good as the sacrifices they give to others. I want so dearly…so desperately…to be good."

"Why?"

And finally her mouth trembled and her eyes began to grow too bright.

"I guess I've never wondered that. Who doesn't want to be good?" But she didn't continue. Growling in aggravation at herself—something Xius was all too familiar with when it came to his own moods—she hid her face from his view again. He watched her shoulders shake with a bitter twinge in his chest. Reaching for her, he coaxed her into his arms and held her tight, kissing the top of her head. Somehow, the pieces came together in his mind and he understood.

"I am sorry for how coarse I was with you, my lily. Forgive me for losing my temper."

"Nah, I did say some stupid stuff."

"No. I understand why you felt that way now. Please, let me…let me at least be with you, even if just as your friend. I promise you, upon the throne of Ra, that I will never leave you. Believe me."

She said nothing. The weight of what lay ahead of them seemed lighter now, and he let out a relieved breath into her hair. He would go with her. She wouldn't be alone, and neither would he. And still there was hope that he would figure something out in the time between now and then. He shouldn't be so quick to bow to Kushites.

After a few minutes, she pulled away from him just enough to see his face. Her cheeks were blotchy, but they were dry. Then, to his amazement, she tentatively tilted her mouth up and kissed him softly on the chin like the touch of a butterfly. The kiss was innocent and soft, as though she weren't entirely sure of what she was doing. It made his heart tremble and his limbs shake. What he wouldn't do for a thousand of such kisses.

"Thank you," she said, and the smile finally reached her too-bright eyes.

"Tell me what you want, I will give you anything."

She laughed. "I don't need anything. Though, now that you ask," she looked down sheepishly. "Could I have my old clothes back? I want to wear them on the day we go out to—you know. I'm sick and tired of wearing this dress up like this. That is, if you still have them."

"Would you like your, uh, cam-thing as well?"

"Nah, you can keep that. The film is useless unless I can figure out how to develop it after it's been exposed by you lot, and I seriously doubt you guys could make the paper for it. Man, if only I hadn't loaned my phone to Leah—biggest regret *ever*. Would've been sick to be able to have pictures to take back. It's probably a good thing she lost it, though. You probably would've freaked out more than ever at me and killed me on the spot."

"I didn't have the capability to kill you from the start, Annette. The moment you entered my hall uninvited and spouting stories like that—"

"Spouting the truth, thank you."

"Truth or not, from that moment I was justified in executing you. But I couldn't."

She smirked, which looked awkward beneath her puffy eyes. "I was just too darn cute, huh?"

"I don't deny that." He tapped his forehead to hers, smiling. "But I don't know if I could have brought the end of any woman as innocent and lost as you were, no matter her slander against me."

"You're just too nice." She tucked her head back against his collarbone. "It's why you make a pretty okay pharaoh, just so you know."

He snorted, but thought for a minute on this, enjoying her smell and the feel of her breath on his bare chest. It was rather cool in his room and she was still damp and shivering. Compared to the unorthodox warmth of the previous days, it was nice to finally feel a normal winter day.

"Annette…"

"Yeah?"

"Do you think, maybe, you could ever love me in return? It…it is all right if you don't." Though, inwardly, he knew he was lying. It would be as depressing as the depths of the underworld Nile if she never loved him too.

“I don’t see what good it would do now.”

“It would make me leap with happiness?”

She chuckled and bopped his head with her own. “You should be eating something. You won’t gain your strength back at this rate.”

“Fine, fine,” he said, and moved away from her. Before he stood, however, he brought her chin to him and kissed her, much more gently this time. Then he began the long process of forcing himself to his feet (refusing Annette’s help, for the Pharaoh was done being an invalid) and making his way to the couch.

Part Six

Of What Changed

Hath had locked herself up in Kasmut's bedroom when she was supposed to meet up with Jee for the final preparations.

She knew it wouldn't stop Jee, even if the door was made of stone, but she tried anyway. She knew it was cowardly, she knew it was pathetic, but the instinct for survival still held sway over her will, and the last of her loyalty was the only thing stopping her from fleeing Egypt entirely.

For it was her blood—Kasmut's noble blood—that Jee now sought. Noble blood was all they needed now to finish the ritual, and Hath had failed to find a suitable sacrifice in time.

And Hath didn't want that to happen. Her prince must live.

A cry came to her throat when someone knocked on the door.

"Kassy?"

She swore under her breath. "Yes, Father?"

"Can I come in? I just received some great news from the palace."

"Can't you tell me through the door?"

"Kassy, what's wrong? If it's about the Pharaoh, that's what it's about! The wedding is back on."

She covered her head with a pillow. Yes, she knew that. She had heard it the moment the Pharaoh had come back to his senses, which was close to unheard of. The victims of ameese died in the grips of their delirium.

"Kassy?"

"Just leave me alone. Please. I...I'll be out soon." She searched her scrambled mind. "It's woman stuff."

That seemed to deter him enough, though he still gave her his sympathies before leaving her be.

Her heart pounded in her ears as she slipped out of bed. She knew what she had to do to protect her prince now, the one sure way to do that, and that lay in the box she pulled out from a locked trunk beneath her bed. Blood sloshed thickly inside, and she felt a bit of its wetness leak from under the lid. In order to annul all that she had done, the plague and the curse, she'd have to empty the box and purify the blood in the Nile. As a representation of the river in the underworld, it would serve as a gate well enough. And yes, the enchantment holding her to Kasmut's body would vanish as well, but that death wouldn't be so bad compared to what Jee had in store for her.

Traitor. Vile whore. You shall find no redemption in your end, whispered the voice of Apep, which had once guided her through her spells.

She slapped her hands over her ears, even though she knew it was useless.

"Stop it. Please."

Shameful wench. Find darkness. Find nothing. Annul the purpose of your birth.

But how would she get the box to the river without Jee catching her? He was huge and she was tiny, and none of her spells could change that. In order to kill him she'd need a bit of his essence, and since the man was bald, getting anything else, like skin, nails, or blood, would be impossible.

Failure, nothing, WORTHLESS.

"Shut up!" she hissed.

There was only one thing she could do. She needed to go to the Pharaoh. As his fiancé, the way to him would be open, and she could tell him what he needed to do. It didn't matter what he thought of her after that, she'd be dead the moment the blood hit the waters. But she couldn't stop this on her own, she needed her prince. The moment Jee found her alone...

He couldn't blatantly kill her in front of others, could he? The risk was too high. He needed to finish this ritual.

She locked the box back into the trunk and pushed it back under the mattress. She knew she wasn't brave, so she tried to make up for it in rashness and moved quickly.

At the door, she met a few guards. As future queen of Egypt, she had been moved to her own quarters in the palace and set with her own guard. She only hoped they'd be enough. Eyeing their arms through their armor and comparing them with the sheer bear-like bulk of Jee, she couldn't be sure. One had the most peculiar scar over one of his eyes.

"Take me to the Pharaoh," she said, trying to stop her voice from shaking.

If they thought her request strange or were alarmed by the look on her face, they said nothing as they lead her down the corridor. She couldn't read their expressions, nor could she tell their ethnicity by the dubious color of their skin. Most likely half-breeds of Kushite and Egyptian.

"Our majesty is doing better, my lady," said one, probably presuming that to be the reason of her pallor. She gave him a weak smile, but kept her hands clutched around her robes.

"Just hurry, please."

They nodded and walked quicker. At some point she had to jog to keep up.

But, just as she expected, a dark figure appeared before her. She really did cry out this time, retreating down the hall. Her guards closed in at her alarm, but only one lifted his sword. The one with the scarred face remained still and put a hand on the other's shoulder. The guard relaxed his blade.

"Arrest that man," she croaked.

Jee looked into the eyes of that suspiciously relaxed guard. Why hadn't they attacked him? Hadn't they heard her? Something horrible birthed itself in Hath's gut and she turned to run.

Hands closed around her arms.

"Unhand me!" she shrieked. "How dare you—" a dark hand slapped over her mouth. She tasted salt and the awful oily flavor of worn skin.

"Priestess, meet the brother who's supplied so much of your favorite juicy gossip."

Hath looked up. She couldn't see the guard's eyes, but she could see the bottom half of that horrid scar and his smile. Instantly, she saw the resemblance. It was the same self-satisfied, curling smirk she had seen on Jee.

In desperation, she looked to the other guard, who wouldn't meet her eye. She couldn't read his expression, but she could see no mercy.

Before she could think of what to do next, she was gagged

and tied up with her own gossamer coats. Jee's brother and his friend passed her over to Jee like a sack of potatoes.

"We'll need to return to our stations," said his brother quietly, "but you can go out the east corridor. That's our post."

She winced as Jee slung her over his shoulder. "I hope you won't get in trouble."

"I'm hoping, once you're through, there will be no one to care."

"Rightly so."

Hath screamed through her gag, panic-stricken, horrified of what she had done. Hadn't there been another way besides the front door? Couldn't she have sent a message? But no, the two guards had always been on Jee's side. She had been trapped from the beginning.

How could she have been so stupid?

"Hush," said Jee, slapping her across the thighs. She felt a flame of rage coil in her chest.

Each of his steps jabbed his shoulder into her stomach. She squirmed with discomfort, yelled through the cloth, did her best to kick, but his grip was like solid stone.

As she felt the last of the winter sun fall upon her back, she thought she saw a flash of white out of the corner of her eye. Positively nauseous with hope, she looked up the best she could.

A white figure, too white, stood at the end of the outer corridor. She wore the strangest shoes and her skirt had been cut almost up to her thigh.

Even as Hath mentally called her a whore, she called her savior. She had seen her! Now, if only she just called the other guards—or ran and got the Pharaoh—

"Oy! Bastard!"

Hath flopped her head against Jee's back. Maybe if she hit her head hard enough, Annette wouldn't have just stood there and shouted like an idiot.

Jee turned.

"Yeah! You! Let her go!" shouted Annette.

Hath yelled through her gag, "Run, imbecile!" But, of course, no one heard.

Jee's back rumbled with low laughter against her chest. “Ah, perfect.”

“If you don't put her down, you die!”

Hath groaned. That bitch's Egyptian still sounded so horrible, like she was gargling water.

“Hey, Jija.”

Hath quickly looked up as Jee's brother appeared out of nowhere, running down the hall toward Annette. The girl twisted, expression hard with determination, and dodged to the side like a deer. Then, she turned to run, legs outstretched—

—just to skid into the arms of Jee's friend.

A loud voice boomed down the hall. Guards were coming, and not the ones who were Jija's friends. Hath thought she could even make out a few familiar voices. Jee cursed.

“Jija, I'll take her.”

And then a rag wrapped around Hath's face. The instant she recognized Jee's signature potion, the same kind that had knocked out the mighty royal general, all fell black.

***

Xius found the courage to have Set arrested that evening.

As he had expected, his friend had not left the palace. Set would not run as long as Annette was here. No matter the strength of his self-preservation, his devotion and investment in the future girl was deeper. Besides, Xius didn't much care to see Set anymore. Nor, he guessed, did Set care to see him due to the rawness of the guilt he must harbor, and then just to see Annette at Xius's side rather than his own…no, Set was better off in the dungeons. Of course he could hear the palace voices wondering about his actions behind his back, but he didn't bother to inform them, and he didn't have to. He was pharaoh.

Denan, though, was a different story. On his next visit, and probably his last for the old warrior was to be discharged soon by the physicians, Xius nearly retreated at the look on the general's face. Lucky for Xius, Denan's wife was gone and there was no sign of any of his daughters. Just a worn, huge, angry warrior sitting on a bed that looked too small.

"So the gods addled your brains, did they?"

"I don't know what you're talking about," Xius said, hovering by the doorway. "I merely came to see how you were doing."

"Badly."

"I'm sorry to hear that."

There was a stiff, awkward pause where Xius forced himself not to squirm like a child.

"They say you had visions in your fevers and threw away your vizier out of paranoia."

"It wasn't paranoia, and you don't have to address me so formally."

"What could he have possibly done in the past few days, Xius? He's hardly left your side since you fell ill—we both thought you would die—he cares about you."

Xius folded his arms over his chest. "Let it suffice to say he doesn't—at least, not as much as you seem to think."

"What did he do that was so awful then, hmm? Or is this your great scheme to get to the white girl before him?"

He stiffened. "Is this where your trust in me takes you,

then? Thinking that I'm quick to throw away my companions out of pathetic jealousy?"

"I wouldn't put it past you."

Fury overwhelmed him and he left, being sure to slam the door after him despite his weakened arms. His guards walked farther behind him than normal.

Now he sat at the close of the day, alone, numb, and stupefied. He stared into the flames of the brazier as though they could tell him something. Two more days, Set had told him. Two more days left to have the white beauty in his world, two more days until they'd meet up with the Kushites for the spilling of her blood, and he was still too angry to confront Denan and explain. Sure he was bad at most things, but he had never supposed his friends thought him disloyal or uncaring.

Xius gazed deeper, watching the embers glow and crack. The alternative he hoped to find still eluded him, and he feared it would never come. It was aggravating just how unfair it was that his people's magic had to be so weak in comparison to what the cult had shown. So far, the only magic he knew of was the scant mind magics of a few, the pathetic illusionist tricks of the court magicians, and lastly his own pendant. But what use was being able to interpret languages against the ability to rip the very threads of time itself? Isis's magic of divination had been more powerful, but even her abilities had been somewhat of a mystery. And though he had yet to hear of her death, she would still be too weak to stand, let alone access her magic.

Why was it now, when Xius needed assistance the most that the gods simply left him with a translating medallion and a traitorous vizier who could see through lies? What use was that against a plague and necromancy? Even if he found how his army could be effective against such power, what good would it do when a large number of his men might very well be overtaken by ameese?

A great maw of darkness seemed to gape about him. He covered his head with his arms. Never in his life had he had reason to doubt the gods as he did now. Always, he had seen evidence of their presence in the bright sun, the burnished land, and the thriving life around the glimmering Nile. But how could gods who proclaimed to love him abandon him at a time like this?

Set's question, which seemed to have been voiced so long ago, rankled in his chest.

Why do the gods care about us?

Doubt snaked into his mind and brought him slipping to his knees. He stared at the shadowed floor, untouched by the moonlight hiding behind the smoky layer of clouds across the night sky. Nut's dress reflected the state of his heart so well tonight. But was the sky really the raiment of a goddess? Like so many other possibilities Annette had brought into his life, what if with their flying machines they had flown up and found something else entirely? Maybe even nothing? What if the Kushites were right in their worship of death—that Apep was the only god and all his own were…

Breathlessly, he clenched his hands before him. Xius prayed every morning and every evening, but this time felt dire, like it could be the last. Others had room to doubt, but not the Pharaoh, who was supposed to be the link between the people and these suddenly dubious gods.

"Great Shu, god of air, I beg of you to hear my whispered prayer and send it up to the divine king of us all, the Great Sun Ra, and Pharaoh Horus, far above in the kingdom of past Kings. Great Shu, hear my prayer and send it to Geb of the earth, the guardian goddesses Isis and Bastet, and to any other god willing to hear me. Please," and he took a shaky gasp for breath, "if there is anyone out there, even if you have never cared to listen to me before, at least hear me now."

A wind hummed as it slipped in to play about the fire and pick up his hair like a caress. The chill touch seemed to whisper to him. Slowly, he closed his eyes, imagining a god, with skin like gold and hair like polished obsidian, standing unseen with arms arched protectively over him. He took another calming breath.

"Dear gods…I know that I am small and of little use to you, forgive me for my weakness. Please, forgive me for my anger, my selfishness, and my foolishness. Please, punish me as you will, but help me save my people, do not let them suffer for any crime I have done, or for Set's crimes. Answer me and guide me as to how I can fulfill my duty as pharaoh and heal my poor, sickened people. I need you, any of you, for..." he gulped, feeling his hands shaking against one another. He clenched his eyes harder. "I am afraid. Good Ra, gracious Isis, I am so afraid. I feel so powerless. What good am I against such power as I face now? How can I stop your displeasure or these killers who hide in the shadows about me? What can I do? Please, I only wish to know...to know that one of you, any of you, are out there...and haven't left me alone to face this. I didn't mean for any of this to happen."

Though he hadn't intended to, he fell silent, listening to the stillness. As he did so, a part of his thoughts wandered. Annette came to his mind, standing in the sunshine as it turned her hair into a brilliant, burnished mane of electrum. He recalled what Set had said about her future and their remarkable medicine. Even if she had been trained as a physician in her time, wouldn't she have done more by now than she already had to help his people? Besides, the few tricks she had used she had considered minor, even practices of the poor and impoverished. But another thought occurred to him: Was he taking her for granted? In his search for tools that the gods had blessed him with, had he failed to consider her as a likely candidate?

But that was impossible. If what Set said was true, Annette was the result of an evil, bloody practice, brought only by the power of dark god. Despite this, a thought struck him deep in his gut: How could anything as pure and good as Annette come from something so horrible? How could a god of death bring a girl from the future who had only brought goodness and life, healed him with something as simple as a river, and saved his general from the brink of death? How did a god of death have any control over the future, anyway?

The colder wind blew against his ears this time and rose into a whistle. Xius shivered, but not because of the chill. His opened his eyes and stared at the edge of his dangling kilt. Could it be possible that someone had lied? That Annette hadn't come from Apep, but from something else entirely? But that would mean she wasn't the reincarnation of Set's wife. That would mean not only had Set been deceived, but the children of Apep didn't have the power that frightened Xius so.

He knelt in wonder, gazing out his open balcony at the waving palm trees. A warmth of peace had filled his chest, and he knew it could only be the touch of a god.

A knock came at the door and his haggard bodyguard stumbled in, face flushed and sweaty. Xius pushed himself to his feet, knees shaking, at the soldier's alarm.

"She's gone. The white woman is gone, your majesty."

"*What?*" The guard winced. "What do you mean she's gone? And if she is, why are *you* not gone with her?"

"Kidnapped, your greatness. We were jumped on the outskirts of the—"

"*Excuse me?!?*"

The guard shrunk into the doorway. "She ran from me, your majesty—saw a noble being held against her will by some huge slave and thought she could help, I suppose, but before I could help, the slave threw this, this...I can't remember, your majesty, forgive me. Please, punish me as you will, oh Pharaoh, I fully deserve your wrath!"

As the man fell prostrate on the floor before his quaking monarch, another man came through the open door, puffing and panting. Denan, clutching a walking stick, hobbled through.

"Your majesty, they used the same trick they used on me. I saw it from my balcony."

"Denan? What are you doing—"

"We don't have time for that! If we hurry, we can catch them. I have already sent out men."

Xius barely had the mind to shove on his sandals as he rushed out the door after Denan, leaving his devastated guard on the floor.

"Have my horse prepared for me and send every man on patrol again. I will go to Set; he may know where they have gone."

"Set? Why would he know where these men may be?" puffed Denan, before his expression blanched. "You're not saying Set…!?"

"Would I have apprehended him for anything less?" He

tried not to pay too much attention to the dawning horror on Denan's face.

"Your majesty, I—about earlier—"

But Xius's feeble legs had had enough and he found himself stumbling to a wall in his attempts to hold himself up, just to collapse onto his knees. He cursed, dropping the side of his fist to the floor.

Denan couldn't kneel yet without pain, so he simply crowded about Xius in baffled concern.

"Are you certain you want me to prepare a horse for you? You're not thinking of joining the search like this?"

"I can ride a horse just fine," Xius spat.

"But you are still weak from the ameese. You could relapse into your sickness."

"I don't care!"

"We'll find her—"

"No!" And to solidify his statement, Xius clawed up the wall to force himself to his feet. Denan rolled his eyes to the ceiling.

"By the gods, you're stubborn. Very well, have it your way."

There was a clatter as Denan dropped his walking stick before him.

"Take this; you are going to need it where you are going."

Xius stared down at the gnarled staff in bemusement.

"But you need that. I can't."

"Take it."

"I will not."

A sound that many men had learned to fear rumbled in the broad general's chest. Despite his wounds, he leaned down to meet his pharaoh's eye.

"Xiusthamus, take the Ra-accursed stick. I am your friend and protector and, Osiris damn it, I will take care of you whether you want it or not. Set was not the only one watching out for you." When Xius just looked at him, unmoving, he barked, "Take it!"

Xius obeyed, awkwardly averting his eyes. The general, satisfied, straightened the best he could.

"I will continue as you commanded, your majesty. I shall keep the men at it until she is found or until you order otherwise."

The Pharaoh nodded numbly as he leaned on the walking stick. He really had needed it. Denan limped with him until they had to part ways, Xius to the royal prison, and Denan to the captain's quarters.

Once he found himself alone, not even followed by his other guard, he found his fear caving in around him. He felt as though the world had stopped breathing, and he had the deranged idea that if he didn't find a way to start its breath again, all would suffocate. Even though Annette may have had to die soon anyway, he feared for her life. He had prepared himself as much as any man could for an event that still felt like an unreal dream, a whispered premonition.

And he had sworn to her to always be with her—to be by her side till the very end. How dare they—how dare they take her before her allotted time! How dare any soul take something of his! The Pharaoh!

He wheeled about the corner of the stairs and into the dank hall of the palace cells. The moment he saw the lanky form slumped in the corner, he grabbed the bars as though ready to pull them out and dropped the walking stick to the floor.

"Where is she!" he roared.

The man, more like a dirty heap of cloth, leaped to his feet in one bound from fright. Set's form could only be seen by the lone, greasy torch behind Xius. His cheeks were blotchy and tears had dried dirty tracks down their curves. How strange it was to see the most logical and level-headed person he knew so emotionally unhinged.

"What do you mean?" asked Set in a dry rasp.

"Annette, you whelp! Your slave friends took her, now where are they?"

As was half expected, Set's expression crumpled and he brought a hand to his face.

"Oh Geb…This is my fault."

"Yes, yes, now answer!"

"I don't know where they are! I already told you! And they probably took her because of me. I broke my pact and told you, so now…now they've taken her as retribution."

Still, his anger could only grow. He gave a shout of frustration, shook the bars, and threw the walking stick at them. Then as his knees buckled, he fell against the opposing wall. He pulled at his hair and clenched his teeth. Fear was beginning to return. *What if*, whispered his heart, *what if…?*

He cursed loudly, reached for the walking stick, and struggled back to his feet, almost missing Set's soft request.

"Take me with you. Let me help."

Xius glowered at him over his shoulder and barked a short, humorless laugh.

"Help? How? Are you going to go back in time and rewrite what you did? But oh! You can't do that, for time is unchangeable. Or are you going to grab a nearby virgin and cut her stomach so you can use her entrails for divination? What a lovely idea that is. I'm sure you've done it plenty of times."

Set's eye twitched. "Correction, I have never participated in any of their ghastly rituals."

"You have as good as!"

"I know you're upset with me, more than you ever will be—"

"Incredible. You really are as clever as I thought."

"—and I know I won't survive after all this is over, and I only have myself to blame. But, please, Xius, please, let me help you this one time. Let me try to fix what I have done wrong. Please, let me help my Annette—"

"Help me? Help *her?* If you had wanted to help, you would have turned over those monsters the moment you found them! Now look what you've done!"

"I know—"

"Half of Egypt dying, the rest just waiting for the chance to vomit up their souls—Denan and I would have been dead if it hadn't been for Annette!"

"Xius, please—"

"Wenamon's dead, and soon Isis will be too! And the gods are raining down their vengeance upon us—dozens of young women are now dead, and for what reason? What would have happened if that had been one of Denan's little girls? What would you tell him? Is Tawaret really worth the pain those girls' families are going through right now? All those innocent lives, Set!"

Pain as Xius had never seen contorted Set's entire body, causing him to fall to the ground with his arms over his head. A whimper escaped him.

"I know! Please, I beg of you!"

"Beg of me what, Set? Beg of me what?" and his eyes burned. It was as though Set's pain had gone through the bars and infected Xius, but he was angry. He had to be angry.

"I don't know," Set wailed. "I don't deserve life, I don't even deserve to have been born. I only wish for a chance, a chance to redeem myself both to you and Annette. I brought her into all of this. I was the one who so blatantly leapt over the lines that should have never been crossed."

"Blatantly? Ha! You defied all reason, you denied everything I ever knew of you! Ra, I don't even know what you are anymore! Have I ever?"

"Yes, Xius. I'm still Set, I'm still your friend, I swear—"

"No!" shouted Xius, and his voice cracked. "You were never any friend! Gods, *I trusted you!*"

Set shuddered and shifted back toward the wall of his prison. "Forget it. Kill me now, if you have to, but continue on with whatever you were doing."

"I don't need you to give me permission!" But whatever indignation he had wanted to portray was ruined by his fracturing voice and the tears trickling off his chin. "I am Pharaoh!"

"Yes, yes," mumbled Set. As Xius stood there, trembling and shaking uncontrollably and not sure how to tell his legs to start moving again, the broken man sighed. "You're the same as always. So overemotional. But I guess it only makes sense."

"Don't—don't talk to me about irrational. You were supposed to be the rational one. You were supposed to be the—the reasonable one, the one who never let his emotions get to him, the one who—who was always *right*."

"Yes. I know that too. I'm very aware of that."

And Xius was melting down to the floor, not bothering to fight down the sobs. He was pathetic. He always had been. But Set had known that all his life. Set was one of the few he could show that to. With him, Xius didn't have to struggle to be the hard, strong and stoic man he knew he was supposed to be, for Set knew him.

But what was he doing? He was supposed to be looking for Annette! But with all the soldiers left untouched by ameese combing the city, what more could he do?

"Why? Didn't you know what I would have to do to you? What I'm going to have to do?"

Set said nothing, keeping his back to Xius.

"Why did you do this to me? To yourself? Set…"

"I don't know," came his traitorous answer. "I just…I just couldn't live another day in such unbearable loneliness. I—I had no one I could feel with and no one to just walk and talk and philosophize with—"

"We were right there, Set! By Ra! Aren't you listening to yourself?"

"I know now it was stupid! But you wouldn't understand. You, the prized child of the gods. Has it ever occurred to you how apathetic the gods are to the rest of us?"

"Don't make assumptions about what I do and don't understand, I hate it! Just because I am a weak man doesn't mean I am a stupid one as well!"

Set paused before saying softly, "I never thought you a weak man. Quite the opposite. If either of us were to be the weaker it would be I, even without this demented, foolish mess that I've made."

Xius snorted but was too upset to think of anything to say to that. He could only wait as his tears subsided and his knees were willing to hold him once more. He breathed in the rancid but stale scent of urine, mold, and earth that made up the prison. The burning torch above his head didn't make a single pop.

There was a rustle of straw and Set pressed his worn and ragged face to the bars. Xius couldn't meet his eyes.

"I do think I can help, though. I know of an old dock we

can try, I just don't know which one it is and I'd have to see it to recognize it."

"Who do you think I am?"

Set's eyes hardened. "I will not flee. The only way I can ever atone for this crime is to face the consequences. I am not as base and cowardly as to escape what I know is inevitable."

"Ah, but you were base and cowardly enough to bow to the threats of lowly Kushites, hmm? Fascinating."

Set winced. "Do you want to save Annette or not? I may know where they are, I was supposed to bring them Annette tonight."

"Then why don't you just tell me and I'll find them?"

"That's the thing, your majesty," Set looked up. "I may tell you, but I'm the only one who has seen these two face to face."

***

Jee glared at Hath as she knelt unmoving on the sand, stick in her hand. A murky blanket of clouds moved across the sky, blocking what stars could be seen, and there was sand as far as she could see. A scorpion stalked its way across a smooth stone nearby to investigate a lone clump of dry, dead grass.

All the while, Apep hissed in her mind, a sound like water on the fire.

You'll never find your father, he threatened, *you'll never find your mother. Alone, alone, alone forever.*

She could smell blood in her nose. She would die if she did not comply, but then, she was to die soon anyway. The moon already sat fat and yellow on the horizon. Near its zenith, the eclipse would begin. Hopefully, the clouds would remain, making the eclipse impossible to see.

A ways away from her, shivering at the edge where the firelight died and the night began, was the pale form of Annette. Her white hair had turned yellow with sand.

"Are you missing anything?" asked Jee. "I was sure to bring all your supplies, and there is plenty of blood should you need it."

"I've had enough of blood," she snapped. "You're wasteful to think I need more."

"Then why don't you start?"

"Because I won't kill him." She had killed enough as it was, and she couldn't even figure out if it was all worth it. Apep hadn't stopped her, but then again, he was a god of death, and the reason to his killings evaded her.

Jee scoffed. "As you've said before."

"I won't do it."

Suddenly, his plow-like hands slammed onto her scalp and pulled her head back to meet his black, narrow eyes, so unlike her prince's.

"I know you still fear pain."

"You can't waste a drop of my blood," she said calmly, as though her windpipe wasn't about to be bent in half. "And you still need my virginity, so there goes your other stupid idea."

Jee only blinked. He didn't smile, he didn't frown, only

stared into her eyes as though he could read her thoughts. Then, he let go of her head and walked away. For a split-second, Hath thought of fleeing and already had a foot out from beneath her, but then a moment later she saw him reach for that sand-stained mane. Annette cried out in pain as he yanked her to her feet and turned to meet Hath's eyes. Then, knife still in hand, he sliced slowly along the girl's arm.

As she watched the other girl squirm, doing her best not to cry out as the blood trickled onto her clothes, Hath could only feel confused pain. This girl had taken away her prince. This girl, the slave, who had made no sacrifice like Hath had, who had done nothing to change herself, and yet still had seduced the heart of her prince.

He pressed the knife down harder and Annette muffled a howl, cursing in that strange tongue of hers. Her eyes came up, her eyes on fire.

Hath saw something then—maybe a trick of the light: a momentary blur of color about the girl's form, unlike anything she had seen. Perhaps it had been like an aura or a cloud.

Could that be what had reflected Hath's curse? Was that the sign of another god?

Before she could get a closer look it faded and Annette lashed out at Jee with her teeth, missing by inches.

The woman who her god hated, Hath couldn't help thinking. *The woman who her god hated...*

Hath sighed. She really didn't want to do this anymore. Besides, should Annette die, the prince would be sad. Who cared about Apep or anything else anymore. She was going to die. Annette was going to die. Jee would probably die as well.

Numbly, she drew the circle, placed the tokens of skin, bone, and hair, and sang the song her mother had sung the night she had died. She wondered dimly how her father would have sounded when he sang that same song.

You'll never see them, whispered Apep, *treacherous daughter.*

Jee dropped Annette on the ground and took his place hovering over Hath's shoulder once more, knife in hand.

You'll be alone in the darkness, said Apep.

"You'll have to kill me when the moon is red," she muttered. "That was another thing my father and mother did wrong—my father didn't have noble blood, and my mother didn't kill when the moon was ripe."

"And I presume the master has told you this?"

"The master, that's a new one."

Jee kicked her away from the circle and took up the box. Carefully, he tied it shut and lowered it into the saddle bags of one of his stolen horses. The horse shifted nervously, skin twitching at the smell of blood from the box. Suddenly, the other stallion, who had already been the more skittish of the two, was bumped slightly by the other. With a plaintive whinny it galloped off, eager to get as far from the box as possible. With a shout and a stream of profanities, Jee mounted the first horse and chased after the other without another word or thought for Hath or Annette.

Die tonight, and forever be alone in the darkness, you who chose to fail.

Hath slid Kasmut's hands beneath her and stood. Annette's form shook, whether from cold or pain or both, Hath couldn't find herself caring. Aching from the emptiness and feeling she might grow mad from the constant whispers in her head, she picked up the blade Jee had dropped and made her way to the edge of the light.

Thinking I would ever give you the cursed son of Horus, thinking I would ever honor the frivolous breathing of life.

Without ceremony, she sliced the cords binding her wrists and feet, swiped her hand along the stream of blood Jee had left behind on Annette, and made her way back to the fire. Humming, singing, trying to drown out the sound of Apep, she flicked the blood into the fire. It hissed and spat. She went to the grass clump, where the scorpion still meandered, and swiped it up by its tail and into the fire in one smooth movement. It's exoskeleton popped.

Annette was still on her side, face covered by her hair. Hath breathed in the smell of the burning scorpion and turned to her. She looked pathetic. How had her prince ever fallen in love with such a weak, fragile thing?

Alone forever, nasty soul, only fit to be spewed out.

Hath yanked Annette to her feet, hands still covered in blood. The fire spluttered and hissed across the broken insect within it.

"Come on. We dance."

The girl flinched, hand over the cut in her arm. "Did you just—"

Hath rolled his eyes. "Where do you think your pharaoh's amulet gets the power to understand languages? What I've done is just a very simple, much less potent spell than that."

"But he said Thoth—"

"Dance with me."

"Why? And why has he brought you here? Isn't that huge guy going to be back any second now?"

"If I meant to tell you, I would have by now, don't you think?"

The white girl stared. A cool desert breeze brushed over them, flicking her hair over her shoulder and making the fire spit sparks into the air. Hath leaned her head back, missing the feel of her own hair upon her head rather than the baldness of Kasmut. Egyptians and their strange fashion sense.

"Breathe. Do you smell it?" asked Hath.

"Smell what?"

"The night."

There was an awkward silence, filled with only the moan of wind across the dunes and the crackle of the fire. Annette said nothing, and Hath lowered her eyes to her.

"No more questions?"

"What you mean to tell me, you will," she said quietly, fists at her sides and blood slowly dripping down her arm. Hath smiled.

"Dance with me, for soon," she breathed the night in deep, "we die."

"Both of us?"

"Both of us."

She looked down to meet the white girl's steady gaze. She had stopped her trembling and just looked at her, waiting. Hath found her respect for the girl increasing.

"Aren't you going to ask why? Aren't you scared?"

"I'm terrified," she said, "but not surprised. I don't belong here."

"No, you don't." Hath raised her arms. Annette, somewhat hesitantly, copied her.

"Where's the music?" she asked.

"In the flames. In the wind. And if you listen, in the drums of my people." Hath thumped her chest. "Since we both die, we need to appreciate everything here in the now. The wind and sky." Hath spun. "The smell, the air, the taste of sand." She brought her hands down to caress the air, then thumped the sand beneath her. "The earth."

Annette followed her clumsily, but with an attempt at the same spirit as Hath. She reminded her suddenly of the child Hath had once been, stumbling after her father's lead. The white girl's docile behavior confused her. She had just told her she was about to die, but here she was trying to dance with her without argument. Hath continued to murmur her father's words, holding them close to her eyes and wishing it was her own black limbs that beat the ground rather than Kasmut's, but for now she had limbs, and that was what mattered.

No prince on the earth held her back anymore. She would move on. To what, she didn't know.

To nothing, said Apep, *to nothing but loneliness, to agony, to nothing.*

But the voice was fainter this time. Her heart was pounding too hard to hear.

She eventually ran out of things to say to the girl and simply moved. For the first time she allowed herself to feel her heritage, swiping the air, beating the ground, flinging arms to the starless night sky and paying tribute to invisible drums and flame. Annette followed her, strange and weightless on her long pale legs and eyes lost.

"You're supposed to marry Xius," Annette said.

"Yes. But not anymore, for it's you he really wants."

"Don't you hate me?"

Hath laughed, but it sounded empty. "Yes, and no."

"What do you mean?"

In answer, Hath only said, "Do you hear it? The drums. It's in our heartbeats, in our breaths. Come now, this is our last chance."

"For what?"

"To make life worth it."

Annette spun after her, stomping sand into the fire and throwing her white hair behind her. Their feet moved together, and Hath thought she could hear something. She thought she could see the whirl of her father's colorful robes as he spun ahead of her, singing loudly. But when she looked, all she saw was the white hair of Annette.

She beat the ground harder with her stolen feet, focused on only the breath in her lungs and the pound of her heart.

There was nothing left. Nothing she could do now. She was going to die...

And she wasn't even sure what waited for her on the other side, if anything. Before she had the assurance of her parents that all her loved ones and eternal peace waited for her in the arms of Apep. But now, the voice of that same god whispered damnation in her mind.

"Why must we do this?" Annette asked.

"To figure it out," said Hath, feeling the Egyptian's body begin to wear far before she knew her own would have. "Death is beautiful because of this. Death is a gift because life makes it so—it teaches us about paradise and suffering. Paradise will help us know what we enter into, and suffering will help us to not fear it."

"Fear what?"

"Death, you idiot, aren't you listening?"

"Forgive me for not being as spiritual as you right now."

"Aren't you?"

She said nothing. Then she suddenly leapt and spun on the ball of one foot, toes bent up to her other knee before returning to following Hath in her furious, and somewhat confused, dance. She flung her long mane of hair about herself like a banner. The fire spat sparks and ash into the sky. Hath eyed the corpse of the scorpion. The spell wouldn't last past morning.

"How do you know it's true?" asked Annette.

“I don't,” said Hath.

“Then why do we have to die?”

“Because I needed to finish what my parents have begun,” Hath breathed sharply through her nose. “And my god hates you.”

“Wasn't it that big guys death god who brought me here?”

“No. Apep had nothing to do with you coming here. Saying that hc had was only to win over the sappy-faced vizier. It is true your blood will stop the plague that had been intended for you, but that is as far as you are involved with Apep.”

The drums were thrumming. Hath lifted off her feet, drinking in the sound. Finally, finally she could hear it. Mother must be to the side, slapping the pig skin stretched taunt across the frame of her drum. The crackling of the fire could be the beads against dried cactus shells.

“Maybe...maybe we can still run for it,” panted Annette.

“We won't make it,” said Hath.

“How'd we get out here, anyway?”

Hath sighed. “Keep dancing.”

“But why does your god hate me?”

“I don't know.”

A dog howled in the distance. Hath caught Annette's dance faltering as she looked over her shoulder.

”I think I can just see the glow of the city,” Annette breathed, drawing her elbows into her sides and turning softly.

“He is on horseback, and you are white.”

“What's that supposed to mean?”

“You'll stand out like a beacon in the dark. Now shh.”

But Annette had stopped, breast heaving, hands at her sides. Hath could feel her alien eyes on her as she tried to ignore how Kasmut's body grew heavier and heavier.

Hath stumbled and caught herself just before she trapezed into the fire. She stared into the yellow orange flames. Something horrible was rising in her chest, and she moved to step into the dance once more, but Kasmut's knees shook and she fell to the ground. Annette knelt before her without a word. Her fingers were long, slender, and clenched so tightly into the sand next to Hath’s.

"I'm sorry," she whispered. "You shouldn't have to die."

Hath snorted. "You don't listen."

"Yes, I did, death is a blessing, blah blah blah, but...a friend told me that death is only welcome to those who are prepared for it."

"You're the one not prepared for it," said Hath, rolling onto her back and laying spread-eagle like she hadn't a care in the world, though the opposite was true.

Annette sighed and lay down besides her. "Can anyone be?"

Jee returned from the shadows with both horses properly cowed. He took one look at Annette and Hath, free, sitting up, dirty, and exhausted, and merely snorted. As he walked towards Annette she looked to Hath in alarm, as though the white girl hadn't considered whether Hath was telling the truth about just how far away the city was.

"I wouldn't try," said Hath.

Annette hesitated. She eyed the horses, then Jee. Before she could make up her mind he was upon her, hand to her neck. His thick fingers went to the back of her head, squeezing until she finally went limp. Hath found she couldn't feel anything, even though she had talked to the girl. Without the energy to dance, Apep whispered damnation in her mind, and only a little compassion could survive through that.

Useless, wasteful, born to rot...

"On the horse," said Jee. "The moon is close."

"And if I don't?"

He kicked her to the ground, where she gasped for air from the pain.

You will die, and death shall be your fear.

Rope cut into her wrists and her hands were yanked behind her. Somewhere, on the desert, she thought she could smell the distant musk of rain. Thunder rumbled, but it was so far away she could barely see the flash of lightning around Jee's bulky form.

Annette was tossed onto one of the horses, dirty and unconscious.

Know nothing but fear. Know nothing but pain.

But why do you hate her so? Thought Hath. *I deserve your hate, but what has she done?*

She didn't expect the darkness to answer her. Why should it? Then again, why should it still be whispering to her after her disobedience? She had already been damned, so now what? What was the use of crushing her spirit now if she was to be crushed the moment she died?

But as Jee flung her next to Annette and Hath once more endured having a bar of bone digging into her stomach, the answer came to her in words made of that same pain, and yet so different and soft compared to Apep's. It took her breath away, it made her hyper-aware of the touch of Annette's skin upon hers.

She is of the only true enemy of death.

Which could only be someone who could not be killed, right? Like a goddess, or some other denizen of heaven. Could it be she was a messenger of a different god, much as Hath was for Apep? A goddess of life? Of light? But what did that mean? Why was she here? Had the words telling Hath that Annette was a true enemy to death come from this self same goddess?

Hath's mind raced, but it was difficult to make out her own thoughts amidst the pain. She nearly fell off as Jee rode down the slope to the riverside. Papyrus and dark, empty farmlands greeted her along with the sides of the pregnant Nile, ready to give birth to a flood any day now. Jee yanked her off the horse to lay arm deep in wet silt, then gently lowered the box to the shore, allowing the river waters to lap at it. Then, lifting his face to the sky, he started to sing.

Hath had never heard him sing before, and the sound caught her unawares. It was beautiful, and as he weaved into the song her mother held so sacred it had become Hath's lullaby, a fire burned fiercely through the numbness of her soul. How could death make her feel so alone? She thought of her father, of his crazed dance. She thought of the feel of desert sand upon her feet as she raced about the fire, arms to the sky. She thought of the air on her skin, the stars against her eyes, and the musk of earth before rain.

Then the kind, warm eyes of the prince came to her mind.

He had saved her life. She had loved him for it. All his warmth, all his kindness, and this is how she repaid him? If death was to be honored, life had to be as well, for it all was a blessing. Saving a life was an honor. Rewarding him with death, however, could not be right.

Trembling with the intensity of her conviction, she looked up at the form of Annette, still slumped over the horse, her white hair dirtier than ever. If she truly were of some god of life, she could not die there.

But what could she do?

Ignoring the pain in her side, Hath wormed beneath the standing horse to where Annette's long hair dangled. Lucky for this wench, she had such an ungodly amount of hair, unblocking the flow of blood to her head that Jee had stopped would be easy. Ears filled with Jee's beautiful tenor, she took a mouthful of the girl's sandy hair and tugged. She pulled till Annette shifted enough to come crashing down on top of her with a moan, knocking the wind out of Hath. Jee, meanwhile, was singing too loudly to hear them.

The clouds parted above them, revealing a single sliver of the moon left over from the eclipse.

A great mouth in the sky, just like the night her father died and the blood fell dark and shiny.

"Wake up, you lazy bitch," wheezed Hath. "Damn, you're heavy."

"Wha?"

"Yes, you!"

"Ugh, my head."

Hath kicked the girl off her. Her shoulders ached something awful and she wriggled her hands, but she had to get this stupid, ugly girl going. Because if Hath was to be an enemy of Apep, she might as well do it thoroughly.

"Run," she said.

Annette looked up at her through curtains of dirty hair, bewildered from the pain. Hath pushed her face through the hair, teeth clenched.

"Run! Waset is just on the other side—he's going to drop the box in the river here, so memorize this place and find the prince."

"The who?"

"The Pharaoh!"

"But what about you?"

A horrible, electric jolt of fear ran through Hath as she heard the song winding down. The time was coming. She would have his hands on her, that knife, sharpest of knives, would be against her throat.

"*Run! Now!*"

Faster than she expected, the girl jumped to her feet and bolted. She couldn't help but smile, the last smile she would ever feel, as she watched the girl flee down the shore and be swallowed by the bulrushes. She hardly even heard the angry, sharp intake of air and final roar as Jee turned around to see her missing. His hands came, hard and unyielding, bruising Kasmut's flesh. He dragged her unceremoniously to the side of the river and yanked her chin back so far she choked for breath. She barely had time to be afraid.

"Stop smiling. They'll kill her before she even reaches the other side."

The knife was as icy on her throat as the last time she had died.

***

The smoky sky blocked the stars and moon, leaving the night a groggy black. The clattering of their horses hooves rang too loud in the quiet. Four soldiers galloped after Xius and Set with torches upheld. The streets were eerily devoid of life and sound. The few windows lit up with candles looked faint and tired, as though the inhabitants themselves weren't quite sure whether they were alive or not.

All the while he prayed in his heart that Denan wouldn't notice that he had run into the darkness without him while necromancers were on the loose, and with a traitor, nonetheless. But traitor or not, Set was the smartest man he knew, and he needed his help.

Xius thought over the conversation they had had earlier as they had readied themselves for the search. Set had mentioned that the cultists seemed oddly too well-informed on the happenings within the palace and suggested they keep this search to themselves.

"There's only two of them, I'm certain," he said, "so we shouldn't need that many men to overpower them."

Set had mentioned that he suspected the two were going to try to finish the strange ceremony they had been trying to complete for the last ten years. Set explained that the markings, number of blood sacrifices, and time of the moon cycle had been consistent with the purge of ten years ago and the night Tawaret died. Information that Set had been withholding from Xius came pouring out: the exact numbers of deaths, symbols he had recorded from the box of Apep, moon cycles, and an arriving lunar eclipse that could be happening this very night.

"You're telling me this all now?"

"Pardon me, your majesty, but you were delirious the last time I saw you, and you didn't bother to visit me after throwing me into jail. They would have killed Annette if I told you before then."

"What are they trying to do?"

"I may have worked with them, but that doesn't mean I'm a child of Apep as well."

Set hunched over the back of his horse ahead of him, linen

kilt flapping in the wind. They had been searching from the moment the moon had come out, though storm clouds threatened to swallow it once more.

"Kasmut is to be their next Tawaret, their sacrifice of noble blood, I believe. If you had just kept her by your side like any normal fiancé would have done—"

"What, like you and Annette? I'm sorry, but I don't find stuffing the woman I want to woo into the apartment next door as the greatest way to cultivate romance."

"You never tried to woo Kasmut, you hardly did anything."

"Shut up and tell me how you think we're going to stop them—if we find them at all."

"Why, with weapons, of course."

"Set, you can't cut your way out of a bag."

"Who said I would have a sword?"

In the faint light, Xius could still make out the bow and arrows tucked away into their sheaths against Set's back. Xius's sword, a fine, gilded khopesh, slapped against his thigh. The homeless and the drunken watched them from the alleys along the docks. Once Xius thought he saw the form of a new mother through a window, rocking her tiny babe by the light of a lone candle.

The moonlight flickered as the clouds peppered across its face.

"This sounds to me like we're going to be running up and down the Nile like idiots."

"Each ceremony was done near the Nile or in it. The old shaman of the cult was slain in the Nile itself, throwing the box of Apep into it. With the number of deaths, the eclipse, and the kidnapping of Kasmut, I'm almost certain they're trying that ceremony again."

"I wasn't that delirious, you know. You really could have told me all this while you were sobbing like an idiot over my death bed."

"For the love of Isis, Xius!"

"Dumb ass."

Set suddenly yanked his horse to a stop. The guards behind them nearly collided with Set's mare.

"Quiet!" he hissed, eyes sharp at a point somewhere across the river. Xius searched along the opposite bank to see what he was looking at. Before he saw anything, though, he heard it: a man's beautiful tenor, echoing across the sounds of waves lapping upon the shore.

Set scowled. "Damn it, they're on the other side."

They? The cultists? At first the beauty made Xius wonder if Set had been mistaken. But the singer's voice grew into an awful wail and all of the riders cringed back. Even the horses lowered their ears and began to paw the ground nervously. Milky moonlight poured into the dark night as the clouds parted. Its silver light was thin, coming from a slice of the moon.

That's strange, thought Xius, *I was certain there was a full moon last night.*

All looked up into the sky, watching the little sliver of a moon with bated breath. Set, however, pointed to a guard, arm shaking.

"Find us a way across."

The guard kicked his horse into a sprint toward the nearest boat upstream. Xius squinted across the waters. He nudged his horse forward as the last piece of the moon vanished. At first Xius assumed the clouds had finally closed in, but then everything glowed with a coppery light.

A full moon, and it had turned red as rust. For some reason, it brought the scene across the waters into sharp contrast, turning the Nile to a deep, almost blood-red. A jolt ran through his gut.

Annette. And Kasmut, kneeling on the ground next to a horse while a dark man stood in the river besides them.

He scrambled with the reins to turn his horse around and saw the guard Set had sent upstream cutting the rope to a small, streamlined boat. Xius would repay the owner later.

But then a strange heaviness filled the air, making it strange to breathe. The horses became alarmed and deaf to their riders' commands. One even tried to rear up and retreat down an alley off the docks.

Right as Xius thought he would lose control on his steed,

he saw a wave of nearby water bubble, then boil. A nearby drunk gave a shout and scrambled up the walls of the neighboring home, too stupid and terrified to take the easier route down the alley.

Set cursed before he and the last guard leaped off their horses. Xius followed, falling less gracefully. Without ceremony, his friend tugged him up to his feet and ran to meet the guard steering the boat toward them.

The singer from before sang a different song, lilting and beautiful once more.

With a running leap, Set flew over the water and into the small boat, rocking it precariously.

"Xius!" he reached out a hand.

Xius jumped and Set managed to stop him from tipping over just as the last guard jumped in. The third stayed on the shore, hands holding to the reins of the unsettled horses. He pointed to the river, however, and cried "Look!"

The guard at the helm pushed the boat roughly to the shore they had just left, eyes white with horror. Xius just had time enough to spot what might have been round stones rising from the frothing red water before Set was pushing him out of the boat. A few citizens, probably woken up by all the commotion, stepped out of their homes and were surprised to see the Pharaoh. The moment they processed his fright, they too grew alarmed.

He looked back, but Set blocked his view.

"To the palace!" he cried to the people. "All of you! Run!"

"Why did you push me out? What about the Kushites?"

But then, above Set's arm, Xius caught the sight of thousands of human forms rising from the water, skeletal, naked, pale—

Two men broke off from Xius, mounted their horses, and kicked their steeds to a sprint. Set pushed Xius toward his horse and swung up on his own.

"What are those things?" His voice was high, even borderline shrill.

Set didn't answer, expression hard.

"We need to get the people to the palace first,"

"But what's happening—"

"Damn it, do you think I know?"

A hand reached out from the water to snake around one fragile back ankle of Xius's horse. The stallion screamed in fright and kicked high at the thing's head while Xius had to hold on for dear life. When he looked down he too gave a strangled scream.

Rolling white eyes. A jaw only half hinged.

He felt as though his stomach had dropped away. Some had missing limbs, others had their faces crushed in, and even more shuffled out with their innards dripping into the river like a flowing train.

Their horses bolted. In the streets near the docks, families had poured out screaming and gripping their children. They crowded the streets, clutching the many sick with ameese as they fled toward the palace, barely displaying enough peace of mind to step aside for the panicked horses of the vizier and pharaoh. A few Egyptians had climbed to the roofs and were now peering toward the river and pointing toward the scarlet moon.

"Set! Annette and Kasmut!" Xius hollered.

"I know! I'm thinking!"

But beneath all the panic in his mind, he knew crossing the river now would be near impossible. He cursed the simplicity of it. Few lived on the west side of the river, where the dead were buried and most of the farmlands were kept. It was a perfect, easy, brilliant defensive move on the necromancers' part, because while there were pieces of the Egyptian army stationed on the west side of the river, there could be little to no way of sending them word of what to look for with the river filled with violent undead.

Through the waves of dark, running bodies, a flash of gold appeared. Xius's horse stuttered to a sudden halt. Though its eyes rolled and its mouth foamed, it pawed in place, refusing to move. Xius moved to kick its sides, but stopped as the eyes of a black jackal caught his gaze. The god's skin glowed gold despite the red moon, and the curve of his staff's end stood tall and sharp above the fleeing mortals.

His guards flowed past, unable to control their horses or the crowds. No one seemed to notice the god who stood in their presence, but ran about him as though he wasn't there.

"Are you so caught up in your fear that you have forgotten something?" growled Anubis. His voice ran though Xius like embalmists' salt and Xius dropped the reins to draw his arms in instinctively. His breath became dry and weak.

"Your majesty!" called Set from up ahead, barely audible above the din of panic.

Anubis waited. It was hard to read the expression on his canine face.

"Is there another way across?" he gasped.

The black eyes flashed, "The box, Pharaoh, which is at the bottom of the cursed Nile where only the dead may walk," he turned his muzzle ever slightly to the side.

Xius jerked. "Annette—"

"Will be with the rest of your people should you fail me." Anubis's hackles rose. "Xiusthamus, you have allowed these heathens of your world to trespass in my realm for too long, and now look what you have done."

"But how can we get across?"

"Does it matter?"

"Your majesty!" called Set. The soldiers they had brought with them had already vanished into the night, hopefully leading the rest of the people toward the palace, which had at least stone walls to protect them from whatever crawled forth from the waters.

"It would also be in your best interests," growled Anubis, "to not discount the opportunities the gods have given you. You risked more than you know in allowing the heathens to touch her."

"So she *is* from the future?" Xius turned away from his approaching guards to look at the god—but he had already vanished.

The screams were rising like mist in the night, filling the air and chilling the soul. The red moon cleared a wide berth through the clouds. The air was wet from rain and too thick with bodies to breathe. Xius sat amidst it all, still feeling the imprint of the god's golden body against his eyes. Elbows and shoulders brushed past his calves like surreal waters.

Set finally managed to make his way back to him, nearly trampling some of the crowd in the process.

"Xius, we should return to the palace—try to think of a way across, maybe find a bigger boat—send out a carrier pigeon—"

"The box is in the river."

"What?"

The screams were deafening. They could hardly hear one another.

"Anubis just told me we have to go into the river and get Apep's box."

"Anubis? But that river is vast! If it wasn't filled with death already, we'd drown just trying to find it!"

"A god told me to go, I'm going! If I don't," Xius pulled his frazzled horse about.

"But—Xius!"

Behind him, back out toward the river, he saw his people. The rotten corpses mingled about them like lions amidst a herd of confused antelope. Their rotten nails were long as claws. Blood stained the street, black in the rusty light. Even as he watched, the undead pounced on their living victims to gnaw on their flesh, unhampered by rotted limbs. They tore out muscles, ripped open stomachs, feasted on the blood-darkened organs within their still living, screaming meals—-

"Xius!" cried Set.

The horse fought him, reluctant to return, but Arabians were not the most revered breed in the world for nothing. Arabians, especially the one Xius rode, were trained to be obedient under any circumstances, be it starvation, war, or even, well, the end of the world.

Thus, it plowed through the crowd.

He had no idea what he was doing, but the vision of Anubis still burned before his eyes. The gods had heard him. The gods were there.

And he was Pharaoh, God on Earth, and child of the gods.

Set pushed after him, calling for him above the crowd. The

stallion trampled at the undead corpses and kicked their flimsy bodies against stone walls with an awful crunch. But no matter how the horses stomped and flailed, the dead kept coming, like waves upon a beach. Their eyes varied from decayed to white, swollen, and bulbous balls that leaked puss and wore caps of foggy, water-rotted irises. Flesh hung on them like torn clothes. Their nails raked at Xius's poor horse.

It pressed on, despite the foam now flecking its sides. Xius silently asked for its forgiveness.

He rode up the docks, searching for anything.

"Xius!" shouted Set.

A flash of gold caught his eye. He looked up ahead, where the river curved slightly, to see a huge, ornate boat, curved like a sultan's shoe. Xius couldn't believe his eyes. He recognized the boat, the same one that Kasmut and him had ridden, the very same one Merkha tried to escape from the plague with. Why hadn't he noticed it before?

The dead ignored all the boats, distracted by the lone pharaoh and vizier riding amidst them and by the living who fled. As Xius came to the boat he leapt off his horse and ran aboard. Set followed suit, heading to the rope tying them to the docks. He pulled a knife from his belt, sawed through the rope, and kicked the gangplank off just as their horses gave up on wondering if they would return and ran for it. A few corpses fell back into the rust-colored water with the rest of their brethren who had yet to touch shore.

"Idiot!" shouted Set. "There's only two of us, it'd take at least twenty to row this thing!"

"I'm open to ideas, *adviser*!" Xius yelled back as he pushed on the rudder.

The sound of fingernails on wood came from the sides. Set ran to Xius's side and pushed the rudder with him. With a groan of wood, the boat slowly, slowly, started to turn. The sail, which had been taken down for the night, was rolled and set along the width of the boat. It would take at least five men to raise it.

The nails scraped harder at the wood, desperate to reach them.

"This isn't going to work!" said Set.

"Shut up!"

A hand appeared on the railing of the deck. Set cursed loudly, left the rudder to Xius, and pulled out his bow and arrows. For a frozen moment in time, Xius thought Set looked like the bow itself, tall, lean, and taut. In a blink Set had an arrow whizzing through the air. It threw off the head of the corpse the moment it appeared, throwing it back into the waters.

The river's currents finally caught onto the boat. It turned into the flow. The sound of the nails never ceased, and whenever fingers appeared Set let another arrow fly.

"I'm surprised," said Xius breathlessly, his arms starting to shake from the weight of the rudder, "that you haven't gotten rusty after all these years."

"Come now, you know me better than that." A whistle, a thunk, another corpse slipped off the edge. "Though I'm afraid to say I didn't bring enough arrows for a horde."

"If I had known, I would have warned you. I'm sorry."

"It's the thought that counts. We'll probably die anyway."

"Your optimism is encouraging."

"I just don't want to be disappointed." Another whistle and the sound of bones cracking broke through the air beneath the screams of the city.

As the boat finally aligned with the rivers flow Xius pulled hard on the rudder, elbows cracking with the effort. Slowly, the boat made an angle toward the opposite shore. As an arrow whistled past his ear to impale another undead crawling up from behind him, he inwardly swore to the gods that, if he should live through this, he would have to build up some muscle. Straining on the handle of the rudder, he couldn't believe he had seen boatmen all his life handle this one-handed without a sweat.

"Xius!" Set pointed over his shoulder. "Annette!"

His head turned so fast he heard his neck pop. There, along the distant shore, her whiteness was unmistakable against the dark silt background of the shores and farmland. She was running up to where they were on the river, followed by staggering, but surprisingly fast, figures that could be none other than more of the Nile-birthed corpses.

Next thing Xius knew, Set was by him, firing arrow after arrow. Some flew a bit off, but about every other arrow he let fly landed on some corpse or another.

"Pull harder!"

"I'm pulling as hard as I can!" Xius looked back to the main deck and felt his heart sink. "Uh, Set—"

"I know."

Rotten fingers, their bones dyed red in the moonlight, were clicking against the railings.

"But she's fast," he said, "and, uh, we're kind of trapped."

"She can't run forever. Just keep pulling." Set turned around briefly to shoot a corpse that had pulled itself over the edge of the boat, jaw missing, and it slipped back over the side.

By now, Xius thought his arms might just dislodge themselves from his sockets. His joints and fingers burned. He peered over his shoulder, teeth on edge, to see the shore almost within reach. Annette had gotten closer, though he couldn't yet make out her expression.

"Get ready to jump off," said Set.

"My legs are shorter than yours!"

"You'll be fine—"

Several corpses flopped onto the deck, their hands mere feet away. Xius got another close up and personal view of the rot and disease crawling within their maggoty flesh and naked bones.

"Now!" Set roared.

Xius let go of the rudder. The whole ship groaned as it gave in to the current of the Nile. They climbed onto the railing and jumped. Dead hands reached for them, their rotten joints creaking.

They missed the touch of the red waters by a hair, tumbled against the wet dirt, and scrambled to their feet.

"Guys!"

"Annette!" they both cried.

She fell into their arms, gasping for breath. They spent no time dragging themselves out of the reach of the monsters behind her and up an embankment.

"Back...back that way..." she gasped. "Kasmut told me—

the box. The box is that way."

When an undead corpse raked at her bare calf, the cry she gave out was strangled with exhaustion. Set whirled on the body with his teeth bared and released an arrow into its skull. Soggy, gray matter and bone splattered out from behind it and it fell limp. Xius watched in horror as the dead behind converged on their fallen comrade and became momentarily distracted from their living prey.

"Aw, gods, this is insane," said Set.

"The Kushite box?" Xius asked Annette.

"I don't know! The box box, the one the big black guy dropped into the river!"

Sounded as close to a good description as any. Xius prompted her to lead the way and she pushed off from his arms and jogged back down the river. They followed at a heated run; Set occasionally shooting a stray corpse that had yet to be distracted by the much bigger living population on the other side of the river.

She brought them to a clear spot on the shore. A lone body lay there with Egyptian features and a slit, bloodless throat.

Xius stomach constricted. *Kasmut.*

Annette slowed with her eyes wide and both hands to her mouth as Set ran forward. Her breath whistled as it rushed through her fingers. Xius hesitated before following after Set, the words of Anubis echoing in his mind.

But no sooner had he reached the bottom of the tall bank besides the river than a dark arm shot out and backhanded the side of his head, throwing Xius completely off his feet and into the silt laden sand just out of reach of the Nile. He heard Annette scream his name.

"Awfully small for a ruler of Egypt," said a low voice.

The whistle of an arrow. He heard it thunk into the dirt behind his attacker. At the same time, Set cursed. Xius pushed his arms beneath him, moving to cradle his stomach, but he was stopped by a foot to his back. His back popped under the weight and his breath whooshed out.

"Oy! Asshole!"

There was a solid thump and the weight staggered off

Xius. He flipped over and reached for his blade. Before him stood a huge Kushite he vaguely recognized who could have been the same size of Denan, or even larger. But he wasn't looking at the Pharaoh. He was scowling up the embankment at Annette, who had crawled up to its top and thrown one of her beloved, duck-like shoes at him.

"Yeah! That's right!" She yanked off her other shoe and chucked it toward the Kushite, where it bounced off his chest. "Freaking dipweed!"

A frightening, inhuman loathing came over his face. Before Xius could move a muscle the man was halfway up the slope, crawling up like some wild ape. Set dashed past, flinging his bow like a spear in desperation. The quiver against his back was empty. Xius unsheathed his gilded khopesh and ran after them, heart in his throat, mind whirling with panic and adrenaline.

Annette bolted. The Kushite pulled himself onto level ground and thundered after her, Set hot on his heels. Xius's sides ached like fire as he climbed up the embankment to a horrifying scene.

The young white woman, who could run faster than any being alive, was spent. Her attempts to flee the huge man were slow and sluggish, and Xius screamed her name as the man's hands grabbed her hair and threw her to the ground.

Set, however, with his long legs, had caught up easily. He fell upon the man with a dagger he had pulled from his boot, expression feral. He slashed his blade across the man's back rather than stabbing to get his attention. Xius groaned inwardly. Even he knew to never do that with a knife. It only made your opponent angry and didn't slow them down in the least. Thus, having never been a fast runner in the first place, as Xius neared he could only watch in horror as the bear of a man whirled on his cousin. Something glinted in one of those paw-like hands.

Set ducked as a long, obsidian knife, still stained with what had to be Kasmut's blood, swiped at his neck. Then Set stabbed down, hitting the man's thigh. Blood flew, black in the moonlight.

The Pharaoh had his bronze khopesh at the ready when he

reached them. While Set stumbled about the Kushite, getting nicked by the knife and pushed backward, Xius wove beneath the huge man's arms and sliced across his right hamstring. With a roar of pain the man collapsed, eyes wild, spittle flying. His dark eyes met the Pharaoh's and, for a horrifying breath of time, Xius saw something foreign, dark, and unearthly in those eyes.

He had never seen such eyes.

The man's curled fist smashed into his skull, sending him flying off him.

The earth hit him next, splaying stars across his vision. A ways away, through the blurred legs of Set and past the Kushite, he saw Annette stumbling toward the river. But the ground tipped precariously beneath her in Xius's vision, and the night closed in.

Set cried out in pain. No, Xius couldn't lose consciousness now. Set needed him. His friend needed him.

Head whirling, Xius stumbled to his feet and raised his blade. Just ahead of him Set battled the kneeling giant, though his weakness with using anything other than a bow made the man's handicap virtually nonexistent. Blood soaked the front of Set's tunic.

Growling and more furious than he had ever been in his life, Xius charged, khopesh raised. This time the giant didn't have the reflexes to ward off the Pharaoh, who took one hard swipe at his neck. The khopesh got lodged into the man's spine, but Xius's momentum swung the curved blade clear through the man's neck, severing his windpipe and jugular in one go.

The Kushite threw up his arms, air gurgling past the blood from his lungs. He seemed to be reaching for something in the sky, perhaps the blood-red moon. Then, with a ground-shaking thud, he collapsed onto the ground.

Set staggered, and Xius caught him.

“We have to get the box,” Xius said.

“Annette?”

“She went back to the river, come on!”

In an awkward, running gait, with Xius supporting his injured vizier, they followed after Annette, who had just vanished over the edge to the river below.

"This eclipse is strange," breathed Set. "The red portion should have ended by now."

They slipped down the slope to the riverside, where Kasmut's body lay and Annette shuffled in the water. A few corpses breaking the surface eyed her, almost as though curious. She, however, didn't notice them, focused completely on the task at hand. Set bleated her name before stumbling, hand to his chest. Xius, momentarily distracted, examined his friend's chest, but amongst all the blood-soaked fabric he couldn't see the wound.

"Help her," Set croaked.

Xius let go and ran toward the water. The moment his foot fell into the water, a searing pain rushed up his leg, the likes of which he had never felt before. Gasping, he stumbled back, vision blurring even from the brief contact.

What the...

Anubis's words rung through his head.

The box, pharaoh, which is at the bottom of the eternal river where only the dead may walk.

"*Annette!*"

But she ignored him, waist deep in the water, arms in up to her elbows. A corpse from the waters right ahead of her rose. Her face showed no sign of pain, no discomfort, only sharp concentration.

Why wasn't it hurting her? She couldn't be dead—she didn't even have anything to do with death! Desperate, he looked down at the water and moved to put his foot into it, just to stop when he noticed blood oozing out of the same foot, as though it had turned sponge-like.

His throbbing mind turned. He started to hyperventilate. She had to get out of the water, quickly. He looked out over to her, hoarsely screaming her name.

"What are you waiting for?" yelled Set hoarsely from behind him.

"No living thing can step in that water!" said Xius.

As she stepped deeper and deeper into the river, his jaw ached with tension and his balled hands slipped with sweat.

But nothing happened. She had gone chest deep and still

nothing happened. The arms she brought out of the water were whole.

Set cried out. Coming down to them from upstream was the horde of undead they thought they had left behind at the boat and with the rest of the city. Through his throbbing, pain drunken mind, he thought he could hear them calling to him, recognizing him, hungry for him.

He pivoted on the spot and fought them back with his blade, despite the aching in his foot and the weakness in his body. He could see nothing, hear nothing but the whispers and the decayed bodies. Hollering in defiance, he swung again and again, beating back the nails and the teeth. A rage had come over him. Passion filled his very blood, though he could feel the leftovers of ameese weighing down on his limbs. His knees wobbled, but he beat down a corpse with a snarl.

He somehow managed to turn in full circle, and as he fought down another corpse, he had a clear view of the river once more. Partially blocked by bodies, Annette stood ragged and wet, shin deep in the shallows beside the dock, a black box at her feet. Wet hair hiding her face, she wedged her pale fingers beneath the lid and opened the box.

All the corpses froze.

She heaved open the box and they turned on her with inhuman shrieks. They sped toward her, sweeping past Xius and Set as though they no longer mattered. But just as their lame feet touched upon the water's edge Annette kicked the box over, pouring a mass of congealed and sloppy blood onto the silt-laden shore and shallow waters of the Nile. Up in the sky the last piece of the rust-colored moon had just begun to wane.

Not a sound came from the bodies. For a breath of time the monsters balanced precariously in whatever state of motion they were in, mesmerized by the thick blood seeping out of the box. A breath of wind blew over the river to pick up strands of Annette's wet hair. With its touch, the corpses crumbled, whether on land or in water. Bones lost connections, flesh dried up, and the white eyes shriveled up in their sockets. When the bones fell to the ground they too turned to dust and blew away with a sudden whirlwind. Xius had to protect his face with his arms and for a moment lost sight of the white girl.

Just as soon as it had started, the dust storm vanished. Annette shivered violently in the river, her foot still besides the box. Normal, clear river water lapped at the edges of the old, spilt blood. Beside him stood Set, worn and bloody, but otherwise alive. The red light had faded to a pale, tired silver. The distant white noise of people terrified out of their minds came from the opposing bank.

"Annette?" he stumbled forward, nearly losing his balance in the river before sloshing over. "Annette? *Annette?*"

Set followed him, but he ignored him as he roughly took her arms.

"Annette, say something."

She peered up at him through curtains of hair. Tremulously, she smiled. It was a tiny, weak little thing, but one nonetheless.

"I may not have a clue about any freaking, whack-job zombie magic, but I think that worked just fine."

"Zombies?"

Then his knees gave way and he splashed down into the water. His vision darkened and spun like a wheel. He thought he could see the stars pushing the world down till he saw back to Set, who had also collapsed into the shallows, breathing heavily, knife stuck hilt deep in the mud. Fingers of icy water ran through the Pharaoh's hair.

"Oh my god, are you guys okay?"

The last thing he saw was the rune covered box, forgotten and still oozing leftover drops of blood.

Part Seven

Of What Ended

Xius woke up in his room to thunder rolling in from the gray down outside. He could smell the crisp, clean air that came after a good rain.

Denan sat beside him.

"Annette?"

"She's resting. Caused some trouble trying to help the physicians care for Set, but her own wounds needed caring to."

Fear pulled up on his reluctant eyelids. "Wounds?"

"She is alright, friend. Just some cuts along the arms, shallow ones."

"Set?"

Denan didn't answer right away. He only did when Xius made to prop himself up and looked ready to run down the hall himself. He was able to spy a still, sleeping figure on a cushion in the corner before Denan pushed him back down.

"Calm yourself, your majesty."

"Is he well?"

"He's as well as he can be with a stab wound to the chest. Lucky to have lived this long."

Xius recognized the peculiar paleness in Denan's eyes. He moved to get up again, but the other's hands held firm.

"Let me go."

"No."

"Let me go to him, damn it! He could be dying this very minute and you're keeping me away! I won't stand for that!"

"Hush, your majesty—"

"I won't—"

"Do you want to wake her up? She's just fallen asleep, and she's more trouble than she's worth awake."

Xius quieted at this and peered off the side of his bed to where just a bit of white hair could be seen. When it became apparent that Xius wasn't going to continue his attempts to leave, Denan sighed and leaned back against his wicker chair, folding his arms across his broad chest.

"You need your rest, your majesty. The physicians are doing the best they can for Set, although…I don't know how much that implies, seeing the accursed hole the idiot's dug for himself. It may be best that he doesn't recover. I'm sure you know what I'm getting at."

Xius's heart skipped over it—had to skip over it. "How did you find us?"

"Wasn't hard, your majesty. You sort of had a white beacon jumping up and down and screaming."

He blanched as the image of Annette came to his mind, screaming at the top of her lungs and waving her arms like an idiot. Absentmindedly he touched his chest, feeling for his medallion. Denan picked up the rough, golden pendant from the side table and handed it to Xius. He had long ago expressed his opinion of Xius's strange attachment to the necklace, but seemed to have accepted it by now.

"If you're up to it, as a friend, I would like to know..." Denan waited. The question in the air was all too obvious.

Images of the nightmare flashed in his mind and he clenched his eyes shut against the nausea it inspired. How many had torn apart and eaten alive? "My people—?"

"Also would like to know," said Denan solemnly. "Including the poor father of Kasmut."

Numb, and finding some sort of strength from his exhaustion, Xius explained, starting with the revelation of Set's trade for the soul of Tawaret.

By the end of it Xius had once more lost his voice to a gravely rasp and Denan had his face in his hands. The general's shoulders slumped, and he tipped almost imperceptibly side to side upon his chair.

"Ra, Osiris, and Amun," groaned Denan, "that poor girl. She loved you, Xius. She loved you so much."

"She was involved with them, Denan. I don't know how, but," Xius sighed. "I wish I had known. Perhaps I could've stopped her, convinced her otherwise."

"Is the Pharaoh okay?"

Xius struggled to sit up again. "Annette?"

A white face appeared on the other side of his bed, resting her chin on the mattress."Yeah. I'm awake."

"I'm sorry, I must have woken you."

"In fact, you did. But Pharaoh speaks as loud as he wants, huh?"

He couldn't help but feel a little sheepish at this. Denan, who didn't catch the English they exchanged, raised an eyebrow at Xius but didn't ask for a translation. Instead he watched Annette warily as she stood up, stretched, and crawled onto Xius's bed. Her arms were lined with linen bandages.

"Relax, General," she said in her awkward Egyptian as she sat next to Xius. He could easily see the dark shadows beneath her eyes.

"Excuse me, my lady." He looked back to Xius. "Set has been useless." His face twisted into a scowl. It was the worst insult he could give. Denan, as royal general, lived his life with the sole purpose of being useful, whether it was to the gods or to his family and friends.

"They tricked him, Denan," croaked Xius.

"That means nothing."

"It has to mean something."

"Yes. That he is stupid, weak, and selfish."

Xius winced. "Denan…"

But he knew the place his friend was in now, having been there himself. No matter what he wanted to believe, it wouldn't change what had happened; it wouldn't change Set's fate.

He sighed and let his face fall into his palms. Had he ever felt so tired before in his life? Annette's small, cool hands rubbed the forearm closest to her in small, cautious circles. His lily. His precious Annette.

He suddenly wasn't sure if he could face his dying friend, even if he did manage to persuade his general to let him leave his room. As pharaoh, he could override the law and Denan, if he wanted to, but that could only worsen the gods' displeasure with him. He couldn't let his people down. He had to face the truth: Set had betrayed him—betrayed them all—and had too much blood on his hands to wash off.

"So," said Denan, slowly easy himself back into his chair, "Annette is not of Apep?"

"I don't think she is," said Xius carefully.

Annette straightened. "Kasmut told me they didn't bring me here. She said," she looked down at his arm, as though suddenly shy, "that her god hated me, but that she didn't know why. And then the way that big black what's-his-face fellow hunted me down like that..."

Xius translated for Denan, who shook his bald, rye-skinned head. Annette preoccupied herself with the circles on Xius's arm. He found it very distracting, but not in an unpleasant way.

"Ra, we're right back where we started concerning her."

"I'm afraid we are." Denan groaned a bit as he shifted in his chair, wincing at old pains.

A knock came at the door and a captain entered, followed by a pair of Xius's personal guard. The captain bowed himself to the ground.

"General, sir, you are needed at the gates. There are people demanding to know of the Pharaoh's welfare. They want it from your own lips."

With one last bitter grimace in Xius's direction, Denan left with his captain and the guards after taking up his cane by the door. The snap of it closing sounded loudly in the quiet murmuring of the wind. After a few minutes Annette stood up to close the shutter doors across the balcony. The room fell into a grey, semi-darkness. He watched as she shuffled to the brazier and examined it. She shook her head.

"Nah, I'm so not hitting rocks together."

"Annette?"

"Yes?"

Though his mouth opened, no words came. There simply were none. He turned away.

The first raindrops pattered against the palm wood of the balcony blinds.

"This is all been quite the week, hasn't it?" she said. "Set pulling his skeletons out of the closet, crazy dudes wanting to bleed girls like a grape for their sadistic gods, you puking up everything you've eaten since you were three—"

"I'd rather not remember that."

"To be honest, no one does. No offense, but you're not very pharaoh-ic when you're upchucking."

"You certainly know how to set the mood for a man."

"Of course."

But he couldn't stop his small smile.

"You have seen me at my worse. If you dare speak a word of my lapse in divinity, I will be forced to kill you."

Through the dim he could see her disbelieving frown. "Why would I want to describe that to someone? To anyone?"

"Well, who knows, you may have a son one day who feels humiliated after a particularly bad stomach sickness and you'll feel the need to tell him that even the Pharaoh has such…unseemly urges."

"Which of course, is not true."

"You are learning faster every day."

Her lily-pink lips were curving into a smile when she sat down at the edge of his bed. He couldn't make out the blue of her eyes, but he could still see the lines of worry shading them. They watched him carefully. Too tired to resist the urge, he reached out and laid his hand across her thigh and was pleased when she didn't pull away.

Her expression changed.

"Xius…"

He snapped his hand back. "No."

"But—"

"I don't want to talk about it."

She bit her lip as though to restrain herself, then sighed and laid herself down across his bed.

"Fine. But I think you're making a mistake."

He felt his jaw pop as he snapped his teeth. "I'm doing the best I can! You couldn't possibly understand."

She glared at him. "And why not?"

"I don't have to explain myself!"

"Oh really?"

"Don't look at me like that."

"Excuse me," she said coldly and turned onto her side.

"Sorry for worrying about you."

"You have a peculiar way of showing worry, then, criticizing my actions."

"You don't even know what I was talking about! You just flipped out on me!"

He clenched the blanket across his knees. "Fine. What were you about to say?"

"I think you're making a mistake listening to Denan. You should go see your friend, no matter what he's done." she bowed her head into her chest. "You'll regret it if you don't."

There was a stunned silence. He let go of his blankets.

"Besides, what ever happened to your damn-huge 'I am pharaoh!' superiority complex? You don't listen to anyone."

"Annette…"

"I mean, you're still worried about him, aren't you? Closure's good."

"Annette,"

"I know, I know, sorry for assuming you care about your friends."

"Annette, I have to execute him if he survives."

She flinched. "I-I figured something…like that…but, still…"

She seemed to shrink at the end of his bed, and in an instant he felt guilty for his outburst. No matter how many times, he never seemed to hammer it deep enough into his head to watch himself. Set had been his safeguard against his anger. What she had said about him wasn't necessarily true: Xius did listen to some. Set had been one of them. One of the few.

Thunder rumbled louder, as though gods were moving furniture above the very palace of Waset. Xius laid out his palms across his bedspread.

"Come here," he said softly.

She remained where she was as though she hadn't heard him.

"I'm sorry, I…I shouldn't have…assumed so quickly," he said.

"It's okay. I should be used to it by now."

He winced. "No, you shouldn't. I've always been hot-headed. It causes my friends grief, I know, and I'm sorry you have to deal with it now. May I…may I hold you?"

She took her sweet time to consider this while he sat feeling rather stupid with his arms open and waiting. When she did move it was to turn enough so she could face him and show him her displeased frown—more of a pout, to which he had to restrain the urge to smile.

"If you're trying to change, wouldn't rewarding you for your bad habit ruin it?"

"Isis, I'm not a dog."

"Will you go see Set?"

Xius hesitated. "I should—"

"No, will you?"

He grunted. "Yes, yes. Not sure how well I'll do at walking there—"

"I'll help you."

"I'm not a cripple! I don't need your—"

But then she had plopped herself onto his lap and cuddled up against his chest. He suddenly couldn't remember what it was he didn't need. He fell against his pillows with a puff of breath. When she nuzzled her face against his neck he almost forgot what it was he had promised to do. Her soft breasts were pressing against him through a new clean dress and her weight was like a cozy blanket. He moved to hug her, but she pulled away and stepped off of the bed.

"There, that's about as much as you get or I might just fall asleep."

"And that would be bad?" he asked, confused. Her scent befuddled him and he felt sleepy. So sleepy. A decade's worth of sleepy.

"You have to see Set, don't you?"

He didn't like that reminder.

Later, he would remember demanding to see Set and being lifted drowsily out of bed by his guard. Annette had long left his bed to fall back asleep on her favorite giant cushion on his bedroom floor, but his arms still held the memory of her softness. A chair or something of sorts was brought in which the men carried Xius out of his room and through the dreamlike maze of his palace before finally setting him down in a fire lit room.

A half-naked man with sharp gray eyes lay in a bed, bandaged haphazardly, and obviously forgotten.

"Your majesty?"

"Set."

The two men looked at one another.

Set gave a weary sigh. "I am so stupid."

"Agreed," breathed Xius, wearily. The chair felt like a cloud, and the crackling of the fire like a lullaby. He could still feel Annette in his arms—the feel of a goddess.

There was a brief moment of silence and then Set said thickly, "Xius… I think somewhere in my heart I knew, even if she had the soul of Tawaret, she wasn't Tawaret. I wish I hadn't done any of this to her. I wish I could have gotten to know her more…" Then, as though thinking otherwise, he said instead, "Are you all right?"

"I'm tired," he said bluntly, as though that should be answer enough.

"You shouldn't have come here. I'm not worth it."

Xius said nothing, though he could feel the broken man watching him carefully. As though seeing through a fog, he noticed the red tinting the clean white of the loose bandages around Set's chest. It took him a full minute to register what the red even was. Were those bandages supposed to be like that?

He felt his chin hit his collarbone and bobbed his head back up with a growl.

"Good Ra…" he mumbled.

"Perhaps you should head back to bed."

"Do you feel much pain?"

Set stared before turning his head to the other side to hide a silent laugh. His tone, however, was sad. "Oh, Xius, you are only making this harder on yourself."

"She made me."

"What?"

"She told me I'd regret it. She made me come down."

"Oh."

The storm sighed against the palm boards. Xius's eyes kept

fluttering open, but not once did he notice Set close his, except to blink. He shook himself—struggling through the fatigue. He couldn't sleep now.

"Set, I…I wanted to come. I just didn't know what to say."

"What is there left to say?"

Xius shoved through his muddy mind.

"I'm sorry," he said.

The tall man's face blanched. "Out of all the things you could think to say—"

"For all those times I lost my temper," he pushed through. "And remember those old, fancy astrology scrolls of yours?"

"Uh…wait, the ivory-handled ones?"

"Yeah."

Set gave him a weak, but wry grin when Xius didn't finish that thought. "What about them?"

"I'm sorry."

"For the scrolls? They went missing years ago," Set paused. "Wait a minute, you didn't…"

"I didn't mean to, they just sort of fell."

"Fell?"

"You know. Out the window. There was all this wind and then the drain happened to be at the edge of the pond—" a yawn broke him off. "And the inlay had been so pretty."

"My father was furious! Do you have any idea how many generations those scrolls have been through?"

"Five gener—"

"*Five generations!* And you dropped them out a window and into a pond that just happened to be connected to the Nile! Isis, Xius…"

But rather than be mad, he shook once more with that quiet, breathless laughter. The red blotch grew. Xius's chin dropped again, as though strung to weights, but he managed a tiny smile. The world felt as though it just snapped back into place. The tension in his chest lessened, and for the first time that week, Xius could take a deep breath.

As another storm-filled silence fell in between them, half-formed dreams skittered across his mind. Black faces with white smiles drifted through them, fingers dripping with blood.

Then he dreamed of Set standing tall, legs apart in a defiant stance, looking just like the bow he held taut in his hands. The Kushite slunk in, dark eyes inhuman, strange, and bulging with hate.

"I forgive you."

"Hmm. Good."

"And Xius?"

"Hmm?"

"I'm sorry."

Set's voice cracked. The bow he held had snapped and he looked down at it in dismay as the smiling, disembodied faces surrounded him.

"It's all right," said Xius.

"No. No it's not."

"But it will be."

"Are you even awake?"

"'Course."

The black faces rippled and Set turned back toward him, blue robes of his office twisting about his legs.

"It can't be all right. I can never…I shouldn't have ever…Xius, I thought the gods had abandoned me. No—I thought they didn't exist. It just all became so pointless. It is all so pointless."

Something very strange was going on. The Set in his dream looked angry and shrewd, as he often did in the midst of a particularly hard game of Aseb with Denan. Xius loved that look. It meant something phenomenal was going to happen. Yet the voice coming from his mouth wasn't determined, but a broken sob. Gold dust glittered past the black faces, which were murmuring inaudible words to him and morphing into the heads of jackals.

"I don't want to be here. I want to go back, back to how it used to be. It's just all so pointless. Why are we even here? If there is a god, why were we even created if it was but to suffer like this? I just...I just wanted to be with her. Annette is not Tawaret, but that doesn't change how much I've grown to love her."

The fire was warm. He could feel it as it crackled next to

him. Set still held his determination to conquer the game. The black faces faded behind the gold dust.

"You'll figure it out," Xius said, and his voice was so quiet. "You always do."

"Xius?" Set's voice was fading as well, as though moving away, or perhaps just thinking very hard.

"Hmph?"

"You deserved so much more. I'm sorry."

"It's all right, Set, it's fine."

"Fine? You can't possibly mean that. You're asleep, Xius. You should have stayed with her...with Annette. You are asleep."

And so he was.

As though waiting for him, a dream came upon him the moment his eyes closed. Set and he were ten years old and running through his mother's bedroom. The queen's quarters were grand, perhaps even more so than the Pharaoh's, and the boys ran about, tearing down curtains and yanking the covers from the huge bed. Xius tried to sound commanding as he ordered Set around the corners of their growing fort, but Set ignored him and did what he wanted anyway. He took chairs for the corners and loaded up each one with statues of Hathor and Isis, though Xius demanded he use the potted plants. His mother had just scolded him earlier for irreverence.

By the time they were finished, a palace of white linen sheets stood before them, barely ruffled by the desert breeze and reminding him of clouds against the blue sky. Set agreed when Xius claimed that the gods would never see such a fine palace. Their fort had rooms upon rooms, and they climbed on the chairs to signify the second floor. At one point Set dangled his legs off of one with his back against the floor, ignoring Xius's protests that it just wasn't right to have one half of your body on the first floor and the other half on the second.

The smell of his mother's blankets mixing in with the sheets they had just stolen from Set's room distracted him. Then somewhere, somehow, Annette appeared curled up in his arms, which were no longer those of a ten-year-old, with the soft white sheets turning into her hair.

He jolted awake—for what, he couldn't tell. No comforting form of Annette lay in his arms, nor was Set before him with his loose bandages. The fire had died out in the brazier and the infirmary was only lit by coals enough to see he wasn't alone. Denan sat across the room, his hands across his face.

The doors were just swinging shut.

"Denan?"

But the general said nothing, nor did he raise his head.

***

The days slipped by. Xius's and Annette's wounds healed, though from then on out nightmares of rotting flesh and Set dropping with blood down his chest frequented him. They dreams varied, but they all ended the same: Xius waking up with the intention to hunt down that sorry bastard of a vizier to prove to himself he was still alive.

But then, the next minute, he'd remember that he wasn't.

Xius and Denan put away Set's body privately. Though his being a traitor to the throne denied him the burial he would have received as right hand to the Pharaoh, Xius made sure to leave behind some encouragement in the tomb so he could hope that Set would somehow make it through the journey down the eternal river to eternal rest. Annette had accompanied them, mourning in the quiet, still way of her people rather than the loud wailing, hair tearing, and breast-beating of the Egyptians, which echoed across the city and west of the Nile as his people took their own dead to their final rest.

Reports came in over the month of those who died at the hands of what Annette had called zombies, and he cringed at the numbers. On the plus side, cases of ameese had also decreased dramatically within the week, if not ceased all together, and many of those sick in Waset recovered well—even miraculously—including Isis. The head priestess came to visit the Pharaoh herself two weeks after the red moon, supported by her fellow priestesses, to give Xius the blessing of her understanding, thick-lipped smile. By now almost everyone knew about Set and what exactly had happened, though the details about Annette's involvement were kept conspicuously unclear.

Even then, why the lovers of death had chosen the victims they did was unclear. With Set gone, any knowledge of their practices beyond the basics was unknown, and any other Kushite slave interrogated claimed ignorance or wouldn't say. Xius was left hanging the promise of death above anyone who dared worship the Kushite's Apep.

Annette was more than she seemed, as Anubis had said, but of course, that was obvious. She was from the future, after all. For now, his only choice was to wait and hope the gods would one day uncover her mysteries.

As Denan grew stronger, he looked after Egypt's recovery process with Xius. His remaining royal guards received the greatest of honors for protecting Egypt in its most dire hour. Their solemnity, though, showed they had not forgotten the eerie way in which their brothers had fallen.

Offerings of food and gold were sent up to Xius from his people as gratitude offerings and he accepted them graciously, as he should, no matter how unworthy he felt. Set would have nagged him until he did so anyways.

Annette returned to learning Egyptian and the ways of Egyptian life. She also decided to take up learning the complex hieroglyphics so as to become more useful, as well as gain her own independence. Besides this, she still often went down to the kitchens to cook, this time with Wenamon's daughter, who had replaced her father as cook. Of course he didn't approve in the least and would have rather kept her in lessons to groom her to be a queen, but the most he could get her to agree to (without running off), was to at least take one of his trusted guards with her to ensure the other servants kept their hands to themselves.

Now and then there came those quiet moments when neither Annette's studies nor Xius's duties got in the way and they would talk of the future she came from. A part of him knew there had to be something about her world that was similar to his, so once when the court musicians practiced outside again, he asked again about the music and its poetry. In the face of Set's absence, he had almost forgotten about the poetry.

And it was then, as they recited poetry and listened to the music of each other's native tongues that his heart throbbed for her the most. He loved her. He loved her more deeply than the confused pain of losing Set. Perhaps that was why she brought much needed peace to him whenever she was around.

On one of these occasions, they had stayed up late talking and she ended up falling asleep at the foot of his bed. He had spent much of the night tracing the lines of her round cheeks and lily-like lips.

As he had done so, he couldn't help marveling how Set had kept his mouth shut and met his death for this paradox of a woman. Though a small piece of Xius was grateful for his friend's devotion, the more part of him wished that Set had never made the choice in the first place—even more so that the vengeful, death-worshiping Kushites had never existed. Then Tawaret would have lived and Set would have not broken as soundly as he had.

Several times when he had been awoken by awful nightmares of the scarlet Nile and Set's loose, bloody bandages, it took all his restraint to not walk to her chamber (the same one as had been prepared for her by Set), and curl up beside her. But he knew if he did, not only might she not take too kindly to being woken up by his intrusion, but he wouldn't be able to keep his hands to himself. She had already turned down his proposal, and he was wary of their cultural differences, but that didn't stop him from musing on ways to seduce her will to his own.

Which in turn amused Denan.

"Haven't you taken her yet? Known her?" he asked one too many times.

Xius would blush heartily at this, which was undignifying for a man of his status. Pharaohs did not do something as womanly as blush. "Is it any of your business?"

And to this, the large man would chuckle. "Oh Bes, you haven't. How do you resist when she sleeps at the foot of your bed? Doesn't she have her own quarters?"

"She only fell asleep once while we were talking. And I just don't want to hurt her."

"Ah…You have it bad. I wouldn't expect any less from you, your majesty."

"Besides, isn't it a bit odd to you that I would be courting the woman Set thought to be his late wife?"

"But she isn't," he'd point out. "And forgive me, your majesty, but you are badly put where ma'at and wives are concerned, and I don't know how much longer those priest's will wait until they usurp you completely, not to mention you are getting older. Don't you want to watch your children grow?"

He made it sound as though Xius wasn't aware of this.

Things changed a bit when Annette bowled into the throne room after spending the day working in the kitchens with Wenamon's daughter.

The two counselors who were discussing possible nominations for Set's replacement looked up in surprise as she impatiently, and sloppily, went through the royal greeting salutations, face flushed. He frowned at her careless work.

"Annette, I thought I told you, left foot forward. How are you going to get anywhere if you can't even do the basics?"

The counselors looked a bit too interested for their own good, even if they couldn't understand a word the Pharaoh had just said.

However, she replied to his English in Egyptian. "Forgive me, your majesty, but I am…flustered."

She must be angry if she was not jumping on the chance to speak her own language with him. He frowned and lowered the list of possible viziers he'd been holding.

"Why are you angry with me?" He continued in English.

To this, she clenched her jaw and finally dropped into her own tongue. "Why does everyone think I'm your own personal little whore?"

"Technically it's concubine, my lily."

"So you've known about this the whole time! And you did nothing?"

"I am above petty gossip, as should you be. We are above them."

"You may be, but I'm no royal. How am I going to start my own life with 'pharaoh's slut' hanging over my head?"

His eyebrow twitched. One of the counselors kept nudging another in excitement and giving him significant looks, which the other ignored as he tried to look like he wasn't paying attention.

Wanting to say so much to her, but knowing too little how to say it, he said softly, "Is that what you want then? To be on your own? To be rid of me?"

He wasn't sure if it had been wise to let that last part slip out of him. It rang too clearly of how hurt he was, and it made his pride smart to admit such things to her. Even though the counselors couldn't understand a word they were saying, the one's constant slapping and the other's faux ignorance were beginning to try his patience.

Annette's anger melted away into compassionate surprise.

"No, I don't want to get rid of you. But I won't be a pet forever; I want to be useful."

"There's more ways to be useful than being a servant," he said more sharply than he intended.

Her eyes flashed ice. "Like what? Having babies?"

To his chagrin, heat rushed up to his cheeks. A particularly audible slap of excitement from the one counselor crossed the last line.

"Out!"

The men flinched so soundly their writing utensils went scattering across the floor. Gathering them as quickly as humanly possible, they scurried out the doors with their tools clutched to their chests. Xius glared after them.

"So Ra-damn nosey."

Though he had meant to say it to himself only, Annette said, "Tell me about it," and folded her arms with a scowl. After a long moment where they both sized each other up, Xius tossed aside the papyrus roll of names.

"Oh all right, what do you want of me?"

"I'd like it if you defended my honor a bit."

"Your honor? How have I not been defending your honor?"

She stared at him as though she couldn't believe what he was saying.

"I'm a virgin!" she said so bluntly it made him blush again. "I don't want 'prostitute' hanging over my head whenever I meet someone! Is that too much to ask?"

"Why would you be associated with prostitutes if you were a pharaoh's concubine? If anything, the rumor only gives you more honor. Even as a lesser wife to the Pharaoh you would demand respect."

She opened her mouth to argue, then stopped as something

dawned on her. She huffed and put a hand to her face.

"Okay, okay, I see what's wrong now." She dropped the hand. "My people are Christian-based, so chastity until marriage is a big deal to us—or at least most of us. We don't believe in concubines."

"Christian?"

"Oh, right, you wouldn't know, um…you should have Hebrews in this time, right?"

"Yes."

"Well, think of it as a religion that's a version of the Hebrew religion without the polygamy."

His forehead furrowed, trying to remember what he had learned about Hebrew religions in his studies. But even as he remembered their God's peculiar laws, he still didn't get what she was getting at. At the bemused expression on his face, she looked to the ceiling in surrender.

"Forget about it. Just know virginity is a big deal to us, okay? If girls sleep around, they're not really thought highly of or trusted much—most of the time. It's a big deal to me that people think I'm," her face quickly pinked, "that I'm intimate with someone who's not my husband when I'm not, pharaoh or otherwise. Does that make sense?"

He nodded, eyebrows still knitted in a bit of confusion. "But…this is not your time. So…why are you worried about their opinion of you affecting what you wish to do with your life?"

Again, she opened her mouth to argue, but gave a sigh of defeat.

"Fine, fine. You win. I still don't like it, though."

He smirked. "You don't like what? Being thought of as my concubine?"

She rolled her eyes. "What have we just been talking about?"

"Well, if you're still not satisfied," and very quickly he found his mouth getting ahead of his thoughts, "there's one good way to fix it.."

"Which would be what? Going all pharaoh rage on their behinds?"

"Marry me."

She blanched and had to take a few seconds to re-gathered herself.

"How is making me a real concubine going to change anything?"

"Because you wouldn't be a concubine. You'd be my first and only wife, and therefore my queen. We've been over this before."

"Aren't you supposed to marry your half-sister or something? Royal line of Horus and all that?"

He shrugged. "I am Pharaoh. I can marry whomever I please—especially since my parents aren't here to have any say on the matter and I have no sisters."

He watched closely as a series of emotions played across her face: shock, amusement, something between a blush and a smile, and then annoyance. He too didn't know what to say. He hadn't thought that out very well, but then again, when had he thought anything out well? Set had been the one to save him from his rashness.

"So you do want to make me useful by bearing babies," she said. Once more her bluntness threw him off. Why did she have to be so straightforward? And didn't she want children? He couldn't understand this woman.

"That's not the point," he said. "Of course you would be more useful than any woman in the kingdom by bearing heirs to the throne, and I would give you children, but—"

"Then that's the thing, then?"

"Don't interrupt me." But whatever he had been going to say flew from his mind and he found himself too peeved to remember. He reached for the roll of papyrus and opened it up to where he had left off. "You obviously don't care for anything important in this world, so you may leave now. I'm done dealing with you."

He expected her to storm off. If not that, then he expected her to give him one of her defiant, determined glares that had somehow, only Ra knew how, attracted him to her in the first place. What he wasn't expecting, however, was for her to come up to his throne looking distressed and then bow her head down next to his cushions. He stared at her balled up form.

"Please, I'm so sorry. I didn't mean it like that, it's just...I still have a hard time believing that you're serious and also I'm kind of afraid of the whole idea. It's not that I don't care at all! I care very much."

As always, he softened when she appeared so small against his feet.

"What are you afraid of? As my wife you would be honored above all women, and I would do everything in my power to keep you happy. Or is it," he frowned as he remembered his previous experience when bringing up marriage with her. "Do you still think you may have a chance to return home and don't want to grow your roots too deep here?"

"Possibly that still. But...it's just I—"

"Come here, lily. There is no need for you to bow to the floor like a common slave."

She gifted him with a smile and climbed up onto a spot on the cushions next to him. She pushed her hair back behind her ears. "I never expected to get married at sixteen. I know it sounds weird, but in my time it's different."

"I know," he said. "Set explained it to me. You gave him the same excuse."

Saying his friend's name aloud was like dropping ice into the conversation. Annette pressed on regardless.

"I don't know what you will expect of me as a wife, I mean, everything is so different here and it took me long enough just to figure out what was expected of me as a slave and we both know how that turned out. Also, marriage never looked too fun where my mom and dad are concerned. If...if hers is anything how the real thing is, I'd rather die single, never touching a man. And many say—in my time, that is—that children only make it worse..."

He gently took her jaw in his hand and carefully turned her face so he could meet her eyes.

"I am not your father, you are not your mother, and this is not South Daka."

She laughed. Though he was a bit exasperated that she did so when he was trying to be serious, it pleased him nonetheless.

"South Dakota, Xius."

"Whatever it is called."

What little apprehension she had left vanished from her eyes to be replaced by a happy glow.

"But I'll take your word for it," she said, but before he could start wondering if that mean she had just accepted him, she cautiously curled up on her side and changed the subject. "These pillows are super comfy, by the way. What are you up to today?"

He lifted the scroll. "Finding a new chief advisor."

"Found anyone yet?"

"I'm finding I don't much care for any of the other counselors. You saw the two who were in here. Bumbling, gossiping nitwits, if I ever saw any."

"I'm sure you'll find someone, Xius. Just don't pick me. I'd make a horrible chief advisor. I don't know anything about war and whatnot."

"You don't have to," he said. "I am happy to tell you that this is, as you call it, 'ancient' Egypt, not South Daka—*Dakota*. Our women are kept well away from war. I hope you don't mind."

"Nope, not at all. Never had any aspiration to shoot people or lose any breasts I have to pushups."

Again, the bluntness. It amused him. Any anger left had been washed away and he now smiled down at her happily. "By the way, lily, you are being evasive."

"What's with the lily thing anyway?"

"Annette…"

She pouted. "Fine. What do you want?"

"You know what I want. Will you give it to me or not?"

She squirmed. He must be getting better at this.

"Jeez, why do you have to be so blunt?"

He laughed. "And I was just wondering that about you."

"I guess we both don't pitter about with what we want then, eh?"

"Another valid reason why you should just agree with me."

She glanced at him, a perturbed expression on her face.

"Aren't you concerned about me loving you as much as you love me before we get married?"

"Generally, yes, but does it matter? Besides," he grinned rather knowingly, "you are not unaffected by me."

"There you go saying things you can't prove."

"Oh?"

The playful turn their conversation had taken had affected him with some strange string of confidence. He found himself above her and placing his thighs outside her own. He watched in pleasure as her face turned several shades of red and her mouth fell open.

"What are you—"

Intoxicated with her presence, he leaned down and kissed her speaking lips. At first she seemed to protest, stiffening in response to his touch. But he tenderly moved his lips against hers until she responded in turn. He could feel her muscles relaxing against his legs. Before he could get carried away he pulled back, a triumphant smirk on his face.

That smirk vanished when out of the corner of his eye he noticed the door move ever so slightly closed. He growled a curse. Annette looked at him in bewilderment, her cheeks still flushed with color.

"What?"

"Damn nosey…"

"Oh," she looked over to the door, where the eavesdroppers had just vanished. "Shouldn't that be punishable by death? I mean, you are the Pharaoh."

"If this continues I'm very tempted to make it so. Rude, impertinent, disrespectful—"

Continuing to mutter just exactly what it was along with a few chosen curses, he pushed himself back to his cross-legged position and tore out the papyrus. He really did have to finish picking out the man he wanted from the list of nominees. If he could, he would just choose whoever he felt the most comfortable with. Being that he was comfortable with none of them, this had been something the two "nitwits" had suggested. He just wanted this over and done with.

Annette sat up. He was all too aware of her eyes on him.

"Yes?" he asked.

"I should probably get going, I sort of left in the middle of a project."

He just nodded and turned back to the papyrus. Perhaps one day he'd be able to get a clear answer. At least now Denan couldn't say he hadn't tried.

She slipped off the throne of cushions and padded her way over to the door. From the sound of her footsteps she had been able to retrieve her duck-like shoes. What had she called them? Tiny shoes? Tennie shoes? On reaching the door she turned, considering him. He lifted up his head to meet her eyes, as though to say "I know when you're staring at me, stop trying to be sly about it." She smiled nonetheless.

"To your question," she said.

Instantly he perked, list forgotten.

"I'm seriously considering a yes."

And with that she stepped out the doors, leaving Xius with the sensation that his head had disconnected from his body, flown out the balcony, and floated up to the heavens where the gods held court. Of course, he would have never admitted to such emotions. Such were unbecoming for one such as the Pharaoh.

Glossary

Disclaimer: The Egyptian religion, like most religions, evolved and changed from century to century based on the ideals and needs of the Egyptians. Gods and Goddesses changed faces and roles depending on the area and period. I have tried to compensate for this by doing my best to keep the setting of my story in a certain time period (in this case, the New Kingdom), in order to keep the roles and religion consistent and easily understandable. However, as I've stated at the beginning of this book, I am no Egyptologist, and even if I were, theories vary from person to person. Please keep this in mind when referring to my glossary.

Ammit: A female demon who stood at the ready in the balancing of the heart. If one did not follow the principles of ma'at (or in other words, their heart proved heavier than the Feather of Truth), she would devour their soul, where they would be damned to eternal restlessness.

Anubis: God of embalming and burial ceremonies and guardian of the boundaries between the living and the dead. He is attributed with the creation of the mummifying process which allows the spirit and body to be reunited in the eternal world. Through Egyptian history he is often made to be the God of the dead for this purpose, though it is usually Osiris who is king and judge of the dead, not Anubis.

Apep: To the Egyptians, Apep is a giant, evil snake demon who preys upon the dead of the underworld Nile, and is adversary to the Pharaoh after death due to Apep's intent on frustrating his journey to the eternal world. Neighbors to Egypt, especially those who were enslaved to or less than Egypt, often adopted Egyptian gods as their own and adjusted them to their own beliefs. Due to this, Apep is also known as the God of Death among the Kushites.

Bastet: Goddess of protection. Cats are considered to be her messengers or avatars on Earth, and so she is often depicted either as a cat or with a woman with a feline head.

Bes: Protector of pregnant women, newborns, and families.

Crook of Anubis: A staff held by Anubis used to open up the mouths of the embalmed dead to release the soul. It is used in burial ceremonies.

Domed ovens: Bread was normally cooked as a sort of scone that was placed on the ceramic sides of a domed oven, which would be heated by the fire within. I would imagine the top of the stove was flattened to allow other means of cooking.

Duat: the Egyptian name for the underworld, or place of transition between death and where the dead are to be judged. From there, based on the way they have lived their life, they will either enter the eternal world, be reborn, or have their souls banished to nonexistence.

Feather of Ma'at: Another name for the Feather of Truth.

Feather of Truth: An ostrich feather of the goddess Ma'at, which is used in the balancing of the heart at the end of one's life. If one's heart (which was to believed to be the seat of one's soul), is equal to the feather, they are judged worthy to continuing on to eternal rest. If one's heart proved heavier than the feather, their heart was fed to Ammit.

Geb: God of the earth; often depicted as the earth itself. Husband and brother of Nut and father of Shu, Osiris, Isis, Nepthys, and Set. Ancient Egyptians believed earthquakes were his laughter.

Hathor: Goddess of love, joy, and protection. She is also the wife of Horus and mother of the Pharaoh. Because of this, she has a special connection as well as a guardianship status over the Pharaoh, who is considered to be the 'living' Horus.

Horus: Egypt's national patron god and son of the King of the Underworld, Osiris. Because of this, it is important for a pharaoh to complete his journey down the underworld Nile, or the river of death, in order to make it home to his father, Osiris, where he will take part in the judgment of the souls of his time.

Imhotep: God of healing and patron of physicians.

Isis: Powerful protective goddess, as she is considered to be a goddess of magic and the one who originally resurrected her husband when he was slain by Set, his brother. She is the wife of Osiris and mother of Horus, which makes her especially important to pharaohs, as they are considered to be the 'living' Horus.

Ka: Egyptian name for one's singular spirit, or soul. In referring to one's soul, it is called ka.

Khonsu: God of the moon, human fertility (specifically male fertility), dreams, and visions.

Kush: The native language of the Kushites.

Kushite: More commonly known today as ancient Nubians. For the majority of Egyptian history, Nubia was either enslaved, occupied, or in alliance with Egypt. Much of Egypt's gold and salt came from Nubia.

Left foot forward: It is considered proper respect to approach the Pharaoh (or any god), with the left food forward, due to it is the foot beneath the heart. The heart was considered to be the seat of the soul, where all thought and emotions occurred. The brain was actually thought to be nigh useless.

Libya: A country bordering Egypt's western border.

Ma'at: Goddess of justice, law, and order, who is known to protect all creation from falling into the ocean of chaos, which all creation originates from. Ma'at is also known as 'the way things are,' law of nature, truth, and moral justice in which Egyptians live by.

Memphis: A major port city in the Nile delta, which feeds out into the Mediterranean Sea.

Nut: Goddess of the sky and mother of Shu. Often depicted as being the sky itself. A common poetic metaphor for her is that the blues of the day and the star studded velvet night make up her dress, which she wears to impress her husband, Geb, who she can never embrace in fear of smothering all life in between them.

Nepthys: Wife of the god Set.

Osiris: God, king, and judge of the underworld. He is also the god of resurrection and fertility. He is the husband of Isis, father of Hathor, and is the giver of barley, which is Egypt's staple crop.

Ra: God of the sun, or the sun itself, and king of the gods. He is one of the great creator gods. He often get's combined with Horus and Amun, though in this time period (and for the sake of the story), he is the father of Osiris and his siblings.

Sekmet: Goddess of war and depicted with the head of a lioness. She is often referred to as the Eye of Ra when she is in her role as goddess of plague, famine, and destruction.

Seshat: Goddess of writing and measurement

Set(or Seth): God of chaos and brother to Osiris, Isis, and Nepthys. He is also the uncle of Horus. Set is also the nickname of Seti, cousin and vizier to the Pharaoh, Xiusthamus.

Shu: God of the sky; often depicted as being the sky itself.

Sobek: God or spirit of the Nile. He is depicted with a crocodile head and is also considered a protector of the Pharaoh. The crocodile is his symbol.

Tawaret: A guardian goddess who protected women during pregnancy and childbirth. Also the name of the late wife of Seti.

The Eternal World: The world where the righteous and noble go to live forever with their loved ones. There they live a life not unlike that of mortality on the Nile, except without disease, pain, or suffering.

Thoth: God of knowledge, writing, and language, and is also connected with the light of the moon.

Waset: The ancient name for the old city of Thebes, which, at the time of this story, is the holy capital of Egypt.

CPSIA information can be obtained at www.ICGtesting.com
Printed in the USA
BVOW11s2338201115

427985BV00010B/57/P